D1045060

THE
PYGMALION
VENTURE

The Pygmalion Venture
Copyright © 2004 by Jean Duhon Hanson

All rights reserved.

Printed in the United States of America. No part of this book may be used or reproduced in any manner whatsoever without written permission from the author except in the case of brief quotations embodied in critical articles and reviews.

This book is a work of fiction. Names, characters, places, and incidents either are products of the author's imagination or are used fictitiously. Any resemblance to actual events or locales or persons, living or dead, is entirely coincidental.

FIRST EDITION
First Printing, 2004

ISBN: 0-9759397-0-X
LCCN: 2004112238

Cover art and design by Carolyn Miller Design

Magnolia Mansions Press
4661 Pinewood Drive East
Mobile, Alabama 36618
www.magnoliamansionspress.com

For my beautiful daughters,
Karen and Adrian-
unique, inspiring, enduring-
with love

and
in memoriam, for my cousin,
Stephanie,
who first loved this story

THE PYGMALION VENTURE

*To Larry
with best wishes*

Jean Duhon

JEAN DUHON

**Magnolia
Mansions
Press**

One man, Pygmalion...

...chose to live alone,

To have no woman in his bed.

But, meanwhile, he made,

With marvelous art,

An ivory statue,

As white as snow,

And gave it greater beauty

Than any girl could have,

And fell in love

With his own workmanship.

—*Metamorphoses*, Ovid

CHAPTER ONE

Autumn, 1981

"HELP you, sir?" The vendor at the newsstand eyed a tall, dark-haired man hovering around one of the card racks. A nervous tic made her facial features twitch in unison every few seconds as she sized him up. He was well dressed, but that didn't mean anything. A fairly large percentage of shoplifters in the busy terminal looked respectable.

Blake Harrison was distracted by the grating sound of the woman's voice as he pretended to browse through the postcards. "No, thanks," he mumbled. "Just looking." Ignoring her, he stared intently between rows of merchandise at the crowd moving along the concourse. He needed only a few minutes more, he thought, and hoped a real customer would come along to keep the woman busy.

Dulles International Airport was a kaleidoscope of sights and sounds as the diverse sea of humanity swirled through it, but his surveillance was aimed mostly at the people who slid into view on the upward bound escalators and in moments his patience was rewarded. He felt a surge of triumph as his eyes riveted on a boyish-looking man in his early forties ascending the moving staircase. Senator Kenneth Raitt. Harrison studied him carefully. The man's sandy hair was cut in a stylish shape, brushed sideways and upward, away from the forehead and sprayed rock solid so that even gusting winds wouldn't dislodge one fine strand. Raitt had launched his career as one of the bold, young politicians in the '70s who had affected the JFK look, convinced by public relations experts that it was a requirement for a successful campaign. The illusion had worked for many candidates lacking real qualifications for the job. Raitt had so far managed to slip past voter scrutiny, but now the Drug Enforcement Administration was seriously questioning the Honorable Senator's honor.

Harrison quickly moved away from his observation post as the worried merchant, with tiny muscles jerking at high speed in a clockwise path around her face, rushed forward to check her stock. He dodged a group of Middle-Easterners, their desert-resistant robes flowing around them as they hurried toward one of the gates.

The DEA agent eased into line behind three turbanned Africans dressed in colorful batiks, who had queued up behind the senator at the United Airlines counter. He watched while Raitt presented his passport for the flight to Panama. The young ticket agent did not appear to recognize him. She chatted easily as she processed the ticket and tagged his garment bag before placing it on the conveyor belt. Raitt responded with only a few polite phrases as he picked up his ticket envelope and put it in the inside pocket of his jacket. He slung the strap of a small carry-on bag over his shoulder, ambled past the currency exchange and across the lobby, dodging a group of European exchange students in shorts and backpacks, anxiously checking watches.

Harrison followed at a distance, wondering why Raitt hadn't stopped at the currency exchange. Apparently, the senator was planning to use US dollars, since Panama's balboas were only issued in coin and decidedly inconvenient to carry.

He had already alerted the DEA office in Panama City of Raitt's arrival time, and a stakeout would be waiting. They had tracked him for months, suspicious of the unusual number of fact-finding trips he'd made to Central and South America with little to show for them. Not any trade deals or aid agreements to speak of, but embassy personnel in several of those countries were familiar with the handsome young senator who slipped mysterious packages into their diplomatic pouches.

Two days ago, a sharp agent had spotted the round-trip airline reservation to Panama for K. Raitt, a simple entry without titles or fanfare of any sort. Harrison directed that a bogus call be made to the senator's office with a request for him to meet with his home state forestry delegation. The female agent who made the call was told that Senator Raitt would be vacationing with his family this week. Obviously he was not with family, and three days for a pleasure trip to a foreign country was very peculiar. Still, the senator traveled in casual clothes—sport coat, open-neck shirt, and a pair of horn-rimmed glasses rarely seen by the public.

Raitt turned into the waiting area for his departure gate and found a seat. He reached for a newspaper that had been abandoned on a nearby table and began to scan the headlines. Harrison sat several rows back, keeping Raitt in clear view as he surveyed the crowd.

The seats were filled, mostly with Latin Americans. Distinguished-looking people, Harrison noted, and well-groomed, from neatly combed hair to highly shined shoes. Many wore rich leather coats. Quite a contrast, he mused ruefully, from their North American neighbors, who seemed to prefer jogging suits and Reeboks for travel.

The loudspeaker announced the flight and Harrison watched while Raitt boarded the plane. Now, he thought, all he could do was wait for a report from the other end. He turned away and headed for the customs office to see an old friend.

"Hello, Mr. Harrison."

"Nice to see you, Mr. Harrison."

The two young secretaries in the outer office beamed as they greeted the frequent visitor.

"Hello, ladies. Is Mr. Copeland around?"

"Out on the floor, sir," one of them said. "A flight just arrived from South America and one of the inspectors called for him. Some sort of problem, I guess. Is it an urgent matter?"

"No, I just wanted to say hello."

"He should be at Gate 7."

"Thanks, I'll find him." He smiled and gave a brief wave as he headed for the door.

The woman who had done most of the talking looked over at her co-worker. "Wow!" she mouthed silently, rolling her eyes heavenward. The other nodded and fanned her face with both hands.

Buzz Copeland, middle-aged and portly, stood behind a customs inspector who doggedly checked through the bags of an incoming passenger. Experience had taught the head of the U.S. Customs Office at Dulles that people had all kinds of ways of being clever. He scrutinized the passport of the fresh-faced young woman with the ponytail.

As Harrison approached, Copeland nodded solemnly and handed him the woman's passport. "Your timing is perfect, Blake. What do you think?" he asked softly. "Tom, here, says he'd bet money she's hiding something but we can't find anything."

Harrison looked at the document carefully, then at the young woman standing calmly on the other side of the counter. College cheerleader type, he thought. She was twenty-five, American, returning from Venezuela and not worried about a thing. "Have you anything to declare, ma'am?" he asked.

"No."

"Three weeks in Venezuela and you didn't buy anything?"

"The leather purse I'm carrying. That's all."

"What was your business in Venezuela?" Harrison continued to question her, observing her closely, watching for any sign of nervousness.

She responded easily. "I visited friends in Maracaibo while I did some research for my thesis." Her eyes didn't waiver.

"Did you spend all your time in that city?"

"Yes. The archives had all the information I needed."

"What is the subject of your thesis?"

The customs inspector continued to search her bag very carefully and the woman began to show some annoyance.

"The Spanish Colonial period in the sixteenth century." The words were terse.

Harrison flipped back through her passport. "And last summer…you were in Colombia for a month?"

"Yes."

"More research?"

"That's right," she snapped, eyes flashing. "In Bogota."

"Beautiful city, Bogota."

"Yes, it is."

Meanwhile the customs man, satisfied that nothing illegal was packed in the bag, had begun methodically feeling along the edges of the lining for telltale signs of alteration. Now and then he pried up the edge and felt underneath, but found nothing.

Harrison continued to hold the woman's passport as Copeland handed him another one. The agent noticed several dates of entry into various Latin American countries and the U. S. were the same as the woman's. He looked up to see a drowsy man with horn-rimmed glasses and tousled hair streaked with gray. He wore a loose shirt over tan corduroy jeans and sandals.

"Are you and the young woman traveling together?"

"Yes. We're together."

"PhD, hmm? Where do you teach?"

"At the American Colonial Institute. It's a prep school in

Bethesda for students entering the foreign-service field."

Harrison nodded. "I've heard of it."

The man's only luggage was a briefcase and a duffel bag weighted down with a load of dirty clothes. Copeland signaled another inspector to come forward to help the one already there. After ten minutes of intense searching, the professor's bags were pronounced clear.

With an uneasy feeling, Harrison handed the passports to the customs inspector to be stamped for clearance. He continued to study the couple as they closed their bags and stacked them on the tubular steel luggage cart. The man stretched the heavy elastic cord over the bags and snapped it into place.

"Wait a minute," Harrison said, "I want to look at the luggage carrier."

"This thing?" The man looked from the agent to the cart like he had heard wrong.

"It will only take a moment."

The professor bent down as if to unload the bags. Instead, with a swift reverse motion, he sprang up and plunged through the crowd, jumping barriers as he went.

Harrison stopped the woman as she started to follow her companion. Handing her over to Buzz Copeland and already running, he shouted, "Notify security!"

The man reached the escalators and leaped down the rolling steps, four at a time. The DEA agent barreled down after him before the startled travelers had time to narrow the path cut by the professor. When Harrison got to the bottom, it took only a few seconds to close the gap between them. He grabbed for the man's hair, jerking his head back. With the other hand, he managed to reach around the man's chest and shoved his foot between the other's running feet. Harrison had him down and handcuffed before airport security men arrived.

* * *

IN a back room in the Customs Office, inspectors had taken the luggage carrier apart. Harrison came in as the men were pulling soft plastic tubes from inside the steel ones. The plastic tubes were filled with white powder.

"Probably almost a kilo of cocaine. That's more than recreational use for our professor and his researcher friend, wouldn't you say?" Harrison asked.

"To be sure," Buzz answered in a droll voice. "But the little lady is denying any involvement, Blake. She'll let her boyfriend take the rap."

"Yes, but she was in Colombia last summer and he wasn't," Blake reminded him. "I have a hunch we'll find they're both mules and that she most likely recruited him."

Buzz Copeland gave a low whistle. "Well! Look what we have here!" A handful of green rocks rolled from one section of tube. "Uncut emeralds. Guess they couldn't resist doing a bit of moonlighting."

* * *

BLAKE turned the agency car eastward, negotiating the heavy traffic leaving Dulles. His mind was on the office, and the paperwork waiting for completion before he took over his new position of Special Agent in Charge. Nice, even though he knew he would miss working in the trenches. Still, he was edging past forty and had been chasing scumbags and dodging bullets for a long time. All the way back to Vietnam, in fact. Frowning, he recalled the dark alleys and bars of Saigon, his own deadly battleground where the quiet, undercover war with Viet Cong spies, drug dealers and black marketeers was waged. A stinking, stealthy, terrifying existence of betrayal and ambush.

He had earned the right to expect his life to settle down a bit, even though he loved his job. Detailed observation and ESP. Damned unscientific, he thought with a wry grin. Whatever it was, he liked the challenge, pitting his skill against that of the devious criminal mind.

The Ford hummed its way back to Washington while his mind shifted gears to the intriguing case he was working on. In a few hours, he'd be taking Kenneth Raitt's press secretary to the opera. Strictly business for him. Getting romantic with Jennifer Judson would be like getting into a pool with a shark. He hoped to glean some information from her about Raitt's activities and associates. If he could wind up his investigation quickly, he would be able to free himself for the new responsibilities, and maybe even have time to live a little.

Live a little. Unbidden, a brief flash of memory forced Blake to see her again. Victoria. Her sunny smile, the way she was. He heard a trace of laughter and her soft voice speaking, felt her hand brush his cheek, and then the warmth of her closeness. It was how she always came back to him—his mind remembering the fragile thing they'd had. Cautious lovers, backing away from their intense feelings, both unwilling to make promises. They had gone separate ways, too busy with careers to have enough time for each other. For a moment, the empty space that had lain inside him since they parted seemed to grow larger, creating pressure against the rest of his body.

He tried to call her only once after that. Her answering machine informed him she was in Thailand on business. He hadn't left a message. There was no way to guess when she would be back, and by the time she could return the call, he would probably be out of town. That had been the problem all along. Would his new position be able to change some of that? Maybe. But what about her life? Over and over he had told himself: *Forget her, play the field, take on more work.*

Hard as he'd tried, he couldn't.

The blast of a horn at the rear jolted him out of his reverie. *Damn! You'd better watch what you're doing, Harrison, if you intend to live through the next ten minutes on the Beltway.*

★ ★ ★

"*¿SEÑOR Raitt?*" The dark-haired man bowed as Raitt stepped off the plane at Tocumen International Airport in Panama City.

"*Sí,*" he managed. He wished these people would speak English like everybody else.

"*Buenos tardes, señor.*" With that and a gesture, the man managed to convey that he would provide escort through customs.

Raitt was pleasantly surprised, relieved to have someone handle whatever red tape there would be. His relief increased when he found that everything had been taken care of. With one look at his escort, customs officials waved him through. His guide was also helpful in translating at the ticket counter when Raitt stopped there to reconfirm his return flight.

In a short while, they were in a car speeding away from the busy airport. Raitt noticed that the Panamanian frequently glanced at the rear-view mirror as he drove. The senator looked out the back window and saw the outline of several cars following at a distance. After the driver made a number of sharp turns, only one car continued to follow them. A few more turns and there was nothing but the long black ribbon of asphalt. Soon they were on a road leading to a small airstrip. He could see a single hangar with an executive jet parked on the tarmac. A man stood beside it.

Raitt's driver hustled him on board. "*Adiós, señor.*" With a wave, he sped away. The man who had been waiting on the airstrip climbed into the pilot's seat and in moments the sleek little plane raced down the runway.

Once aloft, the senator eased back into the comfortable leather seat and looked out the cabin window. The view was spectacular. In the scant light remaining as the sun prepared to sink into the western ocean, the deep green landscape of Colombia unfolded below.

The Andes, the main motif on the South American continent, lay in majestic beauty upon the horizon. Materializing in the dusk, one after another, were three parallel chains—the *cordilleras*, leading prongs of the immense, volatile range of mountains that rose from the sea far to the south on an obscure, frigid island in the archipelago of Tierra del Fuego. There, within hailing distance of the South Pole, it began its continent-long stretch northward. At first dotted with glaciers and fjords, then thrusting bare, rumbling peaks high above the heat of equatorial regions, the rocky mass eventually ended on the warm shores of the Caribbean Sea.

Raitt watched while the plane flew over the first two of the *cordilleras*. As it headed toward the easternmost chain, he leaned back with a smile of satisfaction. He was finally doing it. For years he had carefully studied newspaper accounts of the illicit drug trade. It had to be the biggest income-earning enterprise the world has ever known. Moreover, demand was rising and, from all indicators, would continue to do so. People who wanted drugs weren't going to stop wanting anytime soon. It was the growth industry of this century, and probably the next.

As for his own personal choice in the matter, he had no intention of developing the habit, even though he sometimes smoked pot. He'd even snorted cocaine a time or two. When the parties were in full swing, he liked to have the stuff. He had to be careful, though. A man in his position. If the press got hold of it they'd make his life miserable. He'd have to cover up like hell in the next campaign.

Being on the import end of the business was something entirely different. Raitt smiled at the thought. For some time, he had dabbled in the trade, gingerly testing the market with good results. As a member of the senate, he always had an excuse for being in one

South American country or another. It had been easy to buy a kilo here and there. It was risky, but not impossible. He thought of the thousands of people—educated or illiterate, it didn't seem to matter—who had made personal fortunes overnight. If every other tobacco-chewing, crotch-scratching yahoo could pull it off, Raitt knew he could do it, too. Even better.

He needed money, a lot of it. The cost of media coverage for a successful campaign was enormous. And these days, a candidate couldn't do without it. Hell, he thought, he could study the polls, see what kind of person the public wanted, turn himself into that image and play it on television. Like a damned soap opera. It would be laughable if it didn't work so well.

His wife's personal wealth had elected him in '72 and again in '78. Melanie had managed the purse strings, Raitt remembered with a flash of resentment. In '84, he would have control of his re-election. He had worked long and hard to build a base of power on several congressional committees and he wouldn't give it up. Power suited him and this new enterprise was the way to be sure to keep it.

Luck had dealt him a prime hand when he'd found a willing partner to handle the money laundering in the Caymans. Before long, the two had discussed enlarging the business, and now the pretentious, high-society snob wanted to have his hands on the action. Apparently saw himself as a version of the Scarlet Pimpernel. Well, okay, Raitt thought, but he had better sense. Personally, he'd remain well in the background.

He felt the small jet begin its descent, breaking into his reverie. Looking through the oval window of the cabin, he could see multitudes of lights twinkling below. Bogota. In minutes, the plane touched down at El Dorado Airport.

"*Buenos noches, Señor Raitt.* Permit me to introduce myself. I am Esteban Perea, nephew of Don Ignacio Perea. I hope your flight was pleasant." The thin young man with oiled and wavy dark hair looked at the American with expectation. Small brown eyes set in a narrow face seemed to be sizing up the senator.

"Oh, yes. Very nice, thank you." Raitt was cordial but wary of the emissary. He was anxious to get the business over with. "Where is Mr. Perea?"

"My uncle regrets that he could not be here to meet with you right away. Tomorrow the meeting will be scheduled," the young man said with a fixed smile, while inclining his head slightly. "But for now, I am here to conduct you to your hotel."

CHAPTER TWO

At intermission, the elegant throng of opera lovers swept into the great foyer of the Kennedy Center, knowing they had witnessed the first half of a superb performance of *Don Giovanni*. Blake Harrison strolled through the crowd. At his side was Jennifer Judson—blonde, sexy, and savvy. As usual, she chatted in an uninterrupted monologue and he had become distracted.

"I can assure you there are plenty of people on Capitol Hill who would like to stop Senator Goodman," she was saying.

"Um-hmm."

"Senator Raitt intends to use the party circuit to line up enough support to squelch Goodman's proposal when the subcommittee meets again. Kenneth is adamantly against selling the AWACS plane to the Saudis. He and his wife will be touring the party scene throughout next week. There will be an especially gala affair at Monroe House Saturday evening."

"Monroe House." Blake was suddenly alert. "Doesn't it belong to the big society lawyer, the one with the pedigree all the way back to the crusades?"

She smiled. "Yes. Ian Monroe, the eligible bachelor that most of the single ladies in Washington—and half of the married ones—are after. People absolutely stampede to his parties."

Blake listened with interest. Ian Monroe's name had come up in several suspicious money laundering situations in the past. They'd never been able to charge him with anything and there was no obvious tie with Raitt, other than social. On the other hand, it was a very intriguing possibility.

Jennifer's eyes scanned the black-tie crowd. "In fact," she whispered, leaning near to Blake, "speak of the devil…" She nodded toward a knot of people in back of her.

Harrison's gaze swept over Jennifer's head. Monroe, with steel gray hair and standing taller than others in his group, was easy to spot. His picture appeared in the society pages regularly. Haughty son of a gun, Blake thought. He looked away, wanting his survey of the crowd to appear casual. There were quite a number of other notables, along with the ordinary music lovers, sipping wine and renewing acquaintances.

Without warning, a stab of excitement cut through him as he spotted a very familiar face. Golden highlights reflected off the mass of fluffy curls ending midway down her long, slender neck. Lovely as ever. Even in the chic crowd, she was a standout.

Jennifer's voice faded into the background as Blake willed his pulse rate to slow down. *Come on, Harrison, you're a mature guy. Get hold of yourself.* But he couldn't ignore the gaping hole that had opened unexpectedly in his midsection as he looked at Victoria. She was standing within a cluster of people he knew. Well, he thought, it wouldn't do to ignore fate. With determination, he managed to steer his still-talking date toward the group.

"Blake! How wonderful to see you!" Susan Cornell exclaimed.

Her husband turned to see who was approaching. Major Stan Cornell beamed as he held out his hand. "Hey, old fella, it's been a long time!"

Blake greeted the couple warmly, then presented his date. The Cornells recognized her and launched a discussion about her most recent press conference.

During those moments, Blake was sharply aware of the woman

standing nearby. There was a light fragrance surrounding her, a familiar exotic scent. It wasn't until he heard Cornell making introductions that he could bring himself to face her, knowing he was vulnerable, yet not wanting to avoid the impact. He looked at her and saw, once again, the fair skin with its hint of rosiness, the small upturned nose. She was elegant in a Thai silk theater suit in burnished bronze with a turquoise blouse of the same fabric. Her eyes were a matching blue-green.

"Jennifer and Blake, I'd like you to meet Victoria Dunbar and John O'Leary," Stan was saying.

Blake could tell by her startled eyes and hesitant smile that Victoria was off balance at his sudden appearance, but she looked directly at him as she offered her hand.

"We've met," she murmured, not taking her eyes off his.

Momentarily, he felt a familiar charge at the warm softness of her touch, and then he was shaking the hand of her date, Lieutenant Commander O'Leary.

"Oh, I didn't realize you two knew each other," Stan said in surprise, looking back and forth between Victoria and Blake.

"Yes," Blake answered in a quiet voice. Turning to face her again, he continued, "But, it's been a while. It's wonderful to see you again, Victoria."

She smiled in response, her eyes looking at him only briefly, then away.

"Well," Blake said, taking a deep breath, forcing a hearty voice, "it looks like we've got the army and the navy well represented here tonight."

"Hell, yes!" Cornell said. "We can't let you federals across the river get ahead of us in the culture department."

"Right," O'Leary agreed. "But I must admit Mozart is out of my league."

While the light-hearted conversation continued, Susan turned to

Blake. "Colonel Arrington was just talking about you a few days ago. He remarked that you hadn't stopped by in months. We've missed you."

"I've been swamped lately, drowning under that pile of papers on my desk. However, I've got to check some files in the Army Department. I plan to be in the Pentagon soon. I'll stop in for a visit." Blake paused. "So, you're still working with Bob Arrington?"

"Yes, still feeding the computer."

Stan leaned toward them. "Blake, did I hear you say you're coming to see us?"

"Yes, it's time for me to do some catch-up work."

"Great! If you're still there around quitting time on Friday, we'll round up a platoon of us old retreads and have a beer call."

Blake smiled at the prospect as he recalled the time-honored custom of men in uniform. "I'll look forward to it."

As the conversation drifted to other subjects, he found himself once again looking at Victoria. He thought she must have felt his eyes on her because, almost instantly, she turned to him.

Hesitantly, softly, she spoke. "How have you been, Blake?"

"I've done well," he lied. "Keeping busy. How about you?"

"The same. My job keeps me traveling."

"Are you still with the Smithsonian?"

"Yes, but at the moment, I'm on loan to the Navy."

He looked puzzled.

"The Navy has an extensive art collection—as a matter of fact, all the military branches do. From time to time selected works are loaned out to museums or sent on traveling exhibits. I'm organizing several of those events and making recommendations for new acquisitions."

"Does that mean you're at the Pentagon, too?"

"Yes, for a few months." Her eyes appraised him, noticing a trace of gray that hadn't been evident before in his dark, neatly combed hair. "And you, are you still with Justice?" She knew not to make specific reference in public about his work.

"Yes."

Victoria looked into the dark eyes. They were unreadable. "It's nice to see you're still an opera fan. I always thought it was unusual for your...type...to be a dedicated classical musician."

"And what type is that?" He knew she was teasing, but he was intensely interested in how she would answer his question.

She hadn't expected it and was momentarily at a loss for words. He stood there in evening clothes, looking clean-cut and sophisticated, yet as comfortable as if he had on a sweat suit. She knew very well what a gentle, cultured man he was—an accomplished cellist when he had the time. Yet a sense of strength emanated from him, an aura of unleashed power. In those months they had been together, she had discovered he was a paradox.

"Mysterious," she answered finally.

Blake threw back his head and laughed. "I've been called a few things, but never mysterious!" Still amused, he went on. "And unusual or not, you know how much I admire Mozart. What an incredible musician!" he exclaimed in earnest. "My personal opinion is that this one is his best opera."

"It's one of his greatest musically, but it occurred to me tonight that it is not one of my favorites. I guess it's the tone of the story that disturbs me, the old legend of Don Juan and his cavalier disregard for women's feelings. I think I prefer *The Marriage of Figaro*. It's happier!" A smile played about her peach tinted lips.

Blake studied the range of emotions reflected in her lovely face as she spoke. Momentarily, his attention was diverted by the glint of gold in the hollow of her neck. With surprise, he noted she still wore the tiny, heart-shaped locket studded with small turquoises he had given her. "True, true. Giovanni does have a bad habit of seducing innocent maidens just for the hell of it," he said, almost apologetically.

"Still, the finale of the second act is superb, and...," he continued with a grin, "the fact that he gets what's coming to him should please the outraged women in the audience."

Just then the house lights flickered, interrupting chatter as people put down wine glasses and began returning to the theater for the second act. As their group moved toward the doors, Blake looked at Victoria, not wanting their conversation to end. "It was nice seeing you," he said lamely. To the others, he exchanged the usual courtesies with the promise of seeing them again soon, and began to guide Jennifer to their seats.

Victoria's eyes followed them and saw that they sat across the aisle and several rows back from the place she and her friends were sitting. She felt a twinge of jealousy as she wondered if Jennifer Judson was a regular in his life. It had taken all her willpower to keep her emotions in check, standing there next to him, within touching distance, wanting him.

The theater went dark and the ominous music began. The feeling of foreboding that had begun to grip Victoria at the outset of the opera returned. The action on stage seemed to take on a strange, stark reality that she somehow couldn't disregard. It was almost like a premonition, although she had never believed in such things. As the deceitful Giovanni wove his web of treachery through the lives of the unsuspecting characters, an occasional chill went through her. Even as the finale built to its crescendo of macabre justice, Victoria felt sad and angry that the lives of the innocents had been so cruelly altered.

Trying to distract herself, she glanced back. The press secretary was checking her watch, but Blake sat in rapt attention to the performance. Smiling at his absorption, Victoria recognized the familiar feeling of tenderness that washed over her, and wondered if their unexpected meeting had had as much effect on him as it had on her.

At the end, when the applause subsided and people began moving into the aisles, Victoria watched him search the crowd. He caught sight of her and momentarily their eyes connected and she felt the subtle electricity flow between them. He paused briefly, then nodded and smiled across the distance. Her question had been answered. She would see him again.

★   ★   ★

KENNETH Raitt stepped out of the stately Tequendamo Hotel onto the busy sidewalks of Bogota. He wasn't prepared for the glare. The sky was a bright, brittle blue broken by the dark, sharp edges of towering mountains. Squinting, he reached for his sunglasses. Not surprising, he thought. Colombia's capital lay only about three hundred fifty miles from the equator, and at eight thousand feet above sea level, the city got a lot of pure, uncut sunlight. Shivering in the chilly breeze, he walked briskly along the streets wondering what in hell had driven the original group of settlers to this ear-popping high plain to build a city.

There were interesting contrasts all around him. Silent Indians, some hanging their wares on stalls, some sitting along the sidewalks, were wrapped in colorful *ruanas* to ward off the morning's cold. Their weathered faces wore somber, patient expressions as they hawked leather goods to tourists, while businessmen, wearing their own poncho-like *ruanas* over European suits, walked toward their offices.

A cacophony of shrill voices from a narrow alleyway caught his attention. The senator peered into the dim opening between two buildings and could barely make out some movement. Almost immediately however, a writhing mass came tumbling out of the darkness into the bright light on the sidewalk. They were children, he noted in horror, fighting over what looked like a large plastic Coca-Cola bottle. One of the little urchins broke free with the prize in his hands. He raced down the street with part of the mob following, as he wove in and out of traffic, determined to escape the unlucky ones. They soon disappeared around a corner and out of sight. Raitt lost interest. Looking around, however, he realized many of the young children were still on the sidewalk near him. Covered with grime, wearing ragged clothing and most without shoes, they seemed to sense simultaneously that a new victim was in their midst.

"¡Pesos, señor, pesos!" they shouted, pulling on the senator's suit and pressing close against him. In a panic, Raitt swatted them away and managed to dash into a taxi waiting at the curb.

"Take me to a cafe!" he yelled to the driver, hoping he was understood. The driver nodded and shifted into first gear, sending the little car rushing forward and the crowd of small ones scattering in all directions.

Little vermin, Raitt thought with a shudder, feeling suddenly unwell. His head felt very strange. Too much exertion in the extreme altitude, he told himself. Last night on the drive from the airport to the hotel, the Perea fellow had warned him, but he'd forgotten about it until then.

The taxi halted in front of a cafe. The driver turned in the seat, holding out his hand. Raitt had no idea what the man was saying. He fished in his pockets for some of the Colombian currency he'd gotten at the hotel exchange and let the driver take what he needed. So relieved was he that the taxi had taken him to a safer area, Raitt tipped the man a few extra pesos, then went into the cafe and ordered coffee.

A child, thin and ragged, came in selling newspapers. The senator flinched, but recovered his composure when he saw this boy was older than those he'd just tangled with. Spotting the *New York Times* banner along with several Latin American publications, Raitt beckoned him to come to the table. As the boy approached, the senator saw that it was yesterday's paper and he shook his head to signal that he'd changed his mind. The disgusted look that appeared on the small, street-wise face when the child realized that he wasn't going to make a sale pricked even the lofty senator's conscience.

Smiling in his best public relations form, he managed a *perdón* and gave the boy a peso. The gamin took the coin even as he displayed an obscene gesture, then moved away quickly to look for more promising customers before the startled lawmaker had time to erase his fake smile.

Shrugging, Raitt turned to the steaming cup of coffee placed before him by a solemn waiter. It looked very strong. After a few cautious sips, he discovered the powerful brew had an excellent flavor and he quickly began to feel better. Looking around at the cosmopolitan crowd in the cafe, he felt strangely vulnerable without the cloak of immunity usually wrapped around him when he dealt with non-Americans. For the first time, he fully realized what an enormous chance he was taking by presenting himself in a foreign country for the purpose of doing unlawful business. Especially a country like Colombia, known for its exports of coffee, emeralds, and illicit drugs.

Glancing at his watch, Raitt decided to make his way back to the hotel, keeping a sharp watch for pickpockets. When he arrived at the Tequendama, he stopped at the desk to inquire if there were messages for him.

"No, *señor*, no calls since you left," the solicitous desk clerk assured him.

The American was annoyed. He touched his forehead at the spot where the leaden feeling was reforming. How much longer would Perea keep him waiting?

"Are you not feeling well, *señor*?"

"Just a headache."

"Ah, *el soroche*. The altitude sickness. A pity. It is simply a fact of our environment that this happens. However, it will not be long before you are acclimated. Tomorrow you will be better, I assure you."

"Thanks. I certainly hope so." Raitt paused, trying to think how he could fill the time. Last night, he'd asked Esteban Perea about a trusted jeweler. Who was it the young man recommended? The man had a shop in the hotel.

"Can you direct me to a jeweler named…I think…Pedro Marquez?"

"Perhaps, Pablo Marquez? *Sí, señor*. He has a fine shop, down this corridor and on the left. You will see the sign."

Marquez was a thin, middle-aged man who had the stooped posture of one who had bent over trays of rare things for many years. He was very eager to show the American a superb selection of emeralds, lovingly displayed on a velvet cushion. Patiently, he instructed his customer about the quality of the stones. The finest emeralds, he confided, were not too yellow and not too blue, but an intense true green.

Raitt finally settled on an elegant pair of earrings. His wife would be impressed. They were costly, but nothing compared to prices in the states, making him wonder if he might expand his business venture into the realm of precious emeralds. It was something to consider. He finished the transaction and realized there was nothing left to do but wait. With head still hurting, he went up to his room to lie down.

CHAPTER THREE

IT was almost quitting time at the Pentagon. Bored with desk jobs and eager to get a head start on the beltway traffic, the peacetime warriors had begun to hurry out of the numerous suites situated along seventeen miles of hallways encircling and radiating from the center of the world's largest office building.

Caught up with her work for the day, Victoria Dunbar joined the early exodus. As she walked through the corridor in the Department of the Navy, she saw him, smiling as he came toward her. Blake Harrison was trim in a charcoal gray suit and red paisley tie, an easy stand-out from the men in dark blue or olive drab. Her heartbeat quickened at the sight.

"Hi," she said, as they met in the middle of the corridor. The stream of uniformed men and women, unwilling to be detained even momentarily in the effort to reach elevators and stairs in record time, parted and flowed around them.

"It looks like I almost missed you. But I'm glad I didn't," Blake said, touching her arm affectionately. It was an easy gesture of closeness, an automatic thing that once in existence was not erased by time or distance.

"As you can tell, the place clears out rather early." She spoke laughingly, knowing there was a little tremble in her voice.

"So I see," he said. She wore a deep green coat and her eyes had shifted to the green zone of the spectrum. He was always surprised to see them change easily from blue to green and all shades in between, depending upon what color her clothes were. It was part of her magic. "You know," he continued, fumbling for something sensible to say, "I've been up here a thousand times, but I've never paid much attention to these paintings. I would be honored if a distinguished expert gave me a guided tour."

Victoria smiled. "With that kind of flattery, you'll get the deluxe tour." She linked her arm in his and led the way, eagerly pointing out the most notable pieces in the large collection. Along both walls of the corridor was an unbroken display of artwork. Paintings, busts, and models of ships depicted in various ways the proud history of the United States Navy and its heroes.

Blake listened to her informative explanations and asked questions from time to time, even though he was distracted. Her perfume and the feel of her body close to his filled his senses and the memories flooded his mind.

"During most of my years in the field of art history," she was saying, "I've worked with the art of ancient civilizations. Still, I've enjoyed handling this collection. It's diverse and the quality is very good."

Seeing they had reached the end of the Navy corridor, Blake turned to her. "Could you spare a few more minutes to have coffee with me?"

"I'd love to."

The two of them made their way to a cafeteria in the building. It was almost deserted at that time of day. They went through the serving line then settled themselves at a corner table. Both were awkwardly silent, looking at each other as they lifted their cups.

Blake nudged his coffee cup toward hers in a toast.

"It's an old cliché but I had so many things to tell you and ask you. Temporarily, it seems, I can't think of one," he said, shaking his head.

"I know. Me, too," she admitted with a smile. After a moment, she continued. "You can start by telling me how the drug business is doing."

"Oh, it's booming. We confiscate ten tons of marijuana in one place, but somewhere else that same night, twenty tons slip through." Blake looked disgusted. "It's getting to be just as bad with cocaine. The demand is on the rise, therefore, smuggling is, also. Those cartels in Colombia have learned how to mass produce. They've refined their organizations on every level of the business operation, from the beginning when some cold, hungry peon stomps on coca leaves all night in the wilds of Bolivia, all the way up to the street peddler who sells it to the yuppie stock broker in New York City."

Victoria was sympathetic as she shook her head. "I've never been able to understand what makes people...you know, normally decent American citizens...risk their reputations and their lives to sell illegal drugs or smuggle them into the United States."

"Well, for the low-life types, it's a natural. The most obvious reason is the enormous amount of money to be made for only a few hours of work, especially when that same big money buys them bail and a good lawyer to get them off the hook when they're caught. So much for deterrent. In crookdom, it's one of your better occupations, and it comes with a helluva benefits package." He paused to take a sip of coffee. "But the really crazy thing we're seeing now is the middle and upper class sector getting into it—people with position, respect in the community, and plenty of money!"

"It sounds completely irrational, doesn't it?"

"Yep," Blake agreed. "It's staggering! All I can figure is, life has gotten too dull for some people who already have it made. When the pillars of society feel they need even more money and more thrills, we're in big trouble."

As she listened to him, Victoria's mind switched to the early cultures she had studied. History repeating itself, she thought. There was a pattern in the rise and fall of the great civilizations of the world.

After trying for hundreds of years to survive alone, a group of people would finally decide to work together to build a society with an organized structure. Another long period of time would pass, and if the society succeeded, they had a better existence and a little leisure time to enjoy it. When life became orderly and relatively easy, the arts flourished and things like philosophy and science were explored. The human race in full bloom. Then, little by little, things went into reverse. Energies divided and dissipated and the collective focus was lost, taken for granted and forgotten because it no longer seemed important.

It was happening once again, she thought. That same illusion was pervading modern society, a belief that the "good life" was guaranteed simply because it had been in place for a long period of time. The most recent generations inherited the benefits without any idea of what it took to engineer them, and no longer saw the value in maintaining the framework. Had the present civilization begun the subtle process of decay?

"I agree with you," Victoria said, finally. "Apparently, we don't learn very well from the past." She paused. "I wonder sometimes if it's too late for us to overcome the damage. The problem seems so widespread…almost out of control."

"I don't know that we want to learn whether it is or isn't, darling," he said softly. "We've got to think our efforts in this society are worth the time we put in, that what we do will make the difference. I certainly must believe that, if I'm going to risk my neck occasionally in order to get the job done right."

"What did you call me?" she queried. He had said it so easily, she wasn't sure she'd heard correctly.

"I called you darling, darling, and I've missed you like hell," he said matter-of-factly. His dark eyes met hers as he tried to fathom her thoughts. He noted, once again, she wore his gift around neck. Maybe it was a good sign. He reached out to touch the tiny heart.

Victoria leaned toward him and, as if magnetized, they drew together in a brief, tender kiss. Her senses came alive with the closeness of him and feel of his lips on hers. The familiar scent of his aftershave, a marvelous combination of fresh limes and sea air, triggered a rush of romantic memories. "Blake, my love," she murmured, "I've missed you, too. It seems that nothing is exactly right without you…and…I wonder how many admirals and generals are watching us."

"I wouldn't care if the Joint Chiefs were meeting at the next table," he responded in an amused whisper. "They'd only wish they were in my place."

She looked at him, concern showing in her eyes. "I've worried about you, you know…dealing with the bad guys all the time." Her hand caressed the familiar surface of his face. "You seem to be in pretty good condition, though. Just the same scar on your chin." Her brow wrinkled. "Come to think of it, I never did ask how that happened."

He looked surprised for a moment, touching the tough, whitened ridge of skin. He'd forgotten it was there. "Oh, yes. That was the result of a dangerous attempt to apprehend an escaping rascal. I was chasing him through the woods when my foot caught on a fallen limb. I tripped, fell, and cut my chin all to blazes."

"What happened to the escapee?"

"The frog? He got away," Blake said, solemnly. "I was nine at the time."

She grinned, shaking her head.

"Believe me, Victoria, I don't do John Wayne. Caution is my motto." He looked at her with a wink. "Of course, I like all this attention. I have to admit, however, that my work is mostly at a desk these days."

"That must mean you've been promoted!"

He nodded.

"Oh, Blake, congratulations! That's wonderful!"

"Now, about you. Are you and John O'Leary…?"

"Just friends," she interrupted. "He's a nice guy. And what about Ms. Judson?"

"Just business. But that's confidential."

"Right."

"Really," he insisted, convincing her with his eyes as he reached for her hands. "Victoria, don't you think it would be a good idea if we reconsidered our decision?"

"We should probably talk it over carefully."

"Soon?"

"Very soon."

"How about now?"

★ ★ ★

VICTORIA'S eyes scanned the familiar quarters as Blake hung her coat in the closet. She smiled to herself as she noted that little had changed. One thing was certain, the apartment had not been redecorated by some other woman. There was the same serviceable furniture. Plaid sofa, a couple of overstuffed chairs, bookcase, desk, and a Spartan chair next to the large upright instrument case in one corner.

She was distracted by a yellow streak that darted across the room and down the hall. "What was that?" she asked in alarm.

Blake chuckled. "*That* was a fat, ornery cat. Name's Brutus."

"I see something has changed after all."

"A guy on the next floor was moving out and couldn't take the cat, so I did. Old Brutus lives here, but he lets me know he's his own man. He may come and greet you after a while—then again, he may not. Very cool to strangers."

"What happens to Brutus when you're out of town?"

"He moves in with my neighbor. She's elderly. Says he keeps her company."

"Somehow, I can't picture you with a cat." Victoria tried to stifle a grin but wasn't successful.

He shook his head sheepishly. "Bachelor guys have to stick together. We get set in our ways, you know, and nobody else can stand us."

"Oh, I wouldn't say that."

He was close to her now, the playful mood switching quickly to one of intensity. He took her face in his hands as his eyes searched hers. "Victoria, Victoria," he murmured, "I've been…incomplete…without you. And now, suddenly something has brought us back together. Was it chance? Or fate? I've realized what a mistake we made. I love you so much. I knew I didn't want to be without you anymore."

Victoria could feel his warm breath on her. She found herself leaning toward him and knew the moment was beyond her control. "Ever since we stopped seeing each other, I've tried to forget you," she said softly. "But wherever I went, you were there, always hovering around my thoughts." She paused. "Last night, when I looked up and saw you, my heart actually stopped beating! Did you realize that?" She didn't expect an answer. "Blake…"

"Sh-h-h." He pulled her fiercely against him, his hands claiming her again, exploring her lovely body, seeking her breasts, reconfirming the familiar places that had been his, that he had wanted, had ached for since the breakup.

Victoria heard him whisper her name. His face brushed against hers and she closed her eyes, absorbing the scent of him. She raised her lips to meet his, feeling the probe of his tongue as his mouth crushed against hers. She felt the strength of his embrace and the heat emanating from his body as it transferred to hers, coursing through her in strong, insistent waves.

His hands deftly unfastened her dress, and she felt it slip easily to the floor. His eyes swept the length of her, from the lacy chemise to the tips of her shoes, igniting a firestorm of passion with his smoldering glance. She was unbuttoning his shirt, aware of their rapid breathing, as he swept her toward the bedroom and lowered her onto the bed.

He entered her quickly and she trembled under his electric touch, moaning with the sublime feel of him thrusting inside her. His eyes searched her face as if seeking something more, something divine. Sensing his need, her eyelids lifted and her gaze locked with his. The pale aquamarine light seemed to flow into the deep brown mysterious wells, illuminating the depths, making the final connection, and sending a new shudder through their joined bodies, fueling the tumultuous ascent to rapture.

★   ★   ★

FOR hours, the reunited lovers held each other while they talked, not wanting to postpone, even until the next day, learning what each had done in the months since their break-up. At one point in the conversation, Blake propped up on one elbow to look at her. He needed reassurance, he admitted to himself. He couldn't help it. He was afraid to glance away for fear she'd disappear again. It was absurd, he thought. They were closer now than they'd ever been. "We are the yin and the yang, you know."

"What?" Victoria asked, startled at the words whispered into her ear.

"Yin-yang, darling. Male and female, complete," he said with a smile in his voice.

Victoria thought of the ancient oriental symbol of two forms curving and fitting together to make a perfect whole. "It is what we are, at last," she said, turning slightly to press her lips against his neck. "Yes," she murmured, "my dearest love." His arms went around her and the passion flared once again.

CHAPTER FOUR

The telephone's shrill ring woke the senator from his nap. Another of Perea's relatives was on the line to tell him the time and place of the meeting. Raitt agreed to be there, but declined the escort service for a change, preferring to be in control of the situation. Realizing he felt a lot better, he showered and dressed, called a cab and went to see the elusive godfather.

The red tiled roof and cream stucco walls of the *Cantina de Montserrate,* situated at the base of the great mountain, glowed in the warm brilliance of the late afternoon sun. Walking across the shaded veranda, Raitt stepped onto the clay tile floors of the dim interior.

His eyes adjusted and he noted the middle class clientele—and the fact that the establishment was clean. The senator was amazed. He had pictured the meeting in a place crawling with flies and scorpions, not to mention cutthroats and a gaudy gangster in a white suit with diamond rings squeezed onto fat fingers. So far, the cantina seemed safe enough. Busy red-coated waiters hurried drinks to the many patrons. There were family groups sitting around small tables, talking and laughing. A band played Latin tunes while a few couples danced in the cleared space in the center.

A thin young man approached. He seemed familiar. Raitt knew he had never seen him before, yet the Perea genetic stamp was clearly there. The man seemed to have unlimited relatives to run his errands.

With the usual bow, the current messenger addressed the

American. *"Buenos tardes, Señor Raitt.* My name is Francisco Perea. My father is expecting you. Please follow me." Francisco led the way down a short hall and through carved, heavy double doors which he carefully closed behind them, shutting out most of the noise from the main area of the cantina.

Immediately, two other men of medium height and solid build came forward. Raitt was alarmed by their sudden nearness as he heard Francisco begin to speak.

"I beg your pardon, *señor*, but my father has many enemies. We must guard his safety at all times. I am certain a *norteamericano* like you can understand, especially after the recent attempt on your President Reagan's life." The husky bodyguards completed their pat down search for weapons on the speechless senator's body before Francisco had finished his apology.

The room they entered was very large, but partitioned by graceful arches leading toward several secluded seating areas. Groupings of dark, ornately carved furniture upholstered in tan leather were placed over hand-woven native rugs in deep red hues. In the center of the spacious room was a long dining table surrounded by high-backed chairs.

Their footsteps resounded as Raitt and his escort walked briskly across the tile floor. The table was set for dinner with beautiful linens, fine china and heavy silver. The senator noted it as he went by, producing a frown. He knew that nothing had been said to him about dining. To hell with it, he thought, still smarting from the embarrassment of being manhandled. There were several more young men standing around, watchful and silent. Raitt decided he'd be lucky if there wasn't a shootout with some rival cartel while he was there. This would be strictly business, he decided, and when it was over, he was getting out of there.

The group approached a slightly built man seated comfortably, reading a copy of *El Tiempo*. He looked up, placed the newpaper on the table in front of him, and rose to face them.

Kenneth Raitt found himself staring at a man who had the aquiline features and the proud, straight bearing of a Spanish don. The dark wavy hair had a single distinctive streak of gray beginning at the hairline just to the right of center and vanishing somewhere on its way to the back of his head. Immaculately groomed, he wore a dark suit superbly tailored of fine wool. The sleeves of his white shirt ended in French cuffs secured with heavy gold cuff links set with cabachon rubies, and on his right hand was a large gold ring etched with a coat-of-arms. Judging from its worn, smooth edges, it had been used to seal important communications for a very long time. Even without that tangible proof of an ancient noble house somewhere in his lineage, it was clear to Raitt that this was not a common mob boss. The man oozed a restrained refinement with no trace of the arrogance of new money.

The dark eyes looked at Raitt with a level gaze, never wavering as they assessed the well-known American lawmaker. "So, Senator Raitt, at last we meet. I am honored. Welcome to Colombia." With a slight bow, he motioned for the senator to be seated.

"Thank you," Raitt responded, recovering from his initial astonishment as he rearranged his attitude. "It is a pleasure to be here. A beautiful country you have here, *Señor Perea*. The natural scenery is really quite incredible."

"I hope that your stay so far has been comfortable. I instructed my relatives to be certain that you did not want for anything."

"Oh, yes. Quite comfortable. They were very helpful."

There was a pause while a steward served sherry to Don Ignacio and his guest, then departed unobtrusively.

"It is my understanding that you would like to do business with me, Senator. Exactly what kind of business?"

"I have information that your organization supplies a fine quality marijuana and cocaine for those who would like to import it into the

United States."

"And, *you*," the older man began, feigning astonishment, "a leader in the country which cries loudest against those of us who produce the drugs…while rejecting the notion that its self-indulgent citizenry might learn to curb their appetites…are interested in becoming one of those 'importers'?" He ended with eyebrows raised, looking quizzically at the American.

Raitt felt the flush rising from under his collar. *He's a hell of a one to sound like a righteous bastard!* "Mr. Perea," he said, switching to the English form of address and continuing in his best campaign bullshit, "the financial advantages would allow me to remain in the senate to serve my country in various ways. I'm one of those people who understands that the end must justify the means, or else very little would get done in the end. In the United States, getting elected is a costly process, and it takes several terms to build the kind of power base needed to institute the programs I'd like to create. Those programs are for the good of my country."

Perea's sharp gaze persisted, attempting to fathom the senator's intent. "What of the risks to your reputation? You, *señor*, are in a very delicate position. I am told the cameras of the American press follow politicians and movie stars everywhere. How will you handle the…ah…importation without others knowing?"

"Setting up and regulating the flow of supplies is my only part in this," Raitt said, "and, of course, insuring payment. Someone else, a trusted associate, will arrange for the flights to and from Colombia, or for rendezvous with your ships. My name will be known to none but him. Even my family—especially my family—knows nothing of this. Profits will be hidden through investments in the Cayman Islands, out of reach of our revenue service."

The Colombian nodded solemnly, still studying the motives of the foreigner. "You understand, Senator Raitt, that I am only asking these things to determine whether or not you will be a long range investor. I am indeed interested in cultivating good customers." He reached into the breast pocket of his suit and pulled out a small packet of white powder which he placed on the glass table before them. Smiling at the American, he said, "Tomorrow we will speak of terms. Of course, what we sell for export is pure and you will be able to test it before we finalize our agreement. But now, I think it is time for you to experience some of our product. This little sample has been cut for your enjoyment."

Raitt watched in fascination as the *padrino* ripped open the plastic with a small pocketknife and deftly arranged the powder into two small lines. He turned and snapped his fingers, summoning one of the bodyguards who immediately handed him a silver straw and withdrew discreetly. Don Ignacio offered Raitt the gleaming, slender tube and motioned toward the neat rows of cocaine.

Wide-eyed, Raitt took the elegant tool and bent forward. He sniffed a line of powder into each nostril, feeling the instantaneous hit. After a moment, he leaned back. "I think I can say without any reservations, Mr. Perea, you have an excellent product."

The older man was pleased. "Yes, there is no doubt as to the quality of what we produce. And, now, let us enjoy our sherry, also of excellent quality. Later there will be entertainment, and at dinner you will be surrounded with beautiful *señoritas*. They will be happy to insure your pleasure for the entire evening, during the course of which you might even learn our national dance, the *cumbia*!" He lifted the glass in a toast. "To your health, Senator."

"And to yours, Mr. Perea." Raitt felt elated. It was going to work out just fine, he thought happily, as he dusted off his nose.

"Now, I wish to tell you a little about my business and how it is run, so that you can appreciate my position," Perea said, settling back in his chair. "Two of my brothers are planters. They have vast lands in the northern coastal regions around Baranquilla and Santa Marta. There they grow the finest grade of marijuana that money can buy."

Raitt nodded, impressed. He'd heard about the top quality "grass" from those areas.

"But, for the cocaine, we must reach further and it goes through many stages. The brother of my wife makes the arrangements to buy the coca leaves from cultivators in Peru and Bolivia, and workers there produce the paste before the product is brought into Colombia. It is then transported over the mountains to our work places in Medellín where one of *my* brothers directs the making of the cocaine base and then, finally, the white powder that you just enjoyed. It is a very dangerous process. The chemicals. Sometimes there are explosions. We have occasionally lost some of our people." The man's gaze drifted away as he paused momentarily before continuing.

"In Bogotá, we package it. We have to be extremely clever now to get it past customs, especially in your country." He shook his head gently. "It must be rolled into thin sheets between plastic, then slipped into the lining of suitcases or hidden in furniture as if it were upholstery. There are other ways we have devised as well, but all require skilled, highly trained workers and a lot of time. Usually, the product is taken to other countries by couriers. Lately our 'mules', as we call them, have not had good luck. For example, two were caught just a day or so ago as they arrived in your capital city. U.S. Customs is getting more diligent, so we must become more resourceful." He looked at Raitt once again. "Whenever possible, we prefer to send bulk packages by boat or plane. However, we encourage others to handle the transportation —and to allow us to make more frequent shipments. The demand in America continues to increase."

"Mr. Perea, my group in the U.S. is ready to do that." Raitt was elated. His opinions of the expanding market in America had just been confirmed.

The Colombian looked at him thoughtfully before continuing. "There is just one more thing I want to make clear before we begin our negotiations. For myself, I have not the same concerns with risk as you. It is true that the laws of my country do prohibit the sale of illegal drugs, however, there are some in positions of importance who realize we must do a certain amount of trade in this commodity to survive, and they can be bought without anyone feeling guilt. We are realistic. Many of our people are very poor, as I am sure you've noticed, from the old ones all the way down to the very young *gamines* who live on the streets of Bogotá."

A snort of disgust from Raitt interrupted Perea. "Yes. I came into contact with some of those little jackals!"

"They do what they must to survive, Senator," Perea said sadly. "Many are sent out from their homes to steal what they can so the family can eat. Others are abandoned at very early ages by parents who do not want to feed the extra mouths. They must live in the alleys or in the sewers beneath the city. The very young are often looked after by another child just a little older. For them there is no other way until they are strong enough to do hard work. Soon enough, they discover there is much demand for workers in the drug trade, and they are paid higher wages than for the work of coffee growing, mining for the emeralds, or even drilling for petroleum. It means a better life for many, so, of course, they take it," he said, with a shrug and a sigh of resignation.

"I was brought up in the tradition of wise business. Historically, my family has assessed the products of their environment and the demands for those products, and then realistically supplied those demands. Often great risk was assumed, which always seemed more preferable to them than plodding along in obscurity and poverty. When opportunities diminished for one of my ancestors in Old Spain, he joined the group of *conquistadores* who braved the interior of this continent, gained control of the mountains inhabited by fierce native tribes...who, by the way, chewed coca leaves as a part of their religious rites...took their gold, and established the settlement of

Santa Fé de Bacatá. That was more than four hundred years ago." He paused to allow time for his quiet words to register.

Raitt sat silently, mesmerized by the don's account.

"After this country got its independence from Spain, it was able to engage in commerce for its own benefit. Picture the map of the western hemisphere, Senator, and you will see that Colombia is in a unique geographical position for trade. It would have been very foolish for my family to ignore those advantages of location. Though the commodities might change through the years, we always strive to provide what is demanded. In this era, it happens to be marijuana and cocaine. I am, therefore, a *coquero.* As long as North Americans clamor for our products, I will supply them.

"You see," he continued, "unlike you, I am merely doing what those before me have done as they built an empire, and then a new country. You must realize, by now, that my entire family is involved in this with me. It would be wise for you to remember that I will not be ruined by exposure, as you would be. Understand also, I am a gentleman who operates within a code of honor, in this as in any other situation. If I say I will ship a certain amount, of a certain quality, then that is what will be shipped.

"Likewise, I will expect payment in an agreeable time or I will assume that you are not doing business within the same code of honor." The black eyes, as focused as twin lasers, burned into Raitt's own. "Do not underestimate me, Senator. If I am wronged, I will have my vengeance."

CHAPTER FIVE

VICTORIA looked at her watch. "I told Susan Cornell I'd meet her at five o'clock. We're going to do some shopping."

"I'll walk over with you," Blake said, admiring the way she looked in the marine blue wool suit with its short narrow skirt. Predictably, her eyes were an intense dark blue. It was the first time he had seen her since the early morning hours when he had brought her back to her car at the Metro station in Arlington. "Bob Arrington wasn't there when I stopped in earlier, and I intend to see him and Stan before I leave."

They headed down the Pentagon corridor toward the Department of the Army. "I've promised some Smithsonian friends that I'd help hostess a party tonight for someone who's retiring," Victoria said. "After Susan and I are finished, I'll go on to the Hyatt Regency for the party. Would you like to meet me there later, after beer call?"

Blake frowned, shaking his head. "I'm afraid I'll be working for the next couple of nights, darling. I was trying to think of a way to break the news to you."

"I thought you said…"

"I did, but there's an active case I'm working on. I've got to do some investigating later tonight and tomorrow. I should be all finished by the end of Saturday night or very early Sunday morning. Then, I'll turn it over to my partner." He paused. "By the way, if you should see me somewhere in the next thirty-six hours or so, you don't know me. I'll be undercover." He winked at her as he studied her face, worried that he might see some resentment to the work interfering with their lives, as it had before. "The rest of Sunday is clear though, and there's a new little restaurant in Georgetown. I think you'll like it. Great food and a Spanish guitar. What about dinner and a chance to talk seriously about how we'll put our lives back together again?" His eyebrows were raised in anticipation.

"That will be wonderful, Blake. Will you call me? I've got the same phone number, even though I moved since…" She didn't finish.

"Ah, can I assume you moved because you missed me and the old place had all those painful memories?" he asked hopefully.

"Yes," she deadpanned. "Rather than get a cat, I moved!"

He grinned. "Okay. I'll call you Sunday mid-morning and you can tell me how to get to your new place."

"Good. I love you, sweetheart," she whispered discreetly. "Have I told you that today?"

"Um-hmm. But, it was hours ago, and anyway, there's no law against saying it twice." He let her walk ahead of him for a few paces so he could get a good look at her long, shapely legs. "Um-hmm!" he repeated with emphasis.

When they arrived at the colonel's office, they found the dark-haired young woman, pretty in a red dress, working at a computer terminal.

"Hey, it's after five o'clock. Day is done!" Victoria exclaimed. "Hasn't Retreat sounded yet?"

Susan Cornell turned from her keyboard and smiled wearily. "It isn't sounded at the Pentagon."

"That was supposed to be a joke. But, now that you mention it, I wonder why not. It was mandatory on all those military posts where I grew up. The bugle sound, or at least a recording of it, at the end of the day was as sure as the sunset."

"Victoria, you just haven't been here long enough to know that no one retreats at the Pentagon." Susan laughed, shaking her head. "Isn't that right, Blake?"

"I think it's a fair assumption."

"Give me a minute to shut down," Susan said. "After staring at this thing all day, believe me, I'm ready to go!"

Just then, a middle-aged army colonel came out of an inner office. He greeted Victoria cordially and then turned to Blake.

"Hello, Blake, it surely is good to see you again." The older man smiled with genuine pleasure as he shook Blake's hand. "I hoped you'd get here in time. Stan tells me he made you an offer you couldn't refuse."

"You know I wanted to see you, Colonel," Blake began, "but, I don't deny that the mention of a party certainly was an extra incentive!"

"I'll give Stan a buzz and he'll be right over, that is if Susan will let him have a couple of hours off." Colonel Arrington winked as he glanced at Susan to check her reaction.

"Certainly," she said. "Victoria and I have important business to take care of. Please tell my husband that I'll take the Metro and be home by seven."

The colonel made the call and assured Blake that Stan was on his way. As Susan talked with her boss about some matters that needed attention before the weekend, Blake bent toward Victoria. "I suspect I'm going to have a hard time waiting for Sunday afternoon," he said in a low voice.

"Look at it this way," she responded in a spirited whisper, "it'll give you time to reflect—and to cut and run if you get cold feet."

The intensity of his answering gaze left Victoria with no doubts. That course of action was the last thing on his mind.

★ ★ ★

THE two women headed down the busy concourse toward the Metro station. While most of the crowd did the same, some few moved in the opposite direction, the skeleton crew charged with the awesome responsibility of holding the nation secure through the night.

Susan, who had held her curiosity in check until they were alone, interrupted Victoria's thoughts. "Well…is there an update on you and Blake?" she asked, looking speculatively at her friend. "I seem to detect a new sparkle in your eyes."

Victoria smiled broadly. "Yes, yes!" She couldn't hide her joy. Then her expression changed to one of thoughtfulness. "It took being apart for a while to make us realize what a wonderful thing we'd had, only to throw it away. When you've made mistakes before, you tend to be very cautious. Both of us are carrying some old baggage. I think I've told you I'm divorced."

Susan nodded her head.

"I was married for two years to someone I'd known for a long time, and yet it was a miserable failure." Victoria paused, frowning with the unhappy memory. "We discovered we weren't suited for each other after all. Neither of us was willing to try to overcome the problems. The decision to end it was mutual. Since then, I've really appreciated my freedom."

"And later, you met Blake and…," Susan urged.

"We were so right together, but our careers kept pulling us apart. Loving him like I did, I was so afraid of being badly hurt if it didn't work out. He was concerned about that as well. Like me, he'd had a bad experience with marriage, only his was much worse."

"Yeah, it was sad. I've heard about it. Colonel Arrington has known Blake since their tour of duty in Vietnam. After they returned to the U.S., they both ended up living in the same area in

Washington, D.C. The colonel was around when Blake got married and later, when he was having all of the trouble with his wife," Susan said. "It must have been an awful situation. I gathered that she was adorable and quite the social butterfly. The colonel said she partied much of the time—with Blake or without him, it didn't seem to matter to her."

"Yes, that's more or less what he told me," Victoria said. "And when he found out she was hooked on cocaine, he tried to get her into treatment. She wouldn't stay with it, though. In the end, she left him for another man. Blake divorced her and a year later, she died of an overdose. It turned out that the one she was living with had been her supplier."

"Was that guy ever caught?"

"Oh, yes, the DEA made certain of that. The man will be in prison for a long time. Still, I think Blake blames himself for not being able to help his wife."

Susan sighed. "It's the great tragedy of our time. One person taking drugs not only hurts himself, but many others all around him." After a pause, she continued. "In the meantime, I'm glad that you and Blake have discovered each other again. Will you see him this weekend?"

"Sunday." Victoria's eyes were radiant.

"Good!" Susan said, squeezing her arm. "Both of you are overdue for some TLC. And now, if I may distract you for a while, let's march forward to the first selection on the main menu. I couldn't believe it when I saw the ad for Eugenie's in the Post. That shop has the most gorgeous lingerie in the D.C. area, and rarely a sale!"

★   ★   ★

THE unkempt young man hurried onto the subway just as the warning chime sounded and the doors slid shut with a whoosh. He glanced around, only long enough to see that it would be impossible to find a seat among the rush hour crowd. Grabbing the overhead bar, he braced himself as the train lurched forward.

The temporary discomfort didn't bother Harry Pharr in the least. He felt too much elation right then to worry about the small stuff. The fat envelope of bills in the breast pocket of his rumpled suit pressed reassuringly against him.

It was all he could do to keep from laughing out loud at how easy it had been to pull off the deal. He set up the sale by phone. Remembering to keep some of the white powder for himself, he put the two kilos of cocaine in a canvas tote bag, and then went to the mall. The buyer was waiting for him, sitting on a bench, with a similar bag containing the money. They made the switch and nobody was the wiser.

Pharr recalled how he had strolled to the nearest men's room and settled down comfortably on a commode to count the money. Already primed on amphetamines, he took time for a quick snort of coke from the small bag in his pocket. He still had to pay Dominguez for this deal. No problem. The Cuban could wait on his money. It was time to party.

The subway came to a halt at Pentagon Station. Several military men carrying briefcases left. Pharr moved into one of the empty seats as a new flood of people entered the car. There were more uniforms and several young women in tailored suits. He winked at a couple of the women as they sat down near him. They didn't seem to notice. The train rocked along, then stopped, started again, quickly picking up speed.

Pharr was unaware that his face had twisted into a sneer. It infuriated him when women ignored him. However, his recent promotion in the drug trade had given him such satisfaction that he wasn't able to stay angry for very long. He reminded himself of the large amount of money he'd just made. *A few more deals like that and*

I'll be rich. That ought to impress the babes. I could use one right now. One of these, maybe. Show her what a real man is like. He smiled maliciously at the idea. *Yeah, it might be fun.* Pharr's gaze darted to the two women who were sitting nearest him, across the aisle and one seat forward. One of them was dressed in red and had long, black hair. The other one wore blue. He liked blue. He stared at her soft, dark gold hair. It was cut short, baring soft creamy skin on her neck. He could hear snatches of their conversation as the train sped along.

"...exhibition soon...Renoir..."

"I don't want to miss......."

"...............last week."

Then in a louder voice, the one in red said, "Federal Triangle is next. Let's get off there. I have to deliver a packet."

The women were too intent on their own plans to notice the furtive glances from the other side of the aisle. Nor did they notice when they left the train that the muscular young man with the dirty hair dusting his shoulders followed them.

For a while he lost them as they left the subway and disappeared into one of the imposing stone buildings on the triangle. He thought his little game was over, but while he stood there deciding what to do next for fun, the two women reappeared. He fell in behind them as they crossed the street and headed toward a mall nearby.

Pharr thought it was a good omen. Fate was playing them into his hands. He relaxed as he strolled along the mall several yards behind the two. He pushed the sleeves of his coat up on his arm, turned up his collar, shoved hands into pants pockets, and assumed the fashionable slouch of the current trendsetters. He reminded himself that he needed one more thing to have the right look, and he'd take care of it soon. Image was important if he intended to be a high roller.

In front of a swank lingerie store the women stopped to admire the displays in the window. Pharr could see the women were smiling, and in a few minutes they entered the shop.

He bought a hot dog from a nearby concession stand and lounged against a pillar while he ate. The mall was fairly crowded with people, preoccupied as they hurried to complete their shopping. Working stiffs, he thought. Fools. Rummaging in his pocket, he found a toothpick left over from some other meal and began picking his teeth absentmindedly.

When he saw the women going deeper into the store, he decided to do some shopping of his own. It wouldn't take long. There was a jewelry store nearby, and he knew exactly what he wanted. Within ten minutes, the purchase was made and he sauntered out of the store wearing a very wide, very shiny gold chain around his neck.

He took a couple more minutes to buy a soda and then popped another "speckled bird," his fond term for the oblong, blue-specked amphetamine pills. As he returned to his lounging spot in front of the shop, he saw that the ladies had progressed to the cashier's counter.

Idly, he wondered what they'd look like in those little lacy things that were displayed in the window. Just thinking about it made his body tingle. It had been too damn long since he had had a woman, and tonight was the night to end that losing streak, he decided.

The women came out of the shop, and Pharr boldly headed their way. Coming face to face with them, he smiled familiarly. "He-e-ey!" The toothpick wobbled crazily in the corner of his mouth as he spoke in a deep, rumbling voice.

Victoria and Susan stopped to look at him in astonishment. Then, grimacing to one another, they walked around him and continued on their way.

"Revoltingly sleazy!" Susan muttered under her breath.

"It's obvious *he* doesn't think so," Victoria said, looking over her shoulder.

"Is he following us?"

"No. He's walking very slowly. Probably looking for someone

else to pick up."

What had been idle entertainment for Harry Pharr became an obsession. Throwing the toothpick to the pavement, he resumed his stalking with determination. One of the females would be his.

CHAPTER SIX

PHARR was careful to stay about twenty paces behind the women. When the two stopped to look into shop windows, he did the same. Each time one of the women glanced backward, he managed to disappear in the crowd.

Victoria and Susan were more interested in elegant clothes in the upscale shops than they were in the weird stranger, and they lingered a while longer, enjoying the beautiful displays in store windows. Finally exiting the mall, they walked briskly in the early darkness to the nearby Metro Center where several subway lines intersected.

Close behind, Pharr became more anxious as they neared the busy station. The frenzy of the rush hour crowd forced him to stay near or risk losing them in the crush. Watching as they looked at the route board for information, he could tell that the women would be taking different trains. The brunette was heading south on the Blue Line. The other one was taking the eastbound Red Line. A wicked smile played around his mouth. The Red Line also would take him to his neighborhood in the northeastern quadrant of the city. Yeah! Luck was with him.

"Aren't you going back to your apartment?" Susan asked when she saw Victoria checking the fare to Union Station.

"No. Tonight I've got party obligations. I'll get off at Union and take a cab to the Hyatt Regency."

In a few moments, they had bought the necessary tickets and

waved goodbye as each headed for a different track.

Staying in the background, Pharr shadowed the tall, slender shape through the crowds. Once they'd reached the platform, he continued to keep his distance, but the woman's blue suit was never out of his sight as they milled about in the throng beside the tracks.

The lights glowed on and off along the edge of the platform, signaling an incoming train. Pharr moved in closer, his eyes shifting left and right as he squeezed through the crush until he was right behind the woman. His muscles were taut, ready to spring. When the train rumbled alongside of them and the doors opened, the mass of people moved headlong into the car. Instantly, he grabbed her arm and jerked her roughly to one side where the seats were arranged in an alcove, out of sight of most of the passengers. He shoved her down into one of the seats and sat beside her.

Shocked speechless, Victoria turned her head and looked into a pair of wild eyes set in a menacing face. It was the man she'd seen earlier with the big gold chain around his neck. A movement of his arm caused her gaze to shift to his coat pocket where his hand held something.

Rancid breath flooded her nasal passages when he whispered with a sneer, "That's right, babe. A gun. You'd better not do nothing but what I tell you."

Fighting the panic, Victoria stopped trying to pull out of his grasp and sat still.

Her gaze swept the car, trying to signal by facial expression that she was in danger. No one was looking her way. Some were reading newspapers, others talking, and some had eyes closed, trying to doze for a few minutes.

"Keep your eyes down!" he snarled. "Don't look at nobody." He had one strong arm around her and the other held the gun to her ribs. They might have been lovers having a little spat which he was trying to patch, even though they didn't seem like a well-matched couple. Whatever they did or did not seem to be didn't matter. There wasn't a ripple of interest. Pharr was elated. It felt supremely good to be in control of a woman like that, he thought smugly. He'd pull this off with no problem. When the train arrived at Union Station, he jerked her up, holding her close, and melted into the crowd.

"Why are you doing this?" she managed to stammer. "Where are you taking me?"

"Shut up, bitch! You'll see soon enough." His arm tightened around her as he hurried her through the terminal.

The terrified woman looked frantically about her, again trying to signal to someone.

"Keep your eyes down, I said, or you'll be sorry!" He shoved the gun harder against her ribs and smiled for the crowd. Just a little farther, he thought, and then I've got it made.

The escalator brought them up to street level where a sharp blast of November wind greeted them. Taxicabs were lined up in a seemingly endless row, their exhausts creating clouds of steam in the chilly air while the drivers beckoned to anxious travelers. The crowd scattered in all directions at once, like so many dry leaves.

"Come on, come on," Pharr muttered, shoving her roughly as he hurried her past the great fountain in front of the station. People passed by them with heads bent, huddled against the wind, preoccupied with the task of preventing chilly air from getting into collars and sleeves.

Victoria looked to her right, down Delaware Avenue. She could see the Capitol only a few blocks away, its majestic dome illuminating the night sky. "I can't believe this is happening." She spoke to herself in a tortured half-whisper.

"Believe it, baby," the man responded with a sneer.

They had gone past the station, moving eastward across a deserted, dimly lit parking lot. Realizing her chances of getting help were growing slimmer as they got farther away from the station, the woman panicked. Still clutching the lingerie package, she shoved it into the man's face and tried to pull away. Caught off guard, Pharr lost his grip on her and she wrenched free and broke into a run.

"Help me! Somebody, help me!" Victoria screamed, sprinting across the asphalt. With terror mounting, she quickly realized that high heels and narrow skirt hampered her escape.

Cursing his carelessness, Pharr raced after her, soon closing the distance. He hurled himself airborne and slammed into her, knocking her to the pavement. She lay there, stunned. The man gasped for breath from the exertion in the cold. He kicked her in the stomach and felt better as he watched her knees draw up in pain. Pulling her up roughly, he clamped one arm around her neck and the other around her waist in a vise-like grip. Unable to extricate herself from what felt like steel bands, Victoria cried out in anger and helplessness.

Her breathing was restricted to short gasps as Pharr alternately pushed and pulled her along the darkened streets lined with dilapidated rowhouses. A few cars passed them, none stopped or even slowed down. They went several blocks, making various turns before he led her up a walkway to one of the houses. No light came from the windows on any of the three levels. There was silence all around, except for traffic noises wafting over from a busy street several blocks away.

Instead of climbing the stairs to the front door, he steered her around to the basement stairway and shoved her forward. She stumbled down the steep, metal steps, missing every other one. About halfway down, her thin heels caught the edge of one step and she fell, landing hard at the bottom.

Pharr hopped over her, turned his key in the lock, then dragged her inside. He switched on the overhead light and carefully locked the door behind him.

When Victoria finally lifted her head, she saw through the yellow glare a dingy room whose only furniture was a sagging recliner with a small table next to it. In one corner was a mattress. Clothes and sundry objects littered the floor. In the kitchenette, dirty dishes rose up in tilted stacks out of the sink, with more spread in lesser piles along the brief length of counter. Even in her groggy state, she could see insects moving in and out amongst the clutter. There was no door, other than the one they'd entered. Slowly, she shifted her gaze to the short, muscular man who remained near the entrance, staring at her.

Pharr laughed harshly, his head tilting back in perverse mirth as he saw terror shimmer in her eyes. He moved toward her, speaking softly, but the menace was unmistakable. "Well, Miss Goldilocks, that wasn't so hard, was it? And, now, here you are…and Dr. Feelgood is ready to see you now." Once again, he laughed in a way that promised no mercy.

As in a nightmare, she heard a hint of a scream escape from her constricted throat. Shivering violently from both cold and fear, Victoria got to her feet, instinctively choosing to face her attacker rather than cower on the floor beneath him. Her mind spun rapidly, trying to think of a method of escape as she drew away, walking backward and not daring to take her eyes off him as he approached.

Continuing his advance, he crooned to her in a singsong voice more chilling than if he had been shouting. "It won't do you no good. Ain't nobody else in this here house. Upstairs is just used for stashing—when they got something to stash." He paused. "And the neighbors don't care. So, scream if you want to, baby, 'cause I like it!" He breathed heavily as a leering grin stretched across his mouth. His eyes were glassy, trance-like.

Victoria's back bumped the wall. He stood directly in front of her, blocking her only path of escape. "No," she pleaded, feeling sick with dread. "Please let me go."

Suddenly the expression on his face grew from teasing to savage. He lunged forward and grabbed her jacket, ripping buttons as he pulled it open. In another furious swipe, he split the soft silk fabric of her blouse from neck to waist. Pinning her left arm against the wall, he squeezed a breast.

She swung at him with her free arm, the curving fingers bolstered with a sudden strength that came from within and rocketed outward.

"Ow!" Pharr bellowed, releasing her as the nails raked across his face, leaving lines that oozed red. "You little bitch!" he shouted, wiping his hand along the damaged cheek in disbelief at her defiance. He saw blood and his teeth bared, revealing his evil. An ugly laugh followed. "You're gonna find out what a real man is like!" he taunted. Malevolence blazed in his eyes. "You'll see. More than your soldier boys in their macho uniforms. Fakes. All of 'em. Well, not me, sister. I'm the real thing," he bragged, jabbing at his chest with a thick thumb. "Many satisfied women can tell you that."

He was enjoying his game, laughing again. Then without warning, he slapped her hard across the face. "Understand?" Again he slapped her. "Huh?" And again. "Huh?"

She felt the warm liquid well up from the split in the corner of her mouth. Almost instantly, something in her changed. Perhaps it was the stinging sensation on her face mingled with the taste of blood, or the absolute realization that she was a prisoner without any hope of escape. Maybe it was simply the fact that there were no longer any unknowns. She knew exactly what was about to happen. One of those, or the sum total of them served to break the grip of terror, and as the fear left, outrage took its place. The unconscionable situation was brought sharply into focus. For a brief, heroic moment, her dignity made a stand.

Victoria's pale eyes seemed to ice over as they narrowed and gazed directly, piercingly, into the dark ones of her attacker. Her mouth curved upward into a smirk. The change in her demeanor was so abrupt and so unexpected that for a few seconds, Pharr was held

53

motionless by her bold offensive.

She stepped toward him as she spat out the words. "A real man? No. A mistake of nature. Some kind of mutation that gets its thrills by beating up women."

Courage, however admirable, cannot stand for long against brute strength. The sound of her voice had barely faded when the next blows landed. One knotted fist punched her ribs, the other, her eye. The force of the blows slammed her into the wall, releasing an agonizing scream that hung in the air as her body slid to the floor. She lay there, unable to move. Blood trickled from a split above her eye.

Pharr had regained his confidence. Fueled now with a white-hot rage, he dragged her onto the filthy mattress and tore away the rest of her clothes.

Frantically, she fought him, but with each movement of her arms and legs, the searing pain in her chest left her a poor match for his strength. The weight of his body increased the agony, each breath was torture. Finally she quit struggling.

CHAPTER SEVEN

VICTORIA lay shivering upon a pile of rags where Pharr had tossed her, feet tied and hands tied behind her back. Each time she tried to get up, she couldn't maintain her balance and fell. She fought to gain control of the angry tears that wouldn't stop as waves of nausea swept over her and intermittent sobs racked her bruised body. Her left eye was swollen shut, and blood from the cut above it had dried, trapping some of her hair in its hardened mass. She could feel the taut soreness of her lips, puffed and bleeding from several split places and there was a hideous burning sensation between her legs. With each breath she took there was a sharp, stabbing pain in her chest, overriding any other.

The bare bulb in the ceiling fixture remained on, enabling her to see the naked form on the mattress. The man was sleeping, snoring noisily.

Willing herself to think clearly, she assessed her predicament. Her friends must have wondered why she hadn't gone to the party. But would they think something terrible had happened? Probably not. They would assume she had changed her plans at the last minute and simply forgot to call, although it was unlike her. It would be sometime tomorrow before they would suspect something was wrong. Even if she were reported missing, the police wouldn't treat a disappearance seriously for a couple of days.

"Blake," she whispered, as her thoughts switched to him. She felt like she had been torn from him just as they were rediscovering each other. It was he, more than anyone else, who would know how to track her and free her from this bizarre situation. This was Friday. He had promised to call on Sunday afternoon. Only then would he begin to think something was amiss.

What if I'm not set free by then? If he calls and I don't answer, will he think I've changed my mind about renewing our relationship? I'd teased him about doing that very thing. He might think I was avoiding him by not answering the phone. Surely, though, he knows how deeply I love him.

Another almost unbearable question surfaced to torture her mind. *Will Blake and I be able to overcome what has happened to me? If I live through it.*

The nightmarish hours wore on slowly. Memories of her mother and father flashed before her, bringing on a new wave of sadness. Tears rolled down the sides of her face, spilling across her ears and wetting the back of her hair. Her parents had been killed in Italy five years earlier when their tour bus skidded off the highway and into a ravine. She still grieved over the loss.

I'm so thirsty. How much more of this can I stand? What will he do with me when he gets tired of this game? Will my life end too soon, just as my parents' lives did? Victoria heard herself repeating words she had learned as a child and had depended upon for strength ever since. *"Yea, though I walk through the valley of the shadow of death, I will fear no evil, for Thou art with me…"* Whatever would happen, she was not alone.

Her body grew weaker and more chilled as time went on. She fought to keep her senses alert, ready to grasp at the slightest opportunity to escape. With her one good eye, she kept watch while an untrained army of roaches, undeterred by the brightness and assured of their squatters' rights, ran helter-skelter along the floor, up the walls and across the ceiling. The surrealistic scene was intensified by the drip, drip of a leaky faucet filling the room with its hypnotic sound. In relentless cadence, it seemed to be marking the process of destruction as her life was irrevocably altered.

Something brushing against her feet awakened Victoria from her fitful dozing. She struggled to sit up, crying out as a dark, furry rat scuttled across the floor to the security of a dark corner. She shook with fresh pain triggered by the violent motion.

"Shut up, whore, or I'll really let you have it!" Pharr shouted, startled from sleep, his eyes blinking rapidly to adjust to the light. With a scowl, he got up from the mattress, stumbled to the refrigerator, and grabbed a can of beer. He popped it open, took a couple of gulps and belched loudly. Then, reacting to the cold air, he turned the knob of a small electric heater.

Pharr paced the room until his attention was drawn to an object on the floor. "Hey, whadayaknow! Here's your purse. Lucky it didn't get lost on the street somewhere. Wouldn't be smart to leave a trail." He placed the beer on the small table and bent to pick up the brown leather bag. "Let's see. Keys! Hey, bet I can use these. Looks like car keys…and house keys. Am I warm?" He grinned at her, enjoying her angry reaction to his taunts. "Maybe you've got some money." He continued his search. "Hm-mn, here's your driver's license. Yep, that's you, all right, only without the black eye. And your name is…well, I'm disappointed. It ain't Goldilocks. It's V-I-C-T-O-R-I-A Dunbar. Or is that Dum-bar? Ha, ha! Nah, you don't sound like nobody special." Quickly tiring of the game, he located the money, took it out, then threw the purse with the rest of its contents onto the floor.

In the kitchen area, he pulled some things out of a drawer. He carried them to the recliner and sat, quickly tossing a pill into his mouth and chasing it with the rest of the beer.

Victoria watched while he sprinkled marijuana from a small, clear sandwich bag onto a cigarette paper. Pharr took his time, spreading the little pile of dried plant material evenly along the length of the thin paper. He wrapped the paper around the weed and brought the edges together, looking at her as he slowly slid his tongue across the glued side of the paper. He didn't lower his stare as he flicked a lighter into flame and lit the joint. The smell of acrid smoke hit her nostrils. She tried to control the nausea that had begun again as dread of a new attack consumed her.

After a while he came and stood over her, once more enjoying the disgust etched on her battered face. Dropping down on one knee, he began to remove the tight cord binding her ankles as he crooned to her in a nonsensical babble.

Victoria realized her only chance was about to occur, and summoned all her remaining strength. Speed and surprise would provide the only advantage. The instant her legs were freed, her foot shot forward and landed a kick squarely between Pharr's legs. He fell with an inhuman howl, his body rolling over.

Immediately, she was on her feet, the adrenalin ignoring pain and pumping away her stiffness as she ran for the door. With hands still tied behind her back, she fumbled for the knob. Then she remembered it was locked and looked around frantically for the keys. *Where are they? I can't get out without them!*

She spotted them on the kitchen counter. Glancing at Pharr, she saw him still grimacing with the hurt, but he had managed to get to his hands and knees. Fighting for each ragged breath, she raced for the keys, then back to the door. Her hands shook with urgency. *He's moving! I can't get the key into the lock!*

Pharr stumbled forward. His powerful arms reached out and heaved her sideways against the hard edge of the counter.

Victoria cried out as she felt the bone in her upper arm snap with a new agony that brought her to her knees.

Once again he lunged at her, slapping, punching and kicking. He dragged her by her hair along the floor until he was gasping for air. Delivering one last vengeful blow to her nose, the man lowered himself upon the desecrated body writhing in pain.

Within seconds, Victoria Dunbar released her hold on reality, slipped into a mental twilight, and then lost all consciousness. Mercifully, she was spared Harry Pharr's final performance of the evening.

CHAPTER EIGHT

IAN Monroe looked down from the topmost floor of his stately Alexandria townhouse to Fairfax Street below. Shiny, black limousines were parked along the curb in the autumn dusk, while their uniformed drivers lounged against them, leisurely smoking and exchanging gossip. Patiently, they waited to relay their wealthy and powerful charges to the next segment of this Saturday night's round of galas, those important social gatherings that formed the spokes in the great wheel turning the national government.

It's like a damned fraternity, Monroe thought. There was an air of pride about the men. He doubted they felt any less important in the march of history than the people whom they conducted around the Washington area. Monroe understood the feeling, although on a loftier scale. It was a conviction of those who lived in and around the capital, simply due to the proximity of national and international events swirling around them, that they were intimately connected to those things.

Through the branches of trees fast losing their red and yellow leaves, he could see patches of the Potomac River. Along it to the north lay the District of Columbia. Monroe loved living in Old Town, surrounded by history and old ghosts. Alexandria had been quite a port in its heyday before it was pre-empted by Washington and Baltimore. Some of the streets were still paved with cobblestones that once were used as ballast in the ships traveling up and down the river with their cargoes of flour and tobacco. George Washington himself had helped to lay out those streets and had worshipped nearby at Christ Church.

He smiled as he remembered that he was descended from a long line of Scottish merchants who had made the port what it was in the Eighteenth Century. The first, Angus Monroe, had a daughter who married an English baronet. The title helped to keep the family uplifted in society. The combination of crafty business sense and social prestige created a highly respected Virginia dynasty. Down through the generations, Monroes had continued to play a large part in the republic's progressive march.

He felt a duty to insure a continuity from past to present and into the future. At the same time, he also felt his family had earned for him the right to enjoy his social position, and to use that advantage to further his personal ambitions while helping America—in his own unique way.

At age fifty-two, he had begun reassessing what those particular ambitions were. He had always assumed he'd go into the family business, and then when he was established, run for political office. A reversal of the family fortunes, however, before he came of age made that impossible. His father had made some bad investments and had had the audacity to commit suicide rather than correct his financial errors. Left with the scandal and the problem of keeping Monroe House out of the hands of the creditors, his mother had struggled, managing to keep the roof over their heads while losing everything else. The strain probably contributed to her early death ten years later.

By then, Monroe had entered the legal field, and after some years, he was on sound financial footing. That hardly meant he had the enormous amounts of money available to run a campaign. Until recently. When he'd least expected it, he had become a New Age merchandiser with a cargo infinitely more valuable than those of his predecessors. It was then he realized, much to his surprise, that he really didn't want to be an elected official. Too many constraints on one's life. No, he preferred having the power to pull the strings, rather than dance at the end of them.

He watched a black Chrysler Imperial approach and stop. Its passengers, in evening dress, alighted and climbed the steps leading up to the main floor. Mr. and Mrs. Stanley Timmons, State Department. Monroe told himself it was time to rejoin his party.

The stately Federal Period reception rooms, with walls covered in blue silk damask and original pine floors overlaid with Aubusson carpets, were filled with fashionably dressed people gathered in small groups. Under crystal chandeliers, conversations floated through the air against a background of sweet sounds from a string quartet. Occasionally, there was the gentle clink of glasses as waiters circulated with cocktails borne on silver trays.

"Oh, darling, the Wyeth exhibit was wonderful! His work is so sensitive." The bejeweled matron was adamant.

"Even so, Beatrice," retorted a silver haired man in black tie, "I think he could have found a more fetching creature for his subject, one with a prettier face to paint…or…ah…with whom to while away all those hours."

"Nonsense, Charles, if one carefully studies the entire Helga Suite, one realizes that her face mirrors the beauty he saw in her soul." The woman with the dazzling diamond necklace turned to their host who had just joined the circle. "Don't you think so, Ian?" Attention riveted on the distinguished Monroe.

"Why, yes, my dear Beatrice, I think it does. Perhaps in Wyeth's devotion to Helga, he managed to blend in his soul as well." Monroe's smile encompassed the entire circle of guests. Beatrice beamed.

"However," Monroe continued, "we men do like to look at beautiful faces, I must admit." He winked at Charles, who, after having just fallen from grace for voicing his earthy sentiments, now was reinstated.

"Thanks, Ian, for supporting an honest man's point of view," Charles said with warmth. "How have you been lately? We haven't seen you in a while."

"I've been very well, thank you. Staying busy at the firm, you know, as well as keeping a weather eye on the doings in Congress— particularly the AWACS debate. The Israelis are extremely concerned with the prospect of President Reagan winning approval to sell the planes to the Saudis. I can't say I blame them."

"Yes, but I don't think they have any real worry. The Saudis are among the most moderate of the Arab nations," one of the other men in the group responded. "Besides, we may have more pressing problems to worry about in America than the Israelis and the Arabs and their eternal squabbling. I'm very concerned about the huge volume of illegal drugs coming into this country. According to the latest reports, our country is being inundated by ever increasing amounts. I've even heard a rumor that the President is planning to launch a crackdown on drug smuggling in Florida. Do you suppose that it could do any good?"

"I've heard a few whispers, also," Ian said, nodding. "It's possible that it would help, John. Most of the drugs seem to be coming in through Florida, or the southwest. If we can stop the flood, it should make a difference." He paused. "However, they'll have to cover a large area to be successful. I understand that there are many places to hide down there."

"Some say the President plans to name Vice President Bush to direct the operation. I certainly hope something effective can be done," Charles added. "The young people of this nation are going to be ruined if we don't put the squeeze on those drug lords."

"That may be, but I've always had a somewhat opposite opinion," Monroe responded. Leaning closer, he added, "I think drug addicts are the weak ones in our society. I don't think the country loses much there."

"A good point," Charles agreed, nodding sagely. "I'd never quite thought of it that way."

With a smile, Monroe beckoned a white-coated waiter to approach with another round of drinks and wished the group a good evening. He threaded his way through the crowd, nodding, smiling and shaking hands. Pausing before a cosmopolitan trio, Monroe greeted the French ambassador and his wife.

"Welcome, Mr. Ambassador. Madame Dumont. It is so good of you to come." Then, he turned approving eyes toward the third member of the group. Monroe didn't recognize her. She was petite with dark hair and dressed in black brocade. Unmistakably French.

"Monique, allow me to present our host, Mr. Ian Monroe," the ambassador was saying. "Mr. Monroe, this is Madame Monique D'Aquin, director of the Musée de Mornay in Paris."

"*Enchanté, Madame D'Aquin, et bienvenu chez moi,*" Monroe said, bowing over her hand.

"*Merçi, beaucoup, Monsieur Monroe.*" Deep brown eyes looked directly into his. "*C'est un plaisir.*"

"Madame D'Aquin is in Washington to help organize the Renoir exhibit for the National Gallery," Madame Dumont offered proudly.

"Wonderful!" Monroe exclaimed, beaming at the attractive young woman. "I've heard exceptional things about the Musée de Mornay. I'm sure, madame, that your expertise will be invaluable to our gallery here."

"You are too kind," Madame D'Aquin murmured, charming him with her heavily accented English. "It is a joy for me to be able to do this for the work of my favorite impressionist. Are you perhaps an art connoisseur, Monsieur Monroe?"

"No, I won't pretend to be that, but I do know what I like," he responded emphatically. "I've collected a few things which bring me enjoyment. Although I don't have any of his work, I, too, appreciate the fine talent of Renoir."

"Ah, bien. Then, let me say that, should you want a private showing of the paintings, I am sure I could arrange it."

"I shall look forward to that with pleasure, he said cordially. "May I contact you so that we can set an agreeable date?"

"Bien, sur, monsieur," she responded softly, inclining her head. As Monroe bent over her hand once again, he smiled inwardly. Another more subtle invitation than the one spoken had been issued by her dark eyes. The tour might prove to be a very personal one indeed.

After a few more pleasantries, he continued his way through the rooms with a feeling of deep satisfaction. He had gathered the cream of Washington society—the socialites, the political powerhouses, military brass, foreign dignitaries, patrons of the arts and the artists, themselves. No small achievement, he knew. It was, in fact, a cross section of the cream, a glittering collage of the upper strata of humanity.

"Well, well, Ian, wonderful party!" announced an approaching voice. "Wonderful party!"

"Senator Raitt, how are you? I'm honored that you could come."

"Always a pleasure to attend your parties, Ian!" the youthful lawmaker said, clapping Monroe on the back.

"Where is Melanie? My parties aren't complete without her," Monroe said, expansively.

"Why, thank you, Ian. She's here, circulating, I suppose. Melanie always wanders away to look for other conversation when I'm working. I've been talking business, trying to get a few more senators lined up to oppose this damned AWACS proposal." The personable senator looked around as they talked, nodding and waving all the while, shaking the hands of those who walked by.

"Still campaigning, I see."

"One can't ignore any opportunity to get votes, you know." Leaning forward in a much lower voice, he added, "Speaking of opportunity, can we talk privately?"

"Certainly. Come into the library." Monroe led the way into an oak-paneled room off the salon.

Ten minutes later, the two men emerged. The senator found his wife and made a showy exit, pressing hands and hugging ladies as he worked his way out the door, while Monroe joined a knot of people discussing music. One of the speakers, a short, heavy-set man, paused to greet his host.

"Oh, good evening, Ian. A charming party. We were just commenting on the string quartet. Quite a polished group of musicians you've assembled."

"I'm happy their music pleases you, Steven, old boy. I do find them to be a splendid group, and their Haydn selections are among my favorites."

"Yes, yes! Haydn's music is superb," offered another man, a well-known conductor. "In my opinion, there has been no equal to his genius in thematic development. What he could do with a simple melody was incredible! What fun he had teasing, repeating, breaking it apart then putting it together again! Ah, only then did we have music worthy of these stringed instruments."

"Indeed, Bernard, I'll give Haydn his due. Yet, I think Beethoven's work was superior," Steven countered.

"All the more to Haydn's credit, I say," an elderly individual interjected. He had a quavering voice accompanied by a distinct whistle. Peering at the portly man through thick glasses, he continued. "You may have forgotten…uh-hmm…Haydn, in his later years…um…instructed Beethoven!"

The others were momentarily taken aback. The old man had been standing quietly, listening intently as the others in the circle talked. His white hair was slightly disarrayed, but the beard and mustache were neatly trimmed. Although he was stooped and his movements stiff, it was obvious his mind was still limber.

The conductor nodded his head in surprise. "Quite so, I do believe, quite so. A good point."

Steven remained silent, his pudgy cheeks puckered.

Monroe wondered who the old gentleman was. He didn't know him and assumed he had come as someone else's guest. He was about to engage the man in conversation when he saw Margaret Haynes coming toward him.

Each time he saw her, Monroe marveled at her beauty. She was younger than he, maybe forty or so, he thought. However, her looks attracted even the very young males. She wore a burgundy velvet suit and at her throat was a large garnet pendant. With a mane of glossy auburn hair and deep green eyes, she was the most beautiful woman around. In addition, she was witty, intelligent, polished—and unattached at present. His instincts told him they were well suited for one another, and her manner toward him implied that she thought along the same lines. He knew she would accept if he proposed marriage.

"Ian, dear, I've been looking for you everywhere," she said, trying to pout but not succeeding. A dimple in the center of each cheek lent her face a cheery, angelic aspect.

"Good evening, Margaret. You're a perfect vision!" Monroe said warmly as he embraced her.

"Why haven't I seen you lately?"

Although she smiled in a teasing way, he could see that her eyes watched intently for his response. "Simply the press of business, my dear. I've missed you." And he had. He always enjoyed her company.

"I'm going to the ballet tonight with a group of friends. Nureyev will dance in *Swan Lake*. Why don't you come with us? You know there are always last minute cancellations. I'm sure you could get a seat."

Monroe was tempted. It would be very pleasant, he knew. But, he also knew it would mean complications if he let her, or any woman in his social circle, get too close. He caught a glimpse of Monique D'Aquin across the room. Involuntarily, he sighed. Either woman would want to be involved in every facet of his life…and, if too much were discovered, his whole operation could be ruined. It was a lonely feeling.

"I'm sorry, darling," he said gently, kissing her on the cheek. "I really do have paperwork to attend to tonight in preparation for a case on Monday. Enjoy for me, too, will you?"

As Margaret left with her friends, other guests gravitated toward the foyer in little groups of twos and fours. Talk had turned to supper. It was time for the next stop of the evening. Thanking the host of Monroe House for yet another sparkling party, people began to depart.

The sharp-witted senior citizen left alone, however, quietly shuffling down the dimly lit sidewalk. At the corner he crossed Queen Street and continued his careful pace until he was completely out of sight of Monroe House. There was only one couple walking ahead, almost two blocks away. A glance over his shoulder assured him no one was behind as he turned right onto Cameron. His steps quickened a little, losing some of their stiffness. One more turn and he spotted the outline of a compact car parked about halfway down the block.

In a few vigorous strides, the man covered the remaining distance. He opened the door on the passenger side and got in. "Let's go," he said in a sure voice, without a trace of a whistle.

CHAPTER NINE

MIKE Chapman sat up from his lounging position and started the car. "Anybody after you?" he asked his partner. The tension showed on his dark face as he expertly eased the car onto Royal Street.

"I don't think so. I do believe they bought my act," Blake Harrison said, solemnly. "No doubt it was because I astounded them with my incredible knowledge of music." He winked at Mike and grinned slightly. "Let's get the hell out of here, just in case."

In moments they were on a busy thoroughfare. While Chapman threaded the car through traffic, Harrison gave him a brief report.

"Nice party. All the beautiful people were there including our friend, the Honorable Senator Kenneth Raitt. He mingled with the guests for a while. Made sure everybody saw him—at least twice. Handshakes, hugs, and hot air all the way. Then he and Monroe had a little private meeting in the library. I found that to be an interesting development." He paused in thought. "Did you get anything on your end?"

"I walked around a bit, but I didn't see anything to speak of. There were surveillance cameras mounted all around the upper floor of the house angled at the grounds. That changed my mind about climbing the fence! Do you suppose Monroe needs all that protection?"

"Some valuable silver pieces and a rare porcelain collection are reported to be in the house. Nothing to justify all that excessive security. I don't know. I just have a hunch we'll find Ian Monroe is involved in something else shady, and it wouldn't surprise me if it had to do with Raitt."

"Could be. Our surveillance of Monroe last night and earlier today didn't turn up anything suspicious. Tonight's meeting with Raitt might be the red flag we've been looking for," Mike said.

Harrison waited until they had traveled several blocks before removing the heavy glasses and the wig. Gingerly he pried the facial whiskers from his skin. Rummaging in the glove compartment, he found the packet of moistened paper towels that he'd stashed earlier and began removing the white theatrical makeup from his eyebrows. By the time they reached the George Mason Bridge, he almost looked like himself again.

With a little careful fumbling, Blake managed to get out of the baggy evening suit. The agency had supplied one for him that was two sizes too big in order that he could wear it over his own clothes to give the illusion of extra pounds. From the back seat, he got a sweater and pulled it on over his head. The lean, athletic physique was evident once again.

The younger man chuckled as he glanced sideways. "I'll be damned! Clark Kent. And you did that without a telephone booth. Looks like you haven't lost your touch, my man."

"Never underestimate us old-timers."

"Ha! Old-timer, my ass!" Chapman glanced at the rear-view mirror as he continued. "Man, it's been good working in the field with you these past few years. You've taught me a lot and I'm gonna miss that, even though I'm happy you're moving up. You'd better enjoy the excitement on this case while you can. I'll bet headquarters will reel you in to your desk as soon as it's finished."

Chapman kept one eye on the mirror as he drove. They had reached the District, and after a few sharp turns and seeing nothing suspicious, he relaxed. "Okay," he said with a sigh of relief. "We're home free." There was silence for a few minutes while both men shook off the sense of danger that kept nerves taut during all covert operations.

"Mike, did the other team follow Raitt and his wife when they left Monroe's?"

"Yeah. Surveillance radioed that they were at another party."

"Well, then, unless we get an emergency call, we're finished for tonight. Earlier than I expected." Harrison paused for a moment, as if trying to make a decision. "Could you pull over at the next phone booth? I want to make a personal call." When Chapman eased the car into a gas station, Harrison headed for the phone. He dropped in the coins and dialed Victoria's number. No answer. He left a message, hoping she'd pick up the phone while he was talking. But she didn't. He'd called her that morning also. No answer then either. He was disappointed. He'd only seen her for a brief time yesterday at the Pentagon, before she left to go shopping with Susan, when he had told her he'd be tied up Saturday evening. She was probably out with friends. Your fault, Harrison, he told himself, and headed back to the car.

"No luck?" Chapman asked, seeing the frown on his partner's face.

"Nope."

"What? No date with some gorgeous blonde for the symphony or the ballet?" Harrison's swinging lifestyle was no secret and the envy of most guys at DEA headquarters.

"Hell, no! I haven't thought about anything but this case lately," Harrison answered, averting his eyes. For now, he wanted to keep the new developments in his personal life to himself. "What about you? Is your wife expecting you home soon?"

"Nah. Julia's working the night shift at the hospital this week," he answered, feeling a twinge of loneliness. He hated going back to their apartment and not finding her there. Michael Chapman was one solid man who loved being with his wife. They had been married five years, and he still preferred being with her more than anyone else.

"I guess we'll have to find a quiet, dull place where a couple of wallflowers can have a beer."

"Fine with me," Chapman agreed, turning the car toward Georgetown.

★ ★ ★

Miguel Dominguez sat in a massive leather chair in his Crystal City condominium trying to decide what to do for entertainment. He was tired of TV. He'd just watched the University of Florida lose to a lousy west coast team. Damn! Ruined his Saturday afternoon.

As if that weren't enough, one of his distributors was dragging his feet on completing payment for the last deal. He was annoyed. Why hadn't he heard from him? Surely the little piss-ant wouldn't try to pull something stupid.

Dominguez needed some distraction. Ginger could provide that, he thought, and reached for the phone. He had met Ginger Kopenski a few weeks ago at a singles bar, and they'd been going together ever since. She was cute—brassy blonde and really stacked, a *tamale picante*. He punched in the number and waited, ring after ring, for her to answer. Finally, hearing her recorder click on, he turned the phone off with a sigh.

He had a lot on his mind. Monroe had recently informed him that they were expanding the operation just as soon as the head man set it up with the Colombians. They had bought an old DC-3 and needed good pilots right away. Earlier in the day, he had brought a guy to meet with the others. That was always a worry, wondering if the group would agree to take somebody new in.

A source had recommended Steve Callahan. The man had good credentials. His flying ability was proven after his tour in Vietnam. Before that, he'd played pro football. He'd been famous for a while, first at Georgia Tech, then with the Redskins. Now he owned an air cargo business in Atlanta. Dominguez had been pretty impressed with Callahan's experience and he guessed the man would be dependable. He sounded desperate to make money. Everybody was driven by something and Callahan was no different. The organization had agreed to try him on a few runs. Dominguez knew his search couldn't stop there. He had to find more pilots, and a few more planes. The group had big plans.

In frustration, he stood up and began to pace. He didn't know why he was so restless. At times like this, the old fear returned, a feeling that the world would disappear and he would be left floating in space, alone and empty-handed. Unwanted memories swept over him of an idyllic life suddenly wrenched apart. The hated face flashed into his vision. A stern, bearded orator in olive drab battle fatigues. Castro. The harshness of the man's control in Cuba had left indelible impressions in the memory of a young boy. First there was the outrage expressed by his parents when their home and the sugar plantation were seized. Later, and more shattering, was their terror.

Miguel Dominguez y Chavez learned a valuable lesson in survival from that harsh experience. Never again would he put his trust in the illusion of a protective "polite" society. Instead, he continually reminded himself that only what he could see and touch at any given moment was all he had—not so different from the conclusions of the early cave men. Each day when he awoke, it was with the deep conviction that there were no guarantees.

Nowadays, he kept large amounts of cash in his pockets and stashed in shoeboxes in his condo, his car, and even in his boat— especially in his boat. It was the most likely vehicle for a quick escape. As added insurance against the unknown, he converted some cash into gold and diamonds, wearing as much as he could in case he had to run. He could live for quite a while merely on what he was wearing, not to mention what the Hatteras would bring if he had to sell it. But that would be his last resort.

As he stood at the windows and stared with unseeing eyes at the metropolitan sprawl ten stories below, the phone rang. He was relieved to break away from the troublesome thoughts. Picking it up, he heard a deep, rasping voice.

"Dominguez?"

"Speaking."

"This is Pharr. I'm ready for us to have a little meeting. How about tonight?" The words sounded slurred.

"It's about time I heard from you. I was ready to come looking," Dominguez said peevishly.

"What's your problem, man? It takes time, you know?"

"Yeah, I know. I also know you've been testing the merchandise." Dominguez was unable to keep the disgust out of his voice. He wanted to finalize the business, but it would be the last time he'd trust Pharr. "Where do we meet?"

"Come to the Jade Pagoda in half an hour."

"Where in hell is the Jade Pagoda?"

"Chinatown. Where else? H Street, Northwest."

Pharr hung up abruptly and Dominguez was left staring at the phone, wondering if he should worry. Something felt funny. There was always the danger that someone working for you was DEA. But, knowing that possibility made Dominguez very careful. He personally checked out every new distributor he took on. He knew where Pharr lived, and more or less what he had done for the last five years. He wasn't an undercover agent, just one weird dude.

CHAPTER TEN

MOST of the guests had departed Monroe House by nine, going on to other places. A couple of long time acquaintances lingered for another drink, entertaining their host with idle conversation and bits of gossip. Soon they, too, left and Ian Monroe went upstairs.

The third floor of the house was his private domain. Besides the bedrooms, there was a large sitting room that Monroe preferred to call his study. While the library on the second floor was used for business meetings and conferences, the study was a haven for reading and reflecting, or for personal business.

When the house was renovated recently, an elevator had been installed. Only special guests, arriving in cars with deep tinted windows, drove into the rear courtyard to the canopied ground floor entrance. From there, they took the elevator directly up to the study without risking a chance meeting with anyone from the society crowd who might be on the main floor.

Ches Jackson, chief security observer and enforcer for Monroe's business interests, had just admitted one of those special guests—Ian Monroe's favorite lady-of-convenience. Jackson steered her into the elevator and pushed the button to close the doors. Then he buzzed the valet. "Hey, Dalton, my man. One little hot momma, comin' up!"

His laughter echoed down the hallway as he headed for his office. Located on the ground level near the rear entrance, the small room was filled with monitors relaying information from the surveillance cameras in the reception rooms and the grounds. Adjacent to the office were quarters for the household staff. One room was reserved for him while he was on the job. When he had time off, he preferred his own luxurious apartment in Arlington.

Jackson's duties were an assorted mixture of things, some exciting, some boring, all of which he accepted with good humor and no small amount of pride, knowing that Ian depended upon him, probably more than anyone else, to keep the organization running smoothly.

He was a truly happy man, a rare phenomenon for a Vietnam veteran of some of the most savage fighting of the war. Part of a reconnaissance unit that specialized in night missions operating out of a firebase in the dense jungle, Terrell Jackson of Macon, Georgia, for the first time, had appreciated the beneficial effects of his blackness. Blending completely with the darkness, he became a legend as he stalked the elusive enemy through the tangled growth. His partner swore that, in the deadly stillness, when even the slightest sound or movement would have meant discovery by the opposition, he was able to detect the big man only by his glistening white teeth, bringing to mind Alice's imaginary trip through a fantasy land, and the cat whose grin remained even after the creature itself had vanished. It was as if the very essence of Jackson had mixed with the steamy aura of the jungle, becoming part of it, like a reincarnation. He gained the nickname "Cheshire Cat," but only the first part stuck.

However it had not been any supernatural ability that assured his durability, but merely one of attitude. In the harsh environment of war, he knew that survival was the only reality of the moment. Kill or be killed. The choice was easy. Jackson simply concentrated on getting the job done in order to speed his return to a more pleasant existence. When he was airlifted out of the jungle and transported to Bethesda Naval Hospital, that was that. In time, his wounds healed and for him the problem was all over. Never mind all the peaceniks waving signs and parading. Even the bitter veterans' activist groups didn't interest him. He had wrestled the devils of war, had embraced them, had danced with them. He didn't intend to spend anymore of his life dwelling on the subject.

Glancing at the glowing gray screens, he was satisfied that everything was quiet. Earlier, there had been one suspicious fellow, a brother, hanging around the fence on the edge of the grounds. Jackson had watched him carefully on the monitor. The man looked fairly young, probably early thirties, clean-shaven, medium height and build, had on a light-colored windbreaker and jeans. Normal. But he had looked at the house very carefully, and somehow, Jackson didn't believe he was only interested in the architecture. After a few minutes, the man walked on down the street and didn't reappear. If he was casing the place with an eye to robbery, the cameras must have discouraged him.

He took the foil cover off the plate that had been left on his desk and prepared to enjoy the fried chicken he had sweet-talked a female member of the kitchen staff into cooking for him. Jackson smiled to himself as he reflected on his good life. In many ways he still enjoyed the fame that had followed him after his tour of duty. Women were drawn to him like iron particles to a magnet. His buddies teased him about it, saying that at any given time or place, he could reach out in two directions and pull back a piece of tail in each hand. He didn't have any trouble with the overblown image, he mused, chuckling as he inhaled the delicious smell of the chicken. Sometimes it was downright helpful.

At last, he would be able to relax and eat while keeping his eyes on the activity, if any. It was pretty dull now that everyone had gone home. Tonight, the only action would be on the third floor. He lifted a drumstick in mock salute to his boss. With a look of pleasure deep-rooted in mutual male pride, he propped his feet on the desk, leaned back in the cushioned chair and ate with gusto.

★   ★   ★

MONROE was changing into comfortable slacks and lounging jacket when there was a discreet knock on his dressing room door. Dalton stepped in, his aging frame slightly bent, although the proud head was erect. He cleared his throat softly, waiting for recognition.

Monroe turned. "Yes, Dalton?"

"The…lady…is in the study, sir."

"Thank you, Dalton," Monroe said, returning to his task as he heard the man leave as quietly as he had come. He had to suppress a smile. There had been more than a slight tone of disapproval in the voice of his old retainer. He knew the man despised the women who made the trip in the elevator.

Monroe carefully arranged the silk scarf inside the open collar of his shirt. He wouldn't allow the announcement to rush his dressing. In fact, he needed the time to adjust from the earlier party to the later one. The two were in completely different categories. Thoughts of the beautiful Margaret remained with him. These days, he found himself thinking more often about marriage, and when he did, she was central to those thoughts. She was vibrant and charming. Her family was as patrician as his. However, if they married, in a matter of days she would perceive the real business he was in. The neglected law practice would no longer fool her, and she wouldn't like it. It was impossible. He sighed audibly.

It would be the same with Monique D'Aquin if he should decide to pursue her seriously. Although European women generally tended to be more sophisticated in such matters, still with the same lack of naiveté, she would realize that his illegal career would jeopardize hers. On the other hand, and without any consideration of marriage, he needn't ignore her pointed invitation to a private showing. He had an idea that she would provide him with an unforgettable artistic experience.

Monroe smiled to himself, but it was with little enjoyment. He was beginning to wonder if he would have to choose forever between having a superb income or a superb companion. He wanted both.

He forced his thoughts into another channel. Did Kenneth Raitt's constituents have any idea how many trips he made to Latin American nations? What would they think if they knew how much cocaine the good senator had eased into the country by diplomatic pouch, or in crates with a diplomatic seal to guarantee safe passage? So far, it had worked. And, now, no longer dabbling, the two of them would begin transporting it in large shipments. Tonight Raitt had confirmed that he had made arrangements with the godfather, *el padrino*, head of the cartel in Colombia. The new phase of their operation was in motion.

So far, their loose partnership had worked well enough. The time had come to expand and tighten the business. They had been lucky so far, but if anything went wrong in this kind of poorly organized operation, they'd all get caught. It would be tempting fate to try it much longer. Still, he didn't know if he was ready to give up the excitement of being part of every facet of the operation. Ruefully, Monroe had to admit that the adventure was what he loved—as much as the money.

He had never planned to become involved in the trade. It had begun very unexpectedly when a client asked him to take a large sum of cash to the Cayman Islands. Through a sleight-of-hand shuffling of paperwork, an island bank was very helpful in submerging the cash in one corporation, and having it surface innocently in another. It was all over within twenty-four hours and Monroe caught the return flight home with several checks issued from the new company to his client. Those instant "profits from foreign investments" could not be questioned by the IRS. His commission had been ridiculously high.

It was a package deal—the intrigue, the romantic island scene, the money. He was hooked. After that, Monroe began looking for other opportunities as he gathered a small, select group to work with him, and Miguel Dominguez had proved to be a dependable supplier by way of his relatives in Miami. With his fishing charter boat business as a cover, the Cuban was perfect for the organization.

Through other contacts, it wasn't long before he and Raitt discovered each other. At first, the senator needed someone to launder his profits, then later, to transport and disperse the cocaine down the "pipeline." Monroe had the people in place and understood the word discreet. The highly visible socialite had almost as much to lose as the senator if their business were exposed. Yes, Monroe told himself with assurance, it was a very logical partnership.

CHAPTER ELEVEN

AT last, Monroe went down the hall to the study and entered quietly. The exotic sounds of Rimsky-Korsakoff's rendition of *Sheherezade* drifted about the room. No doubt Dalton's grudging selection. A fire blazed in the fireplace, its dancing light reflecting off the brass lamps. The deep red of the walls seemed to intensify in the warm glow.

Unwilling to announce his presence right away, Monroe remained still, drawing in the ambience of his favorite room. It was large, stretching entirely across the front of the house. The tall windows that earlier had provided him with a view of the river, were draped against the prying eyes of the night. Some fine English mahogany pieces and federal period paintings graced the room, however, the main emphasis was on comfort afforded by its casual overstuffed sofas and chairs. Soft beige carpeting muffled sounds, creating a hushed background, except for the intermittent snapping of the log as it burned in the hearth, and the sensuous notes from an oboe playing the Arabian melody.

Monroe's glance ranged over the bookcases lining one wall, filled with contemporary novels and biographies mingled with a few old leather-bound classics. They were like dear friends and had provided him with many hours of pleasure through the years.

He noted that the staff had placed a buffet supper on the sideboard. Delicacies waited under silver domes. A bottle was chilling in an ice-filled epergne. There would be no further interruptions. What a pity, he thought as his vision focused on the center of the room, to waste this perfect setting.

Gypsy Soldana had draped herself across one of the sofas, her dark curly hair stark against the white fabric. The small, nicely proportioned body revealed her youth in contradiction to the sexual maturity obvious by her choice of skin-tight clothes and the way she wore them. One leg encased in black lace crossed over the other and swung up and down impatiently. She held a half-empty goblet as she stared into the fire.

He took a deep breath and moved toward her. "Gypsy, love, have you been here long?" Gently he pulled her up from the sofa and embraced her.

She allowed him a few moments, long enough to let him feel her body curve against his. Then she pushed away, pouting. "I've had two glasses of champagne already," she said petulantly.

Monroe studied her features. Flawless olive skin coarsened by a heavy coating of tinted cream, dark eyes ringed in fake black lashes, a small natural black mole above glossy, bright red lips. Genuine beauty under too much paint. Why he kept her, he didn't know. Basic needs? No, base needs, he thought with amusement. She was a very provocative child. At first, he had been tempted to make her into a courtesan. On the surface, she could have been as impressive as any of those women of legend. But his cynicism and contempt for the weak-witted prevented him from trying. He was convinced her beauty was only on the outside. Inside, other than a determined streak, there was an absence of any material worth the effort. Besides, she was much too young for him to show her off in public.

"Well then, my sweet, I've got some catching up to do, don't I?" He moved to the sideboard, refilled her glass and poured one for himself, anxious to take the edge off his perceptions. The real enjoyment would come only when he was tipsy enough to forget about the quality he always demanded in other facets of his life.

It was a little game they both played, each for different reasons. She resisted, he delayed. Merely one form of the human mating dance.

"Come over here," he said, patting the cushion next to him as he sat.

Still piqued, she stood, hands on hips and lower lip pushed forward as she stared at the wall.

"You are so beautiful when you're angry, my little gypsy. Please do forgive me," Monroe said in a soft voice, looking at her over the top of his glass. "Will you let me make it up to you? I have something for you."

He reached into his pocket. The black eyes flicked toward him, although the rest of her remained motionless. Amused at her childlike interest, he watched her as he took out a small object made of silver. It was similar to a flask, but much smaller and more tubular. Attached to it by a chain was a tiny silver spoon.

Earlier, during their brief meeting in the library, Kenneth Raitt had handed him the little trinket, a gift from the Colombian *padrino* anxious to furnish a sample of the new supply that was ready for shipment.

Curiosity overcame Gypsy's temper and she sat down next to Monroe.

"Look, my dear, what a friend has given me," he said, holding the delicate object in his open palm. "It is something special, to be savored. Shall we try it?"

Understanding registered on her face as she nodded consent. Her eyes shone as she watched Monroe unscrew the cap and tap out just enough white powder to fill the little spoon. Slowly he moved toward her. She pressed one nostril shut and inhaled deeply. Then swiftly, he refilled the spoon and placed it under her other nostril. In an instant, a look of rapture spread across her face.

"*¡Cielo!*" she cried reverently, closing her eyes for a moment of total enjoyment. She reached for the container. "And now, you?"

Monroe nodded. Although he rarely indulged, he wanted to test the quality. No harm in letting her feel that he was joining her in a soul-expanding experience. When the effect of the cocaine flooded his brain, he knew it was good. Already cut once, its strength could be cut many more times before it hit the streets. Very good for his profit margin. He leaned toward Gypsy, suddenly finding the ripe red lips irresistible.

She returned his kiss with a searing passion, running her tongue along his. Without a word, she rose and walked languidly to the other side of the room, swinging hips barely covered with a short, black leather skirt. She stopped and turned slowly, letting the low cut, red-sequined blouse shimmering over unfettered breasts take effect. She was rewarded when Monroe's eyes swept over her, from the sparkling top down to the place where the narrow skirt ended high on her slender thighs.

Packaged fire, Monroe thought. She was only fifteen, but she knew how to sell her product.

Gypsy began her return trip toward him, sequins jiggling, taut leather undulating forward and back, and sensuous perfume adding to the sultry atmosphere surrounding her as her dark eyes burned into his.

Monroe felt the heat bringing his body to life. As he reached for her, she evaded him coyly.

Turning toward the buffet, she cast a half-lidded glance at him over her shoulder. "I'm hungry."

"So am I, you sexy creature. Come here."

It was what Gypsy wanted to hear. The food could wait. Once again, she'd show him that she was the best little thing big money could buy.

★ ★ ★

DOMINGUEZ entered the bar and peered into the dimness. Seeing no one familiar, he sat on a stool and prepared to wait.

"Give me a B & B on the rocks," he said to the bartender. He watched the man fill a glass with ice and reach for the particular bottle of liquor. "Is Harry Pharr in here?"

"Nope. Come to think of it, he hasn't been here in a couple of days. Unusual."

While wondering what that might mean, Dominguez looked around at the décor. Junk plastic in oriental shapes. There was a large model of a green pagoda sitting on a platform behind the bar, same design as outside. From what little he could detect in the darkness, he was convinced he didn't want to see it in daylight. It reminded him of the Shanghai dives he'd seen in old movies on late night TV.

The bartender placed the drink in front of him. Dominguez had just taken the first sip when Pharr came in. The Cuban stared in astonishment. He had seen Pharr only a few times before, but the man never had looked this bad. His mouth was slack in a wasteland of a face. The eyes were dull, with lids dipping at half mast over distended pupils. A two-day growth of dark beard, thick and bristly, was not enough to hide the deep red gouges on his left cheek.

"Son of a bitch!" Dominguez exclaimed in an agitated voice. "What happened to you?"

"Man, if I tell you, you'll be too jealous," Pharr answered slowly, managing to activate his facial muscles enough to leer. Apparently deciding to risk it, he went on to tell Dominguez anyhow. "I got me this little wildcat, see? And I've been keeping her entertained."

Dominguez looked at him speculatively. "Yes, I see. And I also see this wildcat of yours, she fights back."

Pharr began to giggle. "She didn't want to come with me at first." The expression on his face suddenly changed to anger as he continued. "I showed her she had to obey the man." As muddled thoughts plodded with difficulty through the numbed brain, his face reflected a few hard-gained recollections. A broad smile spread across his mouth. He leaned toward the Cuban and said, proudly, "I tamed her." A cloud of stale beer breath filled the air directly in front of Dominguez' face.

"Exactly what does that mean?" Dominguez snapped, leaning away from Pharr.

While deciding how he would answer that question, Pharr was distracted by Dominguez' sharp clothes. Silk shirt, good-looking leisure suit, lizard shoes. Not bad. The jewelry wasn't bad either. Diamond studded Rolex watch, enough rings to go into the business, and—much to Pharr's pleasure—a wide gold chain around the other man's neck, just like his. The only thing different was the huge gold nugget hanging from the middle of it. Pharr hoped he could remember to get one like it.

"What do you mean, you tamed her?" Dominguez prodded, more gently this time. He damned well hoped he could find out what was going on. There might be a need for some quick damage control.

"Aw, you know, I had to knock her around a little."

"Where'd you pick her up?"

"Where? Took her right off the Metro! Ever hear of anybody else able to do that?"

"Took her?"

"Yeah, I grabbed her," Pharr bragged with another giggle. "She was surprised."

Real alarm began to set in as Dominguez continued to pry more information out of Pharr. "Where the hell is she now?" He pretended to be amused.

Pharr seemed fascinated by his own smug grin reflected in the mirror behind the bar. Finally, he spoke. "At my place." He grinned wider. "Don't worry. She can't get away."

"Well, *amigo*, I hope you two will be very happy," Dominguez said, clapping him on the back. "Now, I am due somewhere else shortly. Go into the men's room and I will follow."

"Okay." Pharr immediately got up and swayed in the general direction of the bathroom.

Moments later the Cuban followed. When they were alone, Pharr handed Dominguez an envelope, which he inspected carefully. Satisfied, he put it into the breast pocket of his suit. As he departed, he assured Pharr that the organization would be in touch with him soon.

Pharr smiled happily around stained teeth. He was on his way up.

★   ★   ★

SOMETIME after midnight, the phone rang in Monroe's bedroom. He had been savoring the comfortable feeling, vaguely aware that Gypsy was still dressing in the bathroom. Through the open door he could hear her mumbling about food. Propping himself up on an elbow, he picked up the receiver.

"Monroe here."

"Ian, it's Miguel. I think we have a problem." The Spanish-accented voice sounded urgent.

"What is it?"

"One of my people by the name of Harry Pharr has gotten into something that might draw attention to us if the police pick him up."

"Pharr? Don't know him. What's he done?"

"He's been bragging around a bar that he grabbed a woman and has her locked in his apartment. Says he's been teaching her a few things," Dominguez said guardedly.

Monroe's voice rose in disbelief as he absorbed what the other man was telling him. "Do you mean that one of our people...this, this Harry Pharr...has *kidnapped* a woman and continues to hold her?"

"Yeah. The bartender at the Jade Pagoda would remember that I had been with Pharr tonight."

"If she's a prostitute, we have nothing to worry about. She'll never talk."

"You're right about that, Ian. But at the moment, we don't know who she is."

"Where are you now?"

"In a phone booth at H and 7th in Northwest."

"Stay there and wait for Jackson. Don't let Pharr get away. When he leaves the bar, pick him up and persuade him to let the woman go. Take him home and be certain he does that. Then hide him somewhere while we see what happens. I'll decide what to do with him later. First, he'll have to clean up this mess without bringing attention to us."

"Pharr is high right now. I don't know how we'll be able to convince him he's in big trouble. We'll have to give him the scare of his worthless little life."

Monroe hung up the phone with a look of deep concern. He wondered why the hell Dominguez was taking on dealers who use. That always meant trouble.

He punched the intercom button on the nightstand. "Jackson, come up here right away, will you? I want to talk to you before you take Gypsy back to her place."

"Yessir," the voice boomed cheerfully. "Will do."

Monroe put on his robe and went to the study. He was closing the door quietly after him when he heard the whine of the elevator.

The big man entered looking refreshed. Monroe hoped he'd had some sleep because there was a job to be done, and it might not be simple. Jackson listened intently as Monroe briefed him and gave instructions. "And, whatever you do," Monroe continued, "don't let the woman see your faces. I know it's theatrical, but put a stocking over your heads or something until the woman is gone." He paused, looking down. "Damn the man! I don't care what you do with him. Just get this thing over with as soon as possible. Understood?"

Jackson nodded soberly, thinking that it was an impossible assignment. They could take care of the woman well enough, but the junkie would be the unstable element. He'd better take plenty of hardware just in case the fool tried to resist. "We'll take care of it."

"Good. Get the car ready. Gypsy doesn't know it yet, but I'm sending her down now."

Jackson left, his deep rumbling laugh reverberating in the elevator on the way down. Now there was a battle he'd better brace himself for, he thought. On second thought, she just might be harder to handle than Pharr.

Monroe returned to the bedroom and found Gypsy waiting impatiently.

"Let's eat."

"I'm sorry, my sweet, but some important business has come up which I must handle right away."

Gypsy stared at him stonily.

"Ches will take you home." Ian went toward her, his arms opening to enclose her in an embrace.

The black eyes narrowed and sparked dangerously. Her small hands opened flat, moved together at chest level, and shoved forward. "What do you mean, Ian? I haven't eaten yet!"

Stepping back, Ian was amused at the fiery nature, not to mention the strength, of the tiny seductress. No question but that he liked it. He keenly regretted there was no time to play out the scene. "My precious, please understand there are times I must take care of business, even when I'd rather not."

Gypsy saw the flicker of lust in his eyes and felt triumphant. She watched him turn and walk to the bedside table. He opened a drawer and pulled out an envelope. She remained still, arms folded across her chest, as he advanced again.

"Besides the usual, there is enough here to buy an even more elegant supper, with my most affectionate apologies."

Still she was silent, her eyes smoldering.

"And…Monday, Gartenhaus' will deliver a mink jacket to you."

Her eyes flew open, only long enough for him to be certain the flames of her Latin temper had been doused.

★　★　★

AFTER she had gone, Monroe showered, then returned to the study. He poured himself a glass of Drambuie and settled in a comfortable chair by the fire, thinking over the events of the past few hours. Dominguez' call had unsettled him. Just the stupid kind of thing you could never foresee happening. Even so, he was completely confident that his two trusted associates would take care of it.

The rest of the room was chilly, but it was nice by the fire, he thought, stretching out his long legs to catch more of the warmth. He stared at the amber liquid in the small faceted crystal glass, and the way the firelight sparkled through it. There was a trade-off in having a large, old house, he thought. It was hard to heat, but that was a small price to pay for living in a beautiful place rich in history. He was meant to be there.

As he assessed the present situation, a sigh escaped him, betraying his inner restlessness. In spite of his social and financial success, a sense of disquiet hovered around the edges of his consciousness. At times like this, in the quiet, still hours before the dawn, Ian Monroe knew all too well he had everything he could possibly want in his life, except for one.

CHAPTER TWELVE

JACKSON turned the rented dark maroon Pontiac into the 600 block of H Street and quickly spotted the silver Porsche with Dominguez sitting in it. The black man pulled in right behind it. They were across the street from the bar, about a half a block away. He could see the green neon outline of a pagoda glowing around the entrance.

"Pharr's still in there," the Cuban said, as he got into the Pontiac.

They didn't have a long wait before the stoned man staggered out. Dominguez crossed the street and talked to him excitedly. Then the two of them walked to the car where Jackson waited and slid into the back seat.

"So, man, what's the next deal you've got for me?" Pharr was cocky, grinning and blinking his eyes, trying to keep them open.

As soon as the Pontiac drove away, Dominguez pressed a gun into the man's ribs. "Okay, Señor Bigshot, I don't guess you figured a little kidnapping could bring down the law on us, did you?"

Pharr was startled at first, then the anger took over. "Hey, man, it's my business!"

"Your business? How? People saw me at that bar with you tonight, man. That makes it my business, too. When the cops find the woman at your apartment, they'll bring you in along with everybody who was seen with you for the last hundred years." At intervals, Dominguez jabbed the gun harder for emphasis.

"She was looking for some action," Pharr said arrogantly. "It wasn't really kidnapping."

"Yeah?" Dominguez gave a short laugh. "We'll see what the FBI calls it when they nail your ass."

Jackson stayed out of the discussion going on in the back seat, driving in silence while heading in the general direction of the Anacostia River.

"The main man wants you to clean up your mess, Harry," Dominguez continued in a voice as sharp as broken glass. "Right now, even before the sun comes up…or you might not live to see the sun do that again." He paused now and then to lend added weight to his words. "You aren't going to keep the woman until the police come knocking on your door, are you? ¡Como, no! Of course, you aren't. Tell you what we're going to do, Harry. We're going to your place and help you take care of the little problem."

Pharr was clearly alarmed. Having spent the major part of his career with street dealers, he knew what happened to the peddlers who crossed them. To him, it was only logical to assume that those higher up would do even worse. He was more worried about the silent man behind the wheel than he was about Dominguez. The big black looked like he could do a lot of bruising.

It was quiet in the car, except for the hum of the engine and the rhythmic thump of the tires as they rolled across the 11th Street Bridge. There was little traffic at that hour, and Jackson was especially careful to stay under the speed limit to avoid attracting the attention of any lone police cruiser in the vicinity.

The reduced speed afforded the cornered man an opportunity, perhaps his only one, for escape. Quickly assessing his situation and deciding it wasn't good, Pharr acted. Without warning, he lunged against the left rear door and shoved it open. With a fast roll onto the pavement, he was out and running in the opposite direction before Jackson could slam on the brakes.

While the Pontiac's tires squealed in an attempt to stop, Pharr dashed into the opposite lanes. As he ran, his back was turned to the one solitary automobile approaching at a high rate of speed. He heard it only in time to turn and stare into the fast enlarging headlights that beamed from the mass of chrome hurtling toward him. His thin scream of terror wasn't enough to save him.

What followed was a series of quick actions like freeze frames in a motion picture film. The impact of the big Cadillac grill flipped the man into the air. Jackson skidded to a stop and Dominguez had one foot out of the Pontiac and onto the street when Pharr's lifeless body came down onto the bridge rail with a crack and slid slowly over the side. The Cuban heard a splash from below even as he ran toward the scene. Already the speeding car's taillights were twin specks of red in the distance. Just another hit and run.

When he reached the other side of the bridge, Dominguez looked down at the black water and saw nothing. Jackson ran to the railing and peered over the side. With eyebrows raised in silent question, he looked at Dominguez.

Dominguez shook his head and shrugged.

"Well," Jackson said solemnly, "I guess we could say that part of the problem has been taken care of."

★   ★   ★

A short time later, the two men arrived at the rowhouse on G Street in Northeast. They entered the chilly basement rooms cautiously and soon realized there was no need to worry about being identified. The battered, blood-caked woman was lying on the trash-strewn floor, shivering with cold. She was delirious, drifting in and out of consciousness.

"Uh-h-h-h." The strange breathy sound issued from the woman's swollen lips.

"That son of a bitchin' Pharr!" Jackson muttered. His face set in a grim mask, he knelt beside her to assess the extent of her injuries. "This woman needs to go to a hospital."

"Whew! This is bad, *amigo*!" Dominguez exclaimed, with a shake of his head. "Ian won't like this at all. Pharr must have been some kind of animal." He scanned the room for clues to her identity. He found an empty purse with what seemed to be her belongings scattered around it. There was a vinyl case with identification cards and a few charge cards. He let out a low whistle as he studied the information.

"Hey, Ches! Things just got worse, man. She ain't no whore. Here's her ID…Pentagon, Department of the Navy, Smithsonian Institution. *¡Madre de dios!* The President himself might come looking for us! We can't be seen taking her to a hospital."

"Let me tell you, my man, if this lady doesn't get medical treatment—and soon—she isn't going to make it." As he spoke, Jackson reached for a blanket lying on the floor and covered the nude woman. "She's in shock and I've seen guys in better shape than she's in die from it. We'll have to risk it…leave her someplace where she'll be taken care of."

"You must be crazy!"

"I seem to remember you and Ian were worried that Pharr's kidnapping stunt could lead back to our organization. We're supposed to cover his tracks, not leave them all exposed."

"Yeah, yeah, okay. Damn that little bastard!" Dominguez paced the room, his brow wrinkling as he side-stepped objects littering the floor. After a few minutes, his steps slowed. "Wait a minute," he said, looking hopeful. There might be a possible solution, if I can contact the right people."

"Any possibility is better than none, which is where we are now," Jackson responded morosely.

"Give me the car keys. I'll find a phone booth. While I'm gone, look around. See if you can find her clothes and anything else of hers."

★ ★ ★

Dominguez pulled the car up to a bank of telephones at a shopping center two blocks away. He flipped through a small book of phone numbers he kept in his back pocket. Hurriedly he dialed a number.

"¿Arturo, amigo, como está?"

"¡Miguelito, hermano! Is that you? What's happening, man?" The voice, dulled with sleep, was friendly.

"Sorry to wake you, man, but I gotta have some information. I need the name of a doctor—you know, one who can keep his mouth shut."

"You sick, amigo?"

"No, but somebody else is who needs help right away."

"Okay, hold on." There was a thump while Arturo put down the receiver and a shuffling sound as he walked away from the phone.

Dominguez was nervous. Damn, he thought, hoping Arturo wouldn't take long. He continually looked around him to see if anyone was on the street. In a few seconds, the footsteps sounded louder.

"Name's Hernan Aguirre. He'll take care of you. No questions asked."

Dominguez wrote the number Arturo gave him and thanked his friend. He broke the connection then dialed the doctor's number. When the doctor heard who had referred him, he agreed to see Dominguez' patient.

★ ★ ★

The porch light was on at the modest home in Bethesda and Doctor Aguirre was waiting for them. Jackson drove into the empty bay of the double garage as directed. Immediately the light went out and garage door closed behind them. A short, stocky man in a sweat suit stepped out of a doorway and beckoned to them. The two men gently lifted the injured woman out of the car and into the house. The doctor led the way into the kitchen and motioned them to place her on the kitchen table.

The woman moaned occasionally as the doctor conducted his examination. After ten minutes or so, shaking his head in dismay, he sat down and grimly faced the men who had brought her.

"Did you do this?"

"No, doc, this is how we found her!" Dominguez began. "We are trying to help her. But if we don't handle this just right, it's going to mean trouble for our organization. Long story, trust me."

"This woman needs more help than I can give her. Even if we took her to my office right now, I don't have all the equipment to administer tests and the treatment she needs. I could set the broken arm, but there's a possibility of brain damage."

"We can't walk into a hospital and ask them to take care of her. That's the problem. We can't risk being identified," Jackson said.

Doctor Aguirre looked from one man to the other, as if contemplating something. Finally, he seemed to make a decision. He took a deep breath. "What I am about to tell you is a closely guarded secret. It requires that you must also guard this knowledge—or forfeit your lives. Are you serious enough about this woman to do that?"

Dominguez and Jackson stared at each other, then back at the doctor. Both nodded in agreement.

"There's a place they call The Clinic. Very hush-hush. It's run by some doctors and nurses who lost their licenses for one reason or another. But, they're good. In fact, some of them are outstanding. They're just illegal. The mob and the drug cartels support them so their people have a place to go for gunshot wounds and things like that. Or, for big criminals who maybe just need to have the gall bladder removed. They want to stay out of regular hospitals so the feds can't find them."

Jackson was dubious. "So, what if we can get her to such a place, then what? She's going to wake up completely at some point, maybe soon, and she'll want to know where she is."

"Ches, we can tell the people there to make up some story about why she's in the hospital," Dominguez interjected. "And, they can keep her drugged. It could work for a little while, at least until we can brief our main man. By tomorrow, he can make a decision about what to do with her."

The woman groaned, mumbling gibberish as she moved her head back and forth.

Jackson knew she was hurting. He thought the proposal over for a few minutes. "All right, man, let's do it."

"Good," the doctor replied. Excuse me a minute while I make the arrangements." He was gone for only a short while. "It's all set. They're expecting you. I'll give you directions. You've got to move fast. Keep her as warm as possible."

Jackson wrapped the blanket securely around the woman. The two men gently carried her out to the car and placed her on the back seat, then climbed into the front. Dr. Aguirre punched the button to raise the garage door, and lowered it again as soon as the Pontiac had backed out.

"My car is still parked in front of the Jade Pagoda," Dominguez said with a sigh.

"We'll get it as soon as we take care of this, my man."

"Yeah. If it hasn't been towed—or stolen."

The two men fell silent as the car headed for Fairfax, Virginia. On the way a light snow began to fall. It had been a very long night, and the weary men knew it wasn't over yet, even though it would be daylight soon.

CHAPTER THIRTEEN

"Hello! Wake up, wake up!" The lilting voice overhead was encouraging. "Can you tell me your name?"

The woman lying on the bed heard the words and wanted to respond, but did not feel an urgency to do so. There was a strong antiseptic smell. On one side of her was a bright light. As she struggled to focus she could make out a face peering at her. It was unrecognizable.

The voice asked again, "What is your name?"

Suddenly ready to communicate, the woman opened cracked lips to speak. "I...I...," she mumbled. There was something attached to her upper lip, and something going into her nose causing an uncomfortable pinching sensation. When she tried to move her mouth, there was pain.

"Just a little stick, now. It won't hurt," the voice said. She barely felt the needle enter her left arm, then the firm pressure of fingers taping the IV in place.

Once more, the woman tried to speak, only realizing in the midst of the effort that she didn't know the answer to the question. No matter. She just wanted to sleep.

CHAPTER FOURTEEN

FIRST rays of a cold dawn squeezed between slats of the Venetian blinds as Blake Harrison opened his eyes. Instantly alert, his mind raced to orient itself as if his life depended on it. For years now, he'd awakened like that, no doubt the result of agency conditioning. He couldn't remember doing that when he was younger.

Deciding there was neither a dangerous threat nor a need to rise just then, he stirred and turned over, burrowing deeper into the warmth. Suddenly he felt a thump, a soft vibration occurring on top of the bed. Then slowly, something crept alongside him, stealthily inching forward.

"Oh, no," he groaned.

The something continued its furtive approach. Blake soon could feel the weight of it on top of his body. In moments, a furry probe extended over the edge of the blanket, curving toward his face. Again and again, in quick motions, it swept downward, seeking to make contact with a solid object.

"Go away!"

The action paused, as if for dramatic impact. Very slowly, two peaked ears edged over the top of the blanket, followed by eyes, luminous yellow orbs centered with round black pupils distended in the dimness.

"Me-a-a-a-ow."

"Go away, Brutus. Let me sleep." The gruff reply caused the

blanket to flutter.

It was sufficient belligerence to provoke an attack. The big yellow tomcat jerked up on its hind legs and pounced over the edge of the covers, diving down into the murk where the man lay.

"Umf…," Blake sputtered grumpily, trying to breathe through the fur that engulfed him.

Unconcerned, Brutus nuzzled his master a few times, dragging the stiff feline whiskers across the man's face. Then satisfied that he was awake, the cat jumped down and began the serious business of cleaning his paws.

Squinting at the light, Blake lifted his head and mumbled toward the arrogant cat. "Why do I put up with you, you old rogue?"

The bath stopped in mid lick and the wise eyes stared squarely at him as if Brutus couldn't believe the man needed reminding that they were good company for each other.

Blake reached down to stroke the warm fur. "Yes, I know. I kind of like you, too, fella."

Still half asleep, Blake delayed the moment when he'd have to meet the chill in the room. He stretched his long body and lingered awhile under the covers. Brutus had finally settled down and was curled up nearby, napping. The room was filled with the muted resonance of the cat's purring—a fairy motorboat idling on a velvet lake. Blake smiled at the sound of contentment. Superimposed over that was the muffled din of geese honking overhead. For several weeks, he'd heard them, the flocks flying in from Canada to their winter nesting grounds around Chesapeake Bay. Nature marking the change of seasons.

It was a rare Sunday when he didn't have any obligations or loose ends that needed tying up at the office. It was funny how quickly people settled into a groove. There was a time when he'd gone to church every Sunday. His Deep South upbringing had assured it. In recent years, other demands had pushed that aside.

A frown creased his forehead. No, that wasn't true, just an excuse he used. Somewhere along the way in his life, the nice world he had known and trusted to endure had vanished. Along with his southern accent, he'd lost faith in what he thought were some eternal truths—some things that a reasonably bright, advantaged young man had taken for granted.

In the last several years, he had seen enough savagery and depravity to vaporize any illusions about the intrinsic good of his fellow human beings. Vietnam was one thing, and although he'd only been on the fringes of the battle zones, he had heard soldiers recount ghastly experiences. It was bad for many of them, but it was war, and everybody knew it wouldn't be a picnic. However, at home there was the general consensus that one man shouldn't blow another's head off to steal a few dollars for a twenty-minute high or a pizza. But, there were fools out there doing it. More and more of them.

Blake thought again about what Victoria had said about human history and knew she had been right. He constantly fought the cynicism within himself, especially when he witnessed daily the frenzied efforts of so many people trying to destroy themselves. The depth of that kind of insanity was staggering.

Only too keenly had he felt the effects of that destruction which defied containment, spreading its damage all around. Involuntarily, his frown deepened and an expression of pain clouded his face as he thought of his wife with her gaiety and warmth. It seemed so long ago, yet it still hurt. She had been his first love, and his only until… What had it been? A lack in the marriage that made life seem empty to her? Something in him that caused her love for him to dissolve? Or was it simply the chemical need in her body, that once having sampled cocaine in fun, demanded it forevermore? He knew he would never find the answers to those tormenting questions. Of all people, he should have been able to see the trouble coming and should have done something to stop it before it was too late. No matter how many awards, how many promotions he had received in his line of work, he was constantly aware of the case he had failed to solve in time.

Blake forced the troublesome thoughts away. He thought of Victoria and smiled. A chance reunion at the opera and they knew, both of them, that their previous decision had been foolish. The closeness they had had before their breakup months earlier, had come back instantly and even more deeply. Thanks to a little luck and a lot of love. He'd see her this evening, he thought happily. A quiet little restaurant, romantic music, perfect setting to ask her to marry him.

He didn't think he could wait until then to hear her voice. Feeling lonely, he had tried to call her several times since they said goodbye on Friday night. Apparently she'd been busy, because each time, he had heard only the answering machine telling him she was out. Funny she hadn't returned any of his calls. But maybe she had tried to do just that. He had never installed an answering machine. Until now, a beeper had been enough. No more. Monday he'd change that. Oh well, he thought, he could wait a little longer before calling. No use waking her early. In the meantime, he would jog around the lake.

The desire for coffee ultimately drove Blake from the warm bed. Shivering as his bare feet hit the hardwood floor, he found the slippers easily, but the robe was on the hook behind the bathroom door. In three long strides he reached it, quickly wrapping the thick terry cloth around his sinewy frame.

He loaded the coffee maker and plugged it in, then went back to the bedroom to dress. The air warmed and the enticing aroma from the kitchen filled the place. He pulled on his running clothes and headed directly for the coffee pot. Then with mug in hand, he walked into the sunny living room.

Brutus sat on a windowsill, warming himself while he peered intently at the activity on the lake below. Twenty or twenty-five

Canadian geese, having taken a detour on their way to the bay, skimmed the water looking for food. Some had climbed upon the bank and waddled about, occasionally pecking at the ground.

The cat's head swiveled toward his master, revealing the great yellow stare spliced by thin vertical lines of black, different in the morning brightness. I'd rather be down at the lake, he seemed to say.

"Sorry, pal," Blake said. He stroked the plump body then turned from the window and sat down at his desk.

While drinking the coffee, he jotted some notes on the surveillance of the previous night. In the back of his mind was the possibility that men like Raitt and Monroe, behind that shield of public respect, could easily conduct clandestine business and remain above suspicion. All it took was greed and enough nerve to do it. He dropped the finished report into his briefcase and was heading for the door to start on his morning run when the phone rang.

"Blake, this is Bob Arrington. Have you seen this morning's paper?"

"No. What's going on? Not a national crisis, I hope." His voice had a hint of amusement.

"There's an article in the Post about Victoria Dunbar. It says she's missing."

"What?" Blake was winded, like he'd been hit in the chest. "Dammit, Bob, what are you talking about?"

"None of us here at the Pentagon knew until Susan read it in the paper. She contacted the friend of Victoria's who was quoted by the paper, then bit by bit, she pieced together the story." Arrington took a long, slow breath, then continued.

"You were there Friday evening when Victoria and Susan left the Pentagon to go shopping. After that, Susan said they separated at Metro Center and each took a different train. Victoria was headed for Union Station. From there she planned to take a cab to meet her friends at a party. But Victoria never arrived at the Hyatt Regency. It was unlike her, but her friends weren't really concerned until Saturday, yesterday afternoon. They still couldn't locate her. She wasn't at home. Her neighbor who had a key to the apartment checked and felt like Victoria hadn't been there at all that day. There was a lot of mail on the floor inside the foyer beneath the mail slot in the door. When they found her car still parked at the Metro station where she leaves it on her way to work each morning, they became really alarmed. It appeared that the car had been there since Friday morning. That cinched it. They contacted her supervisor at the Smithsonian who relayed the report to the Navy Department. Somewhere along the line, the media got hold of the story. They ran a photo and are asking anyone who might have any information to call in."

Blake fought to regain his equilibrium. "My God, do you mean no one's seen her since Friday night?" His mouth had suddenly become dry and he had trouble forming the question. Possible causes, both logical and illogical, raced through his mind. There could be any number of ludicrously simple explanations for Victoria to *seem* to disappear. On the other hand, it could be so. "What about the police?"

"They were notified, but you know how it goes. They listened and took the report, but refused to begin an investigation until forty-eight hours have passed. That'll be this evening. I'm sure Naval Intelligence will investigate due to her security clearance, although it's only a low level clearance, merely because she works in the Pentagon. They will check, though, to be sure her disappearance has nothing to do with national security." Arrington paused. "Susan asked me to contact you. She remembered that you and Victoria were planning to go out tonight. She is hoping to hear that Victoria has been with you all this time…or at least that you know where she is."

"I only wish I did," Blake said in a flat voice. "I tried to call her a couple of times, but I didn't think much of it when I didn't get an answer. I know she stays busy." He paused briefly. "Will you give me

Susan's phone number? I've got to talk to her first, since she must have been the last person we know of who saw Victoria."

The colonel supplied the number. "I'm going over to Susan's now. She's pretty upset." He paused. "I'm sorry I had to bring the news to you, Blake. Please let me know if there's anything at all I can do to help find her."

"Thanks, Bob."

Blake hung up the phone and sat down as the shock washed over him. His legs were rubbery, his insides quivering. All at once, he felt sick and cold with fear. Finally, he stood up and went to his desk and found the number he'd written on the calendar in the Sunday space. He picked up the phone and punched in the digits. Inhaling deeply in an attempt to dissipate the nervousness he was feeling, he counted the rings. 2...3...4...then a click, and her voice came on the line. Blake's heart skipped a beat.

"Hi, I'm not able to take your call right now. Please leave a message at the sound of the tone."

He left another brief message asking her to call him.

Immediately after he broke the connection, he pushed more buttons. A soft, muffled voice answered.

"Hello."

"Susan, this is Blake Harrison. I just heard."

"Blake, I'm just sick over this. What could have happened?"

"Try not to worry. We'll find her," he said with more assurance than he felt. "Do you mind if I come over? I'd like you to tell me everything you can remember, and I hope you can give me her address as well. I can get it from the Navy, along with the usual red tape, but they'll delay my investigation and I don't want that to happen."

"Yes, of course, whatever I can do. I'm so afraid for her."

He hung up thinking he felt exactly the same.

CHAPTER FIFTEEN

THE neighborhood was seedy. Blake stopped the car in front of a rundown, abandoned house and the other agency cars followed suit. It was the last known address of one suspicious character Susan had identified from photographs on file at the police station earlier that morning. The strange man who had followed her and Victoria at the mall was the only thing she could remember that might be meaningful. Blake knew it was a long shot, but it was the only lead so far.

The agents entered the house and fanned out quickly, checking the three levels above ground. There was no evidence of recent use. Cobwebs festooned doorways speckled with peeling paint. Dust covered all surfaces, including the trash littering the floors. Traces of marijuana were found in the rooms on the top level, indicating a cache of the weed had been kept there at one time.

One of the men who had gone to check the basement sent word he had found something. Blake went down to search an apartment— if it could be called that—which had been used in the past few days. His eyes took in the evidence of occupation. The kitchen area was cluttered with dirty dishes, some food was still in the refrigerator. An empty beer can stood on a table scarred with cigarette burns. Looking at the stained mattress and rag-strewn floor, he didn't want to believe the possibility that Victoria had been there.

Examining tattered pieces of cloth littering the floor, he found traces of blood on some and bagged them for lab testing. More blood was found in a smear on the floor, with several fingerprints clearly pressed into it. That was a break that could help in identification. At least it could prove that they weren't Victoria's. Her prints, along with her blood type, would be on file with the Department of the Navy. Pharr's would be easy to verify. Nothing else definitive had been found. Not even the discovery by one of the agents of a tube of peach lipstick that had rolled against the baseboard not far from the mattress. A lot of women wore that color, but it would also be checked for fingerprints.

Concentrating on standard procedure, Blake looked at a map of the city and determined several routes from Union Station to the rowhouse. He sent agents out to walk every step of the way, looking for anything that might provide clues.

When his beeper sounded, he hurried to the car and radioed for a report. The men checking the Metro stops had found a package with merchandise from Eugenie's in the Lost and Found at Union Station. One attendant remembered that some honest soul, an elderly woman, turned it in Saturday morning. Blake radioed the others to report to him at the station, and afraid of what he might find, headed the car in that direction.

★ ★ ★

IN a borrowed office at Union Station, the agent who had been assigned to direct the search in that location placed a package on the desk in front of his boss.

Blake Harrison knew his fingers shook as he reached for the ivory-colored paper bag. On it, the logo of Eugenie's was stamped in gold. Quickly, he emptied the contents. An inner package wrapped in scented floral tissue paper was secured with a gold foil sticker. It released easily.

He stared at the soft, pale blue silk tumbling out of the paper and hoped it would be the wrong size. It wasn't. The long, slender nightgown would fit her. It was beautifully simple, low-cut with thin straps, just as Susan had described Victoria's one purchase that evening. A momentary vision of how lovely she would look wearing it flooded his mind, triggering a mixture of longing and pain that threatened to make him physically sick. Fighting to stay in control of his emotions, he looked at the sales ticket. No name. It had been a cash sale.

His face was grim as the team that had been combing the streets from Pharr's apartment to the station came in. On one route nothing had been found. The other path had produced some possibilities. He was handed two clear plastic bags, the type used to gather evidence.

"Harrison, you okay?" One of the men had spoken, but they all looked at their supervisor in surprise as his face went pale. He stood almost trance-like, unable to move or speak for a few seconds, looking down at the packets in his hands. In one bag was a thin gold chain, broken in the center and the clasp still hooked. In the other was a dainty, heart-shaped gold locket studded with tiny turquoise stones.

Finally, in a leaden voice, he asked, "Where did you get these?"

"They were found along a street only one block from Pharr's place, Mr. Harrison," one young agent said. "The little locket was in one spot beside the sidewalk. The chain was found about ten yards away."

"Thank you for your hard work." Blake's voice was strained. "Keep checking the neighborhood for leads. Talk to some people around here. Maybe they saw something. Some of you, hit the streets where our informers are. Find out what you can and follow all leads." He paused, his head down. "I guess you know this lady is very special to me. She might be hurt. We've got to move fast."

As he watched the agents disperse, the sick feeling that he'd fought for the last hour intensified. No longer could he have any optimistic illusions. He knew what the blood type and fingerprint report would show. Abruptly he turned and went into the restroom.

There was no one in there. He closed his eyes and leaned against the wall, waiting for his pulse to slow and the ringing in his ears to stop. It was the second time in his life he had felt such hopelessness. The first was when he was called to identify the gray, lifeless body of his ex-wife with the needle marks up and down her arms. Now it was Victoria, whom he loved so much.

Finally he steadied himself and went to the lavatory. He turned on the spigot and let the cold water wash over his face until the strange sensations subsided. Looking at himself in the mirror, he groaned in disbelief. His eyes looked hollow and the rest of him looked worse. In his frantic haste to investigate, he hadn't even shaved or showered. *Pull yourself together, Harrison.*

He would find Victoria. He had to—for both of them.

CHAPTER SIXTEEN

IAN Monroe read the *Washington Post* every morning, and especially on Sundays, with something akin to religious fervor. It was his firm belief that any businessman who wanted to stay on top had better know what was going on with the Capitol Hill crowd. The fact that his main business now was dealing in illegal drugs did not change that truism one bit.

As he looked at the headlines, he could see that the big news was still the fight in the Senate over AWACS. The vote would occur next week. There was no official word yet about the crackdown on drugs coming in from South America. Well, he thought, whenever it began, there would be some interference in his operation. However in terms of the big picture, it would be only a ripple. He would be interested in seeing how well the scheme worked. There might be a considerable interruption in the flow of drugs coming into Florida, as there had been along the Mexican border of Texas since that area had increased patrols. But it didn't require an excess of brain cells to realize that there was enough lonely coastline between those two places to allow tons of the stuff to slide in undetected.

The plan was mostly for show, anyway. It was politically expedient to make an attempt on a grand scale to confiscate drugs. The voters demanded it. Certain Congressmen would huff and puff and call for something more to be done, making certain to point out their stand in the next election. The whole deal would die quietly after it had served its purpose, then business could get back to normal.

Dalton appeared in the doorway to announce that Jackson wanted to see him. Monroe frowned with annoyance at the thought of being disturbed while reading, until he realized Ches wanted to report on last night's problem.

"Tell him to come up right away."

"Yes, sir."

Monroe glanced at the clock and saw that it was nearly noon. Jackson's sleeping late these days, he thought. It must have taken longer to deal with Pharr than they'd planned.

The big man entered without his usual smile.

"Good morning, Ches. You look tired," Monroe observed. "Was there trouble last night?"

"I guess it depends on what you'd call trouble, Ian." He paused before going on. "Pharr handled some of it for us."

"Good. Where is he now?"

"Downstream."

Monroe stared at the man for a moment before finding his voice. "What?"

Briefly, Jackson told him of the events surrounding Harry Pharr's death. He talked about the woman, how they had found her, and of the little known hospital where they had taken her. "When we left her at the clinic this morning," he continued, "the doctor agreed to take care of her most serious injuries. I just talked to him a few minutes ago. He's checked her completely and doesn't think she has injuries to her internal organs other than some bruising. After the way that fool beat her, it's hard to believe." He stopped and shook his head. "Anyway, the doc said he can't do much about the ribs, but he's getting ready to stitch the cuts and set her broken arm. And…she has a concussion." Again he paused. "She can't tell them anything."

Monroe was all attention as he heard the last of the report. "That might save us," he said. "She might not remember Pharr, or whatever it was she had to do with him. Do we have any indication of who she is?"

"Oh, yeah. I've got her ID cards here," Jackson said, fumbling in his pocket.

"I don't understand why you didn't drop her off at the emergency room of one of the inner city hospitals," Monroe continued, looking at Jackson quizzically. "They would have taken care of her. What was she? Prostitute? Addict?"

"No, sir. Afraid not," the black man said as he handed Monroe the cards.

Monroe stood up and walked slowly across the room, reading the information. Before he had gone five paces he stopped abruptly. "Good God! What in hell has that little junkie gotten us into? This woman is known! And has a security clearance!"

"Yes, sir. That's why Miguel and I had to do something extreme. We couldn't take her to an ordinary hospital." Jackson took a deep breath. "There's something else, Ian. Her face is messed up. Smashed nose, broken facial bones, cuts, loose teeth. The doctor said it's so bad a plastic surgeon would have to fix it. They do have one out there."

It was silent in the room for a full minute before Monroe spoke. When he did his voice was calm and confident. "A plastic surgeon, you say?" A pause. "I want to see the clinic for myself and talk to the surgeon. We might be able to turn this around. I'll be ready to leave in one hour. Notify the clinic that we're coming."

Jackson looked at his employer, unable to guess what hidden meaning lay behind Ian's decision, but he felt sure there was one.

After Jackson went out, Monroe placed the woman's driver's license, Pentagon security tag, and assorted charge cards in his safe and locked it. Then he hurried back to the morning paper. On an obscure page, deep within the other news, there had been something about a missing woman, but he hadn't bothered to read it. Could it be this one, this Dunbar woman? Probably not, but he wanted to find

112

the article to be sure. Scanning methodically, he finally found what he was looking for.

> **Smithsonian staffer feared missing.** *Friends reported Victoria Dunbar, a highly respected consultant for museum collections in many countries, was feared missing after she failed to arrive at a party where she had been expected on Friday evening. Ms. Dunbar is prominent in the field of art history, specifically that of the early civilized world. Her interest in the field developed after seeing first hand the art created in those countries in which she had lived as the daughter of an army career officer. Both of her parents are deceased. She is a sought after speaker for art and historical societies. Anyone who might have knowledge of her whereabouts in the past two days is asked to come forward with that information.*

Ian Monroe was stunned as he looked at the small photo that accompanied the article. A professional woman of the highest caliber, now practically destroyed by a barbarian. It was sickening. He couldn't tell much from the black and white print that had not been obvious from the color photos on her identification cards, except that she had a pretty smile. That smile also revealed her two front teeth that slightly overlapped—a thoroughly attractive nuance, but one that would be very easy to identify. His brows drew together at the thought.

He stood up and walked toward the nearest window. Early afternoon sunlight streamed in, warming the chilly air around the slightly opened sash. Standing there with hands in pockets, he marveled at how detached he felt three levels above the reality of the street. It kept his perspective where it ought to be, he thought smugly, and his decisions easier to make. He looked out and saw the surrounding rooftops through the trees, where old Angus Monroe's warehouse and wharf had stood two hundred years before, when the Potomac's shores had reached almost to what is now Lee Street. In the distance, he could even see the hazy tops of a few buildings in the District.

A movement to the northeast caught his eye. A helicopter, a big one, rose into the sky from the vicinity of the White House. He watched as it drew closer, heading south. It was distinctive—dark with a white top. The Marines were probably relaying the President, or some other VIP, to an appointment somewhere nearby.

He smiled to himself when he realized it was there again, that feeling of being in on things the rest of the world had to wait to hear. Inhaling with deep satisfaction, Ian Monroe turned and went toward his dressing room.

★   ★   ★

THE first thing Blake noted as he entered Victoria's apartment was the pile of mail on the floor just below the mail slot. He retrieved the key from the lock and dropped it into his pocket, reminding himself to hand it back to the neighbor on his way out.

As his eyes swept the foyer, he half-expected Victoria to appear. There was a faint aroma of sandalwood, and he inhaled deeply to steady his heartbeat. In the serene and spacious main room, shafts of sunlight angled upward through the open blinds and ended in alternating stripes of light and shadow on the vaulted ceiling. Cream-colored walls reflected each ray, turning the scene into one of outdoor brilliance. Blake walked to the middle of the room, admiring the artistry of her creative touch. The overall impression was one of refinement, but comfort, too—an easy sort of elegance, rather than a stiff one. Most of the overstuffed furniture covered in pale blues and greens he remembered from her old apartment.

The paintings on the walls of the big room drew his attention. There were some very nice watercolors, several portraits, and scenes of period houses. Blake paused before an outdoor scene done in oil, a meadow with a profusion of wildflowers, signed *V. Dunbar*. He recognized this charming example of Victoria's "hobby" as she called it, refusing to consider herself a serious painter. Farther along the wall he found several others that were familiar, all outdoor scenes rich in color and detail. One that he particularly liked was of a river, the Potomac, flanked by trees, beyond which the Washington Monument rose skyward.

As Blake reached the dining area at the far end of the room, he saw a tall cabinet filled with her china—delicate, cream-colored, decorated with tiny green shamrocks. There was a small kitchen in an alcove to the left. He turned around and saw that beyond the dining room table, a glass door opened to a private garden. Each day from her kitchen, Victoria had looked at that view.

He stepped out onto flagstones in the small walled area lined with ornamental shrubs. There was a young tree shedding its rust-red leaves, most of which were on the ground beneath the spindly branches. Planted around the base of the tree were remnants of chrysanthemums, their once colorful blooms now dried and stiff. Nearby was a dark green wrought iron chair with its small matching table. He guessed it was her favorite spot.

Back inside, he noted that nothing seemed out of place or suspicious. Her closets were filled with clothes neatly hung and shoes paired in the shoe bags. All the drawers in the chest had stacks of folded items. Bottles of perfume and sundry toilet articles were on her dresser and on the bathroom counter. Jewelry was in the jewel box. The kidnapper definitely had not been there yet.

Blake picked up the phone and punched a set of numbers. Quietly he made his own report to the FBI about the probable kidnapping and asked to have a few unobtrusive guards posted to watch the apartment and the parking lot of the Metro station's parking garage. If Pharr decided to make use of her keys, the FBI would have him.

CHAPTER SEVENTEEN

SWOLLEN eyelids struggled to open. Shapes blurred in front of a starburst of light and moved about the woman lying prone upon the operating table.

She heard the murmur of voices, but the syllables seemed to swirl through the pastel air. None of them was distinguishable. There was another more definite sound, high-pitched and distinct, punching through the hazy atmosphere, repeating itself endlessly in rhythmic beeps.

Unseen hands gently lifted one of her arms, wrapped something around it, then put it down. A band squeezed her upper arm tightly, then released. Her mind groped for clarity, but was unsuccessful. Something moved downward to meet her face, covering her nose and mouth. Her eyes closed once more as she drifted back to another plane of existence, where pink and blue elephants tumbled gaily in freeform.

CHAPTER EIGHTEEN

THE black Lincoln sedan sped smoothly along Route 7, heading west. Sunny skies lent a glowing fawn color to the usually drab, late fall landscape. Along the gently rolling Virginia hills, there were a few patches of white here and there, silent proof of the early morning snowfall.

Not far to the south lay Dulles International. Ian Monroe took note of the air traffic over and around it. The thought occurred to him that this purported "clinic" was conveniently situated near the spot where hundreds of people entered and exited the United States each day. A fugitive could fly in, get medical treatment or a change of identity, and fly out again with little risk of discovery. According to Jackson's information, the patients paid plenty, in cash, and were assured of complete anonymity. Highly skilled doctors and nurses, unable to practice their profession legally in the real world, welcomed the opportunity to continue their work in a well-equipped, out-of-the-way place, secure from malpractice lawsuits and the American Medical Association.

As Jackson turned the car into an obscure, narrow lane, Monroe gave the surroundings his undivided attention. There had been no indication from the main road that anything was there. Even with few yellow leaves remaining, a thick stand of maples totally screened what lay beyond. The car slowed to a stop in front of large iron gates supported by a brick fence running through the forest. Forged into the heavy metal grillwork was the word GOLDENWOOD.

Jackson braked to a stop, got out and walked toward the gatepost on which a small black box was mounted. He leaned forward, talking into it. After receiving a message, he got back into the car. The gates had already begun to swing open. The car continued down the narrow lane and veered to the left along a wide curving drive. It stopped in front of a gray stone mansion.

Monroe was intrigued at the innocent appearance of the place. Nothing was evident to show it was anything but a well-maintained country estate. There was no sign of movement on the grounds or at the windows.

The men alighted, squinting in the sunshine as they looked toward the silent, massive house. Solid as a fortress, it was square and rose three stories. Its severity was softened somewhat by an intricate arrangement of stones forming decorative patterns around the windows and across the top of the structure.

Jackson took the lead as they ascended the great stone steps between two reclining marble lions. Flanking the entrance, large jardinières held ornamental shrubbery. In answer to the doorbell's ring, the heavy door swung open, and a butler observed them haughtily.

"Good afternoon, sirs. May I help you?"

"Good afternoon. We're from the Smith Corporation," Jackson said, gesturing to include Monroe. "We're here to see Dr. Kuntz." He noted in the brief moments of the exchange, the butler's steely eyes had sized them up thoroughly, missing nothing. Obviously the man was no butler. Probably a well-trained security guard, different from the one who had let them in at the back entrance the night before. The man beckoned them to enter.

They walked into a huge rotunda, its gleaming floors inlaid with mosaics of tiny marble tiles. Intricate tapestries hung on the walls that curved around them. As they crossed the spacious area, their steps echoed high in the cavernous, stained glass dome. All was bathed in the diffused pink light from above. Climbing the curved marble staircase, they had a close-up view of several immense Austrian crystal chandeliers suspended in shimmering elegance, their hundreds of prisms casting myriad spectrums over the already beautifully patterned floor below.

On the second floor, the men were led into a large library and told to wait. Before long, the butler returned and again told them to follow. He led them down the hall to a door marked "Private."

Behind the desk in the small office sat a stocky, middle-aged man peering at them above his half-lens spectacles. He nodded curtly, without the slightest pretense of cordiality.

"Dr. Kuntz, the men of the Smith Corporation." After his words of introduction, the butler motioned the visitors to two straight chairs and exited, closing the door quietly behind him.

The doctor regarded them intently. "I understand you're here to see about the woman who was brought in last night."

"That is correct," answered Monroe. "I would like to know the full extent of her injuries and the prognosis for her recovery."

"Even though she was beaten mercilessly, I think she may live," the doctor said with obvious disgust in his voice. "Is your organization responsible for this?"

Ian Monroe had recognized the man as soon as he saw him. The doctor used a different name, but Monroe remembered the publicity a few years earlier. Or was it more than just a few years—maybe five or ten? His mind cast back to recall the details. The doctor's wife was dying of a particularly painful and lingering form of cancer. The compassionate man of medicine, a nationally recognized plastic surgeon, helped her die a little quicker, and as a result, was sent to prison for a while. A brilliant career suddenly snuffed out. It was strange how fate changed things so dramatically sometimes. Monroe thought it was the first good luck in days for the injured woman lying somewhere in the clinic, waiting to be made whole again. This was neither a country club doctor distracted by his investments, nor was he an incompetent who had skimmed through medical school. The man sitting there glaring at him with accusing eyes was a highly skilled surgeon.

"Absolutely not, doctor," he answered. "I can assure you that such methods are not my style. However, my group had a brief association with the one who attacked the woman. When we discovered what had happened, and *who* she was, my men brought her here for treatment. Our desire was to return her to her home as soon as possible—anonymously, of course—to avoid being the targets of an investigation. However, I understand that her condition may make that almost impossible, or at least, make things vastly more complicated."

Dr. Kuntz shrugged and said nothing more, obviously dismissing the explanation as plausible, if not necessarily the truth. After a pause, he proceeded to explain in detail the medical findings based upon his examination of the woman up to the present time.

"She has extensive injuries that, in themselves, might not be life-threatening." He paused, shaking his head slightly. When he continued, his voice sounded grave. "However, shock, infection, and the possibility of pneumonia present a real danger. Of course, we're administering antibiotics. She's suffered significant blood loss, and there is a closed-head injury. She is severely dehydrated which has resulted in some mild renal failure, although I believe we can bring it under control with fluids.

"As the doctor on duty told your associate this morning, the woman's immediate injuries have been treated. He reset the simple fracture of her arm, however the ribs must heal on their own." Dr. Kuntz paused, frowning. "It's a miracle the lungs weren't punctured." Another pause. "The lacerations on her face and body have been repaired, but there will be scars to deal with later. The vast damage to her nose and some of the facial bones will require reconstructive surgery, and that can be done only after she stabilizes. I wouldn't risk it at the present time. Her teeth will need attention, but the jaws are intact." The doctor stopped talking, removed his glasses and rubbed his eyes. Finally, he sighed and looked up. "As you can see, Mr. Smith, there is much to be done to make her physically whole again."

Monroe listened intently to the dismal report then asked the question critical to the decision he must make sooner or later. "What about her mental condition."

"That's the other part of the problem. So far, she doesn't seem to recall where she is, what happened to her, or even who she is."

"Do you think it's brain damage?"

"If you mean a condition that would leave her incapacitated…no. The tests do not indicate such. We're keeping her heavily sedated, but when she does wake up, she's relatively coherent. Her legs and her good arm move, so there's no major nerve damage. It is likely a form of amnesia."

"That certainly isn't surprising after such brutal treatment," Monroe said heavily.

"It is more common for amnesia to occur after severe emotional trauma, rather than blows to the head. By the way, did I mention that she had been repeatedly raped?"

There was silence in the room. Monroe's facial muscles tightened. Ches Jackson stared at the carpet while the gruesome scene he had witnessed replayed in his mind.

Ian Monroe spoke after a time. "She wouldn't recognize anyone she'd known before this happened?"

"It's possible she would not, but it's just too early to tell. A person with psychoneurotic amnesia might have recollection of ordinary things, but the personal memory is blocked. The condition is called a fugue state—a state of mind in which the victim can hide from some horrible event."

"I'm afraid I know very little about it," Monroe admitted.

"It isn't uncommon for a person in a fugue state to wander away from the ordinary environment and go to another place, thereby subconsciously helping the mind to escape."

"How long will this state of mind last?"

"There's no way to know. It could last a week, a month, or even years. In this woman's case, her physical surroundings have already been changed—not by her doing, but by yours."

As Monroe opened his mouth to protest, the doctor raised his hand to stop the objection.

"Even though it was a change for the better, nevertheless, your people did remove her from one location, providing further disorientation. Through a series of shifts, her mind has been helped to escape…and, that may be just what her mind very much wanted to do. Her subconscious may cling to the changes in order to avoid having to confront the terrifying experience. The longer she stays away from her old, familiar places, the easier it will be for her to remain in this fugue state."

"Let's consider, doctor, what would happen if her memory returns. Would she remember everything that she had experienced from the onset of the disorder?"

"No. In most cases, the patient remembers the previous life, but usually not anything from the fugue state."

Monroe sat very still, considering all that he had heard. Finally, he spoke. "Dr. Kuntz, my organization will be fully responsible, financially, for this woman's treatment. Above all, we want the matter to be handled very discreetly. Apparently, she was involved in some government work and the investigation may be intensive."

A look of understanding crossed the doctor's face. "So, our patient is none other than the missing woman pictured in the newspaper this morning? I wouldn't have known her from the photograph." He fell into a gloomy silence.

Monroe continued with a nod toward Jackson. "My assistant will check with you daily on the woman's condition. I will expect you to keep your guesses to yourself as to her identity. As soon as you feel safe in completing the surgery, I want you to do so, but…and on this I must insist…not before you notify me and we discuss the way it will be handled."

"Oh, I assure you that you'll be consulted and informed of every step in the process. And, as for keeping your secrets…," the doctor paused, barely managing to hide a smile, "if we're going to have extensive business dealing of this…ah…delicate sort, I think we've got to establish a level of trust. You must realize that I know who you are. A man whose photograph appears in the society section of *The Washington Post* at least once a month is easily recognized."

Monroe was startled into accepting the obvious, and at the same time, was relieved to drop the pretense. "Surely then," he reiterated, more strongly that time, "you understand my need for absolute discretion."

The doctor nodded. "As you must also understand, I have that same concern. I know that a man as well informed as you has recalled the notoriety surrounding me some years ago. I don't want you to expose my clinic and deprive me of the only means left to practice the profession I love. And I can assure you the rest of the staff here feel exactly the same way. Likewise, you don't want me to expose your other activities, whatever they may be. I'd say we've got each other by the short hairs, wouldn't you?"

"Quite so," Monroe said. A flicker of amusement played across his face.

"Good," Kuntz said with a nod. "It is important that we grasp the situation fully."

"Can you give me some idea of when you will be able to start the rest of the treatment?"

The doctor stared out the window. "I can't give you a timetable."

"See here…" Monroe's protest was interrupted before he could finish.

"I think it would be a good idea for you to see her. Come with me." Dr. Kuntz stood up, brushed past them and out of the room. The two men followed.

They walked briskly down the hushed corridor, rounding a corner as it branched off to the right. The doctor set the pace, having a surprisingly long stride for someone not very tall. The others had to step quickly to keep up with him.

"This is our east wing," he explained along the way. "It's where we keep our most confidential cases. The woman is completely isolated from other patients. No one sees her except the two nurses who attend her in shifts. Those nurses, although highly trusted, are only given details they need to know in order to treat the patient effectively."

When they reached a door midway along the east corridor, the doctor stopped. Jackson signaled that he would remain in the hall, his face indicating that he had seen enough the night before.

The doctor nodded with understanding and pushed open the door, ushering Monroe into a small intensive care unit. There was a nurses' station and two patient cubicles. Only one was occupied. High-pitched, pulsating sounds came from the bank of machines registering vital signs, while a ventilator emitted its own wheezing sound an octave or two lower. A nurse stood monitoring the lighted screens on the equipment hooked up to the figure lying on the bed.

Monroe stood in stunned silence. All that he had been told hadn't prepared him for the grotesque sight. What once had been the woman's face now was a formless, darkened mound of swollen flesh. Here and there, neat rows of stitches held the cuts closed. Prongs of an oxygen tube were inserted into her nostrils and taped into place. Another tube that led into her mouth was secured by a device that wrapped around her neck. Her right arm, encased in a cast, lay on top of the sheet. Except for the rhythmic breathing movements of her chest, she was perfectly still. He felt his knees go rubbery and there was a sudden queasiness in his stomach. He turned quickly and rushed out of the room.

Dr. Kuntz found Monroe, his damp face a strange gray color, leaning against the wall in the silent corridor. Jackson stood by sympathetically, knowing from experience that particular effect and what had caused it.

"My God, Kuntz," Monroe struggled to say between waves of nausea, "are you sure that's a human being in there? How will you ever make her look normal again?"

"It's not exactly what you see at your fancy parties, is it?" Derision sounded in the doctor's voice. Then he switched his tone, continuing softly. "I wanted you to see for yourself in order to understand that the repairs can't be rushed. The swelling makes it look worse than it is. Still, it's one of the factors that will delay the reconstructive work.

Monroe was slowly regaining his composure. He listened intently as the doctor continued.

"During this period, you have some decisions to make. Cosmetic surgery can perform semi-miracles, believe me. I am one of the best in the field." The doctor said it without pretense, knowing it to be true. "Right now, this woman is without face or memory. Her future is in your hands."

CHAPTER NINETEEN

WHEN he returned home, Ian Monroe went back to the newspaper. He clipped the account of the woman's disappearance and put it in the safe along with her identification cards. The best thing to do, he knew, was to let the clinic heal her injuries and give her a new identity. After that, he would see that she was taken in by some charitable institution. Each change of environment, as the doctor had said, would continue to delay the return of her memory.

Monroe smiled to himself at the beauty of the plan. Ever since he had entered the drug trafficking field, he had relished the delicate balance between danger and disaster. There were sweet moments in life along the dangerous path. Disaster, however, was another thing entirely. His ability to finesse a situation away from ruin was where the excitement came in.

After working as an honest man for twenty years, he had analyzed the business aspect of his law practice and realized he would never be enormously wealthy, legally, until he was too old to enjoy it. His mind neatly justified the new career as he recalled some of the conversations at the party last night. A number of people felt illegal drugs were destroying the fabric of American society, and of many other countries in the world as well. Yet, roundly ignored was the fact that a number of countries had built entire economic bases upon the drug trade, and further, illegal drugs were pumping money into many legal American businesses. To disrupt that would also destroy jobs, directly affecting society.

Aside from the profit motive, what America was currently witnessing was as irreversible and as unrelenting as the forward motion of time itself. Survival of the fittest, just as the monk had discovered a long time ago in his experiments with garden peas. For the rest of the Twentieth Century and into the Twenty-First, it would continue happening. The process of natural selection based on the genes, an occurrence of nature that would exist no matter what Ian Monroe did. He was comfortable in the knowledge that his forbears had given him the ability to rise above the lesser beings. He had no doubt he was doing his bit for America by making drugs available to the unstrung legions of societal dregs who were making a fortune for him while they self-destructed. Rather environmentally sound, he thought with pleasure.

He got up and began to pace as he reflected on the situation, this crossroads in his life. This was one of those times that some critical decisions had to be made, and those would dictate some major changes. He and Raitt were already in the process of speeding up the organization's activities to accommodate the newly opened, large flow of drugs from Colombia. They'd accepted the probability that Monroe would have to leave Washington soon in order to keep a lower profile. There was much to be done on the southern coast in order to expand the network. He did not look forward to the disruption, but if it meant he could increase his fortune, it would be worth doing. In good time he could return to his enviable life in the capital.

Dominguez was looking around for a good location somewhere in the southeast, but not in Florida. All indications were that the President intended to begin implementing his plan for a crackdown in that area.

By the time this move was set up, the woman should be healed enough to be taken out of the clinic and placed with some other agency. Monroe would insure the problem was dispatched before he left town. It was far too risky to be left undone.

* * *

Subconsciously, for some time the woman had been aware of soft music lulling her as she fluctuated back and forth between dreaming and waking. She was aware also of pain, sometimes severe pain, but then the sounds eased the hurt. She dreamed she was in a forest, a deep and shady forest where a little brook trickled and splashed over rocks, while birds chirped as they fluttered through the trees. Over it all floated the gentle tones of a bamboo pipe. Everything was at peace.

After a while, she opened her eyes. At first, it seemed like there were swirls of blue and orange smoke about her. Then some of the fuzziness cleared and she saw the sterile white walls of a small room. She lay in a bed, constrained by wires and tubes.

She looked around in alarm and saw no one else in the room. Her gaze rested on a small stand in the corner holding a cassette tape player, and instinctively she knew it was the source of the soothing sounds.

There was a soreness in her chest, making each breath she took uncomfortable. The weight of bandages pressed down on her face, and the tubes going into her nose produced a burning sensation. When she tried to turn sideways, a sharp pain seized her, triggering an involuntary moan.

Immediately, a nurse in white uniform and cap appeared in the doorway. "Well, good morning! It's good to see you awake!" She smiled cheerfully at her patient.

"Hurts," the woman said, wincing as the speaking itself intensified the pain.

"Yes, I'm sure it does," the nurse said with understanding as she bent over the bed to look closely at her patient, "but take my word for it, you're very much better than you were a week ago!"The nurse checked the tubes to see if the liquid medication and nutrients were flowing properly. She analyzed the woman's vital signs and made various adjustments to the tubes. She raised the bed slightly, then with a moistened swab, she gently worked to soften the dried blood crusting on the tubes leading into her nostrils.

The woman lay quietly, staring with frightened eyes.

"Can you tell me your name, ma'am?" the nurse asked.

There was a pause while the woman's gaze roamed wildly about the room. "No. I can't remember anything. What happened to me?"

"You were hit by a car. You have some broken bones and have had surgery. That's why you're in so much pain."

"Where is this place?" Panic overcame her and she tried to sit up. That sudden movement brought on a fit of coughing, and the woman fell back on the pillows.

"You're in a hospital in Chicago," the nurse answered, as she had been instructed to do. "Do you have any family?"

"I don't know. I can't remember that either."

"Well, don't worry too much about it. It sometimes happens when you bump your head. The doctor will be in to see you later. He'll explain your condition. In the meantime, I'll get something for the pain. You must sleep so that your body can heal and strengthen. You've had a difficult time."

In moments the nurse was back and administered an injection. She placed a hard plastic object into the woman's hands. "If you need me, just press the button, and I'll come."

Almost immediately, the pain eased and the woman felt herself drifting back to the peaceful forest. But this time, she fought sleep as the troublesome conversation with the nurse replayed in her mind.

How can I sleep when I don't know who I am? I must try to remember. Do I live in Chicago? Surely someone has come to see me. My visitors would know who I am. Why didn't the nurse ask them?

Doggedly, she willed her heavy eyelids to remain open. It was possible she was dying, she reasoned. The nurse wouldn't tell her that. With her left hand, she explored her body, discovering a cast, patches where her skin had been stitched, tubes attached to needles. Her face was swollen, stretched taut under the bandages over her nose. Everywhere she touched seemed to be damaged in some form. And, that was just on the outside. There was no way to guess what her internal injuries might be. It hurt when her fingers probed her chest. Yes, she could be near death.

Time dragged as she waited for the doctor to come, stubbornly resisting the effects of the sedative, holding tightly to the buzzer, the only life-line to a strange world. She could hear voices talking as footsteps went past her room. Once, someone laughed. She watched the bags of clear liquid, suspended high above her head on a steel stand, and counted the drips as they traveled down the transparent tubes and through the needle intruding into her left arm. What if she moved too quickly and jerked out the needle? Or what if she fell out of the bed? She tightened her grip on the buzzer and lay very still.

In spite of her efforts, the eyelids began to droop, and finally she slept. That time, instead of emptiness, she took with her the memory of a kind nurse and a clean, white room somewhere in Chicago.

CHAPTER TWENTY

THE week before Thanksgiving, two eleven-year-old boys were walking along the Maryland bank of the Potomac, looking for rock samples for a school science project. Now and then, they stopped to examine the pink and green pebbles at the water's edge. At a deep bend in the river about thirty-five miles south of the nation's capital, one of them noticed a strange, bobbing object caught in the brush along the shore. Being no different from any other boys their age, they found sticks and curiously prodded the large mass. With determination, they finally managed to roll it over, exposing a tongue protruding from its swollen face, attached to a round, bloated body. Terrified, the boys raced home with the awful news.

Within hours, Maryland police identified the body of Harry Pharr and notified the DEA. Blake Harrison arrived at the medical examiner's office as the autopsy was being completed.

"Hey, Doc." Harrison frowned as he looked at the gruesome distortion of a human body in various shades of puce. "Whew! I don't know how you do this for a living."

"All in a day's work, Blake," the pathologist said with a chuckle. "It helps if I don't think of these bodies as people. They're scientific questions which need to be answered. This one could have been in the water for about two weeks. The river is cold enough now to preserve a body for that long before serious deterioration takes place."

"Did he drown?"

"Nope. The lungs were empty. He was definitely dead when he entered the water. I can't find any bullet holes...or knife wounds either. And all the cuts and scratches are consistent with marks found on other bodies in a river full of debris. What I do find are severe internal injuries."

"So you think he was beaten to death?"

"I don't think so, Blake. Not exactly. The hit came from one direction, a single blow by something massive enough and with force enough to cause instantaneous death."

"Got any ideas?"

"None at all. Unless he was run down by a big car. But then we usually find those on the side of the road, not in a river."

"Were there any effects with the body?"

"Yeah. Torn shirt, belt, shredded pants, gold necklace. Two key rings were in the only pocket that hadn't been ripped open by sharp things in the water. One held a single key for an older style lock. The other had three keys, for a car and maybe a house or office. That one had a gold initial charm—letter *V*."

As he listened to the pathologist confirming what he had feared, Blake felt the familiar sick feeling sweep over him. The keys would be checked out, but he was forced once again to confront the indisputable link between Pharr and Victoria's disappearance. Earlier lab test results on the fingerprints and blood type found in Pharr's apartment had already confirmed that Victoria had been there.

Now, unanswered questions haunted him. What were the circumstances surrounding Pharr's violent death? If Pharr had Victoria, and Pharr ended up dead in the river, was it possible that *she* might also be in the river?

★　★　★

WHILE the Charles County Sheriff's Flotilla dragged the river for another body, Harrison renewed his search for anyone who had seen or talked to Pharr in the days preceding his disappearance. Again, word went out to informants on the street. As soon as the leads came in, he personally checked them out. Only one proved to be hopeful. He walked into the gloomy interior of the Jade Pagoda and saw the defensive look on the face of the bartender. There were only a few early afternoon customers seated at small tables. Blake sat down at one end of the empty bar. He stared at the man who continued wipe the counter far longer than was necessary.

"Mister," the bartender finally said, "you look like somebody with a badge. What do you want?"

Blake produced the expected credentials. Then he held up a file photo. "Do you know him?"

The man shrugged and spoke readily, without concern. "Yeah, Harry Pharr used to come in here regularly, until a few weeks ago."

"Tell me about the last time you saw him."

"It was nearly two weeks ago, I think…maybe a Saturday night. We were busy. Full house. Pharr came in and talked with some guy. A Latino. Never saw him before, but he wore some sharp threads." He paused as if recollecting the occasion. "Pharr looked bad…like he'd been dragged through hell without an asbestos suit. The other dude was plenty pissed about something. Some woman Pharr was shacked up with, I think, and how he was knocking her around and that could mean trouble for a lot of people. At least that's what I kept hearing—not that I cared to listen or anything. I couldn't help but hear it."

Blake's insides contracted. He took a deep breath to steady himself. "Did they mention the woman's name?"

"No way. It sure looked like she hadn't been too pleased, though. Old Harry had bad scratches down his cheek, but he kept bragging that he would soon have her tamed."

"Can you describe the Hispanic?"

"Dark hair, dark eyes, olive skin, mustache, short. Nothing out of the ordinary. Except for one thing. This guy had lots of gold and diamond jewelry. I mean *lots* of it. Above average dealer or pimp. Who knows, maybe he wanted the girl for his own stable."

"Anything else?"

"Pharr was strung out on drugs. That didn't seem to make his friend happy either. Probably something to do with their business deal, whatever that was. My guess was that he was Harry's supplier, because they went in the bathroom for a while. When they came out, the fashion statement split. Pharr left about an hour later and I haven't seen him since."

I wish I could say the same, Blake thought grimly.

CHAPTER TWENTY-ONE

AFTER a second visit to Goldenwood, Monroe left with a lot on his mind. He had answers to the most important of his questions. The woman was recovering fairly well, weak, but walking and talking. The best news was that she still remembered nothing of her former life. Reluctantly, Dr. Kuntz agreed she could be released in a week or so, although he had made it clear he thought more should be done to help the woman rejoin society. Monroe shrugged away the doctor's moral opinions. In a suitable facility, the woman would be rehabilitated to some level of self-sufficiency. That would end his responsibility for this situation and allow him to concentrate on all the other business matters that were more urgent. His organization must be protected and, after all, he had not done this terrible thing to her. He owed her nothing further.

★   ★   ★

IAN Monroe worked at his law office the rest of the day, seeing a few clients and attending to some unfinished cases. In between those obligations, he called Miguel Dominguez at a hotel in Biloxi to check the progress of his search for a new base of operations.

The Cuban informed him that he had been looking at some property on the Alabama and Mississippi sections of the Gulf Coast, away from the main focus of the government's planned crackdown. He assured Monroe that he would be back in Washington the next day in time to oversee preparations for their first run to Colombia. The organization had bought an old DC-3, and Miguel was negotiating for a Cessna 210. That was just the beginning, Ian thought, with excitement. If they intended to make the most of this opportunity, they would need more planes and a ready supply of skilled pilots.

Contact had been made with a struggling accountant who was more than willing to assume the money laundering duties. The man wouldn't have any trouble, Monroe assured him. Gate 1 out of Miami International was one of a few in the country that still did not have any kind of electronic monitoring devices, and customs people were rarely there to check outgoing bags stuffed with cash.

He went back to Monroe House around six. Dinner guests wouldn't arrive until eight, so there was time for relaxation. In his study, he poured himself a drink, then walked to the windows looking down on the quaint street. Instead of the usually calming scene on the ground, he kept seeing the woman at the clinic. The doctor had arranged for Monroe to watch her, accompanied by the nurse, walk down the hallway without her seeing him. Those glimpses of her that morning had stayed with him and he didn't know why. He tried to shift his attention to other matters, but his mind kept going back to her.

He turned away from the windows and paced for a few minutes before going once again to his safe. He pulled out her belongings and sat for a long time studying the woman's biographical information. Well-educated, well traveled and accomplished, she had been the type that would have attracted him. She seemed to have an ingrained confidence that was evident in her bearing, the way she carried herself, the way she moved, even physically and emotionally damaged as she was. His brows drew together. What really bothered him, he had to admit, was the fact that she was like others he'd considered worthy of marriage to him, the kind of woman he wanted but, at the same time, the kind that would never be able to live with his illegal activities.

Unless she had been conditioned to accept them.

The idea came out of nowhere, almost taking his breath away. The woman had been recognizable, well known in her field throughout the world. Would he dare to try the unthinkable? He stood motionless for a while, unable to completely grasp this thing his mind had presented.

What was it the doctor had said to him? *This woman is without face or memory. Her future is in your hands.*

It was as if his thoughts had gone into warp speed as the notion raced through his brain. An incredible opportunity lay before him. Why couldn't he remake her into the perfect woman for him? Then he could bring her into his organization unnoticed, to be a part of it, to live and work beside him. With her—and somewhere else—his life would be whole at last.

He had to be careful if he attempted this, his riskiest venture yet. It would require meticulous planning down to the tiniest detail. Even though Kuntz could transform her into a new person, there was always the danger of her memory returning.

But even if it did, she would find herself in a new environment, with new names, faces and activities. Could he not lull her damaged personality into accepting her life with him as the real one? He was convinced he could.

If not, there was always the traditional method of getting rid of a problem. He was a businessman, and he would not hesitate to take care of business first.

Meanwhile, it was an exciting prospect. It seemed fate had provided him with the way to have the ideal woman for his needs. Few ever had the chance to turn possible disaster into triumph. Monroe laughed softly, smugly, as he extended that thought. *Few would be bold enough to try.* For him, it was an exhilarating challenge, a novel experiment.

He had a momentary twinge of conscience at the thought of taking complete control of another human being's life. However, in a real sense, Monroe assured himself, he would be saving her from certain misery. Tutored in his exciting business, his cultured lifestyle, surrounded with luxury, she would want for nothing. Her life would gain a new and dazzling quality—and so would his.

*   *   *

"WHAT? *¡Hijo de puta!*" Miguel Dominguez lapsed into vulgar Spanish as his temper flared. He was standing in Monroe's study, staring at the man in disbelief, his face reflecting anger and amazement. "You're going to change the woman's face…and keep her with *us*?"

"Yes," answered Monroe quietly. "I think it's the best thing to do."

"Have you gone crazy, man?" Dominguez gestured wildly, his arms flinging wide as his voice rose. "Ian, you have got to consider all the things that could go wrong. What if her memory suddenly comes back? What will you do with her then, eh?"

"I am told the staff at the clinic is well trained in this sort of thing. The woman can be programmed to believe the life she will have with us is real," Monroe answered, speaking calmly in contrast to the other man's fury. "While her physical injuries are healing, she will be counseled extensively."

"*¡Madre de dios!*" Dominguez swiftly made the sign of the cross. "Do you mean brain-washing? Playing God?"

Monroe looked him in the eye steadily, as if to underscore his determination. "It's a conditioning process."

"Do you really think you should do that with a person's life, my friend?" Dominguez looked incredulous. "It will never work."

"I think it will, Miguel. Subconsciously, her mind 'forgets' in order to avoid reliving all that she went through. If we give her an enjoyable and peaceful way out, she is likely to accept it."

Dominguez glared at him, brows drawn together. "We have brought in our first load without a hitch, with another run in the DC-3 scheduled for next week. The Cessna deal is set. You would take the chance of messing with all that just to have this woman? I do not understand. You could get any woman you wanted."

"I'm not doing this to have a woman," Monroe lied. His voice was cold. "It's to solve a serious problem. And, I don't think there will be any risk involved. We're moving our operation anyway, so she can begin a new life with us in a completely different setting. There will be nothing there to trigger the memory of her life in Washington."

Dominguez shook his head. "There are other ways to solve a problem like this," he muttered. Having pointed out the obvious to no avail, he made no further attempt to convince Monroe to change his mind. He couldn't understand his partner's reasoning. This man who had been so wily and wise in their business dealings had apparently become dangerously foolish. For some reason, Monroe's judgment was flawed where this woman was concerned. It was like putting a stick of dynamite a little too close to the fire.

CHAPTER TWENTY-TWO

SOMBER gray light seeped in around the rivulets of water running down the windowpanes, yet sunny yellow walls and floral draperies in the high-ceilinged room were enough to ward off the gloom.

Only a week before, the woman had emerged from the grogginess of another surgery to announce she was hungry. She had been in a different room, one that was white and bare, where she was tended by considerate hands. Several times she had been wheeled into the operating room, but each time, soft voices had murmured to her, encouraging her to get better, to rejoin the world.

It was a strange world. Her mind continued to scan fretfully back and forth over the few known facts in order to piece together an explanation. The pain was less intense now, but there remained a definite tightness in her face, especially around her nose and cheekbones. The braces on her teeth were uncomfortable, but that was to be expected, she had been told. The doctor had been very nice and sat with her for long periods of time, explaining her injuries and the kind of treatment he was administering. He said the car that had hit her had not stopped to help. She supposed she was lucky to have lived through such a terrible accident. The woman thought she couldn't ask for a better hospital than this one. Everyone had been kind, and had taken excellent care of her.

She lay propped up against pillows in her bed in the cozy room, with a cheerful fire blazing in the grate and the winter rain falling outside. She tried to concentrate on the vivid images evoked by Fitzgerald's translation of *The Rubaiyat* as a nurse read to her.

"WAKE! For the Sun behind yon Eastern height
Has chased the Session of the Stars from Night;
And, to the field of Heav'n ascending, strikes
The Sultan's Turret with a Shaft of light."

There was a soft knock at the door. The nurse rose to answer. In a moment she was back. "Dr. Kuntz has sent word that he is bringing a visitor to see you."

★ ★ ★

JUST moments before, the doctor had greeted Ian Monroe as he arrived at Goldenwood, and together they walked down the corridors toward the woman's room.

"How is she today?" Monroe asked.

"Physically, she's recovering well. Of course, I remind you that it's only been five weeks since she was injured, and three weeks since we began working on her facial reconstruction. Some scars remain, and some discoloration and puffiness, particularly around the nose. But, the healing process is occurring on a reasonable timetable."

"And mentally?"

Dr. Kuntz thought for a moment before answering. "Both emotionally and mentally, she's very fragile. We must be very careful not to upset her at this point. For one thing, although she's healing well, she is still in some pain some of the time." He paused, frowning. "She is also very frustrated that she can't remember who she is," he continued. "The more time passes, the more insecure she has become. You will find her wary and suspicious of everything. As you instructed, we gave her no information, other than the scenario about the accident. I think she's looking for an anchor to hold on to."

"Are you saying that today would be a good time to introduce myself as her close friend?"

"Perhaps, but you must be relaxed with her. She may be frightened of you at first. I recommend that you not tell her many details of your 'relationship', or whatever you've decided to make of this. Just give her a few things to think about…to get used to. She's been asking about her name. Do you have one for her?"

"Yes."

"All right." The doctor had slowed his pace as they neared the room. "I'll go in first and explain to her that we've finally found someone, a good friend, who knew her and has been looking for her. When you come in, be relieved to see her, call her by name, let her know you care for her, but do not pressure her in any way. That includes physical contact. Even after she warms up to you, you must go slowly. Understood?"

Monroe nodded.

They had stopped in front of the door to the woman's room. Dr. Kuntz knocked softly and went in. Monroe didn't have to wait long. In a few minutes, the doctor reappeared and motioned him in.

The nurse sitting beside the bed closed the book she had been reading and murmured to the woman that they would continue later. She stood and moved a discreet distance away.

Monroe was barely aware of those actions. He was focused on the woman in the bed. Her startled eyes were locked with his as if frozen in fear. It was lucky, he thought, that those eyes had not been permanently damaged by the blows she'd received. Although they were fixed upon him with a cold stare, he was amazed at their beautiful color—like pale, perfectly matched aquamarines.

Dr. Kuntz was smiling at her, talking pleasantly to diminish the tension reflected in her eyes. "You're looking well, my dear. A little better each day, I think. How do you feel?"

The woman remained silent, her gaze only momentarily flicking toward the doctor, registering his presence, then back to the stranger.

"We've found an old friend of yours," the doctor said, gesturing toward Monroe. "This is Ian Monroe. He has come to visit with you for a few minutes."

"Erica," Ian said softly, smiling. "I've been so worried about you. It's wonderful to find you, and to know that you're going to be all right. I am so sorry that you've had to suffer so much pain."

The blue-green eyes continued to stare, transfixed.

"Are you feeling better?" The question was automatic. Monroe was merely trying to soothe her and didn't expect an answer since the doctor hadn't gotten one to that same query. He was startled when she responded.

"I'm well...thank you." It was barely a whisper.

"Wonderful! The doctor tells me you've come a long way," Ian said earnestly, thinking that indeed there was no resemblance to the beaten, bruised body he had seen a few weeks earlier. Even with the sickly pallor of her skin, the limp hair, the arm in a cast, and dressed in the wrinkled hospital gown, she still looked a hundred times better.

Silently, Monroe marveled at the skillful job of cosmetic surgery Kuntz had done. Only one large scar above her eye, and a few small ones showed. The nose had been reshaped. Her cheekbones were prominent, giving her face an oval appearance. When she spoke, he had seen the braces on her teeth and recalled how Dr. Kuntz said he would tighten those which had been knocked loose, and straighten the two which had overlapped previously in front. As had been requested, the doctor was subtly changing her looks as he repaired the damage. The face looking at him was not the same one in the newspaper photo.

"I've been sick." She said hesitantly.

"I know, but soon you'll be completely well."

"Yes, I suppose I will." She looked directly into Ian Monroe's eyes. "Do I really know you?" she asked in disbelief. As if she feared what the perplexing response would be, her lovely eyes suddenly filled, then emptied just as quickly, sending tears cascading down her face.

"Oh, now, no need to cry," Ian exclaimed softly. He moved closer to the bed and reached for her hand, patting it gently.

"But…I…I don't remember you…or anyone else, or…or even anything," she said, choking back sobs. "Have I lost my mind?"

"No, no, my dear," interrupted Dr. Kuntz. "You've simply had a loss of memory due to your accident. Please try to calm yourself."

Her voice was pitiful and Monroe felt sorry for her, knowing all that she had been, and all that she had lost—courtesy of Harry Pharr. He offered his handkerchief, murmuring softly that he was certain everything would be all right.

The doctor beckoned to the nurse who came forward to assist the patient now struggling to breathe.

Monroe knew that the realization of her amnesia had hit full force. "I will go now," he said, not wanting to cause her any further upset. He bid goodbye quickly, with a promise that he would come back soon. As he turned to leave, he heard her call out to him with difficulty.

"Mr. Monroe, you called me…Erica. What is my last name?" The eyes, now clouded with pain, were intent upon him, waiting for his answer.

"Your name is Erica Lindstrom." He smiled at her as he went out and softly closed the door.

The pains in her chest and face were so severe that she hardly knew when the nurse gave her the injection. After a few minutes, she felt a blissful ease. Her mind had some moments of lucidity before drifting off to sleep. *Erica Lindstrom*, the handsome man had said. *Erica Lindstrom*. She continued to repeat it to herself, afraid that if she didn't she might forget it again. In her hand, she felt the smooth, soft weave of his fine linen handkerchief and held it up to look at it more closely. It was a large, beautifully woven cloth with a hand-rolled hem. In one corner, the initials *IM* were monogrammed in old English script. Ian Monroe. There was the faint spicy scent of masculine cologne. Could she trust this stranger who claimed to know her? How could she be sure of him? As her eyes began to close, she remembered to clutch the handkerchief tightly so that it would still be there when she woke.

★   ★   ★

Busy with his law practice and the invisible organization, Ian Monroe did not return to Goldenwood the next week, or the one after that. With Dominguez making most of the arrangements, the new Cessna 210 went down to Colombia and brought back a load of cocaine. The little plane came in under the radar at Savannah, then climbed sharply as if it were taking off from the local airport. With so many of those popular Cessnas in the air, it attracted no particular attention. The rest of the flight went smoothly and it landed without problems at a private airstrip, paved and lighted, in the Virginia countryside. With 200 kilos in duffel bags, the unloading was easy and quick, and the craft took off immediately for a busy airport in Richmond.

Still, the woman was very much on Monroe's mind. He was fearful of triggering another painful episode of hysteria in the woman, however, and felt it just as well that he didn't have time to visit for a while. Instead, he wrote encouraging notes enclosed in gift packages that Ches Jackson delivered to the clinic every few days. There were fragrant bouquets of flowers along with things unique and beautiful. Sometimes a lovely new gown and slippers arrived, or an elegant caftan for taking her daily walks, or a bottle of perfume. Always, there were books to read and tapes of fine music for her to listen to, which pleased her the most. Her emptied intellect had an insatiable appetite for discovery and the music soothed her emotions. The woman, who now thought of herself as Erica, was becoming convinced she was healing in both body and mind.

CHAPTER TWENTY-THREE

IT was some time after that when a letter arrived in Dr. Kuntz' office with special instructions for its delivery. He read it thoughtfully then put it in his pocket and rose to make his rounds. When he arrived at Erica Lindstrom's room, he tapped softly and entered.

He checked the chart handed to him by the nurse. After few quiet questions to the patient and a brief examination, he concluded his assessment of her progress. "You can go back to your duties, Nurse," the doctor said. "I must talk with Ms. Lindstrom for a bit."

"Yes, doctor."

As the nurse went out, Dr. Kuntz pulled a chair close to Erica's bedside. "My dear," he began, "now that you are doing so much better, it is time that you learned some things about who you are."

Her eyes were wide and her breathing quickened as she looked at him. "You've found out more? Please tell me," she pleaded.

"I have a letter for you from Ian Monroe," the doctor said. "He said he thought it would be better to explain things to you in this manner, to give you time to think about it—and maybe even remember some of your past life. Mr. Monroe realizes how frightening this situation is in which you find yourself. The last thing he wants to do is to upset you, but he felt that knowing some things would be preferable to not knowing in order to ease your mind." He paused. "The sooner you can get back to your former life, the better off you'll be."

With a mixture of eagerness and dread, she reached for the hand-written letter.

Dr. Kuntz stood and patted her shoulder reassuringly. "Remember, if you have questions—or concerns—you can ask the nurse to send for me." With a smile of encouragement, he left, closing the door softly behind him.

Erica's fingers trembled as she unfolded the heavy, ivory-colored paper with the engraved monogram at the top of the first page.

> *Dearest Erica,*
>
> *Perhaps if I tell you a little bit about us, it will help you to remember. We met in Chicago at the public library where you worked. We began to date and before long, we were very much in love. You came to live with me.*
>
> *Neither of us had any family. My parents had died, within a few years of each other, some time ago. You told me you had never known anything about yours. You had lived in foster homes until you were an adult and able to join the work force. So, you see, we had only each other, and we were very close.*
>
> *Then one day you were gone. You simply didn't come home from a day of shopping. I couldn't locate you anywhere. The next day, you did not report for work, and the library did not receive any explanation from you either. The police searched for weeks with no luck. They told me it was quite possible something had happened to you, but also you might have wanted to disappear so that no one would find you. I realized you might have fallen in love with someone else.*
>
> *Finally, I gave up hope that you would come back to me. I sold the condominium where we had lived and moved into a hotel. Even that didn't block out the painful loss I felt. I had money from my parents' estate, so I decided to buy a vacation*

house on the Gulf of Mexico. I knew I could practice law on the southern coast just as easily as in Chicago.

I couldn't leave without making one last attempt to locate you. I tried the hospitals again, just in case the police had overlooked something. I don't know why it didn't occur to me at the time that you could have lost your memory, and that I should track down each "Jane Doe" case. But that is how I found you at last. You know the rest.

I do not know how I can tell you of all the wonderful things we shared before your accident, but I intend to try, a little at a time. Dearest, let me help you rebuild the memory you've lost. Please know that I understand your fears. I know you don't remember me. I don't expect us to go on as we were, unless and until you wish to do so.

I'm writing this to give you time alone to think about what you want to do with one part of your life.

Your devoted,
Ian

★　★　★

THE letter had left Erica with a feeling of discouragement. Although the doctor had assured her that such a thing was to be expected, she thought her mental condition must be very bad, indeed, not to have any recollection of someone with whom she had shared a romantic relationship.

The only thing she really knew of him was of his one visit to her in the hospital.

She supposed it was possible that the two of them had been close. He was so likeable, so considerate of her every need. She enjoyed responding to his correspondence with notes of her own, thanking him for his thoughtfulness. He always answered them promptly. She found herself wishing he'd come back soon.

And then, there were her friends. Since Ian had found her, word had spread among her former acquaintances. She had had numerous visits from them. It gave her a warm feeling to experience their friendship. They were so happy that she had been found and was recovering from her ordeal. Many pleasant hours were spent in her room as they recounted stories of the amusing times they'd had with her in the past. Still, she did not remember them. That would take time.

★ ★ ★

DR. KUNTZ watched over his patient as she healed physically and struggled to sort through the confusion in her mind. As the seasons changed, he was relieved to note that she was oblivious to the approaching holidays. A celebration like Christmas, so deeply rooted in religious and family life, might trigger some memories. The staff was instructed to isolate her from any mention of the yuletide and made certain there were no radios or TVs to bring it to mind. Meanwhile, the carefully engineered counseling that had been provided during her convalescence was working. Her "former friends" from Chicago and the so-called shared experiences had given her much to think about. She was becoming more convinced that her life was indeed as it now appeared to be.

CHAPTER TWENTY-FOUR

A little thrill of excitement went through Erica as she looked up to see the distinguished man walk into her room.

"Good afternoon, my dear!" Ian Monroe was smiling as he greeted her with warmth.

"This is a surprise," she said, trying to stay calm, but a return grin transformed her usually solemn expression. "How nice to see you again…Ian." She hesitated. "It seems strange to call you that. I think of you as 'Mr. Monroe'."

"Erica," he began softly, "I would be desolate if you did not speak my first name." He was pleased to see the ice had broken between them. The gifts and letters were working and she was making a steady recovery although it was obvious she had been through a terrible ordeal. Portions of her face were still slightly discolored, and her hair was dull and lifeless. "Why don't you come with me for a stroll in the corridor? I promise to bring you back speedily when you get tired."

"Yes, that would be nice. I sometimes feel trapped in this room—even though it is a lovely room." She smiled sheepishly. "Will you help me with my robe?"

"I certainly will!"

They walked at a leisurely pace through the deserted corridors of the east wing, ending up in the sitting room where they stopped long enough for her to rest. She was delighted to have someone with whom she could discuss the classical music tapes she'd been listening to and her favorite books from those he'd sent. They sat for a while in pleasant conversation, and Erica was surprised to discover how easily they laughed and talked—as if they'd known each other for a long time. Maybe she could begin to believe that they really had, she thought.

At a pause in the conversation, he reached into his pocket and took out a slim satin-covered case. Handing it to Erica, he kissed her gently on the forehead. She looked at him in puzzlement.

"It's for you. Open it," he urged gently.

Silently, expectantly, she lifted the lid. Dangling from a thin golden chain was a small aquamarine, clear and sparkling as a drop of water from some fabled tropical sea.

Her breath caught for a moment as she stared at it. "Oh! It's beautiful." She paused to look at him. "Thank you."

"You're very welcome, my dear. When I saw it, I knew it would match your eyes, and I'm pleased to see I was right. Here let me put it on for you."

As he clasped the chain around her neck, the shadow of a thought crossed her face. Slowly, her hand went up to touch the cool object. She frowned momentarily as a wisp of memory hovered, and then was gone.

CHAPTER TWENTY-FIVE

IN the early hours of a morning in mid-December, Ches Jackson pulled a rented Blazer into the small parking area of an apartment house in Occoquan, Virginia. With him was Ian Monroe and both men were dressed for fishing. They got out of the vehicle and hurried toward the riverbank with a cloud of frosty air following them as they talked in whispers.

The sleepy little village just downriver from Alexandria wasn't awake yet. Quaint brick houses and shops were still shuttered and there were no lights, except for the dim ones on the street. Historically, Occoquan had been a fishing and trade center. Now, mostly tourists flocked there, but rarely before ten in the morning.

The men headed toward the Old Mariner's Club, a frame turn-of-the-century clubhouse facing Mill Street. At the rear were several dozen boat slips. They picked their way carefully down the slope toward the wooden pier leading to Monroe's boat.

Miguel Dominguez waited on the deck of the *Liberty Belle*. As soon as the gear was stowed, he started the twin 318 Chryslers. There was a dual rumble followed by deep, reverberating growls as propellers churned through cold water and the boat eased out of the slip. In the open river, the 32' Marinette Cruiser began its effortless trip down the Potomac toward Chesapeake Bay.

Still groggy from the previous night out, Ches mumbled something about making coffee and headed for the galley. Before long, each man gratefully held a hot mug to ward off the icy morning chill.

It was daylight when the boat entered Chesapeake Bay, and in good time they were speeding out into the Atlantic Ocean on a northeasterly heading. The sun was bright with penetrating warmth, and the water was as calm as it got in the open ocean in winter. It promised to be a great day for fishing.

At a spot about a half-mile off the Virginia coast, within sight of several other boats, the *Liberty Belle* dropped anchor. Her three-man crew set up the gear, caught some small fish and used them to bait the large hooks. Before long, they were reeling in bluefish and snapper of respectable size.

Many boats cruised by as the day progressed. Their occupants waved and called greetings when they recognized Monroe who had fished those waters since he was a boy. Even the Coast Guard cutter gave a friendly toot on its horn as it streamed past. The three men on the *Belle* waved and shouted in response each time. High visibility was the number one priority. Catching a lot of fish was icing on the cake. Except for Jackson who was out of his element on water, they couldn't have been happier.

★ ★ ★

AT noon, Occoquan bore no resemblance to the silent, empty place of the pre-dawn hours. Shutters and shop doors had been flung open in invitation to the throng of tourists strolling up and down the historic streets. The smell of spices was everywhere. Cinnamon, cloves, and nutmeg were displayed in baskets of potpourri open to the air. There were candles, soaps, wood carvings, painted tins, woolen shawls, Christmas tree ornaments and simple pieces of furniture. Color was in riot, with festive red and green plaid ribbons adorning the endless variety of handmade items for sale. In the midst of the holiday season, there was a ready and eager market for the Early

Americana that the village offered.

Blake Harrison had been there before—with Victoria. He scanned the crowd, as he did wherever he went these days, looking for her. A couple, arm in arm, walked by and a fresh wave of loneliness swept over him. Through the panes of a restaurant window, he saw a man and woman talking over lunch, obviously intent upon each other. He had to turn away from the sight.

Once again, the torment began as he grappled with the anguish of loss. And guilt. He should have been able to find her. Where had he gone wrong? What had he failed to do as he directed the search? And, could that failure have caused her to die? He stopped walking for a moment, staring into a shop window, as he fought the nausea. *Stop it,* he told himself sternly, *you're no good to her like this.* He reached into his back pocket for a handkerchief to wipe the cold sweat from his face and forced his mind to switch into an official mode.

He only had to examine the facts to know it was very possible Victoria was alive. Her body had not been found in the river. Pharr had been killed, but there was a chance she was still being held somewhere. That thought alone kept him going.

With an effort, he turned his thoughts to the real reason he was in Occoquan that day. Surveillance around Monroe House had relayed information that two men, probably Monroe and his security man, had left before daylight in a previously unidentified Blazer bearing rental tags. To the people in Blake's business, a rental car usually meant a drug deal was going down. The DEA had a fairly complete file on Monroe now. It was known he had a boat, a big one, that he kept in the fishing port. Blake wanted to check it out himself.

He continued to walk through the town until he reached Mill Street. At the Old Mariner's Club, he found a young attendant who was eager to talk. Blake told the fellow he was visiting from Rome, Georgia—not a long stretch of the truth—and was unfamiliar with the town. He asked directions to various sites, and soon the two of them were laughing and talking on a number of topics. The older man turned the conversation around to the marina.

"Y'all got many boats heah usually?" Blake asked, nodding toward the two lone speedboats in the slips.

"Oh, yessir, we have fifteen to twenty here most of the time. But with the nice weather today, most of them are on the bay. I got here at six this morning, and people started casting off soon after. One had already gone even before I arrived."

"Whew! Would you say most of the boats in this marina are about that size?" Once again he gestured toward the two small craft.

"No, sometimes we handle thirty, maybe forty-foot cruisers. In fact, the one that left early this morning was one of those. Those outfits can make runs into the Atlantic with no problem," the young man said proudly. Warming up to his subject, he continued without prompting. "Mr. Monroe likes to take the *Liberty Belle* out to sea, but only for quick runs. He never travels anywhere in it, that I know of. He loves to fish but he's one of those gentleman sailors, you know what I mean?" He paused to chuckle. "He's got a couple of crewmen to handle the boat when he doesn't feel like it. Just likes being out on the water, I guess."

"Are you tellin' me that a fella with a nice boat like that, with all them fancy gadgets and all that it must have, doesn't take the helm himself?"

"Apparently not. Mr. Monroe has a Mexican, or maybe he's Puerto Rican or something—name's Dominguez—to skipper his."

The dialogue had proven to be very informative, and after a while, Blake eased away. He continued his reconnoitering up and down the length of Mill Street. Not far from the Old Mariner, he found the red Blazer.

★   ★   ★

It was shortly before midnight when Dominguez woke the other men. Earlier, with her hold filled with the day's catch, the *Belle* had made for Virginia Beach and docked at the Boathouse Restaurant. Their presence had been duly noted there as they ate a leisurely dinner. Then, they had reboarded to get some sleep.

The Cuban shivered as his stiff fingers fumbled with the coffee pot. "Damn cold," he muttered to himself. "No place for me, that's for sure." His grumbling continued as he pulled on another sweater and a knitted cap.

Monroe laughed at the man's rantings as the two of them climbed up to the lower helm station. "So, *amigo*, you haven't gotten used to our weather here?"

"Definitely not! This is not a natural way to live," Dominguez said, as he started the motors.

"Surely you don't want to return to the land of Fidel, do you?"

"Hell, no! But, there are many other warm places, *compañero*."

"Such as Florida?"

"No, no! My people are there, true enough, but so are thousands of other Cuban refugees. They hang on to the southern tip of Florida like it's the only known dry land in an uncharted ocean. Too crowded for me."

"I agree, although it would have been a good place for our business…until recently." Monroe was thoughtful as he watched Dominguez expertly ease the cruiser out of its berth.

Keeping his own eyes on the maneuvers, Dominguez' voice sounded grim. "Do you think things will heat up soon?"

"I do. At least that's what my reliable source in the Congress insists." Monroe paused. "They're going to make a big show of it. Whether or not it'll work is debatable. But no matter how it turns out, the drug smuggling business in and around Florida is going to be very risky for a while."

They were in open sea, running southeasterly without lights and away from the busy area around Norfolk Naval Station. Dominguez gave his complete attention to navigation. Although it was a very clear night, it was a dangerous way to travel. No doubt about it. It couldn't be helped, though. With lights they'd attract too much attention at that time of night. This way, the only danger would come from other smugglers—and there wouldn't be many. Unlike Florida. He chuckled to himself as he considered the things he'd heard from his friends down there. At night in those warm southern waters, so the scuttlebutt went, there were so many stealthy drug boats skimming across the Gulf that they often rammed into each other. *¡Más loco!* It was crazy, too crowded, he told himself again.

Monroe knew Dominguez felt a sense of displacement. It was not surprising. There was Cuba and there was his family in Florida, and then there was the life he actually lived sandwiched in between. *Hell, in that sense I'm not terribly different. How well I know that feeling of being suspended between two worlds—my highly visible society world and this exciting underworld. I long for a complete life, but I don't want to give up one for the other. I want to straddle the two and have both.*

His thoughts merged into the array of women in his life, and the careful tightrope he walked with them. For a while, he had dallied with Monique D'Acquin. She was sophisticated, as are most middle and upper class Europeans. That she had also been beautiful and willing was nice, too. However, he reasoned, it was just as well that, in time, she had returned to Paris and her busy life there. His long-standing friend, Margaret Haynes, had always been available to be escorted to glittering affairs until one day she announced a new suitor. An Argentine. Ian never thought she might fall for one of those hot-blooded types.

It hadn't even been the same excitement with Gypsy lately. She was beginning to bore him, getting a bit too possessive and hard to handle. He was ready for another conquest, something much more meaningful. His thoughts were interrupted with the sound of a door opening below. Jackson's head appeared on the bridge.

He handed coffee up to the two men, then retreated once again into the comparative warmth of the cabin. The sea was relatively smooth, three-foot swells and not much wind. Still, it was bitterly cold, and Ches had elected to stay below until rendezvous. He was relieved that conditions were in their favor. Better tonight than tomorrow. Predictions for the next night weren't so good, and that would play havoc with visibility—not to mention digestion. He could handle the river travel like he'd done in Nam. The open sea was something else.

On the bridge, the radio began to crackle. In coded transmissions, Dominguez had made contact with the Colombian freighter. The two boats would be able to come together in the darkness without raising the suspicions of any tracking vessel. Monroe flipped the intercom switch and called Jackson. The tension on board had escalated one hundred percent.

Jackson came out on deck. Trying to ignore the churning of his stomach, he scanned the darkness for the other ship. He felt the danger, probably more than the other two men, yet he was not excited by it, merely comfortable, a normal state of his being. All senses were on alert, even the pores of his skin seemed to open in order to gain information. He prepared himself to face the Colombians. With their multi-million dollar cargo, they were sure to be fierce. It was his job to be watchful, and if necessary, very skillful.

In a few minutes, the big hulk of the freighter loomed ahead, a pale ghost against the black background of the night. Monroe could make out the name of it as he took the wheel of his own boat. Dominguez zipped up his windbreaker and pulled on thick gloves, then stepped out on deck.

Jackson positioned himself well away from Dominguez to avoid making a single easy target. As the *Doña Maria Francisca* came within shouting distance, he was able to make out more details. He counted eight men on deck, including one who seemed to be the captain. The other seven stood hawk-like, each pointing the barrel of an Uzi down toward the deck of the smaller pleasure boat. The powerful black man stood taut and ready. In one hand was an AK-47. In the other, and slightly out of sight of the Colombians, was a hand grenade with several more hooked on his belt. If the bastards opened fire, he thought, they wouldn't do it for long. With one easy overhead motion, he could lob a grenade onto the freighter's deck.

The larger ship had stopped, allowing the *Liberty Belle* to pull alongside. Monroe cut the engines and joined his crew on deck. He and Dominguez quickly secured the small boat to lines dropped along the side of the freighter

"¡Hola, la barca!" the captain called softly. *"¿Cómo se llama?"*

Dominguez had been waiting for the opening hail. *"Buenos noches, Señor Capitán. Me llamo Mickey Mouse."*

"Oh, crap!" Jackson muttered.

The Colombian did not seem to appreciate the comic aspect of the pre-arranged code, but was apparently satisfied with Dominguez' response. He immediately answered. *"Bueno, Señor Meekey Mouze. Espera uno momento."*

Having asked them to wait, the captain disappeared from view. There was silence on deck, although some muffled noises could be heard coming from the hold of the vessel.

Jackson didn't take his eyes off the Colombians. A grungy looking bunch of muthafuckas, he observed, about as grungy as the old tub in which they sailed.

The *Doña Maria* had caught the interest of Monroe, too, as he stood tensely, waiting for the next move. He could see patches of rust on her battered gray hull, as well as numerous places that had been welded together during repairs. It was a damn miracle the thing could float, he thought, much less travel. But looks must be deceiving in this case. He knew the cartel wouldn't risk such a valuable cargo in a ship that wasn't seaworthy. Those people weren't stupid. He wouldn't be surprised if it turned out to be a new ship painted to look like a derelict so the U.S. Coast Guard wouldn't pay attention to it.

The captain reappeared as suddenly as he had vanished. *"¡Cuidado!"* he cautioned.

Almost immediately, a crane swung over the deck of the *Liberty Belle* and lowered its first load. Dominguez quickly unhooked the cargo net, then lifted out the plastic-wrapped bales of marijuana. Monroe placed a metal box containing part of the payment into the net, then sent it back for the next load. While waiting, the two men stowed the bales in the cabin. The process was repeated several times until nearly a ton of Santa Marta gold and twenty-five kilos of cocaine were on board.

The transfer was made in little more than twenty minutes from first hail. With a wave, the Colombians dropped the lines holding the ships together and the *Belle* drifted clear. Dominguez started the engines, came about and headed for the bay.

Jackson fought back waves of nausea and prayed for the swift return to still water. Valiantly, he watched as the freighter moved off in search of the next customer on its delivery route. The darkness quickly and completely swallowed it, leaving only the thousands of visible stars overhead, studding the inky sky. Within five minutes, Jackson gave up praying and heaved over the side of the boat.

CHAPTER TWENTY-SIX

THE sleek bow of the cruiser cut northward through the waters of Chesapeake Bay. In the moonless night, its wake was almost invisible. Ches Jackson sat on deck, scanning the dark surroundings, relieved to be feeling a little better.

Monroe had taken the helm. He knew every cove and sandbar, but even from the vantage point of the flying bridge, with the boat's running lights and the points of light on shore, it was difficult to tell exactly where they were. Clouds had rolled in, leaving fewer stars in view. Occasionally a definite landmark appeared. He was certain they had just passed Windmill Point and he'd pointed it out to Dominguez who stood beside him. It wouldn't be much longer before they reached the mouth of the Potomac.

The men were solemn. Tension remained with them, even after the transfer of the shipment had gone smoothly. Long hours in the cold with only brief rest had taken their toll. Dominguez and Monroe talked above the sound of the engines, going over details of the drop plan. The cargo would be offloaded at a small wharf about halfway along their route up the river where another group waited to transfer it to vans.

They were interrupted when Jackson climbed up the narrow ladder. His sudden presence startled the other men.

"What's the matter?" Dominguez asked.

"Cut the engines," came the urgent reply.

Instantly, Monroe stopped the motors and switched off the lights. "What is it? Do you see something?"

"Sh-h-h."

The three of them strained to see through the darkness. Their breathing momentarily stopped as they listened to identify each sound. Nothing was visible, and there was no sound except the wind and the water lapping against the hull.

"I don't know," whispered Jackson hesitantly, "I thought I heard another motor." Again he listened, holding his breath, not moving. Finally, he exhaled. "I don't know," he repeated. "Something doesn't feel right." His skin seemed to crawl. It was the kind of advance signal he had learned to heed.

Monroe's mouth was taut. He trusted Jackson's instincts. Immediately, he made the decision to put in to one of the tiny inlets for a while. If Ches were wrong, it would only be a matter of inconvenience. If he were right, it could save them from big trouble.

When Monroe restarted the engines, he kept them idling for a few moments, then slowly proceeded, hugging the shoreline. Even without the lights, he could make out a fine white outline along the banks. Traces of ice. A gap in the thin line identified the next opening in the land, and he veered the boat westward, maneuvering it into the cove. He recognized it immediately from the general shape. A stream led inland, Hoping the large vessel wouldn't ground itself, he carefully went around a bend and nosed the boat into the camouflage of a cluster of trees and thick underbrush leaning out from the banks.

As soon as their motors were shut off, they heard the other sound. It was distant, but unmistakable. Monroe's mind assessed the possibilities. At that time of the early morning, few boats were on the water. It would be at least another hour before the first fishermen were out. Of course, there was the chance it could be another boatload of smugglers going about the same business as they were, but that wasn't very likely. No, from the way it was behaving, the greatest possibility was that it was a Coast Guard shore patrol boat. Silently, he pointed downward, signaling a retreat to the main deck where they would not be so conspicuous. The men moved swiftly down the ladder and crouched low, listening to determine from which direction the sound was coming.

Suddenly there was nothing. The distant motors had stopped. Once again, all that could be heard was the wind and the water, and the sound of a car with a bad muffler on a nearby road. After a few minutes, the phantom engines snapped on again, and resumed traveling while the sounds got louder and louder. The same process was repeated at five-minute intervals. The motors stopped, followed by silence, then restarted. Each time the sounds drew nearer.

There was no longer any doubt it was a patrol boat. Apprehension mounted as the men realized how close it was. No one dared to speak, or even whisper lest the sounds magnify as they tend to do over water.

Damn! thought Monroe, vehemently. He sure as hell hoped they were completely out of sight. Too late to do anything about it if they weren't. He was grateful that he'd had the *Belle* painted in shades of green. That fact, the thick brush, and the cloudy night might save them. It had better, because they were trapped.

Momentarily, the lights of the unknown craft came into view, then the outline of the hull, as it rounded the point of land at the entrance to the cove. It paused there with engines idling. The *Belle's* crew could see it was a small type of inland patrol boat similar to those used by the Coast Guard. A very bright searchlight stabbed the darkness, probing the estuary.

The men on the *Liberty Belle* stayed low, not moving. All knew that one slight squeak of a deck shoe would be as telling as a pistol shot. In between branches of the trees, Monroe could see some of the people on the other vessel illuminated in the backglow of the searchlight as it swept the area. A tall, broad-shouldered man wore the black windbreaker of a federal agency. When he turned around, big gold letters on his back read DEA.

Jackson felt the pulse thumping in his neck. He could hear the breathing of the other two, sometimes stopping, holding, then exhaling softly. It would be close. Their only chance was to stay hidden. If the *Liberty Belle* were spotted, they'd jump ashore and run through the brush. There was a road nearby. Escape was possible, but he had to admit to himself, not too likely to succeed. The alternative was a firefight. In the event it was necessary, he was ready.

The bright beam of light continued its sweep of the cove, then snapped off. Voices were heard, muffled, with only occasional words coming through.

"...brought in...know another ship...so many...keep checking......find them."

Peering through the brush concealing them, the men could detect occasional movement as their eyes readjusted to the darkness. Now and then a small light flicked on, flared, went out, and came back to life in the tiny round glow on the end of a cigarette. Finally, they heard the engines restart and the patrol moved on, heading south, staying near the shore of the bay. There was the same pattern of stopping, waiting, and starting over and over. As soon as the launch had rounded the point and disappeared from view, the men on the hidden boat exhaled simultaneously.

"I'd say we barely squeezed out of that one, my friends!" Ian Monroe spoke through tight jaws. "Thanks to your ESP, Ches, and a lot of good luck!"

Dominguez' whisper was urgent. "We aren't out of this yet, *muchachos*." In the cold darkness, when the tension was so great even he had worked up a sweat, he'd planned what they would do if they weren't caught. "We're gonna unload this cargo of shit right here. That patrol isn't going to give up and we won't be this lucky twice."

"Sonofabitch!" exclaimed Jackson. "You mean, right here in this muck? Does anybody know where the hell we are? How will we pick it up again?" He could feel the twenty-four hours of hard work going down the tubes.

"Hold on, Ches," Monroe intervened. "It might be the best thing to do. I know exactly where we are, and we should be able to make the pick up from the road. It's not too far away."

Briefly, Dominguez clicked on a flashlight and scanned the shore. There was one spot with a stretch of smooth bank bordered by underbrush about twelve yards from the water's edge. They would be able to hide the shipment fairly well. The crew quickly set up an assembly line, relaying the plastic-wrapped, forty-pound bales of marijuana and the smaller packages of cocaine out of the cabin and onto the deck.

Dreading the inevitable, Jackson finally forced himself into the waist-deep, icy water, cursing softly even as the cold cut off his breath. "Oh, shit! Goddammit!" He kept moving, muttering fiercely, hoping the activity would prevent his muscles from getting stiff in the freezing water. "Man, I'm not cut out for this. Dominguez, this was your idea. I want to see your Latino butt in this water! Let's see what kind of a bad muthafucka you really are!" In spite of himself, he was laughing, the legendary grin visible in the darkness.

Dominguez entered the water as Jackson moved onto the beach and the relay system was put to work once again.

"Ooo,oooh!" the Cuban exclaimed in a high whisper, interspersed with little stacatto puffs of air. "¡Madre de dios! Hurry up, Ian! Keep it going. My balls are freezing!"

A deep, low chuckle was heard from the shore, followed by a loud stage whisper. "Yeah! Your voice is higher already."

"Stop complaining!" whispered Monroe sharply, as he struggled to hand the bales from the deck to Dominguez in the water. "A little bit of cold is good for you. Gets the body tuned up."

"Sure. It figures a blue blood would say that," countered

Dominguez savagely, fighting for breath. "Oh, man! Ian, you're the one who should be in this. If you turn blue, it won't matter. If I do, I'll look funny."

"Don't worry, Miguel, my friend. I'm ready to join you." Monroe handed the last package over the side, then slid into the water as they all moved toward the stash on shore.

"Damn!" Monroe shivered violently. "I suspect we'll all be singing soprano if we don't get out of this soon."

The men continued their verbal sparring but concentrated on finishing the serious business quickly. Cautiously, using a small flashlight, they shoved the packages into the brush, and broke branches to hide anything that was still exposed. Satisfied with the covering, Monroe and Dominguez waded back into the water and made for the boat while Jackson used a thatch of marsh grass to obliterate their tracks on the shore.

On board once again, the three quickly changed into dry clothing. Certain now that the patrol boat had moved down the coast out of earshot, they hauled up a high powered vacuum from a stowage compartment and began to go over every inch of the boat from cabin to bridge.

"Use the light to check it out, Ches," Monroe said urgently. "If we're stopped and boarded, those guys will examine every square inch. One little piece of grass, and they'll have an excuse to confiscate the boat and haul us in." After a pause, he continued. "When we've finished, we'll sink the vacuum, along with our clothes…and all the firepower."

Even in the darkness, Monroe could read the pained look on Jackson's face. It was clear he didn't like that, but there was no other way.

CHAPTER TWENTY-SEVEN

THE DEA agents on board the Coast Guard boat were cold and weary from the strain of searching for the elusive cruiser they knew was out there. They had heard the motors briefly. Somehow, the slick rascals had managed to elude them.

Blake Harrison radioed his men on shore to pick him up at Westland, on the eastern end of Virginia 695. The only thing to do now was to meet the pleasure craft as it tied up at the marina—if it would head there at all. He wasn't sure it was Monroe's boat. It was just a hunch. And even if it were, Monroe might have another plan. Blake was fairly certain they wouldn't find anything. Still, it was possible they could get lucky.

The patrol boat put in at Westland, and in minutes, an agent arrived to pick up Harrison. They headed for a main road where they could make good time, realizing the best thing to do was angle westward and hit I-95 for a straight shot to Occoquan. En route, Harrison's radio crackled. A lookout on the Potomac reported that a boat had just passed him, heading upriver. From the general description, the boat could be Monroe's. It was as good as they could hope for.

★ ★ ★

A couple of hours later, the *Belle* nosed into her slip at the Old Mariner. Her tired crew stepped onto the boardwalk, thinking only of dividing the fish quickly and going home.

Suddenly a shout rang out from the shore. "U.S. Customs! Halt!" Two men appeared from the shadows around the darkened clubhouse and approached the pier, others rose from squatting positions along the bank. The crewmembers were illuminated in the glare of several flashlights as a small force of armed men surrounded them. Some climbed out of nearby boats where they had been concealed.

The three froze immediately as they heard the metallic clicks of guns being readied. Their nerves and muscles went taut. Brain cells frantically searched memory banks for the wisest course of action to assure survival. It was a business visit, and Monroe braced for it. He knew Dominguez and Jackson would let him handle the situation.

"You men mind telling us where you've been?" an authoritative voice called out.

Monroe put one hand up to shield his eyes. "Why, no, not at all," he began affably. He continued with just the right amount of puzzlement creeping into his voice. "But, I'm afraid I'll have to see some identification from you gentlemen." He thought he heard a snicker from the darkness behind him. After a moment's hesitation, the man on the bank stepped closer and a light flashed on his I.D. badge. Monroe, squinting in the brightness, appeared to make a careful study of it. Then, straightening up, he smiled and extended his hand.

"I'm Ian Monroe of Alexandria," he said congenially to the startled customs agent. "And this is my crew, Terrell Jackson and Miguel Dominguez." He paused for a moment before going on. "My apologies to you, sir, but surely you can't blame me for wanting to be certain of your identity. Being surrounded suddenly by a group of armed men in the middle of the night is a bit alarming, to say the least! For a moment there, I thought we were being invaded by another country!" The last bit was accompanied by a widening of the eyes and a nervous laugh.

"No, Mr. Monroe, we aren't invaders. Just your friendly home guard." The agent had recovered from his surprise at the unexpected reaction. Usually he encountered shifty-eyed mumblers who had guilt written all over them. Perhaps this man was innocent—or very, very good at what he did. "Now, I want to see *your* identification."

Looking a little sheepish, Monroe and the other two quickly produced driver's licenses, fishing licenses, and registration for the boat.

"Okay, now back to my question," the man continued, after studying the documents in the glare of a flashlight. "Where have you been?"

"We've been out fishing all day," Monroe responded, "off Virginia Beach."

"And you're just now docking? If you stopped fishing at dark, and headed in with your catch, you should have been back hours ago."

The persistence of the questioner convinced Monroe that they had some information. What it was, he didn't know. It might have nothing at all to do with them. He wasn't going to give anything away.

Jackson and Dominguez concentrated on remaining silent, looking like half-wits who might not be able to speak in sentences, let alone answer direct questions.

None of the three had missed the fact that they were neatly surrounded, and there was one man who had stepped onto the deck of the *Belle* with a semi-automatic weapon. "Hold on, now, fellows! I thought this was a free country. Are you questioning all boaters who come in late?" Monroe's face registered amazement.

"No, sir. This is part of an investigation. We can let you call your lawyer if you prefer."

"That won't be necessary. I *am* a lawyer, and I can assure you I have nothing to hide. It's unusual, that's all."

"Well, sir, these are unusual times."

"Quite so, quite so. I understand that you have a job to do," Monroe stated, nodding his head for emphasis, "even if it inconveniences the innocent." He sighed before continuing. "We docked in Virginia Beach at sundown for dinner. By the way, have you tried the food at The Boathouse?" He paused while his eyebrows raised in question. "No? Their Trout Almondine is superb. Well worth the stop." There was another pause while he seemed to savor the memory of the remarkable dish. "Anyway, after dinner, we headed in. Wouldn't you know, we had engine trouble and had to stop for repairs! Something told me last week to have those motors overhauled before going out again. But I didn't. I thought Dominguez here would never get her going!" He glanced toward Miguel who grinned, looking at his shoes, as Monroe affectionately clapped him on the back. "But finally he did, and here we are." He finished with an expansive wave of his outstretched arms.

Unimpressed, the agent asked, "Did you take on any cargo, Mr. Monroe?"

"Why, no…oh, well…the fish."

"Sir, I'm afraid we'll have to search your boat."

Monroe's eyes opened indignantly. "What in the world for?"

"We've received reports of a foreign freighter cruising just beyond U.S. waters. We suspect some small vessels went out to pick up cargo. In fact, we intercepted one of them loaded with marijuana and we've got reason to believe at least two more came into the Chesapeake."

"You don't say! Well, search away, although I assure you we're not carrying imported narcotics of any kind…unless, of course, you'd consider my bottle of Jamaican rum as contraband." He beamed comfortably at the collective force. Several of the men grinned back at him as they moved to start the search.

Monroe continued to chat amiably with the men, hoping to distract them from searching too carefully, just in case there was something left to be found. It was his particular brand of bluffing, the nonchalance, a polished ploy which had slid him through many tight spots. Even so, he noticed that the inspection team was very thorough when they checked the hold and saw a plentiful catch staring wide-eyed at them. They probed the bottom with gaffs to make sure there were no "square mackerel" bobbing under the real fish.

He knew it was no accident that the force just happened to be watching this marina. Either they'd had a tip, or they had been watching him. Neither idea was comforting. From time to time, his attention shifted to the shadows of the clubhouse where a group of men remained. He could make out one familiar shape. Tall, well-built, wearing a black windbreaker with the collar turned up. The man had dark hair, but his face was obscured by the darkness. Obviously he was someone of importance. Frequently, others consulted with him. When he turned around, Monroe saw the bright gold letters on his back. DEA. It wasn't likely to be the same man that was on that patrol boat. But why did he have the feeling that it was?

Finally the search was completed. Nothing had been found and apologies were offered for the inconvenience. Maintaining his act to the end, Monroe responded in good humor, saying he was happy now, at last, to be able to go home and to bed. Casting a look toward the group still standing in the background, he knew one agency or another would be breathing down his neck from then on.

It was an exhausted, sober trio that climbed the riverbank and trudged to their waiting cars.

★ ★ ★

Miguel Dominguez worried about his unloading crew as he guided the Porsche north along I-95. Earlier, on the way in from the Chesapeake, the *Belle* had moored at the darkened wharf where they waited, only long enough to report what had happened out on the bay, before continuing upstream to the marina. He knew the men would scatter quickly, and hoped they had been able to elude the curious Customs people. The troubled thoughts stayed with him as he headed home, realizing they would have to play catch up the next day if they wanted to salvage the unlucky load.

CHAPTER TWENTY-EIGHT

SENATOR Kenneth Raitt used the yuletide to show his support for the needy. He appeared at one of the toy distribution centers on a busy Saturday, along with a truckload of stuffed animals, food baskets, and the media. While the cameras rolled, he smiled, patted children on the head, and with just a hint of tear-dampened eyes and a catch in his voice, he wished them happy holidays.

As he played at bringing joy to the poor children, it did not bother the senator in the least, that he and his secret associates who piled up fortunes almost overnight had contributed to one major cause of their poverty. Cocaine provided the best profit for the traffickers at the moment, resulting in the greatest financial drain for the users, their families, or their victims.

Raitt and Monroe paid their Colombian sources nearly ten thousand dollars for one kilo, pure. They sold it for as much as thirty-five thousand to a wholesaler who cut it with lactose and sold that same kilo, now doubled, for sixty thousand. This practice continued down the line, with each change of hands expanding the kilo to twice or more times the volume for twice the price, until various street dealers bought eight kilos and sold gram weight packets for seventy dollars per. Which meant, finally, at the end of the line, the original kilo of cocaine ended up bringing a half million dollars on the streets of the United States—but only after eight thousand customers came up with the money.

Even while the white gold dust trickled down the entrepreneurial line, and the multi-colored Christmas lights glowed in thousands of homes, those customers were busy lining up financing for their short-term investment in the magic moment. Some already had the money, those white and blue collar workers alike who spent much of their incomes on drugs without regard for the needs of their families. However, being without money required more creativity on the part of non-workers, a.k.a. "The Crime Wave," who fanned out along the quiet streets of honest citizens, helping themselves to everything from jewelry to lawnmowers to anything else that could be sold for the price of a quick thrill.

Superimposed over the activities in the streets, were the upscale Washington celebrations. The President ceremoniously pulled the switch to light the national Christmas tree and a swirl of festivities commenced. Lavishly decorated shop windows inveigled buyers to be generous, while great houses threw open their doors for memorable fêtes.

Monroe House was the scene of several parties, and Ian Monroe was glad for the diversion. The recent week had been extremely stressful. The load of marijuana and cocaine they had so carefully hidden, and retrieved two days later, was quickly picked up by the wholesalers. It had been a close call, too close to ignore. The success of any endeavor, Monroe knew, hinged on alertness and clear thinking—and knowing when it was foolhardy to plow ahead. Going out in his boat again to meet a freighter was out of the question. Bluffing worked once to get him out of a situation, but the Feds wouldn't buy it twice. Next time he'd be brought in for questioning. That would be entirely counterproductive. Better to play at being nothing more than a society lawyer once again, drawing up wills and property agreements. However, the near capture had in no way discouraged him. There was too much money flooding in to consider giving it up altogether. Two planeloads were due the next week, within days of each other, and it was agreed Dominguez would oversee those. The man in Colombia expected to keep his supplies moving.

Knowing he would be watched now in the Washington area, Monroe felt constrained. He yearned for new scenery and his old sense of complete freedom. The time had come to make the move to another territory for a while. He was developing a plan in which he would quietly fade away. He would offer the two lower floors of Monroe House to the historical society for a temporary museum. His quarters on the top floor would remain undisturbed—Dalton would see to that—and few people would know whether Ian Monroe was there or not.

Dominguez had located several places along the Gulf Coast that sounded promising. Immediately after Christmas, Monroe decided he would fly down and look at them. Location was of first importance. According to Raitt, the President would announce the implementation of his drug task force near the end of January. The action was to center around Miami. That whole area would be spotlighted, including the air and sea corridors between South Florida and Colombia. Their operation would soon move away from that and logically, should be headquartered on the upper coast of the Gulf of Mexico, yet still within easy reach of the point of origin for the shipments. Some quiet place where they would have access to good highways and waterways, and plenty of deserted areas for landing planes.

The coasts of Louisiana, Mississippi, Alabama, and the panhandle of Florida were all good possibilities, and Dominguez knew them well. Lots of inlets and uninhabited areas. The terrain was what Monroe wanted to see for himself. Once he made a decision on that, then he could concentrate on finding the right type of house.

Renewed attention to his legal practice kept him from Goldenwood for a while, but his frequent phone calls to Dr. Kuntz kept him informed of Erica's progress. Her physical condition continued to improve and she seemed to be accepting the life that was being carefully created for her. Monroe continued to send gifts and notes. The doctor had impressed upon him the need for cementing a bond of trust between the two of them. Without that connection established by the time Monroe took her away with him, fear might cause her fragile mind to withdraw completely. Or, worse, she might suddenly remember the past.

Ian knew the last phase of Erica's remake must begin. He felt she should have a sense of her new self, a distinct persona—totally opposite that of her old one—deeply entrenched in her consciousness. He had some ideas and wanted to meet with the clinic's staff cosmetologist. Dr. Kuntz assured him the young man was an expert in the art of redesigning hairstyle, makeup, and clothing in order to completely change the image. He had a plan and sketches ready for approval.

Monroe's schedule was tight. He arranged to conduct all business at Monroe House, including the meeting with the cosmetologist. For security reasons, it would have been better to go to the clinic, but there wasn't enough time and he didn't want to delay.

CHAPTER TWENTY-NINE

CHES Jackson stopped the big Lincoln in the parking lot of the mall at Tysons Corner and turned off the engine. He looked at his watch and wondered how long he'd have to wait. There would be a man and woman. He had their names, but beyond that he knew very little about them.

As he scanned the vicinity, he wondered if this next step would work. He had a soft spot for Erica, and a strange feeling of responsibility for her. The poor woman had been through so much hell, he honestly didn't see how she had survived. But she was a fighter, even though she didn't know it. He knew it wasn't right, the way Ian had taken over her life. It bothered him a lot. However, above all, he was a pragmatist, and the reality was that even if she *did* regain her memory, she'd never be the same. On that point, Ian was correct. Ches wasn't sure what they could do for her that would not cause the woman more trauma. He sure as hell hoped she'd never remember what had happened to her. Maybe this was best, smoothing out her life, even though Ian's primary purpose in doing it was to protect himself and the organization. Ches had to hand it to him. The man had balls.

He had been waiting about ten minutes when a big black Harley roared into view along the perimeter of the parking lot. Bent over the handlebars was a man, dressed all in black leather, with his long hair trailing horizontally, like a yellow windsock in a gale. Sitting on the rear seat was a small, dark-haired woman, her head pressed hard against the big man's back, her arms tightly clutched around his waist and her eyes squeezed shut. The powerful motorcycle banked for a turn, then another as it jockeyed into position to come alongside the black sedan. With tires screeching, it made a sudden stop.

Jackson got out of the Lincoln and stood speechless, staring in amusement at the woman who still had her eyes closed.

"Hello, hello, hello!" the man said cheerily to Jackson, shaking his passenger loose as he unfolded his lanky frame from the machine. The bright, blond hair still stood out wildly around his head. "I'm Maximilian and this is my assistant, Dara," he said, gesturing dramatically at the small woman now standing next to him.

Dara, in carbon-copy black leather, sported a pair of black spike-heeled boots. Even with those, she stood only halfway up the man's chest. A smile appeared on her lips for one split second as she inclined her head in greeting. It vanished as she mumbled, "Um-hmm."

Jackson had trouble imagining that this odd couple would be able to complete the miracle that Monroe hoped to perform. "If you'll get into the car now, I'll take you to meet with…Mr. Smith. He's expecting you."

"Cool," Maximilian said flippantly, as he dug an easel and other materials out of the side bags of the big bike.

"Um-hmm," Dara added as the two of them, with portfolios, moved in the direction of Jackson's beckoning hand.

Three-quarters of an hour later, the Lincoln, with its occupants hidden behind dark windows, turned into the rear courtyard of Monroe House and rolled up to the back door. In minutes, the group had taken the elevator to the study. Ian Monroe was called out of a conference in the second floor library and went to greet them.

"Mr. Smith, call me Max." the blond man said. "I'm the…uh…image re-creator at Goldenwood, and this is my assistant. Dara does all the sketches."

Ian Monroe was as surprised as Ches had been at the strange pair, but by now, he completely trusted Dr. Kuntz. Had Ian known that Maximilian formerly pushed drugs in his up-scale beauty salon and spa, lost all his customers when the word got around, and was wondering what to do next when he was contacted by the clinic with an offer of big money to lend his extensive talent to the enterprise, he would not have questioned it. Nor would it have bothered him to hear that Dara, a talented and well-known artist, had killed her boyfriend in a jealous fit over another woman, a model. She had gone to prison, escaped, and had been "done over" by Max so she wouldn't be recognized.

As soon as Monroe motioned that he was ready to hear their proposal, Dara became a human dynamo. Her slender, five-foot frame moved and twirled swiftly as she set up a small presentation easel and opened the portfolios. Deftly, she flipped through the stack of drawings and selected a few which she placed on the easel.

Max, too, was all seriousness as he spoke. "Mr. Smith, this is the plan we formulated after studying the woman's hair, the shape of her features, the eyes, skin tones, and figure. We think the Nordic emphasis that you suggested would work. It suits her physical characteristics. The hair would be lightened to platinum, almost silvery…you know, a 'Marilyn blonde.' With her light, clear eyes, it would seem very natural. The hairstyle must be simple and sleek. It is just long enough now to brush up and away from her face, and to be secured in any number of ways at the back…like so." He paused and pointed to one example on the easel. "It's a style that will be beautiful with her oval face and classic profile. Her ivory skin is nice, but it will be enhanced with a thin foundation cream."

As Max explained the details, Dara stood beside the easel, her small, black eyes intent, arms pivoting at the elbows as she put sketches on or took them off in rapid, crisp motions like a semaphore. The woman was silent. Except for her occasional humming sound of agreement, she let Max do the talking. Now and then, she looked sideways at the impeccably groomed, gray-haired man to check his reactions.

"The eyes are very important in this woman's case because they are so greatly affected by the colors surrounding them. If the lady wears blue, her eyes look blue, but if she wears green…ah, I see I need not tell you. Neat characteristic, isn't it?" Max remarked with a big grin, clearly a man who loved his work. "Look at these photographs we made when we draped the blues and greens on her. You can see the startling difference the two colors have on her eyes. Either effect is lovely, but what is your preference?" With leather softly squeaking, the expert turned to Monroe for his answer.

Ian remembered the blue clothing found in Pharr's apartment. Then there was the color photo on her driver's license in which she had worn blue.

"I think we'll go with green."

"O-o-o-kay! It's cool," Max said amiably, motioning to Dara, who whisked away the sketches done with blue eyes and snapped the green ones in place at the center of the easel. "That's settled," he said with enthusiasm. "We'll add a touch of green eye shadow on her eyelids to deepen the color, and the wardrobe selections will follow the same scheme.

"Now," he continued, "clothing allows us to perform the last bit of illusion. It will be easy to give her the appearance of a different body shape simply by the style, the cut and the choice of fabric. We can create a tranquil beauty. We could have a sharp, short-skirted career woman who lives in a fast-paced hectic world. Or, a type somewhere in between."

Ian asked some questions, listened to other suggestions, conveyed some thoughts of his own, and then approved the plan.

★   ★   ★

WHEN Ian told Erica that the beauty treatments were making her look like her self again and would help her to feel better, she trusted that he was telling her the truth. The uneasiness at not remembering who she was, the nagging worry that had brought on her occasional panic attacks in the past weeks, seemed to melt away as she gave herself over to expert hands.

Her hair was bleached, conditioned, and restyled. Her whole body was steamed and massaged, with particular emphasis on the skin of her face. She listened intently when the beauticians explained to her how to maintain her hairstyle and how to apply the makeup correctly in order to enhance her beauty.

By the end of the week, Erica was handed a mirror for the first time since entering the clinic. For a long while she studied the face of the lovely stranger, desperately searching for a remembered detail. Finally, she put the mirror down and closed her eyes.

CHAPTER THIRTY

VERY early in the morning, two days before Christmas, Blake Harrison's phone rang, waking him from a restless sleep.

"Harrison?"

"Yeah."

"Mike Chapman."

"What's up?" Blake sat up, instantly awake.

"We've got a plane on the ground near Richmond. A doper. He ran out of gas." Chapman chuckled at the bad luck of the usually elusive smugglers.

"Anybody in it?"

"Yep. The pilot is in custody. Aside from the cocaine in the aircraft, there are some other effects that are interesting. We're holding several guards around it until it's unloaded."

"I'll be there in an hour. Tell me exactly where you are."

Chapman supplied the information. Blake dressed hurriedly, and within minutes, rushed out the door.

He made good time in the darkness on the nearly deserted I-95 and met Mike at the Waffle House north of the city. Blake sat down at the counter next to the agent who was eating sausages and a huge pecan waffle smeared with syrup.

"Hey, Mike. Don't you know that stuff is loaded with cholesterol?"

"I know," Chapman said, smiling. "It's delicious. Want some?"

"No, thanks," Blake answered, ordering coffee. "So, what have you got?"

"A Cessna 210 filled with duffel bags packed with cocaine. About ninety-nine percent purity as far as I can tell. We don't know the pilot. His name is Steve Callahan. Does that ring any bells?"

Blake shook his head. "Does he have a record?"

"Negative. Says he owns an air cargo business. We're checking."

"What happened?"

"He was forced to land when he ran out of fuel. Apparently, he managed to get it down in good shape. The plane's intact, but it was a rough landing and Callahan bumped his head pretty hard. He was a little disoriented for a while. Long enough for the landowner, who was awakened by the sound of the plane coming down over his house, to call the police. This pilot is handing us the usual line of bull about how he didn't know what was in the load. Among the papers and trash in the aircraft, there was one note with a phone number that would interest you."

Blake's coffee cup remained poised in mid air as he stopped to look directly at Chapman.

"We checked the number and—you'll love this—it's the home phone number of Miguel Dominguez, the guy who operates Monroe's boat."

Blake whistled softly. "They're getting careless. First, I want to see the plane, then I'll talk to Callahan."

It was a short drive down bumpy roads to the field where some lights were visible in the distance. Chapman stopped the car and whistled shrilly, then signaled with a flashlight that they were approaching. The two men walked through the wet weeds to the small plane. Chapman nodded to the guards and introduced Harrison as he showed his identification.

Inside the Cessna, Blake saw the passenger seats had been removed to make room for the load. Piles of duffel bags were filled with football-shaped, plastic-wrapped packages of cocaine, all secured with gray duct tape. There was a strong smell of acetone.

"Whew, it smells like they just got through cooking this stuff, doesn't it?" he said. "I don't know how these guys can stand to be cooped up with it for so long."

"Maybe that's why the pilots do such daredevil things," Chapman commented, shaking his head.

In the pilot's satchel were charts and maps, lists of radio frequencies, and notes scribbled on numerous pieces of paper. The one Chapman had spoken of was written in the same handwriting as all the others—probably the pilot's. However, a note bearing someone else's phone number on it would not cause a ripple in a court of law. The poor aviator was the one caught with the goods, no one else.

★   ★   ★

BARELY a trace remained of the once handsome and superbly fit man who had gained gridiron glory in the early '70s. Steve Callahan was a prime example of an athlete after the decline. In the all too common alchemy that occurs when the games cease, what was once beef had become pork. An inflated face almost hid his eyes in its folds, the sight made more extreme with a purple goose-egg rising out of the left side of the man's forehead. Sagging shoulders betrayed his exhaustion.

Anger simmered within Callahan as he sat in a cell at the Hanover County jail. Dammit, he thought. Waiting for some dumb cop to ask him a bunch of questions. Luck sure hadn't been with him on this trip. Just one screw-up after another.

A guard appeared and unlocked the cell door. Another man was with him. Callahan forced himself to be alert and reminded himself all he had to do was act stupid, stall, and hope Dominguez had a lawyer in the process of arranging bail. Cautiously, he eyed the fellow who strode in. Big guy, not young, but tough-looking. Callahan felt a flash of envy at the other man's powerful physique. Like his used to be. The stud must workout all the time, he thought savagely, as the man displayed a badge.

"Mr. Callahan, are you a drug smuggler?" Blake Harrison asked.

"A what?" Callahan responded, wide-eyed and angry.

"Your plane was full of the stuff. Who arranged the shipment?"

"Hell, I don't know. It was just a voice on the phone. Wanted to charter the plane to pick up cargo of a special kind of fertilizer in Aruba. Said he was a friend of Sam Jamison. That was enough for me."

"Who's Jamison?"

"Just somebody I know. Jamison sends me a lot of business—all legit."

"Whose Cessna is it?"

"Mine. But, look now, I'm just a rent-a-plane service. I never know what friggin' cargo is on board."

"With the smell in that plane strong enough to choke an ox, you didn't get suspicious?"

"Nope. Fertilizer stinks."

"Not like that, it doesn't. And it isn't usually packed in duffel bags."

The pilot shrugged. "I don't ask questions."

"A Cessna seems a strange choice to use for ferrying cargo, Mr. Callahan, unless you want to keep a low profile."

"I didn't have another plane available, and I needed the job. So, I went down in the Cessna. I was sure it could handle the small load."

"Where did the flight originate?"

"Savannah."

"Then where did you go?"

"Down to Puerto Rico for fuel, then to Aruba."

"Then what happened? Who'd you contact there?"

"Nobody. I taxied up to the last hanger at the airport like I was told to do, and the cargo was ready and waiting. It was loaded on board, I gassed up and took off."

"Do you know who was in charge of the men who loaded the plane?"

"Nope."

"What about fuel on the return flight?"

"Landed at Puerto Rico again. Got fuel, but I guess they didn't tighten the fuel cap. Must've fallen off in flight," Callahan ended with a disgusted laugh.

"Who were you supposed to contact when you returned?"

"I don't know. I just had a number to phone."

"No name?"

"No."

"Is that the number you just called?"

"I called my lawyer, and I'm not answering any more questions until he gets here."

Within four hours, Steve Callahan was released on bail. Whether or not he had been lying about the details was not yet known to the police, and they couldn't hold him.

The note linking Callahan with Dominguez gave the DEA reason to watch the Cuban, but Blake had no intention of arresting him. The framework of the drug ring was beginning to take shape, and he didn't want to lean so hard the people involved would go into hiding. Instead, he preferred to pay out a little line to catch the bigger fish.

★　★　★

"Aw, c'mon, honey, I'm hungry. You promised you'd take me to a real nice place for lunch." Ginger Kopenski perched on the arm of the big overstuffed chair where Miguel Dominguez sat. Her bright yellow cotton candy hair mass moved as one with her head, bobbing up and down as she talked. She stroked his forehead, leaning into him. The short white knitted dress decorated with sparkling pink beads was stretched tightly over her full breasts which she made sure were positioned at eye level to the object of her appeal.

Dominguez was edgy, wondering if the organization's lawyer had sprung Callahan yet, and at the same time, trying to decide where to take Ginger to eat and not get tied up in traffic jams caused by last minute Christmas shoppers. Distracted by her slender legs clad in hot pink stockings and the sensations triggered by her touch, he closed his eyes. He'd like to skip lunch but he knew that idea wouldn't go over with Ginger. He jumped at the sudden ringing of the telephone.

"Yeah?"

The voice at the other end was cryptic. "We have a mutual friend. He'd like you to call 555-6892." Dominguez hurriedly hung up the phone and raced out the door.

Startled, Ginger stood up and stared at the empty doorway with her mouth open. "Jeez, now where's he going?"

Miguel headed toward the elevators. Reaching the lobby, he walked quickly to the bank of public telephones. He put a coin in the slot and dialed the number.

"Hello."

"Steve, is that you?" Dominguez asked anxiously.

"Yeah. I'm out...and about as pissed as I'll ever be."

"Are you all right? Since you're alive, I assume you made it down okay." Dominguez paused briefly. As soon as he'd heard from Callahan, he had informed Monroe there was trouble, but at the time didn't have any details to give him. He'd been waiting since then to hear. "After you radioed that you were out of fuel and going down, we packed up the crew and left the landing site. Believe me, man, we tried to get to you."

"Yeah, well, the cops beat you to it."

"We were worried about you, man. When you called from jail, I knew what that meant. Did you tell them anything?"

"Hell, no! I made up a cock and bull story. Changed the details a little to keep them confused."

"What really happened?"

"On the downward leg, it was smooth. Refueled at Great Inagua, then on to Colombia. That was where things began to tank. I damn near couldn't find that fucking little airstrip on the Guajira Peninsula. When I did, it was a goddamn zoo.

"The people were waiting for me, all right. Must've been twenty of them, all running around with guns, talking in your lingo so I couldn't understand shit. They loaded the plane while I was taken to a nearby hut. There was food and a cot. I ate and caught a few hours sleep. When I woke up and went back to the airstrip, the jokers were pouring fuel into the tanks—looked like one cup at a time. They had these fifty-gallon barrels that they'd brought in on a truck. And, they were siphoning it...spilling the stuff all over the place! It's a wonder everything didn't blow when I started the engine."

"Did you make it back to Great Inagua without any trouble?"

"Yeah, only something wasn't right. I tried to refuel like I did on the way down, but the airport officials looked nervous. Something was about to happen and they didn't seem to want me hanging around. So, I left in a hurry and the tanks weren't completely full."

Dominguez was thoughtful for a moment before he spoke. "Okay, Steve, catch a regular airline flight back to Atlanta. When you get there, stick to legitimate business for a while. You know the Feds will keep you under surveillance. Be careful. And...your phone will probably be tapped. I'll send a message when we need you again."

CHAPTER THIRTY-ONE

From his favorite spot on top of the bookcase, Brutus stared down inscrutably upon his master. Blake stood at the window, feeling as morose as the weather. It was not the greeting card type of Christmas Eve. No snow. Only rain, and cold enough to be miserable.

He was reminded of what psychologists say about holidays, how they tend to make people feel more acutely aware of their aloneness. Granted, tonight there had been a choice, but he had politely excused himself early from Bob and Gwen Arrington's party. He just wasn't in the mood.

Turning away from the window, he sank down onto the sofa. He closed his eyes as the thoughts drifted, then focused on Victoria. He felt the familiar dull ache in his chest. It had been more than a month and a half since her disappearance, and the trail had grown cold. The surfacing of Harry Pharr's body had been the last of it. The only other information was of the Latino seen with him at the Jade Pagoda. The mysterious man undoubtedly was from somewhere else, at least from another part of the city. Even when Blake took the bartender to the police station to try to identify the suspect from photographs, they'd had no success. Apparently, Pharr's connection didn't have a record.

At least one good thing had happened lately—the first break in the Raitt-Monroe case. Although the phone number found on the plane they'd confiscated the day before was inadmissible in court, from the DEA's viewpoint, it was a tangible link between Monroe's people and the smuggling business. They were on the right track. He would have to be patient.

Meanwhile, it wasn't easy for the hound to be in such close proximity to the fox. Just last Sunday, he had been invited to the White House to attend a concert specially arranged to encourage young, talented singers. In the elegant gold and white East Room, under the admiring eyes of President and Mrs. Reagan—and Ian Monroe who was also in the audience—eight future stars sang operatic arias. Blake wondered what thoughts were going through the deceiver's mind while he hobnobbed with the nation's leaders.

Blake sat up with a sigh and reached for the telephone. He would call his mother in Mobile and wish her a Merry Christmas. In a few minutes, she was on the line.

Elise Blakely Harrison sounded cheerful. "Blake, dear, what a nice surprise. How are you?"

"Okay. I hope I didn't wake you, Mom."

"No, no. I've just come from church. There was a candlelight communion service. Very beautiful and inspiring."

Blake pictured the scene, one he remembered warmly, of the fine old church with the Spanish Colonial façade on the corner of Government and Broad. "I was thinking about you," he said, "and wondered how you were and what the weather's like down there."

"It's pleasant—really balmy. And, I'm doing wonderfully well. My friends and I keep busy, you know. There was a lovely luncheon party today at the restaurant in the Admiral Semmes Hotel."

Blake smiled to himself. It was good to hear her gentle southern voice, gliding easily from vowel to vowel, rounding the harsh edges of consonants. It was a hallmark of the Deep South that had been erased from his own speech after living in other parts of the country.

"Blake, are you sure you're all right?"

He heard the concern in her voice, apparently sensing something was off balance. As old and tough as her offspring became, he supposed a mother never completely relinquished her role.

"Yes, I'm fine. I just wanted to say 'hello' and that I hope your Christmas will be happy. I'd like to spend the holidays down there in Mobile, but right now, I'm in the middle of a case that I can't leave. How's Dave and family?"

"Your brother's well. Tomorrow, he and Emily and the children will drive over from Pensacola. The food is prepared, and all that remains now is to enjoy it. It's so warm we'll probably open the French doors onto the courtyard and dine *al fresco*." She paused. "The tree is decorated and…oh, the presents you sent have arrived and they're under the tree. I don't know when you had time to do Christmas shopping with your work. It was nice of you, dear."

"I'm glad they got there in time."

"Speaking of tree…when I went up to the attic to look for the decorations, I came across some of your old things that I'd completely forgotten—and I'll bet you have, too."

"I guess I have. What did you find?"

"Well, there are two baseball gloves…the ones you used when you played in high school and college, along with some pictures of your teammates. And there was that model airplane you and your father built. Remember how many hours you two spent working on that?"

"Yes, I do. Those are very special memories."

"I also found your old saxophone, Blake. It's still in surprisingly good condition, considering how old it is. I remember how surprised your father and I were when you announced you wanted to change instruments. We were baffled. You had studied the cello for years, then all of a sudden you wanted to play saxophone!" she exclaimed with a laugh. "Of course, when you told us why, it made sense."

Blake laughed with her as he thought back to those teenage years when football fever swept through the high school halls like an epidemic. He could recall as if yesterday his determination to be in a band that could play for the games and parades. Since he couldn't march with a cello, he'd found an instrument that he *could* march with. It had been a lot of fun. Later at the university, his new skill had proven to be profitable when he played with a jazz band several nights a week to earn some extra money.

"I can't believe you still have it after all those years. Next time I come down, I'd like to look through those things." Blake paused, feeling twinges of homesickness. "Believe me, I'd really like to be there with all of you. Maybe I can break away for a visit before long. It would be good to see everyone again. Dave and I could do some fishing."

"Yes, indeed. He needs to get away from the business every now and then, too. It would be marvelous for both of you to spend a few days at the beach house. It's not used often enough. I haven't been down to the Gulf in quite a while."

Blake felt a pang of concern for his mother, knowing she must get lonely sometimes since his father had died two years ago. He knew she was still grieving. Suddenly, inadvertently as if out of control, his thoughts became words.

"Mom, are you really okay? We all miss Dad, but I know you feel it the most—the fact he's gone. Is it still painful?" He needed to know. There was a silence and Blake wished he hadn't said anything. "I'm sorry. I didn't mean to upset you."

"You needn't apologize for speaking about your father. I loved him dearly and, oh, how I miss him…but I am all right. Darling, what Braxton and I had was so wonderful it stays with me as a beautiful, healing thing in my heart. You know, two people who really love each other can have that kind of eternal togetherness." She spoke without wavering. Her words seemed to issue from a kind of quiet strength.

When they finally said goodbye, Blake was reassured that his mother was in better emotional condition than most people. He wasn't so sure about himself.

Brutus had descended from the heights and was curled up on the sofa. Blake reached out and gently stroked the soft fur, gaining some comfort from the warm being. The cat lay still, acknowledging the touch by an intensified purring.

Suddenly, Blake got up and walked across the room. He lifted the cello from its case and picked up the bow. Sitting in the chair nearby, he positioned the large, graceful instrument in front of him, tightened the bow and drew it lightly across the strings, tuning them automatically as his mind recalled details of his relationship with Victoria.

They hadn't had much time to build on that never ending love his mother described, a love which sustains one of a couple even when the other was gone. They had only just met again, but both instantly realized that what had been missing in their otherwise full lives had been each other.

His dark eyes were clouded, and the lines in his lean face were deeply etched in worry. Once again, his hand moved up the neck of the cello to adjust the strings. Then his head bent over the instrument and he began to play. It was a beautiful melody, haunting in its tenderness, deepened by the intensity with which he played. For more than an hour, the talented hands moved along the strings and guided the bow through the majestic legato to the sprightly allegro movements of the sonatas of Beethoven and Mozart.

Finally, in mid-score, the bow slid to a stop as Blake closed his eyes and brought his head to rest against the slender neck of the great instrument.

★   ★   ★

"SENATOR Raitt has arrived, sir. Shall I conduct him to your study?"

"Thank you, Dalton. Let him come up in the elevator. I'll be waiting for him," Ian Monroe said.

The elevator whined as Dalton descended. After a pause, the sound resumed for the return trip. The doors slid open and Kenneth Raitt stepped into the room. His expression was quizzical, and slightly annoyed.

"Hello, Ian. You sounded urgent on the phone. What's going on? My family couldn't understand why I had to leave suddenly on Christmas Day. We've got a house full of company and dinner will be served in an hour, for Christ's sake!" Raitt clamped his jaws tightly together as he finished speaking.

"My apologies for calling today. I tried to reach you several times yesterday as well. Each time I had to go to a pay phone several miles away. I don't trust my own telephone. It could be tapped." Ian frowned.

He took a deep breath and launched into the unpleasant report. "Our best pilot went down two days ago. He wasn't seriously injured...but he was picked up by the police, as was the plane and the load. My man was on the radio with him as he came in over the Atlantic. He thought he wouldn't make it because he was low on fuel and the engine was cutting out five miles from the touch down. We got his position as he landed, and raced to pick him up, but Customs got there first. As soon as possible, our attorney arranged bail and got him out. He'd been questioned but he claims he didn't say anything to connect us."

Alarm registered on Raitt's face as he stared at Monroe. "The load *and* the plane?" He spoke in a hoarse whisper. "What now, Ian? We've got enough money to cover it this time, but if this keeps happening..." He shook his head. "It's only because we've proven to be good customers that our man in Colombia allows us to pay only half when we pick up the shipment. We're lucky he gives us a week for the money to work its way from the street to the top before we must pay the balance. If ever we can't meet that second payment, we're in deep shit. 'El Godfather' doesn't give a fuck about our cash flow problems."

"Calm down, Kenneth. It will work out. This afternoon, we have another plane going out—this time to Acandí. The DC-3. We've put rubber fuel bladders in the cargo area to supplement the tanks. That will give it a longer range and we can avoid the refueling problems in Colombia. We're using two fresh pilots. They'll pick up a load of marijuana, come in late tomorrow afternoon and land at a remote airfield. It's all arranged. There's a hangar there, out of sight, which is perfect for unloading. And, we've got an alternate landing site in case something goes wrong at the primary field."

"Why in hell are you bringing in a load in broad daylight on the day after Christmas?"

"Because that's the best time to fly in undetected. Holidays make for busy air lanes. There will be so many private planes that ours will be just one more blip on the radar."

Raitt fumbled in his coat pocket and pulled out a small packet. "Christ! I've got to go back home and play the congenial host when all this is going on." As he spoke, he pried open the blade of a small gold pocket knife and slit the top of the package. "You'd damn sure better see that nothing goes wrong with this shipment, because if it does, my ass—and yours—will be in a goddamned Colombian sling!" Now that the bag was open, Raitt stared at the white powder inside. Looking at Ian, he asked, "Do you have a straw?"

Ian's brows drew together. "No, there isn't one up here. Shall I ring for Dalton?" The sarcasm in his voice was unmistakable.

Raitt glared at him and unceremoniously dumped the cocaine onto the back of his hand. Awkwardly pressing his nostrils shut one at a time, he inhaled the powder.

"Why, Senator, if you keep sampling the product we sell, you may end up clamoring for it like the rest of the fools on the street." There was a haughty look of distaste on Monroe's aristocratic features.

"Absolutely not," Raitt said. He laughed as he wiped his nose with a crisp linen handkerchief. "I indulge only now and then to steady my nerves. For medicinal purposes, you might say." He winked slyly, already feeling mellow.

After he left, Monroe sat thinking over the arrangements for the planned flight, mentally checking the steps that must be taken to insure success. Finally, assured that all would be carefully handled, he rose and went to dress. He, too, had guests coming for dinner. Unlike the senator, he relished the thought of charming twenty-four of his acquaintances during an especially dazzling holiday feast.

CHAPTER THIRTY-TWO

The start of 1982 saw the usual upheavals around the world, varying only slightly from location to location. Poland's Solidarity labor union strained against the injustices of the Communist regime. The Arab League debated ways to bring peace to the Middle East as Airborne Warning and Control System planes were delivered to Saudi Arabia from the United States. The Ayatollah Khomeini continued to rule Iran with a self-righteous iron hand. In Libya, Americans packed up and moved out in response to their own government's strong recommendation to do so, even as Libyan death squads managed to sneak into the U.S.A. with the notion of killing the president and other high government officials.

Aside from those threats, the average American citizen knew there was another danger to the country's welfare—one that had become a great source of concern. The nation, founded upon independent strength and a solid work ethic, was being invaded by the core-rotting, fast-spreading plague of illegal drugs. Something had to be done.

On January 30, 1982, with the announcement of the newly created Drug Task Force, the President declared war on drugs.

CHAPTER THIRTY-THREE

WHEN Ian Monroe returned to Goldenwood and tapped at Erica's door, he was admitted by a smiling attendant.

"Good evening, sir. How are you?"

"Very well, thank you. How is the patient today?"

"Oh," the woman said, looking back over her shoulder, "you'll have to see her to believe it." With a nod she went out the door and closed it softly behind her.

Erica shifted slightly at the sound of the door closing as she stood looking out the window at the last weak rays of January light playing upon the evergreen trees in the distance. The chill of the approaching night had crept into the room and she hugged her arms against the soft warmth of the jewel-toned paisley velvet vest.

Ian inhaled and stood still, scarcely breathing, as his eyes drank in the vision. Under the vest, she wore an ecru satin blouse with a long skirt of deep green velvet. She seemed taller, more regal than Ian remembered. "Erica." His voice was only a whisper.

She pivoted to face him with eyes, darker and greener than usual, that probed his.

He could almost believe she had been sculpted by an artist, but this exquisite statue had life. Classic oval face, delicate nose, sensitive and clearly defined lips, flawless ivory skin. Her platinum blonde hair was brushed smoothly upward and braided in French-style, starting from the center of her forehead to the back of her head. The ends were neatly secured with a tailored, dark green bow at the nape of her neck.

"Hello, Ian." She saw the admiration on his face. "Do I look all right?" she asked, still needing to be convinced.

"All right? You're a Michaelangelo, a daVinci…a masterpiece!" He realized with surprise that he sounded a little breathless. It was no wonder. Her beauty was the kind of thing poets write about. In all of his experience, he could not think of any woman who surpassed this one standing before him tonight.

"You look very nice, too." Her gaze took note of his finely-tailored navy suit. She liked the fact he had gray hair. He was very good-looking and such a distinguished, courteous gentleman. It made her feel safer somehow.

He made a courtly bow as he handed her a small nosegay of yellow roses.

"Oh, they're beautiful! Thank you." Her lips parted in a shy, half-smile of appreciation, revealing even teeth. The braces were gone.

"Now, my lovely, I'm going to take you out to dinner."

Her eyes looked startled and she spoke haltingly, suddenly off balance. "Out? I've never been out, at least, not that I remember." The perfect calm she had exhibited only moments before had vanished.

"Well, at least as 'out' as I can take you until the doctor is certain you're strong enough." He took her hands in his and spoke reassuringly. "Dinner fit for royalty waits in a special room at the end of the wing. Won't you be my date for the evening?" This last he said playfully as he smiled at her.

"Well, I suppose so," she agreed with a return smile, visibly relaxing.

"Good! We'll have a fantastic time," Ian said cheerfully. "And now, Ms. Lindstrom, may I have the pleasure of escorting you to dine?" She allowed him to tuck her arm into his and sweep her into the corridor.

In the center of the cozy dining room, a round table was set for two with a white damask cloth and fine china. Spreading warmth over it all was a fire blazing in the hearth. "I think I like this better than eating in my room!" Erica exclaimed, as a waiter served the first course and poured the wine.

The mood was light and romantic throughout the meal. When their eyes met and held, Ian sensed that Erica was trying to reach something through him, trying to plumb that unknown he'd told her they had shared. She seemed to be weighing the odds, whether or not to accept it as truth, to put herself completely into his hands. He must be careful. She trusted him in one sense, but emotionally, she was reserved.

The talk, as usual, centered around literature, poetry, and music, and Ian wanted to keep it that way. Those were safe subjects. He nervously waited for the right time to broach the important subject. That, too, would require great care.

"This was delicious," Erica said with satisfaction. They had finished dessert and Ian was filling their glasses with champagne the waiter had left chilling nearby. "I don't remember really enjoying a meal before tonight."

He smiled, adoring her beauty with his eyes as he lifted his glass in a silent toast.

She sipped the champagne, eyeing him critically. After a moment, she spoke. "Is my name really Erica Lindstrom?"

"Yes it is." He concentrated on looking directly into her eyes.

She sighed deeply, shaking her head. "I've tried so hard to remember, but I don't have the slightest recollection of it." Her voice was suddenly heavy with sadness, although her face remained composed.

He reached across the table and covered her free hand with his, wondering what she was really thinking. As quickly as he could, by steady conditioning, he must dissuade her from the tendency to question things. The quicker he could build her new life, the less she would think about the previous one.

"Erica," he began tentatively, "I have wonderful news."

Her eyes appraised him warily.

He stood, extending a hand to her. She rose and let him lead her closer to the fire. He looked into her eyes as he tenderly kissed the palm of her hand. Soft light from the dancing flames seemed to encircle them in its cozy warmth.

"Remember the first letter I wrote to you in the hospital? In it I told you I'd bought a vacation home. It was to be my only escape from the pain I felt at losing you. Now that I've found you again, it will be our vacation home. Not a place to hide from pain, but a place for us to enjoy. It's on a quiet bay off the Gulf of Mexico where the climate is mild and sunny most of the year. We can go down there and stay as long as we wish."

Ian paused, letting his words seep into her consciousness. She had listened carefully, showing no emotion, her eyes wide but not wavering as she looked directly at him. Taking a breath, he went on. "That's where I've been for the past few weeks, making the arrangements for the furnishings. It's done and Dr. Kuntz believes you are almost well and can travel in a private plane without danger."

He sensed she was drawing up her courage in the face of yet another unknown and his admiration for her grew. This woman had an inner core of strength to go with her outer layer of beauty— beauty that had been created to his specifications. A sudden, desperate sense of wanting flooded his thoughts, not unlike the feeling which often overtook him at an auction while bidding for something priceless. *She must be his!* This most important acquisition had to be gained in a different way, however. He willed himself to proceed slowly.

"Darling," he whispered, "wherever we go, I will take care of you and protect you. Do you believe I mean that with all my heart?"

"Yes," she responded. She heard the sincerity in his voice and saw it in his eyes. "I do."

"Then, will you come with me?"

"Yes."

Ian scarcely dared to believe her ready agreement. Reaching into his pocket, he brought out a small black box and opened it.

Resting in the velvet folds, was a ring with a large, deep green emerald, square-cut, surrounded by brilliant baguette diamonds set in a starburst pattern. Erica was stunned at the beauty of it. "Oh, Ian," she began, not knowing what to say as the exquisite jewels winked in the reflected firelight. "It is...so marvelous!"

"Just like you, my sweet," Ian whispered as he slipped it upon the third finger of her left hand.

A jumble of thoughts and emotions went through her as he gently lifted her trembling chin and kissed her. He pulled her close to him and enfolded her in his arms. She let her head rest against his chest. The familiar scent of his cologne reminded her of the first visit he made to her hospital room—the first memory she had of him. Her life had been barren, empty of everything but pain, when he came and brought light and hope. He had always been kind and encouraging. Everything that she saw and heard indicated she could put her trust in this man. Perhaps she had had a life with him previously. If so, it must have been ideal. She should feel grateful—and lucky. The troublesome thing was that she didn't know it for certain, and it was the wondering that haunted her. But, what were her choices? She couldn't stay in the hospital forever. Where else would she go when she had never even walked down these halls alone?

Outside, a heavy snow had begun to fall. Through the window, the large, white flakes were bright against the darkness. Standing there in that sheltering room, held in a wonderful man's affectionate embrace, Erica felt secure. There was hope for her. Surely, with Ian's guidance and this fabulous symbol of his solemn promise on her finger, she would be able to overcome the misfortune that had befallen her.

★   ★   ★

MIGUEL Dominguez was the first of the group to move south. He sailed down in the *Buena Vista*, taking Ginger Kopenski with him for entertainment. He knew he'd be very busy for a while, but now and then there would be a lull in the activity. If he got tired of her, he'd just tell her to shove off.

He had turned down Ian's invitation to live in the big house on Mobile Bay, preferring instead to rent a condo on the Gulf itself, just east of the town of Gulf Shores. He didn't want to be anywhere near the mentally unstable Erica. Anger flashed through him as he thought about her. Ian's growing obsession with the woman had increased the risk to all of them, no doubt about it. Miguel knew he would feel more secure in his own place.

With the boat docked nearby and easy access to either the Intracoastal Waterway or the open Gulf, he could get away in a hurry if he had to. Besides, it fit his cover better. It had been agreed he would continue his deep sea fishing charter business to divert suspicion, even if he took parties out only occasionally.

Meanwhile, it was his job to pick a staff for Ian's house. He preferred to hire people already involved with the drug trade so he'd have some insurance against having the whistle blown on their operation. With the help of some of his Florida cousins who had their own business contacts along the Alabama coast and the Florida panhandle, it didn't take long to find out who was and who wasn't mixed up in it in some way. The staff would be installed by the time the rest of the group arrived from Virginia.

At the same time Dominguez took care of three other important details. He carefully recruited teams of loaders, people who wouldn't mind using their vans and boats to make a lot of money on the side, and he bought a small automobile repair shop. Having a legitimate operation such as that would provide good camouflage for a fleet of assorted vehicles. He'd also scouted out several more aircraft available for sale. The groundwork was laid for a new start.

CHAPTER THIRTY-FOUR

THE Task Force had been in operation for a month when some hopeful announcements were made. The seizure of drug shipments had markedly increased. The various governments of South America and the West Indies, where most of the drug activity flourished, had offered their cooperation to the United States. Officially, at least, everyone said it would work. Those who fought the war in the trenches were not so certain. On the third floor of DEA headquarters in the center of Washington, D.C., a skeptical group of supervisors met to critique the results of the new policy.

"Since the new plan went into action, we have indeed confiscated boats, planes, cars, houses, jewelry, cash—enough loot to start a kingdom." Howard Scott, one of the special agents around the conference table, shook his head as he spoke. "You'd think that's got to be hurting the dopers, yet they keep pouring it in. The importation of cocaine, particularly, is on the increase. Even with all the seizures, I can't see that we've made a real dent in the problem."

"Starting a kingdom is what some of the smugglers have in mind, it seems," said another. "Remember those two we arrested in New Orleans last October? They'd financed a group of mercenaries to take over the island of Dominica in the Caribbean. If we aren't careful, we may have several new dictatorships on our hands."

There was an uncomfortable silence at the thought.

"As a matter of fact, it looks like one of our old dictatorships is being used as a supply station and loading facility for ships smuggling the stuff from Colombia to Florida," Scott added. "I've just gotten word that our guys have several high-ranking Cuban naval officials under investigation. The Task Force intercepted a shipment of methaqualone tablets and marijuana en route to Miami a few days ago, and the evidence indicates the Cubans are involved. At this point, we don't know if their government is mixed up in it, or just a group of independent operators."

"Remember the Walsh Report that came out in '79?" Blake Harrison said. "It stated that when a large volume of drugs is shipped, somebody in government knows about it. That not only applies to the countries that might be relaying the stuff, but it goes back especially to the countries of origin."

"Um-hmm. Bolivia and Peru produce way too many coca leaves for legitimate purposes."

"Yes. We know what huge profits are made in the U.S. from the time it's imported to the time a kilo hits the streets, but Walsh calculated some equally phenomenal profits before it ever got here. He reported that an amount of those 'surplus' leaves needed to produce a kilo cost only a few hundred dollars, but by the time it was finished and ready for export, it sold for a price well into the thousands. No other commodity there makes that kind of profit." Blake paused. "When the price of cotton fell on world markets, there was a noticeable shift from cultivating cotton to coca leaves. It is an economic thing and you can bet your reputation the governments of those countries have condoned it."

"Oh, sure!" Scott's eyebrows rose. "That couldn't be kept secret. They must import huge quantities of sulfuric acid, alcohol and acetone to produce cocaine hydrochloride in volumes measured in metric tons!"

One agent gave a low whistle. "I wonder what *that* would be worth on the streets of New York."

"Billions," Blake said quietly. "A country can't put a stop to trafficking with that kind of money involved. Even people in high places want in on the get-rich schemes."

"Keep in mind," Scott added, "Walsh came up with those figures three years ago. At the time, he warned that the evidence pointed to an increase in production in the future, not a decrease. The Task Force is now trying to deal with those increases. We'll hope that the promises made by the various countries involved will stick."

Blake's mind shifted to a nightmare he'd had recently. White powder was piled up ten and twelve feet deep in the streets. It was irrational, of course. Yet, if all the cocaine that law enforcement had confiscated were dumped out into city streets, it would form a hefty pyramid. Add to that all that wasn't intercepted, and it might approach the proportions of his mad dream.

The discussion had returned to the problems along the Florida coast. Restless, Blake got up to refill his coffee cup. He looked out the window, down onto quiet Franklin Square with its neat shrubbery. People in overcoats sat eating early lunches while downtown apartment dwellers pushed baby carriages. There were well-dressed businessmen who perhaps just wanted to break away for a few minutes to enjoy the sunshine as they fed the pigeons.

Through the spindly branches of the trees, the brilliant gilded temple facing the north side of the square caught his eye. Although the other buildings of stone or brick were nicely maintained, the golden one made all the others look drab.

The report had moved on from Miami to the coastal areas along the Gulf of Mexico.

Blake sighed as he studied the gray branches. No sign of buds yet. The winter seemed dreary and long this year, more so than usual. He wondered if spring, with its rebirth and renewal, would help him to feel better. *Why haven't I been able to find her?* He lived with the constant reminder that there was no trace of Victoria four months after her disappearance. A light in him had gone dim since then. He glanced again at the temple. *Keep a bright hope,* it seemed to say. Was it possible that she was alive?

His random thoughts were interrupted when he heard someone mention the name of Ian Monroe. Wheeling around in sudden interest, he headed back to the table.

"Monroe, and four of his associates—Miguel Dominguez, Ginger Kopenski, Terrell Jackson, and a woman named Erica Lindstrom—are now living on the Alabama coast, near Mobile."

"Well, I'll be damned!" Blake exclaimed, sitting once again. "How did the Mobile office turn up his trail?"

"A tip from one of those associates turned confidential informant," Scott said. "You know Mike Chapman transferred down there a few weeks ago. Since he'd worked with you on the Monroe surveillance here, he quickly followed up on the new lead."

Blake listened intently as Scott continued.

"The CI is Ginger Kopenski—Dominguez' girlfriend. She was picked up for selling in an adjacent county. With the information Kopenski gave him, Mike found the whole nest of them. Monroe, Jackson and the new woman are in a big Frank Lloyd Wright-type house on the bay near Fairhope. Dominguez and Kopenski are living in a condo just outside Orange Beach, near the Alabama-Florida line. Chapman made a deal with her and she agreed to save herself and rat on old Miguel from time to time. It could prove to be very helpful in the future." Scott paused, grinning at Blake. "By the way, Mike sent word to come on down. He thought you'd want to put yourself in the field again."

It was a lucky break. Blake felt almost normal again, like an Indian tracking. "Who is this woman with Monroe?" he asked. "Don't tell me the poster boy for bachelors finally took up with a permanent girlfriend! Very unlike him."

"Strangely enough, Blake, we don't have anything at all on her,"

Scott said, perplexed. "There's no record of her in any files anywhere, not even with social security. It's obviously an alias."

"Anything else concrete? How are they operating?"

"We don't know that. We've got them under light surveillance so as not to tip our hand. With the CI in their midst, there's no need for more. Chapman feels like she will keep him informed."

"Is there much drug activity—importing, I mean—in this area?"

"Chapman says there is."

"You bet," added another agent, a white-haired veteran of the agency. "You could almost hear the shift when the crackdown started in Miami. Hell, the entire coast from Texas to Florida is tailor made for smugglers. It's like Mother Nature was feeling generous and said, 'Here, boys, this is for you.'"

"I want great care exercised so we don't lose them," Blake began. "Besides the CI, we'll place a couple of undercover agents on Monroe's staff. I already had Dominguez in my sights. We can dig up that pilot again, and he would probably talk if I put the screws to him. But, we want the whole network, not just one or two." He paused. "Come to think of it, I'm on vacation in April, and I was planning to head that way. I'll go down early and tiptoe around a bit…see what I can find out. Maybe Mike and I can wrap this one up before my vacation starts."

"Right-o!" Scott exclaimed. "Good plan." Then grinning, he went on. "I heard that you originated somewhere down there in South Equatorial Alabama. You ought to know the terrain and the drawl pretty well, eh?"

"I can become a splinter in driftwood," Blake assured him with a pokerface, "…a grain of sand on the beach…the red on a redneck…."

CHAPTER THIRTY-FIVE

Erica Lindstrom sat in a lounge chair on the sun deck over the boathouse. Her long slender body showed the beginning of a tan, noticeable even in its early stages against the white bikini. She stretched lazily, feeling languid in the warmth of the March sun and the quiet surrounding her.

A small formation of brown pelicans flew by, scanning the water for breakfast. Nearby, but out of their sight, a splash heralded a mullet breaking the surface as if in mockery. In the distance a huge, ocean-going freighter came into view, plowing its cumbersome way toward the Alabama State Docks at the northwestern rim of the bay. Picking up a pair of binoculars, Erica adjusted the focus and smiled as she saw a sailor looking at her through his own binoculars. In moments, several crewmen were waving at her and she waved back. Finally, when they faded from her vision, she put the field glasses down and leaned back in contentment.

Life was idyllic in and around the big house of concrete and glass situated on the bluff rising to the east of Mobile Bay. Ian told her he had purposely chosen that side of the bay for its beauty and peace, and its distance away from the city. The azaleas had suddenly burst into riotous bloom. The usually non-descript green shrubs had taken center stage as the air warmed, each one producing hundreds of lovely fuchsia blossoms. Through the branches of the surrounding dark green forest, white dogwood and bridal wreath were visible, and lacy lavender bunches of wisteria released their fragrance into the air as they wound high into the trees. It was a world-class floral exhibit.

For Erica, being in such a place was a healing experience. Her body, whole again, was almost completely free of pain. Only occasionally did she feel a vague discomfort in the bones of her face. The brilliant southern sun glinting off the water dispelled the uneasiness she sometimes felt. Ian was devoted to her. Through him, she felt very special and cared for.

She enjoyed going with him as he made acquaintances up and down the shore. He was congenial and knowledgeable about many things, and everyone seemed glad to talk to him. She, on the other hand, was unsure of herself with strangers and preferred to confine her conversation to general pleasantries.

The sound of footsteps coming along the pier below interrupted her thoughts. She turned her head and saw Ian. He was smiling as he climbed the steps.

"Good morning, my sweet."

"Good morning, Ian."

He sat down in a chair beside her and took her hand. "Did you sleep well?" They had adjoining rooms, and only fear of triggering some sort of panic in her kept him from going through the connecting door. He would give her a little more time, but it wasn't easy. His eyes ranged over her lithe body, clothed only in the scant suit, and he felt the tempo of his breathing increase.

"Yes, I did, thank you. What about you?"

Wisps of blonde hair, dislodged from the French braid by the breeze, played along her cheeks. She was looking at him, but her eyes were hidden behind dark glasses. He had no idea what she was thinking. "Fairly well." Gently, he squeezed her hand. "I thought about you."

Erica left her hand in his, feeling the sensation of warmth, studying the man as he looked out over the water. As always, she tried to find something about him that she could remember. His face, the slender hands, the way he walked, the way he looked in the shorts and polo shirt, or even his feet in the deck shoes. He looked wonderful, tanned and fit—but not familiar. If they had been very close before her accident, wouldn't she remember *something*? It was a question she constantly asked herself, but the answer always came up blank. Her gaze returned to the bay. "It's beautiful here."

He noted she was smiling slightly. It was one of her mannerisms he had learned to read. She never laughed at something funny, but a smile came easily when she saw or heard something especially pleasing. "Yes, my dear, it is."

"I'd like to paint this scene," she said suddenly, turning to face him, "and the lovely sunsets we watch each evening…and…the flowers. Do I paint, Ian?"

He looked at her in alarm. Was she having flashbacks? He saw the childlike smile of delight and a softness on her lovely face which too often had a look of coldness. No, he decided after a moment. She was merely waiting for a simple answer to her question. It might be good to give her some distraction aside from the business in which he was slowly training her.

"I believe you occasionally did some painting," he began cautiously. "If you wish, I can have Ches pick up some art materials for you. Then you can paint all the sunsets you like."

"Tomorrow?"

"Yes, tomorrow. Meanwhile, today looks like a good day for an outing. Let's take the *Sunflasher* and explore the coastline a bit. We'll anchor somewhere and have lunch. Alice is packing a hamper for us. We could swim if the water's not too cold, and then have a picnic on the boat."

Without waiting for an answer, he stood, holding out his hand to help her up. Together, they gathered the beach towels and sunscreen lotion and walked down the steps to the level below where the boat was docked.

A woman in a maid's uniform came toward them, hurrying from the main house and down the bluff on the terraced steps. She carried a large picnic basket on her arm.

"Thank you, Alice," Ian said as he took the hamper from the maid.

"I hope you like it, sir. And, there is also a cooler of iced drinks in the boat. Have a good picnic." With a wave, she turned away and headed back toward the house.

Ian guided Erica aboard and handed the hamper to her. Lifting the heavy rope mooring the craft to the dock, he jumped on board and started the motors. They roared to life and he maneuvered the craft away from shore and out into the bay.

He felt pure pleasure as he admired the trim lines of the new, thirty-one foot Bertram he had bought since the move to the Gulf Coast. It was sleek and luxurious. And, even more satisfying was the fact that Erica truly enjoyed going out in it with him.

Picking up speed, the boat skimmed the water southward, traveling past miles of forest and numerous houses tucked in along the coastline. After a time, the bay cut deeper into the land, and Ian steered southeastward as he throttled the motors to cruising speed.

They crossed the opening to Weeks Bay and continued past it, skirting the wooded shores. To the south, they could see the hazy outline of the Fort Morgan peninsula separating the bay from the Gulf of Mexico.

Ian reduced speed as he looked for a place to stop. Finding a spot of calm water along a narrow beach on the edge of the thick forest, he cut the motors back to idle, then turned them off and dropped anchor.

"It's a good place, Ian," Erica said, looking at the deserted surroundings. The only living things in sight were a few herons, still as statues, as they stared at the intruders. "Can we swim here?"

"Yes," he answered. "Don't dive in, though. There might be submerged tree stumps this close to shore."

Erica looked at him in apprehension.

"Just be careful," he said with a shrug, as he disappeared into the cabin to get his swimsuit.

She slipped out of the terrycloth robe she had put on for the boat ride, and lowered herself cautiously into the water. "Hey!" she cried. "You didn't tell me how cold it would be!"

In a few minutes, he climbed over the side of the boat and joined her in the water. They swam out about twenty yards, then back again, repeating the laps several times.

"Well, I think that's enough bracing exercise for me," Erica said breathlessly. "I'm hungry. How about some lunch?"

"Good idea. After you, milady." They climbed the short ladder into the boat and toweled off quickly. In the warm sunshine, Ian set up a small table and chairs while Erica opened the picnic hamper.

Alice had done an excellent job with the chicken sandwiches. There were also crisp vegetables and a creamy dip, wedges of cheese, and golden pears. From the cooler, Ian pulled a couple of icy, cold Coronas.

They sat companionably, enjoying lunch while the noon sun dried them. Occasionally, they talked, but much of the time they were quiet as the boat rocked gently on the calm water. Ripples broke softly on the shore, while a cicada, playing its scratchy violin, managed a crescendo as it sustained a single, solitary high note before diminishing to pianissimo.

Erica was fascinated by the herons standing on their tall legs along the water's edge, patiently waiting to catch a fish. Others perched on lower branches of trees near the banks, napping with their heads tucked under blue-gray wings.

As her gaze swept around the southeastern section of the bay, she noticed another break in the coastline south of them, just above the peninsula. "Ian, where does that lead? Is it another small bay?"

"That's the Intracoastal Waterway. It's a channel that runs along the southern coast of the United States. Boats can travel it to avoid the rough water of the open Gulf."

"Do your boats use it?" she asked.

"Sometimes." Ian was thoughtful as he studied her face, always trying to guess what she was thinking. She knew he planned to join a Mobile law firm if they decided to remain on the coast, but for now they were on vacation. She also knew Miguel and Ches were directed by him in some secretive project which required them to disappear, sometimes in cars, other times in boats, at any hour of the day or night. He had told her only enough about his activities to satisfy her curiosity. He'd been waiting for the right time to explain more, in order that he could bring her fully into the operation. He wanted her to work with him.

"Erica," he began tentatively, "there's something I want to discuss with you."

"What is it?"

"I haven't told you a great deal yet about our business. I wanted to be sure you were feeling well and wouldn't be frightened to hear this." He paused to study her face. She was calm, and he went on. "Shortly after we came here, I was approached by an FBI agent. He told me that a Colombian businessman had brought him information about a powerful drug cartel in Colombia which was shipping drugs into Alabama. He said that by providing information, the Colombian hoped to help bring an end to the manufacture of drugs in his country. The FBI agent asked for my help. I would be in a perfect position to attract some business from this cartel, he insisted, and that would help our FBI and DEA track down some of the key people who have been directing the drug distribution networks once the narcotics come into our country."

Her startled eyes were fixed on him, waiting for him to continue.

"Well, naturally, I was surprised and not a little hesitant," he said. "After all, it's a dangerous game. But the agent appealed to my patriotism and finally convinced me that it would be enormously helpful to both the Colombian government, which is trying to stop the problem at the source, as well as to our government, which is trying to put a stop to the drug activity that ends up on our streets. I could hardly say no."

"I see," Erica said quietly, with a frown. "You're pretending to be a drug smuggler."

"Yes, that's correct." Ian's face was tense.

"Exactly what do you do?" Her gaze was direct, unwavering as she sought to understand.

"All right, I'll try to explain." He paused for a moment before proceeding. "We're working independently, Erica, but under the direction of the DEA and the FBI. One of our people contacts the drug lord in Colombia for a shipment, we import it and wholesale it to the people who will distribute it in America. Our government informs the Colombian government so that it can build a case against the cartel, and at the same time, the DEA will be able to gather enough evidence to catch and convict those who are involved here."

Erica remained silent, listening, her large green eyes wide.

"The important thing is not to get caught by local police, because our work is unknown to them. As far as they're concerned, we *are* drug smugglers. We'd be arrested and might be held before the DEA could step in to explain things. So, you see, there is an element of risk."

He leaned forward, taking both her hands in his. "It's important work, darling. I feel it's my duty to do it. At the same time, it's exciting—a little dangerous, yes, but still exciting! And, Erica, I do need you with me in this. I want you with me in everything." His eyes probed hers, plumbing her thoughts, knowing it was a critical moment. He must convince her in order for his plan to proceed smoothly.

"It scares me." Something had jangled in her memory when Ian mentioned the DEA. Had she had dealings with them before? Honest or otherwise? If the FBI had contacted Ian for help, it must be all right. She certainly couldn't object to that—even though she knew it might be a little frightening. "What would I do?"

"You know how busy I am at certain times. I want you to take over some of the responsibility—if you feel well enough."

"I feel fine, Ian, and…I'd like to help you if you think I can."

"We arrange to import the drugs, then store them in safe places while we contact the people who want to buy them. It all must be done very carefully." He paused, thoughtfully. "You know the big parties we give…?"

"The parties where we know only a few of the people we invite? Are they involved in this?"

Ian nodded. "Those parties are critical to our operation, so that our contacts—actually the suspects—can get information about a shipment and indicate what they want to buy for their distribution networks without attracting a lot of attention." He breathed deeply before exhaling. "It would help greatly if you would inventory the shipments, then set everything up for the distribution."

"I don't know how to do that."

"I will show you how. You must promise me you will be very cautious, while keeping in mind that what we're doing is performing an important mission." He continued to press her hands in his urgency. "It would be…lonely work…without you, my love."

He was surprised at the fear he felt that she might not agree. The past few weeks of serenity—having her near, drinking in her beauty as she moved gracefully through each day, watching her in the enjoyment of her surroundings, seeing her devotion to him—had been very fulfilling. After experiencing such companionship and the promise of a deeper intimacy, it would be hard to give it up. Ian Monroe knew he stood, precariously, on the brink of a perfect life.

Confused thoughts tumbled one over another in Erica's mind.

Ian was asking her to work in something that was dangerous and illegal on the face of it, and that it was for the good of the United States. She studied the handsome face and the conviction that burned in his gray eyes as she recalled all she knew of him. The affection and warmth he constantly showed, his considerate treatment of her, his willingness to give her whatever she wanted as he patiently waited for her to overcome her fears and become normal again.

Tears stung her eyes as she realized that he was everything to her. Without him, she wouldn't exist. How could she *not* trust him? It was unthinkable.

"Of course, Ian," she began, blinking back the tears. "I will work with you. It's just that I feel afraid at any new thing, and I depend on you to help me understand."

Feeling a surge of relief, Ian stood and pulled her up against him. Swiftly, his arms went around her, reassuring her, holding her close as he whispered into her ear. "Erica, Erica, I'll always be here to help you, my darling. I adore you. Do you know how much I want you?"

She lifted her head, looking into his eyes. His lips touched hers and she felt the excitement zigzag through her body. For a few moments, Erica was lost in the sensations aroused by his kiss. Then, without warning, something else registered in her consciousness. Nerves, she supposed, frowning and not knowing why.

Ian, who had been hopeful that the sensual warmth of her return embrace invited him to intensify the moment, was disappointed as he felt her body suddenly stiffen. If he rushed her now, he could lose everything. There was nothing to do but wait. With a deep sigh, he rested his chin on her head nestled beneath his shoulder, while his face registered the discomfort of a primal want still unsatisfied.

CHAPTER THIRTY-SIX

BLAKE Harrison arrived in the Mobile office of the DEA and homed in on Mike Chapman. Over coffee, they exchanged news.

"How's Jan?" Blake asked.

"Couldn't be better. She's pregnant."

"Well, congratulations! You'll be a great father…with a little practice," Blake said, teasing.

Mike laughed. "You're right, it will take practice. But I'm ready to learn. The idea of having a family is great. I don't know…it's funny how you feel about things when you've found the right woman to spend your life with." He stopped abruptly. "Sorry, man. I didn't mean to hit a nerve. Has anything turned up about Victoria's disappearance?"

"No, nothing," Blake said, staring down at his coffee cup. "We've still got informants out with their ears to the ground. Maybe one of them will hear something soon."

"I know it's tough."

"Yes…not knowing if she's alive or dead. I hated to leave Washington in a way…didn't like the idea of getting away from the investigation. But it's dead-ended. I've checked every lead several times, and wracked my brain for new angles. Finally, I couldn't shake the depression. When Monroe and his gang moved, I jumped at the chance to change the scenery for a while." After a pause, Blake continued. "So, what have we got here? Any action from them?"

"The CI checks in once in a while. She's kept in the dark—or so she claims—about their operations. She knows they're importing, but can only guess how they're doing it. I may have to lean on her a little bit more. In the meantime, we've placed two agents on Monroe's staff, as you wanted. One inside the house and one outside. They're blending with the scenery at this point. Later, when you're ready, we'll set their jobs in motion."

"What about the new woman Monroe has with him?"

"Erica Lindstrom?"

"Yes. Where and when did he pick her up? The name isn't familiar from his Washington scene."

"Damned if we can figure that out. All we know is that when their trail was picked up here, Lindstrom was with Monroe. Everything else is unknown. There's no record, good or bad, of her anywhere in the United States. She and Monroe are definitely together. Inseparable, in fact. Must be love."

"Hmm," Blake murmured, as he considered Mike's opinion. "So, she's just along for pleasure…like Kopenski?"

"No…not quite. She's more than Monroe's main squeeze. Our plants think she's working with them. It's just an impression though, since we haven't picked up any hard evidence yet. There is one thing they're certain of though. She's one good-looking blonde, but tough as nails."

"How's that?"

"Her usual expression is a cold stare. Around the agency, we call her the Ice Queen."

Blake listened with growing interest. Something didn't compute. Monroe's choice in women usually ran to high society fluffs, and he held them at arm's length, not letting them get too close. For him to bring someone like this Lindstrom woman home to live with him was peculiar. "It might be time for us to go undercover. See if we can't get a few more tips," he said. "How would you like to troll for big fish?"

"Yeah, it's a good idea. We can bait some hooks around the night spots."

"Right. I'll get set up in an apartment somewhere to establish a new identity. You'd better do the same. I know you don't want to spend time away from Jan, but at least look like you're a swinging bachelor who occasionally returns to his pad for a change of clothes. If you're a party animal, you're not supposed to be at your apartment very much anyway." Blake flashed a grin but his face quickly became serious again as he continued to formulate the plan. "We should get acquainted in a bar somewhere, and be seen hanging out with each other from time to time, just in case we have to work together at some point. If someone starts snooping around, asking about either one of us, that should satisfy them."

"Okay. Now to figure out just who I'll be." Mike grinned at the thought of several possibilities.

"Ah, that's the fun part."

"Yeah, man, so you've taught me. Let's do it!"

★   ★   ★

IT was after midnight and the *Sally Anne*, shrouded in nets, lay moored at the docks in Bayou la Batre, the sleepy little fishing town southwest of Mobile. The day's catch had been unloaded earlier and sold to seafood outlets in the area.

A dark red van drove up, its engine humming, softly parting the stillness surrounding the docks. Through the darkness, a tiny light blinked three times from the deck of the vessel. The van proceeded until it was beside the shrimpboat. Someone stepped out of the shadows on deck and, with a low whistle, beckoned to the occupants in the van.

Two men opened the rear doors and waited, while two others went on board and disappeared down the companionway. In moments, they reappeared carrying the first of the load, bales of marijuana neatly wrapped in gray plastic. The precious cargo was relayed to the men waiting on the dock. When the van was filled, the two on the dock closed the rear doors, got into the front and drove away.

That was the signal for the second van to move forward. Another pair of men got out and immediately reached for the bales handed to them from the those still on board the *Sally Anne*. Once again, the loading was completed quickly, and all the loaders headed for the van and departed.

Miguel Dominguez kept watch from a rented Toyota parked a block away, ready to signal if anyone approached. When both vans were gone, he started the engine of the little car and rolled away from the dock.

The captain of the shrimper was pleased as he went down to his cabin and lit an oil lamp. He opened the shoebox Dominguez had brought him just before the unloading began and recounted the money. Smiling in satisfaction, he realized he'd found something much more profitable than the shrimping business. In the morning, his crew would be well paid for their participation. He pulled off his boots, turned off the lamp and went soundly to sleep.

In another rental car parked in front of a convenience store, Erica Lindstrom sat with Ian Monroe. They watched the first vehicle go by, traveling north toward the city at a normal rate of speed, followed in ten minutes by the second one. Ches Jackson waited farther up the road, ready to radio a coded warning to the others if a police car or any suspicious vehicle went past him. So far, he had been silent.

"The pick-up operation is going well," Erica said.

"Yes," Ian agreed. "Everything is right on schedule, just as Dominguez planned it." Even with that reassurance, the tension was evident in his voice. "The vehicles will peel off onto different roads. If one should be stopped, at least the others will get away."

It would be easy to hide two vans in the parking lot of a busy apartment complex in Mobile. There the load would wait, innocently, within view of a lookout to guard against random car thieves, until the next day.

Ian turned to face her. "You'll be on your own tomorrow, Erica. I have to set up another shipment. Are you ready for the transfer of this shipment to the stash house?"

"Yes. I've gone over it in my mind so many times. I know what to do, and the crew has been briefed. I think I'm ready."

CHAPTER THIRTY-SEVEN

AROUND noon the next day, the vans waiting in the parking lot were ready to move. Stationed nearby were two old cars Dominguez had dispatched from the repair shop to follow the vans in case there was a need for damage control. They were battered relics that looked like they needed to be tied together with baling wire. Each young driver had his seat belt secured, and a pint of whiskey stashed between his legs.

The first escort pulled out behind the red van as it got underway. His old Chevrolet had spots of missing paint. The front bumper hung askew and the right rear fender was dented in. The back end was pop art. The license plate was encased in a frame decorated with multi-colored paint sprinkled with glitter dust. Bumper stickers pasted all over proclaimed their diverse messages. Wild Child, Bad to the Bone, I Superlube My Car, If You Can Read This Get The Hell Off My Tail, and Honk If You Love Jesus. A Ford Fairlane in similar condition followed the second van.

Erica watched from her car in the parking lot of a strip mall. The vans and their escorts left separately, staying in the right lane, blending into the heavy noonday traffic. They carefully maintained some distance between each other. Erica's driver pulled away from the curb and turned onto Airport Boulevard, settling into the middle lane about a block behind the procession. The vehicles moved smoothly along the busy street in bumper to bumper traffic.

Patrolling the same segment of road was a middle-aged veteran policeman feeling extremely pleased with himself. After years of waiting, he had finally been issued a brand new patrol car. It was a happy day indeed for someone nearing retirement. Years on the job had dulled his enthusiasm and idealistic notions about law enforcement. The work was discouraging—always more crooks than they knew what to do with. No matter how many were sent to jail, there were still a large number out there doing their mischief and needing to be caught. About the only rewards an old hand had were a few creature comforts. He leaned his portly body back against the soft cushions and enjoyed the feel of the car's interior as he carefully threaded his way through heavy traffic. There were always fender benders along the boulevard, and he didn't want to be a victim of one.

Just then, as if his mind had conjured up the real thing, there was a screech of tires and a loud thump as one car rear-ended another about fifty yards behind him. The patrolman was in the far left lane. He immediately radioed for an approaching patrol car to come to the aid of the small wreck. That would be easier, he decided, than for him to make a U-turn and try to get back to the scene himself. He knew there would be no injuries, only locked bumpers. Pain-in-the-butt category. "Damn fool idiot," he muttered to himself, "driving with one finger up his ass and his mind in China."

He began to move the patrol car to the right, toward an exit, not wanting to risk the noontime crush any longer than necessary. He eased into the middle lane, then with more difficulty, edged once more to the right, squeezing in just behind a dark red van. Right away, the policeman noticed something peculiar about it. The rear was dragging.

"Well, looky here. This ole boy seems to have a problem," the policeman chuckled. "Either the tires are going flat, or the load's too heavy." He noted it was a rental and decided to pull it over. It was always a good idea to check out those. Besides, it would give him an excuse to test the flashing lights mounted on the roof. It wouldn't take more than a few minutes, and then he'd be out of there and on to Burger King for lunch.

With extreme pleasure, he saw the blinking of intense blue light reflected in the van's windows as it slowed to a halt. The officer stopped behind his quarry and began to get out of the car, coaxing his bulk from behind the steering wheel.

The first escort car, which had dropped back when the patrol car moved in, approached the scene and its driver was ready. Quickly, he took a swig of the whiskey and sloshed some on his clothes. Then, his foot pressed down on the accelerator and, just as the startled officer stepped onto the pavement, plowed the ragged car into the shiny, bright new one.

"Ho-o-o-ly shit!" bellowed the policeman, wagging his head from side to side in anguish. He watched in horror as the trunk popped open and the pristine rear bumper clattered to the pavement. There was a considerable dent across the back.

Enraged, he stormed toward the Chevrolet, catching the smell of whiskey at ten paces. Looking at the drooping eyelids of the scruffy, teenage driver, he knew the cause of the problem.

"Oopsh," the young man said thickly. A half-smile formed around his slack mouth as his eyebrows floated upward.

"You sorry little prick! Look at what you've gone and done!" the officer yelled, red-faced and barely able to bring his flailing arms under control. He couldn't decide whether to write a ticket or pull his weapon. Damn little wet-nosed bastard deserved to be shot two or three times. "Exit your vee-hicle!" he roared, with his hand on the gun butt at his waist. "Get your hands on top of the car! Spread your legs!" The tension eased a little as the teenager did as he was told. "You know what I'm going to charge you with?" The policeman grinned maliciously. "Driving under the influence, reckless endangerment, destruction of municipal property…" At that point his face crumpled, looking as though he might cry. "And," he growled, recovering, "just being too purely stupid to operate a motor vee-hicle!"

During the entire tirade, the drunk driver leaned limply against the car, blinking frequently and murmuring rapid agreement.

Erica's car approached the scene soon after the crash, in time for her to see the forgotten van rejoin the stream of cars on the boulevard. She felt a tremor of panic when she saw the uniformed officer and the lighted patrol car, but she forced herself to focus on the goal. The decoy had served his purpose. He'd have to spend a couple of days in jail, but he knew it was his job and for that, he'd be well paid. Meanwhile, the policeman was oblivious to all but his problems. With fears under control, Erica stared indifferently at the events taking place on the roadside. All other organization vehicles were once again moving easily toward the stash house.

Soon they turned off the boulevard and ended in a quiet neighborhood of modest brick houses. The second van and its escort were waiting, parked along the street a block apart. The whole group then merged into a tight caravan and proceeded two more blocks, turned left, then right, and pulled into the driveway of a house with burglar bars on the doors and windows, and a neat lawn. The two vans drove into the double garage and its electronic doors closed after them. The one remaining escort car left. As a security precaution, Erica's driver also turned into the driveway and moved the car forward until its bumper was pressed tightly against one garage door. Almost immediately, Ches Jackson drove up beside them in another rental car and did the same.

The front door of the house opened and a pleasant looking woman beckoned them inside. She was half of the "couple" who pretended to live normal, nine-to-five weekdays and suburban weekends. She had made coffee and was preparing to serve it, as if she were an ordinary housewife rather than a prop.

The unloading had already begun. From the garage into the kitchen, then through the house to one of the bedrooms, the men carried the fragrant packages. When they had finished, they went back to the kitchen for the promised cup of coffee while the woman vacuumed up any trace of plant material dropped on the floor.

In the back room, Erica counted the stacked bales and opened several at random. From these, she pulled handfuls of marijuana and examined them carefully. There was none of the poor quality green or the dark brown marijuana she'd been taught to guard against. Ian had stressed that in the charade in which they were involved, they must demand best quality or the Colombians would become suspicious. She relaxed when she saw that the weed was the pale gold type, proof that it was grown in Santa Marta. Making notations on a clipboard, she finished her inventory and announced she was ready to leave.

Ches had stood around with his hands in his pockets, waiting for Erica to complete the inspection. "Looks like you're ready to have another party," he said to her with a grin. He had to hand it to the main man for inventing novel ideas. Smuggling drugs was still smuggling drugs, but Monroe did it with class. It gave the operation a cleaner feel somehow.

"Yes, I'll get started on the details for this one immediately. Ian will be glad to hear everything went well." Erica felt a new confidence. She had proven she could handle a delicate transfer skillfully. This operation had gone like clockwork, even with the potentially dangerous run-in with the police. Damage control had been tested and it had worked. Ian would be pleased.

CHAPTER THIRTY-EIGHT

"How ya doing, Ginger?" Mike Chapman asked as he seated himself on the barstool next to the frizzy blonde at Peg Leg Pete's in Gulf Shores.

Startled, she jumped, then stared at Chapman for a moment. "Hey, I didn't recognize you with the whiskers."

Chapman felt surrounded by a choking mixture of smoke and perfume. He signaled the bartender to bring Ginger another drink. "I got your message. What's up?"

"I can't stay long. Miguel will be looking for me. I told him I was going shopping," she said, nervously lighting a long thin cigarette from one she was finishing.

Chapman noticed two other stubs bearing her dark lipstick in the ashtray. He looked at the stark, painted face and bright bleached hair. Not a young babe, he thought, but the figure was dynamite and she dressed to show it. In the middle of the afternoon, she was ready for night life.

Ginger took a slow pull on the fresh cigarette and inhaled deeply. After a pause, the smoke flowed out of her mouth in a narrow, translucent stream. It seemed to calm her nerves, but still she spoke very fast and in a hushed voice. "The organization is in full operation now. They've been bringing in boats and planes from Colombia for about a month. I don't know where they unload the stuff. Miguel doesn't tell me anything. I only get what I overhear." She paused.

"But I know they're looking for more airstrips. They don't like to use the same place more than twice. Also, Miguel says their best pilot— the one in Georgia—is flying in for a meeting."

"Is he coming in for a particular job?"

"I don't know. I just know he's flown for them before—that's all."

"What else can you tell me? What kind of stuff are they shipping?"

"They're shipping a lot of both—m.j. and coke. Miguel is happy about the money. He's buying me all kinds of things. Not bad, eh?" She paused to flash a diamond ring for Chapman's benefit. "But, he's really pissed off about one of the other guys...or rather the woman he's brought with him...says she's dangerous to all of them. I don't have any idea what that means."

"You mean Erica Lindstrom?" Mike asked quickly.

"Beats me. I don't...wait...yeah, I did hear Miguel mention the name Erica. But I don't know anything about her. I've never had the pleasure of meeting her, I'm sure," Ginger said, sounding peeved. "I really gotta go now."

"Okay. Thanks for the info," Mike said. "I want you to call me when that pilot arrives."

She stood up to leave. "Yeah. My favorite thing is to call the drug cops."

Mike grinned. "Take care of yourself. You know, things could get a little rough."

"Gee, thanks, Mike. Ain't it nice to be loved." Ginger hit him playfully on the arm and walked away, trailing the toxic cloud in her wake.

"Damn!" Chapman muttered to no one. "I don't know how she finds any oxygen to breathe." He sat a while longer, eating peanuts as he thought over the information. It could be a concrete lead. He'd authorize increased surveillance at Monroe's house as well as that of Dominguez. He had a feeling they'd soon find themselves following a hot trail. It would have to be hot in order to catch those guys holding the dope in their hands.

★   ★   ★

STEVE Callahan never tired of the view of the world from an aircraft cruising at six thousand feet. The sense of power could only be understood by one who spent many hours observing tiny structures on the ground from that lofty vantage point. To his left the Gulf of Mexico was a smooth expanse of mercury shimmering in the afternoon sun. Beneath him the green terrain had patches of other colors where the forest had been scooped out and replaced with buildings and parking lots.

Before long, he would begin the descent to Pensacola. The flight from Atlanta had been effortless. He had trimmed out so he could think, letting his thoughts run without interruption, something hard to accomplish on the ground. He was on his way to talk to Dominguez about another job. A wry smile creased Callahan's face. After his little visit to the jail in Virginia, things had quieted down. The group's lawyers had taken care of things nicely, making a plea of innocence on behalf of an honest businessman who had been duped into carrying illegal cargo. He was sure a lot of money had changed hands somewhere along the line. It was good to know the organization kept their promise to protect him. All he had to do was not get caught again.

His air freight business was doing well. Callahan loved flying, and really loved pulling in money with ease. He had a nice life, even if it had taken a long time to make it happen. His wife was happy, finally living in the luxury a former Miss Virginia deserved. His beautiful daughters were in good schools. The worries were disappearing. It was a way of life he intended to maintain—and enrich whenever possible.

★   ★   ★

BLAKE was in the office when the surveillance team watching Monroe's house called in to report three occupants in a tan Jeep Cherokee had left the house and headed south along the scenic road skirting the bay. The agency car was following at a discreet distance.

"Who's in the car?" Blake asked, grabbing the radio.

"Monroe and the Ice Queen, herself. Jackson's driving."

"Good going, Levin," Blake said. "I've been waiting for this mystery woman to surface. Monroe keeps her pretty well hidden. Any idea what they're up to?"

"Negative." Levin's voice sounded raspy as it came over the radio. "It's too soon to guess. We've just driven through Fairhope. Ahead is the Grand Hotel, along with a lot of private bay houses. The group could be meeting with someone at any of those places. On the other hand, they could be just out for a drive."

"Is Harding with you?"

"Affirmative."

"I'm on my way. Radio your position every ten minutes," Blake ordered. He left the office immediately, speeding eastward across the I-10 Bayway in an agency undercover-issue gray Toyota Celica. At the Highway 59 exit, he headed south. It was a more direct route than the one the others were on.

Blake toyed with the new mustache he'd grown as his mind tried to second-guess where the group was going. The last report had Monroe's vehicle proceeding at a leisurely rate. Apparently, its occupants were enjoying the scenery. When he reached Foley, he decided, he'd turn back to the west and intercept them at some point. Just as he made the decision, the radio crackled. It was Mike.

"The CI just called and said the pilot is on his way, flying in to Pensacola."

"Okay!" Blake filled in the details for Mike of the current surveillance. "It's a very good bet the group is going to meet with him. If we don't lose them, we'll be there, too."

"Good," Mike said. "I'm coming over there. I'll stay in touch. The team following Dominguez says he's heading toward Pensacola. Maybe he's picking up the pilot."

Mike signed off and Blake concentrated on maintaining his speed. Before long, the radio squawked again. The Jeep had passed Point Clear, heading east for a short distance, then had turned onto 59 and resumed its southerly course. Good news. He could stay on the same highway, Blake thought with relief. He sped past the little town of Loxley and calculated that Monroe couldn't be more than fifteen miles ahead of him. Ten minutes later, he received another message. The Cherokee had turned and was headed down the Fort Morgan Road—a road that led to only one place. He was eight miles behind them, and closing.

CHAPTER THIRTY-NINE

Two fortresses commanded the approach to Mobile Bay. From the west, on the tip of Dauphin Island, what was left of Fort Gaines faced its sister across a two-mile stretch of water. On the eastern shore at the end of a long, skinny peninsula, Fort Morgan sprawled, its massive bulk hugging the ground.

The latter had met with kinder fate, surviving the years of use and abuse in a more complete condition. Built in the shape of a five-pointed star by a French engineer, it had withstood assaults from the English, the Indians, and the Spanish, until finally, it was claimed by the Americans after the War of 1812. The Union and the Confederacy squabbled over it during the Civil War, with the Union finally seizing it after the famous Battle of Mobile Bay in 1864. Subsequently, when two world wars broke out, its job once again was to guard that portion of southern shore against attack from the Gulf.

As many times as Blake Harrison had entered the long, dank, brick-lined tunnel leading into Fort Morgan, he was always struck with a sense of history. For that awareness, he was grateful to his father, the history buff, who had been his chief guide on frequent visits. All the memories registered in one part of his brain, even as he strolled along with a different purpose this time. His gaze nonchalantly swept the throng of tourists in search of Ian Monroe. He'd already located Agents Harding and Levin. When they saw him arrive, they moved away from the group of tourists so he could get close to the three suspects. The men showed no recognition of Blake, but Harding nodded imperceptibly toward the middle of the fort grounds.

The first one Blake spotted was Ches Jackson, head and shoulders above most of the crowd milling around the grassy parade ground. He stood comfortably, hands in pockets, laughing and talking with a beautiful black woman. In moments, another adoring lovely gathered around, and the three engaged in a lively conversation. However, the agent noted that the big man's eyes continually swept the area. He watched the crowd, and at the same time, kept a close eye on a couple standing on top of the surrounding walls.

Blake had managed a quick change in the restroom outside the fort, pulling a few pieces of clothing out of a bag he always threw into the trunk of whatever car he was driving. Now merging into a group of sightseers heading toward one of the stone stairways leading to the ramparts, he felt confident that he looked the part of a tourist— perhaps a traveling salesman grabbing a few hours away from his hectic schedule to relax and see some things of local interest.

The rest of the tour group was typical. There were gray-haired women in tennis shoes and polyester pantsuits. Most carried big purses, which in all likelihood were stuffed with rain bonnets, relief shoes, and an array of pills for any eventuality. The men had cameras slung about their necks and wore various types of clothing for comfort. Walking shorts and pale legs on holiday.

Blake maneuvered through the crowd to get close enough to Monroe in the hope of overhearing any bits of conversation, but the wind blew away most of the sound. He couldn't see the blonde woman he presumed was Erica Lindstrom. Someone blocked her from his view.

The guide shouted information over the howl of the wind. "And if you'll look over there in the waters just beyond the western wall of the fort, you can see where the Union ironclad *Tecumseh* sank at the outset of the Battle of Mobile Bay during the Civil War." Everyone peered in that direction, trying to visualize the formidable weapon of war hitting a Confederate torpedo—as underwater mines of that day were called—and going down with ninety-three of its crew. Pausing to be certain that her flock was suitably impressed, the guide continued. "Now, then, the Union's Admiral Farragut watched the action from…"

Encompassed by the roar of the Gulf's waves hitting the beach and the sharp sounds of the historic flags snapping in the fresh breeze, Blake's mind was flooded with memories of the account heard so often in his childhood. Braxton Harrison's voice seemed to take up the narration. *"…the rigging of the Hartford. He watched the Brooklyn turn aside, its captain unwilling to risk his ship on the deadly torpedoes and wooden pilings placed across the opening of the bay. Frustrated that his massive Union fleet, poised and ready in the Gulf, might be prevented from doing battle with the few Confederate ships guarding the bay, Farragut shouted his famous command to 'Damn the torpedoes,' and his ship led the way through the dangerous passage."*

Blake smiled as he recalled how his thoroughly southern father, while stressing the heroism of the Confederates battling insurmountable odds that day, gave Farragut his due. Bravery was bravery, his father had said, no matter which side it was on.

★   ★   ★

IAN Monroe was pleased at Erica's intense interest in the information given by the guide. He felt a strange warmth in his heart as he looked at her. After a moment, she turned and smiled at him. When her attention went back to the narrative, he looked around at the general layout of the fort and the surrounding land. He spied Ches below them in the crowd and nodded to him as their eyes met. His gaze then swept the crowd and focused on the people near him. A herd of sheep, he thought, looking at their bland expressions.

Except for one who was eagerly listening to every word, and snapping photographs at everything the guide pointed out. The Virginia aristocrat frowned in particular disdain as he noted the man's tasteless outfit. He wore a baggy shirt vividly printed with scenes of boats and anglers battling leaping sailfish, plaid walking shorts, dark mid-calf dress socks and black leather shoes. A neat, small-brimmed baby blue poplin hat perched on the man's head. One would think that nothing could be added to make the costume more noteworthy, Monroe mused. But, in fact, there was one more thing—a pair of lime green sunglasses with reflective lenses forming what looked like dual oil slicks spreading their rainbow sheen. Monroe picked out a number of other ludicrous costumes in the crowd. Visual pollution, he thought in disgust.

His mind switched to tactical matters. The fort and its grounds were filled with crowds milling about every day. The ferry from Dauphin Island docked nearby, crossing the waterway every twenty minutes, shuttling people and cars back and forth until dusk. At night, both the ferry and the fort shut down. After that, there was little or no traffic on the peninsula road. Small boats could pull up on the beach, unload, hide the goods inside the fort wall until vans could pick it up a couple of hours later. Some sections of the road were completely uninhabited, and for that matter, straight enough for a plane to land on, if necessary.

★ ★ ★

BLAKE noticed Monroe staring at him and eased away. He took a picture of the alleged spot where the Tecumseh lay. He pretended to adjust the setting of his camera and resumed photographing, panning the camera in other directions, as if scanning the horizon for good shots. In that way, he was able to take pictures of Ches Jackson and his admirers, still down on the ground.

The guide moved to another location, beckoning her flock to

follow. During the shift, Blake snapped a photo of Monroe and of the woman in olive green who stepped into view just as the shutter clicked. He immediately took another picture at a slightly different angle and quickly lowered the camera to get a good look at Erica Lindstrom.

When he did, he felt the hairs rise on the back of his neck. He had no idea why his senses reacted that way. The woman was just as the surveillance team had described—tall, blonde and aloof. Big sunglasses and a straw hat, its brim curved down in front, shielded her face from the midday sun.

Watching her with Monroe, Blake thought they made a very striking couple. Both were dressed in the expensive type of clothes found in trendy outfitting shops—the kind of clothing in which trekkers might go on safari through the bush country, kill endangered wildlife, and still be found at sundown, crisp and fashionable, sipping gin and tonic on the veranda of the Norfolk Hotel in Nairobi. Just the thing Ian Monroe could pull off with aplomb.

As the group descended the steps, Jackson joined them. Together they inspected several small chambers off the arched brick passageways, darkened rooms with mineral formations pointing down from the ceiling. Some parts of the outer wall of the fort were broken completely through, providing easy access from the beach. Blake wondered if Monroe had some things in mind other than history.

Erica appeared to be cataloging details as carefully as Monroe. Blake watched her take off her hat and glasses. Determined to get a good look at her he crowded closer and managed to bump into her. Stern, pale green eyes bored into his and he felt his skin prickle again as he apologized. Those eyes reminded him of someone else's—only Victoria's were bluer and softer. This woman was the same height as Victoria, and there was something about her walk that was similar. *Steady, Harrison*, he told himself, and forced the ramblings away from his mind. It was nothing new. He had searched for her in every woman's face he'd looked at since she disappeared.

Blake was careful to stay with the tourists as they left the fort and strolled briefly around the outside walls. Monroe, Lindstrom, and Jackson continued their inspection. Soon after, he watched them get into the Cherokee and leave, followed by Levin and Harding in the surveillance car. He went into the restroom again to change into his own clothes. Glancing in the mirror, he was startled to see a man with a mustache. Hell, he almost didn't recognize himself, he thought, taking off the silly hat and sunglasses.

As he climbed into the Toyota, the radio squawked with the news Monroe and company had stopped at a small boat dock along the road, looked around a bit, then headed east toward Gulf Shores. The tour wasn't over yet.

CHAPTER FORTY

UNDER the watchful eye of the DEA, the Cherokee continued east through the Alabama resort town of Gulf Shores, crossed the bridge over Perdido Bay and entered Florida. It traveled a short distance along Perdido Key before nosing in among the Jags and BMWs parked at the Flirty Flounder. Ian and Erica entered the restaurant, along with Jackson who carried a briefcase.

It was a typical upscale beachy establishment of weathered wood and bamboo, designed to draw well-heeled beachcombers. Against the background of nets, shells, and flickering hurricane lamps, the relaxed voice of Jimmy Buffet sang about a laid-back existence in a place called *Margaritaville*.

Outside, agents Bernie Levin and Frank Harding concealed walkie-talkies inside their windbreakers and quietly merged into the surroundings. Levin strolled the beach in the late afternoon sun. Harding laid his fishing rod on the sand, squatted down and opened the tackle box. He attached a spooner to the line, and began to cast in the surf. Blake soon joined the other agents on the beach, carefully noting the group gathered on the beachside deck of the restaurant.

Miguel Dominguez arrived with a heavy-set stranger—none other than Steve Callahan, who had crash-landed in Virginia some months earlier. Blake wasn't surprised. He'd expected as much. On the deck, the men shook hands and Erica nodded in greeting. As the five sipped drinks, Blake strained to catch any bits of conversation, but the sound of the surf blotted out all else.

His eyes focused on Dominguez, and on the array of gold and diamond jewelry the man wore, exaggerated in the reflected light of the sunset. Other than photographs the surveillance teams had shot of the Cuban, Blake had only seen him once, the night Monroe's boat was searched at Occoquan. This time, he had a better look at the man, and the way he dressed. Something nudged at his memory. The Jade Pagoda. Could Dominguez be the bartender's "Latino"? Was it possible that Harry Pharr had worked for this man? His pulse quickened.

Erica Lindstrom sat quietly among the group of men on the deck. She seemed to listen, but did not enter into the conversation. Blake studied her face as carefully as he could from the distance. She showed no emotion, only a hint of wariness, even when the others laughed. The woman was definitely strange. Gorgeous—and somehow familiar—but strange.

★   ★   ★

ERICA was more absorbed with the sights made mellow by the amber glow of the setting sun than by the small talk going on around her, the men reminiscing about the football career of Steve Callahan. She supposed he had been famous. A few lone vacationers fished in the surf, patiently casting, then reeling in, hopeful of seeing a flash of silver on the end of the line. Only one was having any luck.

In the exposed wet sand of low tide, an assortment of people, some in pairs and some singly, walked on the beach and children played while the ever-present sea gulls circled overhead. Their skreeing cries seemed to direct the children where to find the prettiest shells to fill their colorful pails.

As the dusk settled around them, a waiter lit the torches mounted on the railing of the deck. Erica remained silent, her eyes now studying each man as he spoke, her mind going through the usual torment. If Callahan had been that well-known, she might have heard of him, but once again, she had no memory of it. She looked at Ian and Ches, their animated faces illuminated in the strong, yellow light of the surrounding flames as they rehashed some notable games in Redskin history.

Her eyes rested on Dominguez and a little frown appeared on her brow. Silently, she observed him as he talked, slouched down in the deck chair, one foot hiked up, resting on the other knee. He had made it clear many times that he did not like her. She didn't understand why, and it made her uncomfortable when he turned his dark, brooding eyes upon her. When she spoke of it to Ian, he told her not to be concerned about Miguel, explaining that he had a lot of emotional problems because of his experiences in Cuba. She would try to do what Ian said, to ignore all her worries about Miguel and their risky mission, and concentrate on the job they had to do.

It was important for her to learn exactly how the sting operation was being conducted. Ian told her he would probably be out of town soon, which meant he'd be depending on her to receive the next shipment. She could do it. Just that morning, he'd told her again how important their work was. In fact, Ian had said his occasional trips to Washington were for the purpose of meeting with key government people to assess the progress of their secret operation.

The conversation switched to baseball, then to deep sea fishing. The sun was only a memory on the western horizon, and the wind had turned stiff and chill. The beach fishermen gathered up their gear and departed, along with all but a few of the walkers. Erica's thoughts were interrupted as the group stood to go inside.

★   ★   ★

BLAKE heard the two-way radio crackle and Levin acknowledged the incoming message. Mike Chapman had arrived and announced he was going into the restaurant. At that point, the others left the beach and huddled out of sight, deciding the next move. One would remain outside in the car to observe and report. Two would join the diners in the Flirty Flounder.

The aroma of freshly cooked seafood greeted Blake and Levin as they entered the warm eatery. Seated at a table near the entrance was Chapman, who managed to tilt his head toward the open doors of a private dining room where Monroe and his group were studying menus. The agents sat at an obscure table a distance away, but in clear view of the private room. Knowing they were in for a long wait, the three settled down to the pleasant business of choosing from an offering of succulent, broiled shrimp, stuffed flounder, and blackened redfish. This night, they would be the lucky ones, unlike poor Harding eating a ham sandwich in the car. There was no guilt. Another night, it would be their turn for the cold sandwich.

★　★　★

"OKAY, Steve, let's get down to business," Ian said. The waiters had served coffee, cleared away dessert dishes, then disappeared, closing the door to the main dining room behind them. "We've got to make some changes. I want to try some different routes other than the ones we've been using."

"Ditto," Callahan agreed.

Dominguez spread a detailed map of the Western Hemisphere on the table.

Callahan bent over and peered intently at the map. "From Atlanta, the best route has been east over the Atlantic, then south to Great Inagua. Most of the time, it's a good place to refuel," he said, tracing the path with his finger. "Then, through the Windward Passage just east of Cuba, and after that, due south to Colombia." He paused, still studying the map. "Or, sometimes, I leave Inagua and continue on a southeast heading until I reach Puerto Rico and cut through the Mona Passage. Either way has been okay. We've been able to avoid trouble. But now, with this damned Task Force, they're tightening their hold over all the eastern Caribbean."

Jackson took a pencil and ruler from the briefcase and drew straight lines on the map to connect the points on the flight. "Considering the fuel problems, it's still the shortest route. On the downward leg, the plane is empty. It won't be any big deal if you get intercepted."

"Maybe." Callahan looked dubious. "But I don't want to get picked up again.""Right," Monroe agreed. "It's not worth the risk of going near Florida anymore."

The men nodded.

Callahan borrowed Jackson's pencil, aligned the ruler on the map from Acandí, on the northwestern coast of Colombia, to Alabama, and drew a straight line. "Okay, here's the straightest path. There's just one problem."

"Yes," Dominguez said, grimly. "Cuban airspace."

Callahan continued to stare at the map. "Okay, what if I left Atlanta and flew to Mississippi or Louisiana, and then south? There's always a lot of traffic heading for those oil rigs in the Gulf. I'd keep south toward the Yucatan Peninsula. Then, southeast to Colombia. We'd use the fuel bladders on the way down. Can you arrange for refueling on the Yucatan Peninsula for the return leg?"

"I'll have to check on that," Monroe said. "We probably could, at least for a couple of times. If we can't arrange it, what then?"

"Find an airplane with more range. Like a Piper Navajo, for instance. It would be worth it to you. That's a clean little route we're looking at here, and with a longer range aircraft, I could travel it both ways without a problem. We'll still have to refuel in Colombia, though."

"Why do you prefer to pick up in Acandí?" Monroe asked. "The runway there is shorter. Why not Montería? We hear the facilities are better."

"Yes, but the folks are friendlier in Acandí. It's smaller and there's not so much official snooping." He fell silent, studying the map. "What about your local landing site? Is it paved and lighted?"

"The one we've used in the past is, but it's hot right now. We're looking for several others—at least two. For each run now, we set up a primary landing site and an alternate in case of trouble," Monroe answered.

"How will you warn me if there is a problem?"

"We'll have our spotters stationed a few miles south of the primary site. If they hear a plane following you, they'll direct a spotlight upward as a signal." Erica's voice was firm and clear, startling everyone. They had forgotten she was there. "If you see that, veer away and go to the secondary site. Land the plane and get out of there. Our people will stay just long enough to pick you up."

Hearing the emotionless voice, Callahan felt a chill as the cold, clear eyes looked at him.

Dominguez turned to Monroe. "What do you think, Ian, should we look for a better plane? I like the idea. The old DC-3 won't stand the stress much longer."

Monroe nodded in agreement. "Yes, it would be good business. We'll need to bring in at least one or two more loads with the old Gooney Bird, but let's begin looking for a Navajo."

★   ★   ★

THE agents quickly re-organized as the group emerged from the private room and walked outside. Harding followed the Cherokee, and Chapman turned his car over to Levin who followed Dominguez' rented car.

Mike Chapman rode with Blake back to Mobile.

"Looks like we should keep advertising our real-estate service around town," Mike said. "It's a good bet Callahan was the pilot

Ginger talked about. They're in the market, and sooner or later, they'll take the bait."

"Yep," Blake agreed, thoughtfully fingering his mustache. "We've already established a pretty good cover. But, I think I'll branch out a bit."

Mike looked sideways at his partner. "Branch out?"

"Um-hmm. When we get into town, let's stop by my mother's house. She'll be glad to meet you…and I've got to pick up some equipment."

"Okay." Mike knew the mystery would be cleared up in good time.

CHAPTER FORTY-ONE

THE glare of neon beer signs barely cut through the haze in Lula's Bar as Ches Jackson stepped inside. He stood near the door for a while, taking stock of the crowded place. The clientele was mostly black, but there were some whites and Hispanics mixed in the crowd.

The Port City Blues Band was in full swing. Many of the patrons were vocal in their approval as they held up white handkerchiefs, letting them sway in the direction of the musicians as they wound up their big number.

Jackson turned to get a good look at the band. The group was multi-ethnic. There were two on steel guitars—one black guy, one oriental—a Hispanic drummer, a white sax player, and a black singer. The men were older than the usual run of nightclub musicians and they looked like they were having fun.

He sat at the bar and looked around him at the faces in the crowd. Instantly, his eyes went to a woman in red, beautiful enough to be on the cover of *Ebony*. She sat on the opposite end of the bar, staring at him. Reminding himself why he was there, he looked away and ordered a beer.

"I hear somebody who comes in here a lot has some land for lease," Jackson said. "You got any idea who I want to talk to?"

The bartender kept his eyes down as he carefully wiped the counter. "Not right off, brother, I can't think of nobody. But, I'll sure pass the word around. Maybe somebody can help you."

Jackson didn't comment further. He'd heard of some dude down from D.C. who had been advertising in the bars around town. This bartender knew more than he was saying. Someone would surface. He would just sit tight and wait.

A member of the band announced the next number featuring Sm-oo-oo-th Terry Sm-oo-th on the sax. Waiting wouldn't be bad, Jackson thought. At least he'd hear some good music. He glanced across the bar and noted with a twinge of regret the woman was gone. Just as well.

Ches Jackson smelled the perfume before he felt the body curves press against his back. A head bent over him, and a sultry female voice whispered into his ear.

"Now what's a big hunk of man-meat like you doing all by himself?"

He swiveled his head to the right, grinning easily, knowing who it was. "Hey, baby." His eyes ranged along her skintight dress. "You are one good-looking woman. What's your name?"

"LaTonya's my name. Can you guess my game?" She broke out in loud laughter as she sat next to Jackson.

"Well, it would be fun to try, little momma. But, I'll have to take a rain check. I'm here on business tonight."

"Say what? What do you think I'm here on?" LaTonya exclaimed, then began to laugh again. "A rain check? Have mercy!" She slithered away, one hand on a hip, shaking her head in mock disgust.

Smooth Terry Smooth had just begun to blow it cool when Jackson became aware of someone on the barstool to the left of him. He turned to see a smiling black man with a pointed goatee, dressed in colorful African-type clothes and pillbox hat. The brother was looking him over. Jackson was annoyed. That was all he needed to screw up a deal. "Sorry, bro', this is my week for girls."

The man snorted. "My name's Ali Abu Amin. And you, like, read me wrong."

Jackson laughed and straightened up on the stool. "Uuh-huh. And, I'm your Cousin Idi. Do we have something to talk about?"

"We might. I hear you're looking for some real estate."

"Hm-m. Man, I gotta hand it to that dude behind the bar. He works fast."

"Think of me as your, like, real estate broker. What kinda land you interested in?"

"Private, out of the way. About a mile or so in length. Hard-packed."

"Like maybe solid enough for anything from a bike to…uh…an airplane to use?"

Jackson decided the man was out in the open now. "Yeah, that's the idea. What've you got?"

"Well, you know, man, I don't have all of it memorized like my shoe size. It'll take some thought, you know."

"How much thought?" Jackson persisted.

"Like, man, I have a partner I work with. He's got local connections. I'll have to, uh, like, consult with him."

"All right, where's your partner?"

The pseudo African tilted his head back, causing the goatee to point toward the raised platform.

"Your partner's in the band?"

"Yeah. That's my man on the sax."

"The white guy?" Surprised, Jackson took a better look at the saxophonist. He was dressed in dark clothes, like all the others, but he was the only one wearing a baseball cap and cowboy boots. With a full mustache wrapped around the mouthpiece, cheeks puffed out and eyes closed, the musician was in his own world, completely absorbed in his music. Grudgingly, the big man said, "He's pretty good at blowing notes in the air, but can he come up with what I want in a hurry?"

"We've made lots of deals, man," Amin assured him. "You can count on it."

Jackson thought a moment. "I have a partner, too. He wants to meet with you—if you've really got something to deal with. What about tomorrow night, same time, same place?"

"Sounds cool, man."

The crowd was on its feet shouting and applauding. Index fingers stabbed the air, white handkerchiefs fluttered dizzily. Smooth Terry had been confirmed.

★ ★ ★

SOFT, ethereal light of early morning filtered through the leafy canopy overhead as Erica sat painting on the terrace. She loved this time of day, when the world was still waking up. Water lapped gently against the pier and boathouse in the distance below her, and myriad birds twittered as they convened in the stand of trees high up on the bluff where she sat.

An annoying racket distracted her as a mockingbird angrily defended its nest from some luckless squirrel that happened by. Dive-bombing while squawking raucously seemed to be the most effective method of defense. Erica paused in her work long enough to smile at the drama. In moments, the same combative bird, now satisfied that the threat had been banished, had perched on a branch and was singing its copycat collection of songs with all the melodic intensity of an Italian tenor.

Alice arrived bearing coffee on a sleek silver and ebony tray. Erica thanked her and eagerly reached for the cup while she studied the painting propped against the easel in front of her. It revealed a small, walled garden. A single tree displayed fresh green leaves through which sunlight filtered. A wrought iron chair and table stood on flagstone pavement. Curious, she thought. This was the second time she had painted a variation on the same garden, and yet there was no similar place here to give her this idea. It was as if the brush had guided itself. Was this something from the past surfacing in her mind? Perhaps if she painted more, her paintbrush would remember what she could not.

She finished the coffee and turned back to the canvas. With a skill she did not understand, Erica dipped her brush in a cream shade of paint, and expertly shaped a delicate cup and saucer on the table in the painting.

"My, you're out early this morning, darling."

Erica turned to see Ian coming through the open glass doors of the house. "Hello," she said, smiling pleasantly. "You know I love this time of day. And the light is so good for my painting."

"Yes, it is a nice, clear light. He sat down in an adjacent chair. "Do you mind if I have breakfast out here with you?"

"Not at all," she responded with a distracted nod. "Tell me, Ian, what do you think of my latest work?"

He leaned over to get a better look, marveling at her talent as the brush formed tiny green shamrocks on the cup and saucer. "It's lovely, Erica. You have a special touch."

She smiled her thanks. It pleased her to realize she could do something. So far, that was all she did know, but she was certain of it now. *She was an artist.*

Ian offered her a Danish pastry which Alice had just brought, along with more coffee. They ate quietly, his thoughts rambling as he watched her. She was completely absorbed in her work.

He was glad Erica was painting. It gave her something tangible with which to occupy her hands, and allowed her a satisfying way to express herself. There probably was no risk in that, although at times he wondered where she got the ideas for some of the artwork. It was true she had painted sunsets, and had done several scenes of boats on the bay. But, sometimes he had come upon her sitting on the lawn, painting a scene that he couldn't find anywhere in the surrounding landscape. There would be a river with small green and pink pebbles on its banks, with hazy white buildings rising beyond the trees. At other times there were fields of wildflowers that did not grow in the area. But they did grow in Virginia. He also knew where the colored rocks were found. And, now, this garden she was painting again today.

The first version of it was in an autumn setting. Ian frowned at the troublesome thoughts.

★   ★   ★

THE police department's early evening sweep of the streets of Washington, D.C., turned up an especially diverse array of hookers. They ranged from young to old, and came in a variety of colors and costumes. The bored precinct sergeant had seen it all, however, and his voice was one long drone as he gathered information and typed out the arrest reports.

"Next!" he intoned.

A whiff of expensive perfume reached the harried policeman as the next prostitute flopped down into the chair beside him. "Name?"

"They call me 'The Gypsy'."

"Really?" he said, looking up but obviously unimpressed. "The only title you get here with 'The' in front of it is 'The Detainee.' What's your real name?"

The very young woman pursed her lips and gave an impatient shrug of her shoulders as she rearranged her luxurious mink jacket. "Gypsy Soldana," she snapped, crossing one dainty leg over the other.

"Age?"

"Nineteen."

The sergeant's fingers paused on the keys. He looked at her sharply. "Age?"

"Eighteen."

"Do you have any proof of that?" he persisted.

"Do you have any proof I'm not?" she countered in a taunting voice.

"The charge is soliciting by a minor and possession of a controlled substance. Do you intend to make bail?"

"I'm not going to need bail, mister. I want to talk to the top man," she said, imperiously. "I've got some information he'll want to hear."

CHAPTER FORTY-TWO

THE next night Jackson returned to Lula's with Monroe. Straining to see through the smoky dimness, they noted the bandstand had been vacated and was strewn with temporarily abandoned instruments. A few couples gyrated to rock music from the jukebox, while others sat at tables surrounding the dance floor. Most of the large crowd milled around, killing time during the break. A word from Jackson directed Monroe's gaze toward the far side of the room, and he headed that way.

Preferring the vantage point of distance to scan the crowd for anyone suspicious, Jackson settled down at the bar, much to the pleasure of a familiar female huntress who had already drawn a bead on him. LaTonya, apparently not one to give up easily, approached with the speed of a hot silver bullet and sat down on the stool beside him, flashing her siren smile. Her shiny lamé dress with its very short skirt caught and held his attention. Jackson had to remind himself he was a working man who was supposed to remain cool and not relax his vigil. It would be tough, he thought, as his eyes ranged over the bounteous, shimmering curves. She was hard to ignore.

Monroe wended his way through the crowd, stopping at a table where a bearded black man in a colorful African dashiki lounged, staring cynically at the bobbing dancers.

"Are you Ali Abu Amin?"

The arrogant head slowly swung around to face the speaker.

Several gold chains and an earring glistened with reflected light.

"I could be," he said lazily, with a lack of interest. He glanced away quickly, as if he were more curious about others in the place. "Like, who's asking, man?"

"Somebody interested in leasing some land."

"Yeah?" came the still disinterested reply. The man lifted a can of beer to his lips and took a slow drink. "Why do you think I've got land to lease?"

"My partner talked to you last night," Monroe said, noting a second beer on the table.

"Oh, yeah…the big brother," Amin said, noncommittally.

Just then, the thumping music stopped. Monroe saw that Amin's eyes were on one of the dancers, a tall white man dressed all in black. He had his arm around a woman as he led her back to a table where several people were sitting. He hovered, flirting awhile after she sat. Finally, he straightened up and adjusted the baseball cap, and ambled easily toward his own table. Monroe, still standing, studied the man. The stacked leather heels of his cowboy boots thudded loudly against the floor as he approached. A rooster motif stood out proudly on the large brass belt buckle riding on the snug jeans.

The man, grinning under an overgrown mustache, extended his hand as he noticed the visitor at his table. "Hey, good buddy! Terry Lee Wilson's my name." He spoke congenially in a nasal twang, as he chewed vigorously on a big wad of green gum. "What's yours?"

"Smith." Monroe glanced down at the black man and waited for him to open the discussion.

Amin chuckled and gestured at Wilson. "This is my main man. We work together like real good, you know, when he's not tooting his horn or shaking his tail with the lady turkeys."

Wilson stood, arms folded comfortably across his chest and a crooked grin on his face. "Don't pay any attention to Ali, here. He's just real jealous 'cause he can't get someone cute to dance with."

Wilson looked down at Amin, then back to the stranger. "I keep tellin' him he's too damned serious." The rapid chewing resumed as he sat and motioned Monroe to a chair between them.

"Dance! That was dancing?" Amin laughed scornfully, stabbing a thumb toward the dance floor. "It looked to me like you were mostly groping the woman." He continued to chuckle to himself. Then jerking his head sideways toward Monroe, he said, "The man's looking for land, Terry Lee."

"Uh-hmm. What kind you looking for?" Wilson's dark eyes looked speculatively at Monroe.

"I need a good piece of ground. It could be grass, but solid, up to a mile long. And, of course, it must be isolated."

"Well, now," Wilson said slowly, "let me see. There's a section northwest of Mobile, but it was planted in corn last year and still has some in the field. Those cornstalks might be kinda rough on an airplane." He grinned slightly as he smoothed his bushy mustache in careful thought. "Nope, we may have to do a little searching—that is if you really want it bad enough." He cut his eyes to the right to see what Monroe's reaction was to that probe. Wilson reached for the greasy bill of the cap that bore a John Deere patch, lifted it a little, then settled it back down on the unruly brown hair. "What kind of money are we talking about…say, for a one-night lease?"

Both men leaned forward, arms on the table, and looked intently at Monroe, waiting for his answer.

"Fifty thousand," he responded quietly, without blinking. The two sets of eyebrows opposite him shot skyward and the teasing slick grins dried up as jaws dropped open. The large green mass, suspended as if by inertia, leaned out of Wilson's mouth. Fascinated by the sight, Monroe couldn't help but wonder at what moment it would lose its battle with gravity and plop down upon the table.

Inhaling noisily and glancing at Amin, Wilson deftly reeled in the gum. "Whoa! We ought to be quick and find some land for our good buddy here!" He began working on the gum again. "As a matter of fact, Mr. Smith, I've just remembered a nice little strip of dry pasture out to the southwest. Maybe three-quarters of a mile at best and it's flat. It's mostly grass, but the far end of it is red clay. Too hard-packed to farm. Nothing grows there. It's off Highway 90 near Grand Bay. It might work for your purpose."

"What's out there?" Monroe asked.

"Not much. Cows, mostly," Wilson grinned again. "The few people who live around there are accustomed to hearing planes overhead. The municipal airport is nearby, and another small airfield, also. But, hey, you'd have to be careful of the radar along the coast— that is, assuming you'd be coming in from the south. Wouldn't it pick you up?"

"No. That's no problem," Monroe said. "We come in low, under the radar. Nothing shows up on the screens."

"I don't know," Wilson said, shaking his head. "It's dangerous around here. There's a lot of shipping traffic in the Gulf, big suckers, heading for the bay. You fellas gotta watch out for them if you're flyin' real low. Hell, in the dark, it would be easy to paste an airplane upside one of them babies."

"Let me worry about that. You just get me a couple of fields. I need more than one. And understand, for that price, I want a lot of careful advance work. Find out about the people who own the land. My group will want to stake out the place for a week prior in order to know what goes on there and in the surrounding areas on a daily—and nightly—basis. We'll only land a plane in a secure spot. But first, I'll expect you to screen it."

"It's cool, man," Amin assured him solemnly. "We'll check out the sonofabitch from one end to the other and give you whatever information you want—including, uh, like, what time the farmer lays his wife every night."

Monroe nodded. "There must not be anyone around when we

come in. I'll expect you two to arrange it. Nobody around. Period. We'll need a couple of hours, at least, to set up the field before the plane lands, and another hour afterward for unloading and getting all our vehicles out of there.

"No sweat. We'll clear it out for you," Wilson said. "We can have the place deserted for as long as you want."

"All right. One more thing. Does this site have several access roads? We don't want to get bottled up."

"There are two roadways leading out of the place, and the farm road that runs alongside intersects I-10," Wilson said.

"Good. I want that one, then scout for a second location. I need an alternate strip in case something goes wrong at the first one. I'll call you in a couple of days to arrange another meeting. I want to see the place. Give me a number where I can reach you."

Wilson wrote his apartment phone number on a scrap of paper and gave it to the man.

As Monroe stood, Wilson extended a hand without getting up and Amin casually touched two fingers to his forehead in a parting salute. He walked away thinking he himself had some checking to do. On the way out, he spoke briefly with Jackson, who was, literally, all wrapped up in some little whore. Monroe knew he'd have to wait until tomorrow to find out more about those two clowns he'd just met. It would be soon enough.

Ches, relieved that Monroe had completed his business for the evening, turned back to the insistent woman. She was breathing against his ear, whispering that they could go to her place. He thought it sounded like one hell of a good idea.

The other two men stayed at their table, beating time to the music and sipping beer. Seeing that Jackson was out of earshot, the white guy leaned over and said, "Well, what do you think? Did he buy it?"

"Oh, we're good," the black dude said. "He bought it. I'd say the countdown has begun."

"I hope so," the other one said as he took the gum out of his mouth and rolled it in a paper napkin. "I don't think I can stand these damned high-heeled boots much longer." Wincing, he stood and clomped back to the bandstand for the second set, just as Jackson and the hot momma departed.

CHAPTER FORTY-THREE

A week later, Blake Harrison and Mike Chapman parked a pickup on a dirt road and settled down to wait in the humid midday heat. The sweating men felt the strain as they swatted curious flies straying in from the pasture. This second stage of the operation was important. If there were a slip of any kind, it would blow the deal. They'd carefully chosen the vehicle from a number the agency had confiscated. The truck was metallic red with the words PARTY TRUCK painted in huge black letters across the tailgate. A gun rack hung empty in the back window.

Blake saw movement in the rearview mirror. A car approached, billowing up clouds of dust. In minutes, a dark green Mercedes pulled to a stop behind the truck. Instead of Jackson with Ian Monroe, Blake was startled to see Erica Lindstrom in the passenger seat. Damn, he thought. Her presence would throw him off if he weren't careful. The woman was enveloped in some kind of weird aura that was confounding to him. Worried, but smiling broadly, he made the mental switch into Terry Lee Wilson and prepared to get out of the vehicle. "Ready, Amin?" he whispered to his partner.

"Yeah, man, yeah," Mike muttered.

Monroe looked over the red truck in amusement as he and the woman stepped out into the dusty road to meet them. He nodded curtly then gestured toward his companion in trim white walking shorts. "This is Erica Lindstrom. She works with me." She stared at the men through her sunglasses, nodding her head only slightly to acknowledge them.

Blake stepped forward with his amiable Wilson greeting. "Ma'am," he said in a twanging voice as he tipped the baseball cap. He wondered what it was that affected him every time he saw this woman. Something about her reminded him of Victoria and it was unsettling. He examined her face more closely. It could have been Victoria except for the nose. Different shape. And the face was thinner. He wished he could see her eyes. There was something strange he couldn't put his finger on—vibrations, maybe, as the psychics say. It was eerie.

A small aquamarine, suspended from a dainty chain, lay in the hollow of her throat, reminding him of another tiny pendant and a broken chain that swam before his vision. Pain sliced through him at the graphic reminder. He struggled to push away the thoughts.

"Well, this here's the place. It's a large dairy farm." He made a broad sweep of his hand to indicate the boundaries. "You can see that there's three roads borderin' the property—two dirt roads that cross state highways. The paved county road goes all the way to the interstate." He lifted the baseball cap, and rearranged it on his head, waiting for a response from Monroe.

The man studied the roads carefully before he spoke. "So far it looks good, but I want to walk the length of it." As he said this, he reached for Erica's arm and guided her across the ditch. He separated the barbed wires of the fence so she could step between them, and relaxed only when he saw her slip through without a scratch.

Mike and Blake stepped between the wires after them, and led them to a place under the trees where they could view the property and still remain unnoticed. The land was fairly flat with nothing but tufts of wiry grass growing. With a herd grazing daily, the grass was short. Several cows paused in their munching and turned to stare balefully at the intruders, while their tails continued to swish flies.

"We're like on the eastern edge of the place. There are a few barbed wire fences across the field. The farmer uses them to contain the herd. They will be taken down a couple of hours before the plane arrives, then afterward, we'll hook them back up," Mike said slowly. "You can see the house only if you look hard. It's, uh, you know, on the far side. Some workers come in early every morning to do the milking, and again in the evening around six. Another crew works the dairy during the day, processing and shipping. Everything cools down at sunset. They bring in the cows and won't be nobody jankin' you after that."

"This road ain't used much," Blake added, "and at two or three in the morning, there won't be no traffic. Country boys all home in bed—or at least, in somebody's bed." He paused to lift his eyebrows and grin. "Only trouble is, there's no extra barn to hide the crew in or stash your equipment."

"That's not a problem. We'll bring enough vans with mechanized off-loading equipment. Just like the airlines use. It's quick and convenient. Our vehicles can park on the edge of the property until the aircraft is down. I just want to make sure it's not marshy or deeply rutted."

Blake and Mike waited while Ian and Erica zigzagged back and forth across the area until they were satisfied it was firm and there were no major bumps or craters. After a while, the two retraced their steps to the coolness under the trees. As they reached the shade, Erica took off her sunglasses and stared at Blake. Their eyes held for a disturbing few seconds. He noticed her green eyes were deeper in color today, reflecting her bright green polo shirt. The Ice Queen was definitely studying him. There was an electric current, but it wasn't warm. He sensed an element of danger. Who was this woman, anyway? Is it possible she recognized him from somewhere? He'd better be careful, he told himself as he heard Monroe speaking.

"There is not really enough length to assure a safe landing," Ian commented with a frown. "But, the pilot is good. I think he can manage." He paused. "The other problem is, without nearby buildings, there will be no electricity to hook up even the most rudimentary landing lights." Ian's brow creased, displaying concern as he glanced at Blake and Mike. "On previous sites we've had lights or at least a source of electricity somewhere nearby. We'll have to be very resourceful."

Before Blake or Mike could answer, the Lindstrom woman leaned toward Monroe and spoke so softly the agents couldn't hear. "I think we can rig something, Ian," Erica offered. "It shouldn't be too difficult to set out a line of reflectors, and the trucks could be situated to shine their lights where we need them to illuminate the strip, just long enough for the plane to touch down. I've heard Ches tell about how people have done this. We'll work it out."

Squinting in the brightness even under the shading brim of his Australian bush hat, Ian beamed at her. Gently he squeezed her arm as he spoke. "Yes, I think it would work, indeed. Darling, you're not only beautiful, you're clever, too."

A flush rose in her cheeks. Erica basked in the warmth of Monroe's compliment as he turned back to the men.

"Nevermind, gentlemen, the problem is solved, thanks to the lady. What about that alternate site I asked you to find?"

"Yeah, man, we got a second site," Mike answered. "It's, like, just a logging road that nobody uses much. It'll be cool in case you have an emergency."

"All right," Monroe said, looking at each man in turn and sounding pleased. "Lead the way. We'll look at it, and if it's okay, then we're in business."

Blake spat on the ground and looked at Mike with a grin. "Hot damn!" he exclaimed nasally, lifting his cap one more time.

"Far out," Mike said, shaking his head slowly, eyes staring at a point slightly above the horizon. His goatee was a short, fuzzy pendulum swinging through the air.

* * *

HOURS later, Erica sat propped against the pillows in her bed. A book of poetry lay in her lap, forgotten. Her mind kept going over the meeting with the two men. Something about the Wilson man had caught her attention as they'd inspected the field. Was it the general outline of his body in the tight, faded jeans and plaid shirt? His posture, his build, the shape of his head? Something had struck her as familiar. Yet, she didn't know him. Or did she?

Something else had bothered her when they were first introduced. A fragrance. She'd picked up a faint scent of his after-shave when he'd leaned forward to greet her. Recently she had smelled the same scent. Where? It wasn't Ian's cologne, of that she was sure. This one was unusual—a fresh breeze off the ocean mixed with the scent of limes.

She'd looked very closely at Wilson's features. She couldn't tell much about his mouth under the bushy mustache, other than that he laughed a lot. In the glare, his face had twisted up, shielding his eyes and forming little lines at the corners. She sighed, wondering if he'd be caught and arrested with all the others when the DEA completed its sting operation.

The lamp had been turned off for some time and Erica was drifting toward sleep when she sat up in bed. It had been the funny-looking man at Fort Morgan. He'd bumped into her and that's when she had smelled the after-shave. How strange, she mused, that two such different men chose the same lotion, and…that she would remember it so clearly. There must be hundreds of them on the market. Why did this one in particular impress her so?

Perhaps Ian could shed some light on the mystery. She'd ask him tomorrow.

CHAPTER FORTY-FOUR

MONROE was at work in his office in the bay house early the next morning when a member of the household staff buzzed. There was a phone call for him. He picked up the receiver and heard a familiar voice.

"Good morning, Ian," Kenneth Raitt said. His voice had a forced sound. "How's the fishing off the southern coast?"

"Very good," Ian responded. "In fact, I'm planning another trip tomorrow. We'll leave early and return tomorrow evening."

"I see. Do you think you'll catch much?"

"Oh, absolutely."

"It sounds really super, Ian, however, I think you'd do well to come and personally check out the waters around here. They're a little different, you know, but always exciting."

Ian tried to read through the twisted sentences to get to the meaning of Raitt's conversation. Did he want him to stop the run? "Are you sure that it's necessary for me to come at this time? I'd really hate to cancel my fishing trip."

"I don't think you should cancel it. Put someone else in charge of the boat. He could fish for you, so you wouldn't lose the catch and you would still be able to meet with me. What do you think about that? We must prioritize, you know. I can't stress enough how important it is for us to compare fishing techniques at this particular time."

Well, that was stunningly clear. "Fine. I'll fly up in the Lear this afternoon."

"Good enough. I'll meet you at six o'clock this evening at your house."

"All right. See you then."

Ian stared at the phone for several minutes in disbelief. What in hell was going on? It must be serious for Raitt to call and tell him to turn over the operation of the drug run to someone else. He had no choice. It wouldn't be too difficult, however, since everything was in place, ready to go. With luck, he'd be back in plenty of time to receive the shipment. Miguel should have secured most of the loading crew by then. Ches was out at that moment notifying Wilson and Amin to have the area around the dairy farm cleared by midnight tomorrow.

His mind shifted to those two characters. He'd been concerned about them for a while, still worrying that they might be Feds. But, during the week, he'd put out inquiries on them and the information coming back had been satisfactory.

He'd ask Erica to run the last minute checks and assure that everything was coordinated at the field, but Ches would really be running the show. If Erica thought she was responsible for the operation, she'd learn quicker.

He picked up the phone again, dialed the number of his pilot and told him to be at the airport at noon. Next he called Miguel Dominguez and arranged to meet with him shortly at the Fairhope Marina. Then he went downstairs to look for Erica.

Ian found her in the swimming pool on the terrace. He stood quietly absorbing the lovely sight, watching her glide smoothly through the water with the graceful movements of a natural athlete. She'd been swimming laps each day for exercise since they'd moved into the house on the bay. It had helped her body to strengthen, and had provided one more thing for her to focus on while getting her bearings in the new surroundings. As she got to the edge of the pool, she saw him and waved.

He held her towel ready and watched as she climbed the ladder. Water rolled off the slender form encased in a smooth, one-piece knit suit.

"How is my lovely mermaid this morning?" He wrapped her in the large, terrycloth rectangle, realizing as he did that there was a considerable amount of sensual pleasure involved in patting her dry, tempting him to linger. She was breathing heavily from the exertion, and droplets of water ran down her face and neck, into the hollow between her rising breasts. It took enormous control for Ian to keep from running his hands over her body.

"Wonderfully well," Erica said, smiling. "It's a beautiful day, isn't it?"

"Darling, I must talk to you for a few moments before I leave." Ian motioned her to a lounge chair nearby in a shady spot of the terrace.

She looked at him with a puzzled frown as the familiar insecurity pervaded her. "You're leaving?"

As he often did when he wanted to reassure her, he took both her hands in his and sat beside her. "I've got to make an unexpected trip, my sweet. I'll leave this afternoon. It's only for one night. You know we have a load coming in late tomorrow. I want you to take over until I return, to make certain that everything is in readiness for the shipment."

Apprehension showed on her face. "Oh, I don't know if…"

"Hush, now, darling. Of course you can. Haven't you been with me as we prepared for other runs? You know how it's done."

"Well…I suppose so." She looked doubtful.

"I've gotten word to Wilson and Amin about the landing area, and I'm going to meet with Miguel shortly to see if everything is going smoothly on his end. Ches will be here with you."

"All right, Ian. I'll do my best."

"Thank you," he said softly, leaning forward and kissing her gently at first, then with more desire. "Erica...Erica, I want you so." His hands pulled her close to him and settled along the sides of her breasts. "I need to have you in my arms at night, and to see you when I open my eyes each morning."

The intensity of the sudden change in him triggered the old uneasiness, leaving her in confusion. She looked at Ian's passionate face. He was almost begging, and she felt guilty at continually resisting his advances. The man was so good to her and she adored him, yet she shied away every time he wanted to make love to her. It was something even she didn't understand.

"Would you think about it, darling? After I return and this next operation is over, promise me you'll consider it." He looked at her hopefully, knowing he must be cautious.

Erica nodded mutely in response to his plea. She was unwilling to say anything.

★　★　★

WITHIN the hour, Monroe waited at the marina, scanning the bay for a sign of Dominguez' boat. He spotted the flying bridge first, then the white hull of the big Hatteras as it rounded a point of land just to the south and headed in. The powerful motors churned the water as the boat came alongside the dock and slowly eased to a stop. He watched as Dominguez threw lines fore and aft to secure it.

Ian waved a greeting and stepped on board.

"Good morning, *amigo*," Miguel said, pleasantly. "Welcome to the *Buena Vista*. Come into the cabin and we will have some coffee." With a nod, Monroe followed him in and sat at a small table.

The Cuban filled two cups then looked at Ian expectantly. "What's up?"

"Are you set for tomorrow night? Do you have the unloading crews lined up?"

"Yes, most of them. I have one or two more guys that I have not contacted yet. But I will have them by the end of today. I have three vans with hydraulic cargo lifts. They're parked in the repair shop."

"Good. My mind will rest easier," Ian said.

Miguel nodded his head, still waiting for an answer to his original query.

"Something has come up that requires my personal attention," Ian continued. "There is no avoiding it. I will leave in a few hours for Washington, but I feel certain I can return before the shipment comes in."

"No problem." Miguel spoke with confidence. "Callahan is ready. I talked to him this morning. He takes off late tonight from Atlanta. We'll maintain radio contact with him whenever possible in order to revise the arrival time if necessary. Jackson and I will keep in touch and make sure everything is a green light here."

"Sounds like it's all set." Ian nodded his approval. "Ches has met with the men who scouted the landing strip and informed them of the ETA. Erica will coordinate everything else. She'll have to use your people to set up some form of lighting system on the field."

As soon as Ian had spoken Erica's name, Miguel's expression changed. It went from surprise to fury in seconds, about as many as it took him to jump to his feet.

"You gotta be kidding! I thought you were crazy to bring her down here with us in the first place. She is a walking time-bomb. And now, as if that is not dangerous enough, you say she is going to take control of this job!"

Ian raised a hand to stop the tirade. "It will work, Miguel. She's been watching and learning all this time."

"Will she keep her cool if something goes wrong and she has to make some quick decisions? Hell, no!" the angry man said, shaking his head. "You'd better let Ches handle it. Tell her to go shopping, or something."

"I'm convinced she'll be able to do it. Haven't you noticed? She's come a long way since your…associate…nearly destroyed her," Ian said acidly. "I've given a lot of time and effort to help her overcome the handicaps Pharr left her with." He rose then, nostrils flaring.

Miguel was beyond caution. Pent up resentment boiled to the surface. "I can see you are very proud of your role in this fairy tale."

"What do you mean?"

"Oh, yes, Señor Pygmalion, you heard me right. It seems you have created a living doll to play with, your very own Galatea."

"That's absurd!" Ian's face was a frozen, defensive mask.

Miguel laughed without humor. "Is it? As a schoolboy in Cuba, I studied the classics. Even then, I had sense enough to know a myth was just that—a myth. But, here you are, big man of the world, pretending this woman is real."

An uncommon rage tore through the usually composed aristocrat. Ian wanted to flatten Dominguez. The son of a bitch had one hell of a nerve, he thought wildly. "My orders stand!" he snapped.

Dominguez remained silent, glowering at Ian under dark brows. Resentment and disgust were evident in the set of his mouth. Let the bastard screw himself if he wants to, he thought, already knowing their partnership wouldn't last much longer.

After a moment of tense silence, Ian turned quickly and lunged through the cabin door. Striding out on deck, he jumped onto the pier and hurried to his car.

CHAPTER FORTY-FIVE

"MAKE mine a double, Ian," Kenneth Raitt said as he sank down onto a sofa in the study at Monroe House.

A double martini sounded about right to cure his own ill humor, Ian thought darkly, adding another measure of gin to the pitcher. As he poured the drinks, he studied his guest. The senator didn't look well. His eyes were dull and red-rimmed. Several times he had taken out his handkerchief to blow his nose. Perhaps the man simply had a cold. He hoped to hell that was all the senator had.

Ian walked to the sofa where Raitt sat and handed him the drink. Mindful the meeting was at the senator's request, he settled in an adjacent overstuffed chair and waited for Raitt to speak. The warmth from the fireplace felt good as he sipped the cocktail. He had been cold ever since he'd stepped off the Learjet into a sharp wind at Washington's National Airport. Coming from the sunny Gulf Coast, his body had rebelled at the sudden change. That fact, along with seething memories of Miguel's arrogance, had put him in a foul mood. His unpleasant reflections were jarred by Raitt's voice cutting through the silence.

"I've just returned from Colombia. The jewelry you asked me to buy this time was sent from Panama by diplomatic pouch. I didn't want to risk getting caught with such a valuable piece in my pocket. I'll have it delivered to you by courier tomorrow morning before you leave." He paused long enough to accept Monroe's murmur of thanks. Then he got down to business. "The man in Colombia wants us to handle some of his stuff on our return flights."

"What do you mean 'handle'?"

"Along with what we buy for ourselves, he wants us to ship some extra cocaine, then turn it over to his own distributors once it's in the U.S. Two reasons. First, the demand is so great, the Colombians have trouble getting it to the customers fast enough. They could produce a lot more if it wouldn't get bottlenecked coming out of their country. Second, he wants a piece of the really big money once it hits the United States. So, if we agree to take his shipment, he'll make it worth our while."

"What is he offering?"

"Eight thousand dollars a key—just to transport it. Besides that, he will have the airport sealed off from other traffic while our plane is on the ground. His organization has the power to do that. It sounds to me like an easy extra profit, since the plane's going anyway."

"Maybe," Ian said, dubiously. "I don't know if it's wise to get too chummy with his group. They're probably a ruthless bunch." He paused, staring at the glass in his hand, his eyebrows drawn together. "If our plane was loaded with a distribution value of fourteen million in cocaine—half of it being this godfather's—and something happened to it, we'd be in a considerable degree of hot water. He'll blame us and we'd have to cover his losses as well as ours."

Raitt was silent, sipping the martini thoughtfully. Finally, he spoke. "Well, I think we can risk it. How much can your planes carry?"

"In one of our small Cessnas…around two hundred kilos. In the Navajo, we can take a larger load, although we don't like to overload the plane when we have the weight of a co-pilot and a short runway. The DC-3 could hold plenty, but it's giving us a lot of trouble and we plan to sell it after tomorrow's run."

"Montería has a runway long enough for the Navajo, and if the cartel runs interference for us with the military there, everything should be fine." He paused. "Do you realize how much money we're talking about, over and above our usual profit? If we transport two hundred keys for the Colombian, that's a million six. We'd be fools to turn our backs on that!"

"Certainly, that's a good bonus. But do *you* realize, if we brought in the additional two hundred kilos for ourselves, we'd make an extra five million dollars, instead of just one million six? On *one* load, after expenses, we'd clear eight million. We could retire a tad more quickly doing it that way."

"Look," Raitt said rudely, "we could double our profit, but he wants to double his first. True, he needs us to do it, but we need him more. He wants air freight, and we're going to give it to him. If we don't, we may lose *all* the business."

For a long time after Raitt departed, Ian stood at the windows looking out at the night. It had begun raining and looked as if it would get worse. Only a few restaurant seekers hurried toward King Street this evening, and Monroe was reminded that he hadn't had a decent meal since breakfast. He was famished and reached for the buzzer mounted on his desk.

Moments later, Dalton stood in the doorway in answer to his ring.

"Get the car ready, Dalton, I'm going to dinner."

"Very good, sir. Will you require evening dress?"

"No. Just tweeds and a sweater will be fine. I'm going to Gadsby's Tavern tonight."

★   ★   ★

A half hour later, Dalton steered the big Lincoln from Monroe House just two blocks to the old tavern on the corner of Royal and Cameron Streets. Monroe alighted in the worsening rain.

"Good evening, Mr. Monroe," the headwaiter beamed, taking the distinguished customer's dripping raincoat. "We haven't seen you in quite a while. Your usual table, sir?" In response to Monroe's nod, another waiter was summoned and led him through the sparsely filled dining room to a small corner table situated between windows that looked out onto the street.

The blond young man in colonial period dress stood patiently beside the table, his order pad ready, while his customer perused the menu. "May I suggest the duck, sir? It is especially good this evening." He spoke with an English accent.

"That sounds excellent," Monroe said with pleasure. After selecting the wine, he watched as the waiter hurried away to the kitchen. Smiling, he settled back in the chair, relishing the quiet surroundings. It was a unique, simple place of white walls, blue wood trim and bare pine floors. The cozy public rooms of the tavern were filled with early American furnishings, from pewter candlesticks on cherry tables and the tied-back curtains on tall, narrow windows, to the great fireplaces giving off comforting warmth.

He preferred to dine alone here, to be able to absorb its aura of the past without distractions, easily imagining himself transported back more than two hundred years. In the early days when Alexandria was a bustling seaport, Gadsby's Tavern was an important stage stop between Williamsburg and Boston. Ian was certain a number of Monroes—from the famous political one to the merchant branch from which he was descended—as well as other colonial leaders like Washington and Adams, had patronized the tavern and its hotel.

Yes, he had roots here in this structure, too, and each time he entered, he felt the whispers of the past, his ancestors encouraging him to boldly carry forward the American tradition of adventure and free enterprise that they had begun, in ways that were most advantageous to him.

Rain beat against the windowpanes, strangely intensifying his comfortable feeling. It was a wonderful place to be on a rainy night. He wished that Erica were with him.

His thoughts shifted to her and to the shipment coming in tomorrow, and knew he would worry until he got back. He had arranged to meet with the Colonial Heritage Commission first thing tomorrow. The group had agreed to maintain and operate the main floor of Monroe House as an historical attraction in his absence. After the meeting, he'd take care of some business at his law firm.

By midday, or thereabouts, he should be able to take off for the southern coast before the next wave of thunderstorms rolled in.

★   ★   ★

THE following afternoon, the small group of conspirators gathered in the dining room of the Spyglass Inn on the causeway that traversed the northern shore of Mobile Bay. Through the restaurant's broad windows, which provided a bright panorama of the bay, they could see a few scudding gray clouds moving across the southern horizon. Someone commented on the weather, but no one was worried. The local meteorologist had predicted the clouds, but only a small chance of rain.

A waitress arrived with sandwiches and beer and the conversation branched off from the weather to fishing and to speculation about the outcome of the Argentine-British tug of war over the Falkland Islands.

Erica Lindstrom ate lunch in silence while the men's talk flowed around her. She was distracted, worried about the success of the evening's mission—and her head was hurting. It would be a relief when Ian returned. The fact that severe thunderstorms up and down the Atlantic coast had prevented him from flying back sooner added to her unease. There was plenty of time for him to make it, but she knew she wouldn't feel well until he was back and could take the responsibility from her. Jackson's deep voice interrupted her thoughts.

"I've been in radio contact with the pilot on and off all day. He left Atlanta on schedule early this morning and the flight has been okay." He looked around before continuing. The late lunch crowd was thinning out and the restaurant was almost empty. No one was near enough to hear, but he lowered his voice anyway. "Right about now, Steve should be in Colombia, loading up the bird. In another hour, he'll be taking off for the return leg."

"I've got the crews standing by," Dominguez added. "Most of the men will be at the primary site, and a smaller bunch at the alternate place. The vans are gassed up and ready. I don't think the weather will be a problem. It looks like a 'go' to me...unless you two haven't done your homework—or you're getting ready to set us up." The Cuban glared at the men he knew as Amin and Wilson. He didn't trust them. Jackson had hauled them up from a bar in Mobile. "For all we know, you're undercover cops."

"You don't know," rumbled Mike, in his most casual tone, concentrating hard on his role. "Like, you'll just have to take the chance, fool."

"Leave it, my man," Jackson said to Dominguez. "We had them checked out. They're clean."

"You don't have to believe us, jack, but our asses are covered. That property is all set up and ready," Mike said, emphatically. "All you have to do is, like, drive to it."

Blake finished a piece of pecan pie and reached for his coffee, sipping it thoughtfully. "Yep, it's a funny thing. That ole dairy farmer just happened to win a trip to New Orleans for a couple of days. Buddy, he was one excited fella." The undercover agent paused for effect, long enough to put the coffee cup down and rearrange his baseball cap. "He and the little woman are already gone and the rest of the work force will knock off by nine. Just like we told Smith...hey, where is Smith, anyway?"

"He had to make a little trip," Jackson answered. "He'll be here tonight."

"He'd damn well better be. This is his party. We'll expect him to be there or we might get a little bit suspicious." Blake stood, preparing to leave.

"No problem," Ches assured him again. "He'll be there. Meet us at ten. The Frederic Motel on Highway 90. We've rented a couple of rooms."

Wilson and Amin—a.k.a. Harrison and Chapman—left the restaurant and drove to a shopping center about five miles away. Each had kept a sharp eye on the road and knew they weren't followed. Blake stopped the red truck at a pay phone and called the DEA office. He asked to speak to Agent Harding and in a few minutes, the voice answered.

"Hey, Harrison, what've you got?"

"The shipment will come in tonight. Put the interception plan into effect as of now. Get as many people as you can, and have them in place by ten tonight. I know it'll be a long wait, but it can't be helped. You can't risk being seen by Monroe's people arriving later."

"Okay. What about the alternate site? Do you want that one covered as well?"

"Yep. They'll have only a skeleton crew there and no evidence, so it'll probably be a waste of time. However, we might get lucky and get some information from one of them. Aside from that…and this is damned important…make *certain* there's no DEA or Coast Guard plane on that doper's tail to spook him or the ground crew. We don't want them to abandon the primary site. Contact whomever you need in order to be sure it doesn't happen."

"That's a copy," Harding responded.

"Mike and I will be with the group all evening, so this is the last you'll hear from us," Blake reminded. "We won't be able to signal from the field either. When the plane is down and they've started unloading, that's when you move in. We'll try to get loose as soon as that happens."

"Sounds good."

"And, Harding…there will be a lot of big fish out there. Let's scoop all of them into the net."

★   ★   ★

CALLAHAN took off and climbed steadily to cruising altitude and began the long flight over the dark Caribbean Sea. The pick-up had gone fairly well and he had managed a short nap before leaving. Acandí was primitive, but at least he didn't have to contend with the military police giving a show of force as had often happened on the Guajira Peninsula or at Montería. His muscles were knotted and he was anxious to get this big load of grass home. Too much stress. He was glad to have someone along with him, he thought, glancing sideways at the co-pilot. The older he got, the harder these long flights were. He'd make good money on the shipment, but he made a lot more when it was cocaine.

To add to Callahan's uneasiness, the DC-3 was giving trouble again. One engine was running rough and oil pressure was erratic. The organization had promised to retire the old workhorse soon. He was pleased that Ian had taken his advice and had bought a modified Navajo. It was ready and waiting for him.

Hours later, ahead and off to his left, Callahan saw some tiny lights twinkling in the darkness. Honduras, according to his position. He began the descent. Time to wake up his buddy in the seat beside him and look for the friendly airstrip near the coast that Dominguez had set up for refueling. The Yucatan would have been a better mid-point, but the area wasn't reliable. After takeoff, they'd head due north over the Gulf and drop slowly to one thousand feet. When they got near the coast, he'd ease it down, less than a hundred feet off the water, and put on the starlight goggles. He'd be able to keep a lookout for the big boats, and it was a cinch the radar boys wouldn't have him on their screens.

CHAPTER FORTY-SIX

ACCORDING to a poster tacked on the wall of the lobby, the claim to fame of the Frederic Motor Hotel lay in the fact that its cinderblock construction had survived the fierce hurricane of 1979. The motel, already twenty years old at that time, had been renamed in recognition of the event. Otherwise, there was nothing remotely special about it, except that it provided its diverse clientele with a cheap night for whatever purpose.

Jackson had reserved two adjoining rooms in the rear for a command center. Maps were spread out on one bed, radio equipment rested on the dresser, empty hamburger cartons and drink cups with straws protruding through the plastic lids were scattered all around. People that Blake and Mike didn't recognize milled about, in and out of the two rooms.

Erica Lindstrom, carrying a clipboard, monitored the preparations. Blake noted she was dressed all in black—jeans, sweater and lace-up boots. Perfect costume for night crawlers. She didn't talk, although he noted she was closely observant of all that was going on around her. Her mouth was set in a grim line and the tiny black dots centered in her pale eyes seemed to leap outward in their agitation. Who was she? The agency had compared the photos he'd taken of her at Fort Morgan with all the others in their files and came up empty.

Jackson stayed near her, even as he gave the crew precise

directions in short phrases. At one point, he bent close to her while Erica whispered something to him. He turned to look at the undercover agents, then moved quickly toward them. Without preamble he questioned them. "Is the field all set?"

Mike nodded in agreement. "We looked around, you know, and at nine the dairy crew knocked off, right on schedule."

"Yep," Blake said emphatically, tugging at the bill of his hat. "We checked her out real good. Fences across the field are down."

"Good," Jackson said. "When we get out there, I want you two to help set up the reflectors on the landing strip. They're in one of the vans, along with some mallets for driving them into the ground." He waited for a reply.

"Sure. We can do that," Blake said as he looked around with a quizzical glance. "I thought Smith was going to be here tonight. I don't see him."

"He hasn't made it yet. Bad weather."

Blake had to struggle to hide his disappointment. Dammit, he thought, one of the biggest fish in the operation might get away this time. Rotten luck. It couldn't be helped, though. DEA policy was strict—no shipment of drugs was allowed to go through while waiting for a more opportune time for seizure. Even if Monroe did not appear, they'd have to close in as planned. As for Monroe's location, he had a pretty good idea. Earlier in the day, Blake had talked with headquarters and knew at least one area of the country was inundated by fierce thunderstorms. The eastern seaboard, and that included Washington, D.C.

Ches Jackson fended off the possibility of further questions with a grin. "So, everything's cool, brothers?"

"Like ice, man, like ice," Mike assured him. "And your man over there tells us that the pilot's, like, right on schedule." He nodded toward the radio operator who was turning dials on the equipment.

"Yeah. It's all on go. He's already refueled in Honduras and he's heading toward the Yucatán. I figure he should be here around two o'clock. We'll go to the site at midnight to get things ready."

Just then, Miguel Dominguez walked in from the next room. Silently, he stood in the doorway and glared at Erica. The handsome Cuban's features were twisted with hatred. The woman, seeing this, glared back then turned away, ignoring him after that.

Blake observed with surprise the degree of animosity between the two. He wondered if it was a macho thing for Dominguez, that he couldn't handle being directed by a woman. Then he recalled what Ginger Kopenski had reported—how the Cuban felt the Lindstrom woman was a risk to the operation. As he continued to study the man, he noted once again that Dominguez wore an unusually large number of gold chains around his neck. There was a ring on each finger, some of them set with diamonds. He heard an instant replay in his mind. "…lots of gold and diamond jewelry," the bartender at the Jade Pagoda had said of the Hispanic who had met with Harry Pharr. Once again, Blake worried about the possibility that Dominguez was the one. His skin prickled, heightening his alertness.

Still pointedly distrustful of them, Dominguez barely acknowledged the presence of Harrison and Chapman. He muttered something to Jackson about taking two men with him to the alternate site and went back into the other room. After that, Blake did not see him again and assumed the Cuban had left.

Two men were dispatched to a location twenty miles south, directly under the flight path, to listen for a chase plane. In the event one was heard, it would be their job to warn the pilot to land instead at the alternate site where the plane with its cargo would be abandoned. There was no other way. If they were being chased, they'd never have time to unload. The two or three men stationed there would help the pilot escape. The main thing was to avoid giving away the location where most of their people and equipment were gathered.

Shortly before midnight, the first cars moved out, spacing themselves about a mile apart. As they arrived at the field, Blake noted that other cars, vans, and pick-up trucks were approaching from various directions, slowly converging on the dark, deserted pasture. Someone opened the gates at each end of the strip, and the vehicles drove in and parked under the sheltering trees near the roadside fence. Lindstrom and Jackson swung into action, giving orders in hushed voices. Blake's truck and two others moved onto the field. Two stopped on one end facing the strip, and one on the other end, positioned so that the two sets of lights would shine across to illuminate the landing area. Lights flashed on very briefly to check positions, then snapped off.

Out of a van, the group unloaded stakes with shiny foil pie pans nailed to the sides. The agents drove the stakes in two parallel rows along the length of the temporary runway.

Soon, all was ready and, except for the soft sounds of night insects, a strange quiet settled on the field. Small clusters of people stood around whispering, finding it hard to have nothing to do but wait after the frenzied preparations. In the darkness, the earthy smells of the pasture wafted upward, a combination of dew-soaked grass and cow manure. The tension was an electrical thing. Most of the people were sweating, although the damp air was chilly. Muscles grew taut and ears strained to pick up the first faint sounds of an airplane.

Far across the pasture, the farmhouse and out buildings were dark and still. There were no lights on the ground, except for an occasional glimmer nearby as someone took a drag on a cigarette. Some few bright stars twinkled between big patches of clouds, while in the east toward Mobile, a soft pink glow illuminated the horizon. The moon would not make its appearance for several more hours.

Erica was near enough for Blake to see. Her face with its cold beauty was expressionless as she repeatedly looked at the flowing dials of her watch. He wondered what was going through her mind.

Jackson hurried over from the van containing the radio equipment. "The surveillance team just reported. The pilot is coming in. No chase plane," he said, emphatically. "Get ready."

Erica nodded to him and he gave the order to move into position. Headlights on the three trucks clicked on, lighting up two rows of silver circles stretching between them. Drivers got into their vans and started the engines, ready to move them closer.

At first the sound was barely audible. As it grew louder it became identifiable. Aircraft engines. Squeaks sounded along the field as shoes moved on wet grass. The loaders positioned themselves, ready to rush forward.

Jackson was tense, frowning as he looked around to spot trouble, even though he had armed surveillance crews at the gates, and other locations along the road. There would be at least some advance warning if unknown vehicles approached the area. But he knew this moment, while the plane was trying to get down, was the operation's most vulnerable time.

Suddenly, a darkened apparition materialized above the trucks on one end of the strip. Blake could see the churning propellers as the shape of a DC-3 appeared in the glow from the ground lights. It was coming in fast and at a steep angle. With only a little more than half a mile of runway, it looked like the pilot intended to use every inch.

"Son of a bitch!" Blake muttered in astonishment, certain that the plane would crash at that speed and rate of descent. His disbelief changed to admiration as the wheels skimmed the truck tops and touched down near the beginning of the illuminated rectangle. The air was torn by the squeal of brakes as the pilot struggled to bring the aircraft to a stop on the grass. A pale cloud billowed up in its wake, dust scattered by the skidding wheels. Finally the dark metal bird came to a halt, just before the end of the makeshift runway.

Immediately all lights on the field were doused. Crews raced forward. Vans drove in near the plane as one of the engines was shut off. Within moments a cargo door popped open and a head stuck out, then a ladder was lowered. While the co-pilot stayed at the controls, the pilot climbed down and sauntered over to the little knot of people standing nearby, as a few raindrops began to fall.

"Okay, you guys!" Steve Callahan hollered over the noise of the one engine still running. "How's that for setting her down on a dime?"

"A-OK, my man! A-OK!" Jackson shouted back, slapping Callahan on the back.

"Did you have any problems in Colombia?" Erica shouted to make herself heard as she watched the progress of the unloading.

"Nope. None at all."

In the misting darkness, the men swiftly relayed bales of marijuana from the plane onto the raised platforms of waiting vans. At the same time, from another van, fuel for the final two hundred-mile run to a safe hanger in southern Georgia was being pumped into the nearly empty tanks of the aircraft. Other workers stood by with high-powered vacuums to sweep the plane clean before it took off again.

The two undercover agents had edged away from the group in the darkness, each moving into position near the opposite gates where the loaded vans would drive out. Blake, nervous now that rain threatened, was wondering why the agency units delayed moving in when he heard the sound of a scuffle and a few muttered curses. He wheeled around, squinting into the darkness, until he made out the shapes of several men. When he heard the metallic click of handcuffs, he called out softly.

"Harrison here. Who's out there?"

"Harding, at your service, sir," the voice whispered jovially. "We've got these two guys, and…" The walkie-talkie crackled as a garbled voice squawked its report. "Sounds like they've plucked the two on the other end. What do you say we have a party?"

"We'd better do it. This rain is getting ready to screw us up. Let'er rip."

Harding spoke quietly into the small piece of radio equipment held in his hand. From somewhere, a flare shot high into the darkness, spreading its Martian daylight over the proceedings, even as the quiet was split by the sound of shouts and stampeding boots.

"DEA! FREEZE! YOU'RE UNDER ARREST!"

Caught by surprise, the smugglers paused. Just then, the clouds dropped their moisture in earnest. It was a timely bit of luck for the culprits and they snapped into frenzied action, scattering quickly.

Erica Lindstrom stood rooted to the spot, struggling with the confusion in her mind. Ian had told her they must not be caught by police. But, this was the DEA. *We work for the DEA!*

"Erica!" The deep voice called to her urgently through the accelerating downpour. "Run! Get out of here!"

She knew it was Ches and turned to tell him it was all right. "No…"

"Get moving! We've got to get away! Hurry!" His voice was imperative. Jackson tried to see what direction the government agents were coming from. It was hard to be sure through the dense rain, but it looked like the field was almost completely surrounded, and access to the road running along the eastern edge of the property was cut off. But, the Feds hadn't figured on the heavy rain to mess up their visibility. He swung around to look for Erica. She was gone. Frantically, his eyes swept the scene, but he couldn't find her. In the remnants of light from the flare, he thought he saw Callahan running toward the silent buildings of the dairy farm. Swiftly, he moved in that direction, hoping Erica had done the same. He had a car hidden several miles away for just such an emergency. In between flares, the three of them would be able to slip out of the noose—if only he could find her.

Blake watched as agency personnel and local law enforcement people surrounded the field, knowing it would be hard to sew up the large area in these conditions. They had the plane, about five thousand pounds of marijuana, and with luck, most of the traffickers.

Another flare went off, but it wasn't much help. The sudden shower had come at precisely the wrong time, and people were getting away. Shots rang out overhead, intensifying the panic. It was enough to slow down a number of the loaders. Government agents quickly intercepted them. They were handcuffed and led to police vans.

Mike walked over to where Blake stood, observing the operation. "We got most of the worker ants and the co-pilot, Blake, but we seem to have lost the soldiers and the queen. Callahan's missing, and so are Jackson and Lindstrom."

"What about the others at the alternate site? That's where Dominguez was."

"The agents radioed in that when they closed in, no one was there except three rented cars. They must have been warned and hid in the woods. Probably had other cars stashed somewhere else."

"Set up roadblocks all around," Blake ordered. "We may get them, but you know how it is. They'll have alibis and claim innocence as long as we don't catch them with their hands in the stuff." His voice registered keen disappointment.

★   ★   ★

WITH Ches Jackson's words slicing into her mind, fear coursed through Erica as the red glow descended through the rain and the ground shook from pounding feet. With quaking hands, she negotiated the barbed wire fence and bolted for the deep protection of the trees across the road. Once inside the surrounding darkness, she stopped to look back, crouching as she heard gunfire. What she saw renewed the alarm she felt. Through the steadily pelting rain and the eerie light of a second flare, the plane was slightly visible. Bales of marijuana lay in disarray on the ground around it, vans stood with their doors ajar and their cargo lifts half-filled, while her crew was led away by others with weapons.

She turned away in terror and charged straight ahead. Wet leaves slapped against her face and branches scratched arms and legs. Occasionally, she tripped as her feet hit some sharp undergrowth. The darkness intensified her fear. There was a screech overhead, followed by the sound of large, flapping wings as something was disturbed from its roost. Erica's heart pounded and there was pain in her chest as she struggled to breathe, but still she fled headlong into the unending blackness.

CHAPTER FORTY-SEVEN

SPECKS of brightness dotted the black sky, paled by the great orb of a full moon as it drifted serenely westward. The clouds, which earlier had produced heavy rainstorms, were gone.

Suddenly aware of the dampness penetrating her shoes, the woman stopped walking. She stared down at the shiny leather boots glowing in the moonlight. *They weren't her boots. Why were they on her feet?*

A car sped by, rocking her with its windrush. Startled, she jumped back from the edge of the highway. The quick, involuntary action set off shockwaves of alarm through her mind. She looked around frantically. There was nothing but forest. The road was empty except for the receding lights of the vehicle. She was in the middle of nowhere.

Panic consumed her and she broke into a run, racing toward the red taillights winking in the distance. Faster and faster she ran, as if her life depended upon catching up with them, the only animate objects to which she might appeal for help. Her body finally forced her to halt as its muscles tried to stabilize from the sudden exertion. Painfully, she drew in gasping breaths, insufficient to satisfy her demanding lungs. She dropped to her knees until the agony subsided.

The fright which had sent her hurtling through the darkness was gone, replaced by confusion. Her head felt strange and it was hard to think clearly. As she worked through the turmoil in her mind, she struggled to her feet and resumed walking along the roadside. The squishing boots and the occasional croak of a bullfrog from somewhere in a muddy ditch became familiar sounds, taking away a little of her terror.

Along one side of the road, she could see the outlines of a few scattered houses, some illuminated by the moon and others shrouded in the shadows of great pines. In the distance, small lights flickered. It might be a place where she could find help. In desperation, the woman headed toward those pinpoints of hope.

As she trudged through the weeds, her mind groped for clarity. *What was this place? What was she doing here?*

There had been a train with crowds of people, and a hazy blur of moving stairways. Perhaps she had wandered away somehow and was heading back to that same place.

Drawing nearer to the lights, she could see that they were attached to—not a brightly lit train station—but a run-down cinderblock building on the opposite side of the road. Two dilapidated gas pumps stood bathed in the sickly glare emanating from fluorescent lights mounted on the pump island. The center window of the building displayed a large sign with a sleek dog running against a red, white and blue background. There were more lights inside the building that housed a convenience store. On the outside wall of the building was a pay phone exposed to the elements, and a newspaper rack beside a rusted oil drum overflowing with trash.

She could see a man leaning against the wall. He appeared to be asleep standing up. A crumpled cap was pulled down over his eyes and a blue work shirt was hugged against his short, wiry body by arms crossed over his chest. A young couple paced back and forth, their duffel bags resting on the grimy oil-streaked pavement.

The woman was hesitant, realizing her vulnerability to danger if she announced she did not know where she was or even why she was there. Caution, that basic instinct of survival, told her it would be better to say nothing.

While she debated what to do, a bus bearing a destination marquee that read MOBILE pulled into the parking lot. The man who had been slouched against the wall came to life and stretched lazily. The two others hurriedly picked up their bags and walked to the door of the bus. They were soon joined by several people coming out of the store.

Mobile. *Alabama? Is that where she was? How could she be that far from home without knowing it? But, then, where was home?* She wasn't sure, but it wasn't at this place. There could be no simple explanation for finding herself near a city on the Gulf of Mexico. She stood woodenly, paralyzed temporarily while her mind tried to process the information.

Finally she made a decision. Strange as her predicament was, it was absurd to keep standing in wet grass. At least the bus was going somewhere. As the eastern sky began to lighten in advance of sunrise, the woman ran across the road and joined the knot of people ready to board the bus.

★   ★   ★

WHEN his bedside phone rang, Ian was already awake and staring into the early morning darkness. He knew it was trouble even as he picked up the receiver and held it to his ear.

"Call me at 555-9624," the deep voice said.

"Damn," Ian said, slamming down the instrument as he got up hurriedly. He knew Ches would have given him a coded message if everything had gone well with the shipment. This meant he was at a phone booth somewhere and there was a problem.

Ian pulled on sweat pants and jacket and took the elevator down. In a few minutes, he was in his car and driving in a downpour through the southern part of Alexandria on Highway 1, looking for an all-night shopping center. Soon he spotted one and pulled into the parking lot, stopping near a phone booth. He dropped a coin into the slot and dialed the number.

"Hello?"

"What's happened?"

"Plenty. The DEA moved in on us. Got the whole thing—load and plane, and a lot of the ground crew. I think the two screwballs fingered us. They disappeared about five minutes before the raid. Later, from where I hid I thought I could make them out, walking around like they were directing the show. Man, I'd like to put a tight squeeze on their muthafuckin' necks!" His husky voice intensified.

"Those bastards! I should have trusted my instincts," Ian exclaimed in fury. "My luck isn't running with this one. Stranded here in this weather—and, added to that, the pilot has found a problem with the plane. He's got someone working on it right now." He paused. "Is Erica with you?"

"Afraid not. When the Feds popped up, she didn't want to run. Kept saying it was okay since it was the DEA. I hollered at her to come with me—told her we had to get away. Then I think she got scared. Before I knew it, she was gone. Instead of coming my way, she must have run toward the road."

"Do you mean you don't know where she is?" Ian's voice quavered slightly.

"No. I hope she made it across the road into the trees."

"You hope? You hope! Ches! She may have been arrested!"

"Hold on, Ian. I don't think so. I didn't see her with the others they rounded up. Listen, if she managed to hide in the woods somewhere, she'll make it back here once it's daylight. Erica's got money with her. She'll be able to get some transportation."

"No, no! She may not be able to do anything!" Ian was shouting angrily. "Do you realize it's the first time she's been alone since…?" He couldn't finish as his thoughts spun back to the past several months. After a pause, the anger was back. "How in hell did you let this happen? I trusted you to take care of her. This could affect her, you know."

"I know. If she doesn't turn up soon, I'll go looking for her. It'll be less risky after daylight. I'm sure the cops are still patrolling the roads looking for strays."

"I don't care about the risk. She's more important. Just find her—and fix the story. Tell her whatever you must to explain to her what happened."

★ ★ ★

Squinting in the artificial brightness, the people waited patiently while the driver loaded assorted packages and a suitcase into the cargo bay. There were a few people in the store which looked like it carried a small selection of food items and basic supplies.

Not knowing what she should do next, the woman looked around, trying to absorb details from everything around her. The man in the blue shirt was talking on the phone. Next to him, newspapers in the rack carried the banner of *The Mobile Press*. It was the late edition dated Thursday, April 15, 1982. As her gaze swept the scene, she saw a hazy reflection of someone in the dust-coated window. *Was it she? No, it couldn't be.* She glanced down at her clothing, then back to the reflection. It was the same. *The strange face looking back at her must be hers.* She looked terrible—frightened, disheveled, and not at all like herself. Everything was different. Wisps of blonde hair hung down around her scratched face. In disbelief, she touched a finger to one of the scratches and felt the sting of an open cut. Then her hand moved to the crown of her head and felt the distinctive lumps of a braid running along the back to the nape of her neck. If it was a nightmare, it was a very real one. A coldness went through her, as if someone had opened a tap and ice water flowed into her veins.

The startling discovery somehow stilled the panic and alerted her senses. She didn't know what had happened to her, but she must find out. In the meantime, she must be careful. *Survive*, something inside her said. *In spite of the shocks—be wary, move very carefully, survive.*

The surrounding noises demanded her attention and she caught drifts of conversation from among the group standing near.

"...just a couple of hours ago. There was sirens'n police cars'n ever'thin', all over the place. Some feller said there was a drug bust."

"Yep. I heard all the commotion. Some of them troopers was in m'pasture with flashlights looking for somebody, I reckon. One of 'em told me there was a drug plane, bold as all get out, parked in my neighbor's field."

"They was more than state troopers," said one man whose cheek was distended on one side. "I saw FBI and DEA on some of them jackets. It was a big deal. You betta' believe I was scared shitless! There was guns ever'where!" For emphasis, he spat a long, brown stream of tobacco juice onto the concrete.

"They even set up roadblocks. Wonder if they caught anybody?"

"Prob'ly not. Them drug dealers is damn near invisible. They can disappear quick as lightning."

The bus driver slammed the luggage compartment shut and began collecting tickets. When he got to the frightened woman, he smiled. "Ticket, please, ma'am."

"I don't have one."

"Well, little lady, you'd better go in and buy one. Don't worry now. I'll wait for you, heah?" Looking at her more closely, he asked, "Ma'am, are you all right?"

"Yes," she answered, looking away. "I'll get a ticket." She turned and went into the store.

"How near are we to Mobile?" she asked the clerk behind the counter.

"About thirty miles. Do you want a ticket?"

"Yes."

When the cashier told her the price, the woman automatically reached into the small purse that had been hanging by a thin leather strap around her neck and under one arm. Until that moment, she hadn't been aware of it. Fumbling through the bag, her hand grasped a wallet. Quickly opening it, she found money and paid the clerk.

With ticket in hand, she ran outside, almost bumping into the man in the blue shirt who was still yawning as he entered the store. Nervously, the woman handed the driver her ticket and boarded just ahead of the slow-moving sleepy man, who had somehow managed to buy his ticket in time. There were only a handful of people on the bus at that early hour. She made her way down the aisle and easily found a row all to herself. Grateful for a chance to rest, she sank down into the double seat and closed her eyes.

CHAPTER FORTY-EIGHT

As the bus jerked forward, the woman realized her head was pounding and her stomach felt queasy. She breathed deeply several times. If she could only calm down and think carefully, maybe she would remember why she was there. But the date…that newspaper had said April. Where had all those months gone? The last thing she could remember was a train station, an underground train station. She and someone, a friend, had gone shopping. She even remembered what she had worn—a blue wool suit. It was in autumn.

She sat up and clicked on the overhead light. She opened her purse again, taking out the contents one at a time to examine them. The slim, green leather wallet had quite a bit of cash in it—she had seen that when she paid for her ticket. The woman looked around to see if anyone was watching. There was no one sitting directly opposite her, and the man who had boarded after her was one seat back and across the aisle. From the sound of soft snoring, she knew he was asleep again.

The woman counted the money. More than four hundred dollars and some loose change. A neatly typed identification card bore the name and address. ERICA LINDSTROM, #13 JUBILEE LANE, BAYSHORE, ALABAMA. She looked carefully through the pockets and compartments, but couldn't find a driver's license or credit cards. A small calendar notebook had many handwritten entries, and in some cases, only curious symbols had been drawn. The handwriting resembled her own—at least, she thought it was hers. At that point, she didn't know if anything she thought was valid.

There was a key ring in matching green leather with the initials *EL* in gold, a dusty-pink lipstick, compact, comb, and nail file. Except for a few tissues, that was all. It made no sense. *Why did she have things belonging to this Erica Lindstrom? Her own name was Victoria.*

In those few moments, she was able to internalize three irrefutable facts. There was a gap of time she had lived through and didn't remember. Her appearance and her name were changed. And, she was in a different place. She had to find out what it all meant.

Her feet were cold in the wet boots, and for the first time, she realized her clothes were wet also. Triggered by frustration and discomfort, tears came silently and without warning. She didn't try to stop the onslaught as her body shook with sobs, knowing for a time at least, she was safe and could afford herself the luxury of releasing some of the tension. When the spasms were over, she wiped away the tears, blew her nose on one of the tissues, and felt a little steadier. She put all the things back into the purse.

Memories were coming back to her now…a large city…Washington…and the train station was the subway—the Metro. There had been danger…danger of some kind. A tremor of fear went through her, but she didn't know why. There were only those few mental pictures that were far from clear.

Victoria was exhausted and knew she'd fall asleep as soon as she leaned back in the seat. The soft roar of the bus was soothing, but something else kept nagging at her. What was it? She forced herself to continue thinking. All of a sudden, her eyelids swung wide as she recalled what the people at the bus stop had said. A drug bust nearby. Police, FBI, DEA chasing drug smugglers in the middle of the night. An airplane. Roadblocks. *Surely she hadn't been mixed up in that. Or had she?* Questions continued to torment her as the bus hummed and rocked toward the city.

Dark pine forests alternated with stands of oaks. In the graying light of early morning, the first stirrings of life became visible. A small lake came into view, and as she watched, two men clad in windbreakers set out from the pier in a small boat, cutting through the layers of mist that hovered over the quiet water. A bright yellow school bus, still empty, lumbered toward them, getting an early start on its mission for the day. Clusters of buildings and houses came into view. Shopping centers, their huge asphalt parking lots still vacant, waited for the hordes to advance.

Soon they were rolling smoothly along a wide thoroughfare lined with graceful mansions, silent and brooding in the dim light of dawn. Along each side of the street, huge moss-draped oak trees stood with their great branches reaching across to meet high over the center, forming a green canopy above the traffic. Signs told her what was ahead. Just before Government Street dead-ended into the banana docks along Mobile River, the bus pulled into the station.

By then, Victoria had used the comb and cosmetics in an effort to improve her appearance. She stepped off the bus and went into the station and approached the portly ticket agent.

"Is there a bus to Bayshore?"

"Sure is, ma'am. We've got one that would let you off at Bayshore on its way to Gulf Shores and Pensacola, but it won't leave for three more hours."

Her face reflected disappointment. The man felt sorry for the woman who looked like she'd had some hard times. "If you're in a hurry, why not take a taxi? It wouldn't be a long trip—just across the bay."

"Thanks," Victoria said, smiling gratefully. The sooner she got to the bottom of the tangle she'd found herself in, the better. The ticket agent signaled an eager cabbie and Victoria hurried out after him.

★　★　★

AT a pay phone in the station, the man in the blue shirt quickly dialed a number. A pleasant voice answered. "Good morning, Drug Enforcement Administration, Patsy speaking."

"Patsy, this is Levin. I'm on stakeout, calling from the bus station downtown. Relay this message to Blake Harrison, ASAP, will you? Tell him I picked up the trail of the Queen herself, not far from the landing site. She got on a bus and rode to Mobile. The first thing she did when we arrived was to ask the ticket agent about the schedule for Bayshore, then she got in a Yellow Cab. Call the dispatcher. He can tell you where cab #369 ends up."

"Will do. Anything else?"

"You bet. How about sending a car to pick me up? I'm ready to go home for some real sleep. Playing possum is exhausting."

★   ★   ★

THERE was little traffic on the interstate at that early hour. The taxi traveled easily along I-10, through the twin tunnels beneath the Mobile River, then eastward onto the Bayway curving above the arch of land at the northern tip of the bay. Victoria looked to the left and right, vainly trying to spot a familiar landmark. But not even the huge battleship docked beside a park triggered any recollections. The only thing that seemed familiar was the bay itself, but the one she remembered was the Chesapeake.

Chesapeake Bay. Virginia. She lived in Arlington. Yes! And…her name was…Dunbar. That was something. *But whose face was she wearing?* There was also a ring on her finger—an expensive one if the gems were real, and they looked it—that she didn't recognize. She fought against the tears, not wanting to give in again to the despair she felt. In a short time, the taxi, its meter marking the distance with rhythmic clicks, was heading south along the Eastern Shore. It followed the coastline for several miles and finally turned into a circular driveway.

"Here we are, ma'am. Number thirteen."

Victoria paid the driver and stepped out onto the pavement. Nervously, with a quick intake of breath, she turned and looked at the house. She was still staring, as if in a trance, long after the sounds of the departing cab had died out.

What she saw was unfamiliar. A low, contemporary structure of concrete, stone and glass bricks, masterfully combined and composed into a harmonious blend with its surroundings. All was silent until she was startled by a faint shrieking sound. Looking up, she saw a seagull soaring overhead. The bay must be just beyond the house, she thought, although the view was blocked by trees and shrubs on either side. There was no other sign of life. Victoria walked up the low marble steps leading to the magnificent entrance and paused in front of massive double doors carved with a sunburst design. In her hand was the key ring with two keys.

Her heart pounded. She could leave and simply walk back down the road to the nearest pay phone and call the police…and there was someone else she could call, just out of reach of her memory. Whoever it was, it was someone to whom she had been close. The police would have to clear up the mystery, and then her life could resume normally.

Yet, she couldn't shake the nagging worry over the talk at the bus stop. *What if she were mixed up in an illegal situation?* It was certain there had been a period of time when her mind was out of kilter. If somehow, she had become involved with criminals, she would have to clear her name or the police would put her in jail to await trial for the unthinkable. Once that happened, if it happened, she would not be able to do much from a jail cell.

It was absurd to even think like that, she told herself angrily. She wasn't a criminal. Still, it would be best to try to find out what she could on her own before contacting anyone else.

Taking a deep breath, she selected the larger of the two keys and inserted it into the lock. Silently it turned, and one of the great doors swung inward.

Victoria stood perfectly still, listening. She looked beyond the doorway. Seeing no one, she stepped noiselessly inside and closed the door. Daylight filtering through the curved glass-brick walls reflected off the gleaming pink-veined gray marble floor of the foyer. Lush tropical plants, encouraged by the soft light, grew out of beds sunk into the floor. The only pieces of furniture were a few richly upholstered benches.

She walked forward to the end of the foyer. Ahead of her, the two-story glass wall along the back of the house framed a magnificent panorama of the calm bay. Victoria could see that she was actually on the second level of the house. Part of it must be resting on top of the bluff, she thought, while part was built against the side. The stairway directly ahead descended to the main room where the ceiling soared to the full height of the house. A balcony, supported by ornate molded cement columns, circled high above the immense room. Other rooms led off from the balcony to form the upper floor of the north and south wings of the house.

With apprehension, she approached the stairway and looked down onto more gray marble floors. The great room was done in Art Deco style. Beautiful rugs outlined intimate groupings of sofas and chairs in neutral colors with touches of black here and there. The impression was one of sophistication and spaciousness.

Outside, a terrace stretched from the house toward the bay. There was a swimming pool and, nearby, a hot tub. Beyond the terrace, stairs led down the bluff and out to a pier which ended at a boathouse. Still no one appeared.

Victoria looked at the key ring that was gripped tightly in her hand. More questions raced through her mind. *Why was the key to this house in her possession when she couldn't remember being here before?*

Undaunted, she descended the dramatic staircase, looking for something familiar. Under the balcony to her left stood a bar and several small game tables. On the opposite end was an elegant dining area and, beyond it, a door through which filtered kitchen sounds.

Wary once again, she turned toward the muffled but unmistakable noise of dishes clattering, and of a faucet being turned on and off. She had only a few seconds to consider this new threat and brace for the inevitable confrontation when the kitchen door swung open.

CHAPTER FORTY-NINE

A solemn-faced maid in a crisp gray uniform swept into the room carrying a stack of freshly laundered table linens. Glancing toward the center of the room, she spoke. "Oh, good morning, Ms. Lindstrom. I didn't hear you come in. Mr. Monroe has been very worried that something might have happened to you. He's called from Washington three times this morning." She turned toward the china cabinet, pulled out a drawer, and carefully placed the linens in it. Then she closed the drawer and came forward.

Victoria stood frozen, finding it difficult to breathe, unable to believe the woman had accepted her presence without blinking. Numbly she studied the woman, much as cornered prey would assess its predator. Sounds continued to come from behind the door. Someone else beside this maid was in the house.

"Would you like some breakfast, ma'am?"

There was a coldness in her expression. Victoria instinctively knew this steely woman was not the one to confide in. "No, I'm not hungry." She wondered how much longer she would be able to keep up this act. Her muscles quivered from the tension, and there was a huge lump in her throat.

"I'll just bring you some coffee, then," the woman said briskly. "While you drink it, I'll fill you in on today's schedule." She turned back toward the kitchen door.

"All right." So much for the first round. Still shaking, Victoria eased her tired body onto the soft white sofa and took off her soggy boots. She was exhausted but the adrenalin kept pumping. Everything was so twisted. For all she knew, her life might be in danger. If at any moment she felt she couldn't play out this role—whatever it was—she would leave.

The maid had said something about a schedule. Perhaps the woman would give her some helpful information—like who the Mr. Monroe was. The more she could learn quickly, the less chance someone would have to discover her confusion.

Above her, on the second level just to the right of the foyer, a door opened sharply. Victoria sat immobile as a tall, powerfully built man hurried down the stairs toward her. His dark face registered concern.

"Erica, am I glad to see you! Damn, we've been so worried! How did you get out of there last night? When I tried to find you, you'd disappeared."

"Oh, I don't know." Victoria hardly knew what she was saying, once again amazed that people in this house knew her. Her tiredness caused her to mumble the words and helped to cover the panic. "It's all a blur." That certainly was the truth. How had the man known she was in the house? The maid must have notified him.

"Hell! You're covered with scratches," the man said, sounding genuinely concerned. "Looks like you went through the woods. I thought that was what you'd done. I went out again about an hour ago to try to find you. Glad you made it back." He emanated a friendly kind of warmth, unlike the distant attitude of the maid. "They caught most of our loading crew, you know. Only a few of us managed to get away. I wish you'd stayed close to me. Callahan and I high-tailed it to the car I'd hidden." He shook his head as he talked. "Of course, the Feds got the load…and the plane, but they messed up the sting. They were on top of us before we knew what was happening and the principals got away clean."

Victoria shook her head sympathetically as he spoke. It seemed to be enough of a response. She had not missed the reference to distinctly illegal activities and…a sting! What was *her* part in it? It was impossible to accept that she was here, with these people she did not know, involved in something very fishy.

"Mr. Jackson, would you like some coffee also?" The maid had returned.

"No, thanks, Alice. I've got work to do." He waited until Alice was gone, then faced Victoria. "There's some land I want to see. We've got to find some new locations." He stood with his hands in his pockets, looking down, wondering how long she would believe Ian's story. Finally, he glanced up. "You know, Erica, in order to catch the bad guys, we've gotta act like the real thing. That's why we can't let the DEA pick us up."

Victoria nodded passively.

He stopped in the act of turning away, as if he had second thoughts, and looked at her closely. "Are you sure you're okay? You're shaking, and…sort of pre-occupied."

"I'm okay."

Reassured, he smiled at her and turned once again to leave. "I'll notify Ian that you're back safely. Get Alice to help you doctor those cuts."

She watched him walk down the hall of the south wing, and presently she heard a door open and close.

"Here you are, ma'am." The expressionless woman arrived with a silver coffee service, which she placed on the pearl-inlaid oriental table in front of Victoria. She filled a cup and continued talking. "As I told you, Mr. Monroe has been calling since I got here at six this morning. He said he'd call again later. Dinner will be at eight, unless he changes his mind." She handed Victoria the cup. "I couldn't get the flounder you wanted, so Henry is preparing a Shrimp Meuniere, with potatoes and a spinach soufflé. Mr. Monroe suggested a dry

Chablis. Before I leave, I'll bring a bottle from the basement storeroom. Is there anything else you wanted me to add to the menu?"

"It seems to be fine as is," Victoria murmured, trying to sound calm while more questions shot through her mind. The steaming coffee tasted good and helped to clear her head a little.

"Marie will come in at five-thirty to set up and serve dinner. Henry will take his rest from one until four, as usual, before finishing dinner preparations. Have I forgotten anything, ma'am?"

I'd better leave that one alone, thought Victoria, forcing herself to concentrate. "No, I think not."

"Now, about the party tomorrow evening—the party service wants your final approval concerning the arrangements." The woman took a breath, then went on in monotonous fashion, as if reciting something she'd memorized. "And, the florist wants to know if he can substitute another type of flower for the tulips. He can't find a source for them at this time. He said he cleared the change with Mr. Harper, but he wanted to be sure you had no objections."

Victoria knew she must let this woman, and the others on the staff, handle as much of the routine as possible. It would lessen her risk. Who was Mr. Harper? She realized now, even more than before, that she needed information if she were going to live the life of Erica Lindstrom, however briefly. "Anything else?"

"No, ma'am."

"Tell the florist the changes will be okay. I'll wait for the party service to call again. I've got to get some sleep before I talk to anyone." She said the last with conviction.

"Yes, ma'am, you look tired. I expect you'll want to clean up first," Alice said, frowning down at the boots defiling the exquisite silk rug. "I'll get your bath ready."

Victoria watched the gray-clad figure climb the stairs. Through the balustrade, she observed Alice's progress along the balcony on the north wing of the house, past the first and second doors. She entered the third one.

I guess that's the mysterious Ms. Lindstrom's room, Victoria thought. She wondered who had the other two rooms on that side of the house. Turning her head, she looked upward at the opposite balcony on the south wing. The house was symmetrical—unusual for a house of contemporary design. That side of the balcony also had three doors. Perhaps those were the guest rooms.

She poured herself another cup of coffee and sat for a while longer, wondering how long she'd have to walk the tightrope before she found the answers to her questions. Maybe she shouldn't worry, she thought, as she watched several gardeners tending the lawn and flowerbeds beyond the terrace. Apparently, this Monroe man was wealthy and had enough friends to invite to large parties. There was a chance that someone might recognize her and help her out of the peculiar situation in which she'd found herself.

Feeling stiff and sore, and suddenly too weary to think at all, Victoria stood and climbed the elegant stairway. When she reached her bedroom, what she saw was a soft blend of pale colors reminiscent of seashells and sand. Transparent windows looked out over the bay. In the corner, the glass bricks were repeated, probably the architect's favorite building material, strong, yet translucent, illuminating the room as it formed a concave wall of soft light. Set against this dramatic curve was natural rattan furniture.

The smell of a perfumed bath filled the air. An inner door was ajar and through it came the sound of running water. She could see what looked like a dressing room, and somewhere beyond was the bath.

Just then, a phone rang. Victoria's eyes followed the sound to a table beside a lounging chair. She stared at the telephone, not knowing what to do, too sluggish to react. However, in seconds, the older woman appeared and crossed the room to answer the insistent ringing.

"Yes, Mr. Monroe, she's here. Just one moment," the maid said, and handed the instrument to Victoria.

She reached for it stiffly, hoping there would be some way to get past this new trial. If only she could get some sleep. "Hello?"

"Erica, my dearest, are you all right?" The deep, cultured voice on the other end was tense.

"Yes, I'm all right. Just very tired."

"How did you get home?"

She hesitated. "On the bus to Mobile…then I took a taxi to Bayshore."

"Good." He sounded relieved. "That was a close one. Ches called me early this morning to give me the report. But, we won't discuss that now. Darling, I'm so sorry the weather prevented me from leaving yesterday. Those fronts have just kept rolling in, and then there was a problem with the Lear. Bad luck, I'm afraid. But, at least you're okay."

"Yes."

"I suppose Alice has told you that I won't be able to get to the coast before late this afternoon. The pilot tells me the repairs are almost completed and the Weather Bureau reports clear skies in this area very shortly. We should be able to leave in a few hours. So, I'll see you soon, probably around six."

"All right."

"You sound strange, Erica. Are you sure you're all right?" The voice was probing.

"My head hurts. I'll feel better after I sleep," she answered truthfully.

"Well, sleep the day away, my love. I'm very much looking forward to having dinner with you across the table from me. We'll talk then."

"Okay." Victoria hung up, even more confused. Were they

married? She looked down at her left hand, again taking note of the emerald and diamond ring on her third finger. There was no wedding band with it, and their last names were different, therefore, she assumed they weren't married. That was a definite relief. Could he be a business partner? No. He'd spoken the words of endearment with extreme tenderness.

"Everything is ready for you in here, ma'am," Alice said as she came from the bathroom, "and, there's some ointment for those cuts in the cabinet. I've laid out your gown and robe, and if you'll tell me what you want to wear for this evening, I'll hang that out in the dressing room before I leave this afternoon."

"Oh, Alice, I'm too tired to decide. I'll leave it entirely up to you. I know you'll pick something suitable." Victoria felt certain Alice would know, better than she, what kind of clothing a supper-for-two in this household called for.

Alice nodded with a slight smile, unable to hide her pleasure at the compliment, as she went back to her work downstairs.

Victoria followed the heavenly scent through the dressing area and found the elegant bathroom. Along the exterior wall, where the tub sat, more glass bricks transmitted a luminous glow into the room. The three other walls were mirrored from floor to ceiling. Soft light bounced from one steamed wall to the other, giving an illusion of a larger space.

She immediately unfastened the tight braid, shaking loose the strands. Picking up a hairbrush, she pulled it through her hair, forcing out bits of leaves, pine needles, and other debris. It was a relief just to do that. Then she peeled the damp clothes off and sank into the immense square tub with its gold plated faucets. Even though the water stung the scratches on her arms and face, the heat eased tensions and the perfume soothed her spirits. She leaned back, immersing her hair in the cleansing water and recalled that a hot, scented bath was good therapy, something she had always enjoyed. In a flash, she could picture a bathtub, not elegant as this one, but *her* bathtub at *her* apartment. Clear, distinct memories. A good sign.

A recollection of her face as she'd seen it in a window glass, caused her to sit up abruptly. She turned to look at the mirrored wall at the foot of the tub. Wiping away the condensation, she stared at herself intensely for the first time since those shocking moments at the convenience store.

The face resembled her, yet it was different. In mounting panic, her eyes and fingers probing every inch, she studied the stranger in the reflection. Instantly obvious was the change in style and color of her hair. But that was not what upset her so deeply. More frightening were the permanent changes in her teeth and her nose…and something else she couldn't pinpoint at the moment. Was the actual shape of her face changed also?

Who did this to her? Everyone here recognized her as this new person named Erica. As tears of frustration welled up in her eyes, she wondered how she had gone from Victoria to this Erica who gazed out at her.

"No!" Fury boiled up and out of her as she shouted at the reflection. "You aren't me! Who are you?" Her anguished cries were muffled in the steamy room. She slammed her palms flat against the mirror, trying to block out what she didn't want to see. "Have I lost my mind?" That was it. She was going crazy.

Moaning in helpless misery, Victoria leaned her head against her extended arms as sobs exploded from the center of her body. The sounds came out of her unchecked, speaking in place of words for all the vulnerability and desolation she felt.

When the wave of emotion had spent itself, she lifted her head and looked in the mirror once again. Staring into her own eyes—eyes which were the same—she whispered, "Find out what happened to you. Find out." Drained of energy, Victoria slid down into the healing water once again. In the quiet solitude, she bathed, feeling her muscles relax. Only when the water began to cool did she climb out of the tub and towel dry. Walking across the thick carpet, she looked in the medicine cabinet and found a tube of ointment. Carefully she applied it to the cuts and scratches. Satisfied that she had tended to each one, she slipped into the pale green crepe de chine gown and slippers that had been placed within easy reach for her.

She returned to the bedroom where a framed picture on the dresser caught her eye. Walking over, she picked it up and saw herself—or rather the face she'd just seen in the mirror—with a good-looking, gray-haired man, smiling and fit at the helm of a boat. She was smiling, also, but the eyes were remote. The photo had been autographed, "To Erica with love, Ian."

"Ian," she said out loud. The name that Jackson had spoken. Mr. Monroe, Alice had said. "Ian Monroe." Victoria had seen the face often in the newspaper. This was a very confusing state of affairs, she thought. Very confusing.

Victoria continued to look at the picture, knowing she had not known Ian Monroe personally before then. There had been someone else…someone very important in her life, and she knew it wasn't Ian Monroe. She told herself to stay calm. It was encouraging that she was remembering things, a little bit at a time. Maybe later she'd remember more. Until she found out what she was mixed up in, what could she tell anyone? Finding that information was the most important thing she must do.

Too tired even to pull back the covers, Victoria Dunbar sank down onto the bed and went soundly to sleep.

CHAPTER FIFTY

BLAKE was going over details of the raid with the Mobile County Sheriff when the phone rang. The sheriff picked up the receiver, listened, then handed it to Blake.

"Harrison here." He paused to listen. "Thanks, Patsy."

He hung up the phone and turned back to the sheriff. "Erica Lindstrom came out of the woods just before daylight and rode a bus to Mobile. Then she took a cab directly to Monroe's bay house."

"That's good news, Harrison. Hell, it wouldn't have been surprising to discover the whole organization had vanished overnight to start clean somewhere else."

"Since none of the big guys was caught, they're not in any panic at the moment. Apparently, they don't know we've had them under surveillance—other than the deal with Mike and me. Supposedly, we only knew Monroe as 'Smith'." Blake stared at the desk for a few seconds. "I'd like to get authorization to have Monroe's phone tapped. We need some solid leads to catch this guy."

"And soon." The sheriff nodded his head slowly. "I'll contact the judge in Baldwin County and get the ball rolling. Monroe lucked out once and thinks he's still unknown. But, he'll get nervous before long and move his operation again. Then you'll have to start all over."

"Right," Blake agreed, grimly. "Would you excuse me, sheriff, I want to debrief one of my men."

Immediately he dialed a number and a sleepy voice responded.

"Yeah?"

"Levin?"

"Yes." The voice became alert. "Harrison?"

"I heard you managed to pick up Lindstrom's trail."

"Yep. She boarded a bus not far from the landing site. She was a mess. I figure she hid out in the woods until she saw her chance to get away clean. But…funny thing…she didn't seem her usual self. It's hard to explain, Harrison, but from the moment she showed up at the bus stop, she seemed confused…or something. After she got on the bus and sat down, she opened her purse and went through it like she'd never seen it before. I mean she studied every little thing! Is that weird, or what? And, then…you won't believe it…damned if the Ice Queen didn't melt. The lady cried! I guess it was a delayed reaction to the raid, but I'll tell you, it was the last thing I expected to see."

"You're right, it doesn't sound like her. Let's hope it means we're putting a strain on their operation." Blake paused a moment before continuing. "Get some sleep. I'm going to need you later."

★ ★ ★

THE jangling of the telephone woke Victoria. She jerked upright, staring around the unfamiliar room brilliant with sunlight.

"Oh, my head," she said aloud, clapping her hand to her eyes to shield them from the glare. It was an automatic reaction to try to stop the pain. The ringing continued. "Why doesn't someone answer it?" she asked. The clock on the bedside table registered two forty-five. Then she remembered the maid…Alice…must have gone for the day. And the cook rested until four, she'd been told.

Victoria got up and reluctantly picked up the phone. "Hello?"

"Erica, darlin'! Benton Harper heah. Gulf Coast Party Service. I'm callin' to go over last minute details for the party tomorrow evenin'…ah, that is…if it's convenient. I always like to be absolutely sure everything is in order, don't you?" His voice, slowed by the

Southern accent, rolled on soothingly, like lotion on a sunburn. "Do you have any concerns about our plans at this point?"

"No-o-o, I don't think so." Victoria realized this caller could be another source of information. "However, I've been very busy and I might have overlooked something. Are you certain we've planned for enough food?"

"Oh, sugah, yes," he assured her with a sigh. "You won't have to worry about that. With two hundred invited guests, we always plan for two hundred-fifty in case you have more heavy eaters than not, and…heaven forbid…a few gate-crashers." He made a clucking noise of disapproval before continuing. "As usual, we'll provide you with a staff to serve and clean up, along with two parkin' valets."

"That sounds fine." Victoria paused as she remembered something Alice had said earlier. "I received the message from the florist about substituting the flowers, and I've relayed my approval. Whatever you think is okay will be fine with me."

"Excellent! Now then, doll, I'll arrive with my decoratin' crew tomorrow at precisely one o'clock to create the scene. I want it to be absolutely different from the last party, don't you?" he asked, again not allowing time for her to answer. "On the small tables inside and out, we'll have lighted white tapers under hurricane glass chimneys. The swimmin' pool will have a veritable flotilla of lotus candles. It will be simply divine, Erica, I assure you! The caterer and her staff will be there at four, and the musicians at five—although they're the absolute worst for bein' on time." Another clucking sound. "I think the best place to station them will be at the glass wall in between the big double doors openin' onto the terrace, don't you? That way the music can float in and out. Mm-m. Simply, simply divine!"

His soliloquy had continued without interruption for so long, that a moment or two had passed before Victoria realized Benton Harper had stopped talking. She almost missed the cue to respond. "It should work well," she said, finally.

"Good! Now, don't worry about a thing, sugah. Once again, you'll have a perfectly lovely party. Until tomorrow, then. Ta-ta."

Victoria hung up the phone and sat down on the chaise lounge as she felt a new wave of panic. What in the world was this party going to involve? Two hundred guests! Musicians! And she had so little time between now and then to find out what was going on. As her thoughts raced, her gaze rested on the key ring she'd left on the table earlier. It reminded her of another question that needed answering. Two keys. One opened the front door. What would the other one open?

Alice had placed a tray of sandwiches on the dresser. After the hours of sleep, she was famished. She ate quickly, on her feet most of the time. Pulling back the sheer linen panels draping the spacious windows, she saw sailboats on the bay and all the bustling activity on the grounds. There was a whole platoon of gardeners planting flowers in little islands on the lawn. She supposed that must be in preparation for the party, too.

Moving about the room, inspecting the furnishings, she looked once again at the photograph of the man, and of herself alongside him. Without warning, another face flashed through her memory. Another handsome man, but with dark hair and dark eyes, and an easy smile. It was as if he stood before her with his arms open wide, ready to envelop her in safety against his body. She felt his warmth, smelled his cologne, heard his voice whispering her name, and felt the tender love flood her senses. *Blake*!

Suddenly, it came back...great shock waves of recollections crashed through her mind, competing for her attention all at once. She felt dizzy, as if she might faint, and grabbed the edge of the dresser for support. Weakly, she groped her way back to the lounge chair and sat, lowering her head to her knees, hoping to still the roaring noise in her ears.

She had seen so much in those few seconds. She and Blake, their months together, the lonely time of separation, their chance meeting at the opera and then…the night of renewed passion. Without realizing it, Victoria was crying again as the memories tumbled rapidly through her mind. Her work in the art world and, most recently, with the Navy. The party her friends were giving…but, she didn't go…why? What had happened? She remembered shopping with Susan, then the subway, and that was it. Try as she might, she didn't know why her life had stopped at that point. For a long time she sat, with her fingers pressed against her eyes, as if the tactile sensation could draw the images out and into focus.

The face of Blake Harrison kept reappearing, and her heart felt a familiar tug. Where was he now? Had he looked for her…was he *still* looking for her? With another rush of clarity, she recalled his profession. Of course he was looking for her!

The telephone was in front of her. All she had to do was pick it up and call him, let him get to the bottom of this mess. Yet the underlying worry over the extent of her involvement in some strange business stopped her hand. It was a twisted situation that the black man's words hadn't been able to smooth out for her. He had looked uncomfortable when he tried to explain to her about the "sting." Could she believe him? Nothing made sense. Why was she there in the first place? She certainly couldn't remember getting there. From the Metro station in autumn until early this spring morning, there was nothing, like a book with a few chapters ripped out. Had she wandered away from Washington—or had she been brought here? There was too much strangeness for her to believe this was a group of upstanding citizens. Maybe they were drug smugglers themselves and she was taking part in it with them. That was extremely unlikely, but if so, she had no real facts with which to counter any charges that might be made against her. Blake might be convinced she was in it willfully. He would despise her. *And she'd go to prison!*

Victoria knew she must try to clear herself even though it could be dangerous. Her mental change had gone unnoticed in this household so far. Perhaps, for a little while longer, she could play the game. One cautious step at a time.

Feeling steadier, Victoria went into the spacious dressing room to look for something to wear. On the far end she found a pair of cotton slacks, a knit shirt and sneakers. As she changed, she noticed another door in the wall, beyond the door to her bathroom. She turned the bolt above the knob and found it led to an adjoining dressing room, a twin of hers except for the men's clothes. Yet another door opened to someone's bedroom. It was dim, in stark contrast to the rest of the house. Only two narrow glass brick panels let in soft light. When she tried a light switch, she discovered that indirect lighting made up for the absent natural light. Black lacquered furniture in the Art Deco style, placed against fine walnut burl paneling, gave a sophisticated masculine stamp to the setting.

The wall between the two glass brick windows jutted forward several feet providing a dramatic backdrop for the bed. It was an odd arrangement, she thought, although clusters of large potted plants softened the look. She noticed heavy silver accessories on the dresser, including a silver framed photograph of her, looking more pensive than happy. It was signed, "To Ian with love, Erica."

There were two other doors to try. The one leading to the inside balcony opened easily. The other, which probably accessed an adjoining bedroom, was locked. This door had no manual bolt. Instead there was a dead-bolt lock. She turned off lights and went back through her own room to the balcony.

The house was quiet. Victoria glanced down into the great room and saw no one. Bypassing the door to what was probably Monroe's room, she tried the next. That same room was locked from this side also. The long hall which ran the length of the north and south wings of the house was deserted. She moved quickly, trying to get her bearings before someone saw her. Somewhere along this hall was the room Jackson had come out of earlier. There were two narrow flights of stairs on either end of the hallway. Silently, she went down one flight that led to the main floor. She noted it also continued down to a basement.

Opposite the kitchen was a pantry, and beside that, a closed door. Victoria tensed as she heard the soft rumbling sound of snoring. Probably the cook. He would awaken soon to begin preparations for the evening meal.

Hurrying back along the same route, Victoria went upstairs to her room for the key ring. She felt elation when the smaller of the two keys easily opened the outer door to the room next to Monroe's. She didn't know who else had keys to the room, but at least she knew that Ian Monroe wouldn't be back for several hours. If she intended to find out anything, this was her only chance. Once inside, she locked the door again and pivoted slowly while her eyes scanned the furnishings—two desks, file cabinets, and a word processor. The more massive, carved desk sat between two glass brick window panels. A delicate ladies desk was placed along one of the walls.

Victoria approached the smaller one. On top was a neat stack of stiff, peach-colored cards with matching envelopes. They were form-printed invitations with Monroe's name and hers—or rather, Erica's—and details of the address, with some lines remaining blank for other information to be filled in. They were bordered with an intricate, artistic design of vines. The unusual stems seemed to be blooming with a profusion of asterisks alternating with symbols of three horizontal lines. In the upper left hand corner of the border was a sun, while in the lower right hand corner was a crescent moon.

Something the same color lying crumpled in the bottom of the wastebasket caught her eye. She reached for it, smoothed out the wrinkles and saw that it was the same paper with an identical border as the paper on the desk. However this one wasn't blank. It had been filled in, but a single misspelling of the word "cocktails" had caused it to be discarded. The card read:

> *Mr. Ian Monroe and Ms. Erica Lindstrom*
> *Invite you to join them for*
> *Cocktaits*
> *On*
> *Saturday, April 17th at 7:00 P.M.*
> *#13 Jubilee Lane in Bayshore*

So, Victoria thought, this was the invitation she had sent to two hundred people. Which people? She looked for a guest list, pulling open one drawer after another in the desk. There were more invitations printed on blue paper in the same format but with a slightly different border. The blooms were made only with asterisks. A separate package of sage green cards had only the three-line symbols "blooming" on the ends of the vines. How curious, she thought.

In the next drawer, she found several pages of what must have been the guest list. None of the names was familiar. She hadn't really expected them to be. She was certain she had not lived here, at least not before her memory loss. The people on the list had addresses from Louisiana to Florida and the titles left no doubt as to their distinction. A mayor, several judges, a state senator, representatives, numerous doctors, and their spouses. Pencil notations followed some of the names, supplying the occupation or name of a company affiliation. Bankers, lawyers, artists, writers. Altogether, an impressive chunk of area society and influence. Were these friends, or just business associates of some kind? Maybe that's what this party was all about—entertaining business clients.

Victoria was reminded to hurry as the elegant clock on the wall chimed five o'clock. She opened the last drawer and found a small, canvas-covered ledger. What she saw when she opened the cover caused her to inhale sharply. The entries were written in her handwriting. In confusion, she turned the pages. There were listings for the nine planets. Under each were dated entries, numbers and letters that made no sense. This was followed by a series of columns with clear headings—distribution dates, designations showing one or both of the small symbols that were on the invitations, dollar amounts, and one final column noting dates paid. The codes meant something, but at the moment, she didn't have any ideas.

She recalled the drawings in the little notebook she'd found in her purse and realized they were the same as the symbols for the planets. From her field of expertise, she knew enough about those symbols, some of which had been used since pre-history. Her notebook was somehow linked to this ledger.

Victoria risked a few more minutes, knowing she was pushing her luck as she tried unsuccessfully to open Monroe's desk drawer and the file cabinets. Her key didn't fit any of those locks. Giving up, she grabbed the ledger, the guest list, and the one ruined invitation and moved toward the door. Her fingers were closing around the small key when she stopped. Someone standing on the other side of the door was breathing hard. It could be the cook, or Jackson, maybe. There was a soft knock. Her breath caught. She wheeled around and lunged toward the door that must connect to Monroe's bedroom, grateful for the soundless plush carpet, as she heard the jingle of another set of keys.

Victoria's heart seemed to pound in her throat as her own key slipped silently into the lock. In the space of three seconds, she had the door open and she was in the bedroom, locking the deadbolt from inside. She ran into her own room, shoved the confiscated materials under her bed and flopped down on top of it, pretending sleep as she tried to bring her raging pulse under control. Sounds of doors opening and closing echoed through the interior of the house, but no one came to question her.

CHAPTER FIFTY-ONE

VICTORIA sat in front of the lighted mirror in her dressing room, studying her reflection. The frustration and fear she'd felt hours earlier had returned and remained in her throat as she tried to swallow. She turned her head and looked sideways at her reflection. Her hair was very different from what she could remember, and so blonde it was almost white. She could see the darker roots when she looked closely. Even her eyebrows were lighter. All of that was easy to change. But, her face. What had happened? The shape of her nose, slender and straight. She leaned closer to the mirror and examined her teeth. Perfectly aligned now. Those things were not illusions created by cosmetics. Involuntarily, her hands went to her face. Fingertips slid over the contours, searching for the places where the mysterious changes had been made. Her fingers stopped suddenly when they felt a small, thin ridge, just behind the left ear. Then she saw it. A scar, barely visible. Immediately, she felt behind the right ear and found the same thing.

For several minutes, Victoria was still, stunned by her latest discovery. *A facelift?*

If she were mixed up in a real drug operation, she might have had her appearance changed in order to hide her identity. It was as unthinkable as the mess her mind was in. The missing time before she found herself on that dark, unfamiliar road in the middle of the night. The confusion. The crushing discoveries. She would drive herself mad, if she weren't already. The pulsating feeling of uneasiness, of danger, wouldn't leave her. She must focus on finding the truth. To do that, she had to keep her emotions under control and proceed with all the inner strength she could muster.

With shaking hands, Victoria explored her way through the array of make-up and toiletries on the dressing table, looking for something to cover the scratches on her face. She smoothed on ivory-tinted liquid with her fingertips, blending it carefully over her skin. The automatic procedure of applying cosmetics had a calming effect. She debated how to fix her hair, remembering the French braid she'd found herself wearing earlier, knowing she couldn't manage that. Better to brush it and wear it in a simple style, she thought, as she dressed in the pale green silk pants ensemble Alice had laid out. It was chic and tasteful, decorated only with delicate black piping along the seams and mandarin collar of the tunic. She was hooking the tiny black buttons at the edge of the collar when there was a knock on the door.

"It's Marie, ma'am. I've come to help you with your hair."

"Come in," Victoria responded, relieved to know one problem would be taken care of.

"Good evening, ma'am." She was a pretty young woman with deep dimples in her cheeks.

"Good evening, Marie. How are you?" It was an easy response. Victoria hoped she would get enough cues to continue the conversation.

"Oh, very well, thank you," the maid said, already reaching for the hairbrush. "Mr. Monroe has returned, ma'am. He said you should not hurry dressing. He'll see you downstairs." Marie's efficient hands worked quickly. She separated Victoria's soft hair into three skeins, and skillfully formed the neat braid along the center of the head, starting at the forehead and working to the back. "It's a beautiful evening, ma'am. Would you like cocktails on the terrace?"

A small, cold dagger of dread stabbed into Victoria's mid-section. "Yes, that should be pleasant, except I have an awful headache." She pressed her fingertips to her forehead.

Marie coiled the thick braid at the nape of Victoria's neck and fastened it with Oriental hair ornaments of black lacquer inlaid with mother of pearl. Then, without hesitation, she went into the bathroom, got the aspirin bottle and returned with it along with a glass of water on a tray, which she placed on the counter.

While Victoria swallowed two aspirin tablets, the maid opened the jewelry box. She selected an apple green jade and diamond pin with matching earrings, placing them on the counter. She waited until Victoria put the glass back on the tray. "Will there be anything else, ma'am?"

"I don't think so, Marie, thank you."

"Very well, ma'am." She returned the aspirin bottle to the cabinet, then picked up the tray and left quietly.

Victoria realized there was no real purpose in delay. She would have to go downstairs. The message was courteous, but he would expect her to be there. She was anxious to avoid any suspicion. A little shiver went through her each time she imagined the confrontation. She had no choice. She had to know what kind of business was conducted in this house. Nothing would convince her she was here of her own choice. It was too strange. How could she explain to the police—and Blake—that she came here after a drug bust, but had no idea why? Who would believe that?

Once again she fought down panic as she put on the earrings and attached the large, asymmetrical pin near the shoulder of her outfit. She suspected the beautiful jade was Imperial Burmese, some of the finest in the world. Victoria stood and stared at her reflection in the mirror, subconsciously refusing to focus on the face. The overall look was stunning—simple, superbly tailored, and elegant.

Determined to remain calm, she stood straight and walked out of the room. The soft swish of the pants' edges lapping around her high-heeled sandals somehow gave her a feeling of comfort. She felt alert. She hadn't been in a play since high school, but this role had better be enacted flawlessly.

He wasn't visible to her until she rounded the curve of the balcony. Then she saw him. Standing at the open glass doors, looking out toward the water, he was obviously lost in thought.

Some sense of her presence, or maybe her reflection in the glass made him turn around. When he looked up, it was the Ian Monroe of the photograph—and of Washington, D.C. His handsome face showed concern, but even with that, his admiration was plain to see. He advanced to the foot of the stairs to meet her.

"Erica, darling, come and let me look at you."

Victoria descended slowly, keeping her eyes on him. He was very distinguished in his gray pinstriped suit, appearing more vigorous and much better looking in person than in the newspapers.

"Are you all right?" he asked for the second time that day. As she reached the bottom step, he kissed her forehead tenderly and his arms went around her.

"Yes," she answered simply.

He didn't let go of her. Whispering into her ear, he said, "I was so afraid something had happened to you. I should never have left you to do such dangerous work without me." Finally, he stood back, holding her at arm's length. His intense, gray eyes searched hers, wanting proof that all was well. He gently touched her face with one hand, and felt the scratches almost hidden by the cosmetics. A quick frown formed on his brow. "You must have gotten these while you were going through the brush around the airstrip. My poor darling."

Victoria had momentarily forgotten her terror in the

unexpected intensity of the man's affection. Hearing his last words, the anxiety returned. "I'm fine," she said, trying to smile a little.

He returned her smile as he squeezed her hand. "Come, let's sit out on the terrace." He guided her through the open doors to a glass-topped wrought iron table, pulling his chair close to hers as they sat. Beyond them, the bay glowed in the pink-orange rays of the setting sun.

"I blame myself for the fiasco last night." There was concern for her in his voice, and in his eyes as he looked at her. "But, there is so much chance in this business—and sometimes, it's dangerous." He paused, eyes staring into the distance. "Ches said he told you this morning that the operation was less than successful."

She nodded, thinking it must be the man whom Alice called Mr. Jackson. Ches Jackson. Another piece for the puzzle. She remained intent upon every word.

"He also said when the Feds closed in, you managed to disappear into the woods." Ian looked at her intently. "What happened after that?"

Marie arrived to place martinis and hors d'oeuvres before them. Victoria used the interim to form her answer. Why did she have the uneasy impression that they weren't really working with DEA? What was her particular involvement in the activities around the airstrip?

The maid had withdrawn before she spoke. "I…I don't…know. It all happened so fast. Before I knew it, I was walking along the road, wondering how I would make it back here. I got to a bus stop, a bus arrived, I bought a ticket and got on it."

Ian held her hand while she talked, shaking his head as if trying to imagine her lost and alone in the middle of the night. With his free hand, he raised his drink in a toast. "Here's to you, my darling, for skillfully exiting from that tight spot. I'm very proud of you."

Victoria forced a smile of acknowledgment.

"It's a bitter blow, of course," he went on, "but we'll get by this one and go on to do greater things. Don't you worry. Our attorney has already gotten the crew out of jail. He made sure it looked like the real thing. Remember, our whole purpose is to pretend to be smugglers in order for our government—and the Colombian government—to track the shipments back to whomever is supplying the stuff, as well as who is operating the pipeline here." He paused, again deep in thought. "Dominguez will be here after dinner to talk about the next shipment, and I hope we can plan carefully enough to change our luck. We'll have a new plane. Faster, with a longer range."

He fell silent as soft breezes played about them in the hushed sounds of early evening. High up in the surrounding trees, birds gathered to wind up their chattering in the last rays of light penetrating the deep green bower overhead.

Victoria wondered what motivated a society lawyer to devote so much time to such adventures. The conversation had made clear the nature of their business, and her deep involvement. Could it possibly be all right after all? There was still too much she didn't know. Her heart was with Blake, yet she found herself living with Monroe. As his mistress? It was preposterous. There was no logical explanation.

One thing was obvious. This man meant her no physical harm. On the contrary, he seemed very devoted to her. As Victoria watched the sun set, she considered for a moment the possibility of talking to Ian—she had begun to think of him as that—telling him of her strange memory loss. She felt like he could answer her questions, at least some of them. The answers might not be as bad as she imagined. It might be better to meet the problem head on.

Caution won again, as it had before. She decided to keep her worries to herself, playing along until she was on sure ground. There was no doubt they were involved in a sensitive operation.

Judging from the talk of DEA, loads and planes and hidden airstrips, it was certainly the drug trade. The type of involvement was the unresolved question. In spite of the beautiful house, the elegant clothes, the jewels, and the courtly admirer, Victoria thought it was possible she was caught in the middle of a deadly business.

CHAPTER FIFTY-TWO

Ches Jackson joined them as they went into the dining room. Marie served dinner while conversation around the gleaming black lacquered table focused on the event that held the world's attention at present.

"Have you heard tonight's news?" Ches asked, picking up his fork as he looked at Ian. "Argentina's navy is at sea. They say they've busted through the United Kingdom's blockade around the Falkland Islands. Man, oh, man! Those Argentines seem determined to hold on to their captured territory no matter what the cost." He shook his head in disbelief. "Hell, they ought to know there ain't no future in that! It's ants against elephants!"

"I heard the report earlier," Ian responded.

Victoria remained quiet. Although she knew nothing about events taking place in the South Atlantic, she did know how an ant felt fighting against elephants. She pretended to be absorbed in her dinner.

"More of the British fleet is on its way to retake the islands," Ian continued, thoughtfully. He paused to taste the wine. "Mrs. Thatcher is a tough Prime Minister. She will play cat and mouse with the Argentines for a while, then end it with one grand swat."

Victoria repressed a shudder.

They ate silently for a while. After Marie picked up the dishes of the main course and disappeared into the kitchen, Ian turned to

Victoria.

"What about the party arrangements for tomorrow? Is everything all set?"

"Yes," she answered. "I talked with the director of the party service today. We went over the details. Everything is under control."

"And contacts with our wholesalers?" He paused only a second, not giving her time to answer. "See that everything goes perfectly. After last night, we can't afford another foul up. What we have at the stash house, and what comes in late tomorrow night must be distributed as soon as possible." His eyes were cold steel. "Every step must be flawless."

"Yes, Ian, I know," Victoria said, because she didn't know what else to say. Contact with what wholesalers? The headache, eased only temporarily by the aspirin, had returned in full force. She ate mechanically while trying to assimilate the last few comments and Monroe's change in demeanor.

Marie re-entered with dessert, and talk switched to other subjects.

"I've neglected to tell you, Erica, that I arranged to have your paintings hung tomorrow morning…that is, if you have no objection, darling. Our guests will enjoy them, I think." He stopped, looking at her expectantly, waiting for some response.

Victoria's thoughts raced furiously. She had seen only a collection of seascapes done in oil and a few large Chinese silk-screen prints in this room. Which paintings of hers was he talking about?

"Of course, I have no objection," she murmured finally.

"Splendid. I think the bay scenes would look nice upstairs along the balcony, and the gardens and wildflowers in here…perhaps grouping them against that wall." He waved his arm in the general direction of the front of the house.

She nodded, breathing easier.

With dinner over, the three moved into the living room where coffee was served. Dominguez arrived shortly afterward, looking moody. Nodding curtly to Monroe and Jackson, he completely ignored Victoria.

Without preamble, Dominguez unfolded the map he had brought with him and spread it out on the coffee table. "Callahan's ready to make the run tomorrow. We'll send the plane to Montería since this load will also include the shipment of *El Padrino*. It's a regular airfield, with lights, paved runways and good refueling facilities." He paused. "He'll get back here early Sunday."

Ian nodded, pleased. "That will be a great advantage. The Colombian can control things down there much better than we can. He'll make certain fuel is ready and waiting, and the officials at the airfield will be bribed so that no questions are asked. Callahan's job will be a lot safer."

Victoria sat quietly, listening with intense concentration, trying to pick any information that she could use. She knew enough Spanish to catch the reference to "The Godfather." He must be the head of the cartel they were working with. Her internal alarm bells clanged loudly. They were dealing with the big boys. Involuntarily, she massaged her temples.

Ian looked at her intently. "Darling, what is it?"

The throbbing of her head threatened to make her physically sick. "I have a headache. I guess I need sleep. Would you mind very much if I went up to bed?"

"Why, of course not. I'm sorry you aren't feeling well." There was concern and disappointment in his voice. "I'll look in on you later."

"All right," Victoria said, rising and nodding to each. "Excuse me, gentlemen. I'll see you tomorrow."

Dominguez waited until she was at the top of the stairs, then resumed talking. He kept his voice low. "Wilson and Amin screwed us good last time. We've got to find a completely different landing site. I think the pickup ought to be by boat. If they're watching us, vans would be the first thing they'd spot. The boats can take the load to a safe stash where we can leave it a couple of days before moving it out to the wholesalers."

"Not the Colombian's load," Ches said, firmly. "It's too risky. We've got to deliver his part right away. He'll have our asses hanging sunnyside up if the location is raided by the Feds—or by some dumb-lucky shithead who just happens to stumble on it."

"I think so, too," Ian added. "We should have two or three boats—one to transport only the Colombian's part of the load. Miguel, we'll arrange for you to meet with the cartel's representatives within an hour or two of Callahan's arrival."

Rounding the balcony on the way to her room, Victoria leaned over the railing and peered downward. She could only pick up bits of the conversation drifting upward. "It's a long straight stretch…good spot…boat pickup…" The three men sat hunched over the map. Their fingers traced imaginary lines across the paper, ending up on the tip of a peninsula that formed the southern boundary of a bay.

The tension of the past hours tore at her muscles as she went into her room and shut the door softly. Victoria's thoughts blurred as she got undressed. She took more aspirin, crawled into bed, but a half hour later, she was still awake. The drug deal was real, she thought groggily. She now knew it for a fact. In the DEA's undercover world, no "stash house" would be allowed to remain without confiscating it. Blake had told her that many times. The elaborate lie about a "sting" had been concocted for her benefit. There was no one else to convince. Victoria stared into the darkness with the searing headache now joined by a knot of anger stuck in her throat. It was a long time before she drifted back to sleep.

She was awakened by a soft tapping at the door connecting her room to Ian's. Startled, she lay very still as the door opened and she heard him call out to her in a whisper. Not wanting to face a new confrontation, she pretended to be asleep. Her heart raced as she willed herself to breathe deeply and evenly. Quiet footsteps approached the bed and stopped. Victoria was close to panic. After a few moments, the footsteps retreated and the door closed once again. She could hear Ian moving about in his dressing room. Even after the sounds stopped and he had apparently gone to bed, it was impossible for her to sleep again.

CHAPTER FIFTY-THREE

AT one o'clock sharp on Saturday, Benton Harper's entourage unloaded numerous boxes of materials from three vans and swept into the house on Jubilee Lane. The invasion did not sit well with Alice. "Tinker Bell and his crew," she muttered, elbowing Marie who watched in fascination as the workers, clad in lavender jumpsuits, began their preparations.

Approaching Harper, Alice growled, "See that everything is picked up when you're finished. I don't intend to clean up a messy place."

"Alice, sugah," Harper sniffed, "by now, you know that Gulf Coast Party Service never makes a…mess. Quite the contrary. Our work is art—pure and simple." He stood regally, wearing a fashionably crumpled, natural linen suit with a lavender tank top. His intense red hair was pulled back in a small ponytail. With eyebrows arched high and eyelids dipped low, he looked annoyed and offended at the same time.

Alice glared at him. It was a standoff.

"I'll tell Ms. Lindstrom you're here," Marie said as she hurried upstairs.

Victoria was still in her bedroom when the maid came in. It had been a restless night. This morning, she had used exhaustion and the same headache as excuses for having a late breakfast in her room. She recalled the uneasiness of last evening as Ian had stood over her bed, and as a result, she no longer trusted herself to play a convincing role while around him. He was very perceptive. She knew she should get out of there before he realized part of her memory had returned.

"Mr. Harper is here, ma'am."

Victoria had forgotten. "Marie, is Mr. Monroe at home?"

"No, ma'am, he and Mr. Jackson left about half an hour ago. They won't be back until late afternoon."

"I see." Victoria glanced at the clock. "Tell Mr. Harper to get started. The house is at his disposal. I'll be down soon."

Marie left quietly and went downstairs. She found the effervescent party director standing in the center of the great room, his arms folded across his chest and head tilted back, surveying in all directions. She delivered the message.

"Well, of course, doll," he said. "I don't work any other way. Now, stand back and let me get started. Shoo! Shoo!"

★ ★ ★

ALONE again, Victoria left her room and quietly walked around the balcony to the room opposite hers across the open space over the great room. She'd noticed it earlier when she had toured the house. It was a library, as she had guessed, lined with books and comfortable chairs. Sunlight streamed in and the view out the windows was the same as her own.

She noted a large dictionary open on a stand. Flipping to the "S" section, she found an entire page of symbols. Mathematic, scientific, planetary, weather, linguistic. Scanning the list, she located the two that had been incorporated in the border design of the invitations sent for tonight's party. The asterisk signified snow. Three horizontal lines denoted fog.

Was it just a coincidence, or did their meaning provide a connection to the parties? Ian Monroe was obviously clever. He would leave nothing to chance. Of course, snow was the street term for cocaine. The other one might represent marijuana. Fog – smoke – marijuana.

If that's what it was, the invitations advertised the sale of both drugs. To all those people on the guest list? More likely to just a few, Victoria decided. In the little book she'd found in her purse, those two weather symbols were used repeatedly next to numbers which could signify amounts sold. There was also the symbol of one of the nine planets drawn along with each transaction in her little book. Those "planets" had to be the people who were the buyers.

Victoria went down the stairs into the maelstrom of feverish activity. Benton Harper rushed toward her and kissed her on both cheeks.

"Erica, doll, what do you think of it, so far?"

The voice she'd heard on the phone was unmistakable. "It's very beautiful." Victoria had to force herself to concentrate. Fresh worries of what unknowns the evening would bring had her distracted.

"I think these linen cloths are just scrumptious, don't you? Just scrumptious!" He beamed with satisfaction. "Believe me, Erica, when I tell you I had to absolutely fight that dragon lady at the linen shop to find these for me. But I simply insisted. Nothing else would work. We *had* to have this *very* shade of pearl gray." The diamond in his right ear twinkled as he shook his head with the force of conviction.

"I really do appreciate all your effort, Benton."

"Thanks, doll. At the risk of seeming immodest, I think the whole scene is so…harmonious…it fairly sings!" His nose tilted upward as he flung his hand into the air and hummed a few bars of *Some Enchanted Evening*.

★   ★   ★

JUST before sundown, the party staff lit the multitude of small candles. Benton Harper was everywhere, nervously checking and rechecking the table settings from the exquisite, contemporary china and silver down to the burgundy napkins with an intertwined *I* and *E* stitched in silver threads.

On the raised bandstand, Blake Harrison tuned a borrowed cello. He was clean-shaven and his hair freshly cut. He wore horn-rimmed glasses and was outfitted in a tux. Nothing about him resembled Terry Lee Wilson except the build.

He had eased into the quintet at the last minute. The other musicians thought the cellist had taken sick, but actually the fellow was quite well. The DEA had appealed to his patriotism and convinced him they needed the spot more than he did that particular evening.

Blake was pleased to discover he would be able to keep a sharp eye and not worry too much about sight-reading the music. The repertoire for the evening was easy—tender, romantic songs, especially good for dancing.

Earlier, Ian Monroe had walked about, looking over things, but he had gone back upstairs. Ches Jackson was stationed at the entrance in the foyer, along with Henry, who had no cooking duties that evening other than to guard his kitchen against alien caterers. Henry had received his orders within earshot of Blake. His main job was to take up invitations at the door, and turn them over to Jackson. There was no sign of Erica.

The quintet began to play *Fascination*, a nice number made memorable by a talented violinist. Early arrivals came in, already sampling the lavish buffet and sipping the wines. The party had begun.

CHAPTER FIFTY-FOUR

UPSTAIRS, Victoria put on the softly draped white silk sheath and looked in the long mirror. The ankle-length dress, slit up one side to expose a slender leg, clung to her body in a very becoming way. The neckline framed her head and shoulders, and plunged to reveal an expanse of lightly tanned cleavage. She sat at her dressing table and searched through the jewelry box for a necklace, but couldn't find one that seemed right. Instead she chose a pair of large diamond earrings and was pleased with the uncluttered effect.

Marie arranged her hair and was slipping white silk shoes onto Victoria's feet when there was a quiet knock. The maid opened the connecting door and, seeing who it was, inclined her head respectfully and left the room.

Ian Monroe came in and stood behind Victoria. His reflection filled the mirror and she felt apprehension. For a moment he was still as his eyes scanned her body. Then, reaching into his pocket, he brought out a necklace. Wordlessly, reverently, he put it around her neck and secured the clasp at the back. His face was beside hers as his hands came to rest on her shoulders.

"I am the luckiest man in the world to have you, my darling." He spoke in a hushed voice.

Victoria stared speechlessly at the dazzling gems. Magnificent, large emeralds surrounded by hundreds of tiny diamonds encrusted an intricate filigree framework of gold. Resting at the base of her neck, it resembled a collar of brilliant light. "I've never seen anything so beautiful," she said finally, almost in a whisper. It had to be worth a fortune, she thought, her head spinning.

Mistaking her astonishment for gratitude, he bent down and kissed her neck. The intensity of his feelings was exposed, showing clearly on his face as his eyes drank in the vision of her in the mirror. "Tonight, darling, later tonight, after our business is over," he murmured into her ear, "I will prove how much I adore you." He showed no surprise at the stiffening of her body. "I've wanted you for so long. I've been patient, and I must assure you there is no reason to be afraid of me, my love." He let his hands glide over the curves of the dress. Then both hands moved under the thin fabric, curving around the softness of her breasts.

With anger and an unexplained fear out of control, Victoria suddenly jumped up, knocking her chair sideways. Without realizing how it happened, she felt her back pressed against the wall and her arms out in front of her like a shield. Unable to say anything, she stared wild-eyed at Ian, as her mind belatedly warned her to be cautious.

"Erica, what is it?" Ian asked, startled.

Victoria fought to regain control of her emotions as she watched him. His first reaction had been that of hurt. Then, suspicion flickered across his face. It was there only for a moment, but she had seen it and sensed danger.

"Oh, Ian, I'm sorry. I don't know what's wrong with me." She brought one hand to her face. "I guess I'm a bundle of nerves tonight. The party, you know. I really want everything to go well. Can you forgive me?" Victoria's words tumbled out automatically as she groped desperately for excuses to cover her actions.

"Of course, darling. As you say, just pre-party jitters," Ian said smoothly. He extended his hand. "Now come, my beauty, we have guests." Before Victoria had time to hesitate, he guided her out of the room and along the balcony. All eyes turned toward them as they descended the stairs.

Blake had been waiting expectantly for the entrance of Monroe and the Lindstrom woman. He looked up from his music score when a movement on the stairway entered his peripheral vision. They were a stunning couple, he had to admit. Monroe always managed to look distinguished, and in a tux he was even more convincing. It was when he looked more closely at Erica Lindstrom, however, the DEA agent caught his breath momentarily. He had never seen her dressed like this. The narrow, clinging evening gown revealed her beautiful body as never before. He stared at her graceful neck and the gently sloping shoulders, her bare arms and hands ending in slender fingers.

So much of what he saw seemed familiar. He felt the pain of loss at the back of his throat and confusion in his mind. Who was she really?

His vision focused on the blinding brilliance of the jewels accenting her cool features. Damn. That bastard Monroe was obviously showing off his latest acquisitions—Erica and the fabulous necklace. The crowd at the foot of the stairs parted in awe, as Ian and his lady began greeting the elegantly dressed men and women.

Victoria kept her senses sharp, fearing disaster at any moment. She recognized the names that swirled around her, important names, names from the list she had found in the office. She wondered how she could find out which ones were actually involved in the drug activities.

After a few pleasantries, Ian broke away from the crowd and led her to the dance floor. He took her in his arms and they moved gracefully around the room in time to the music. All the while, he smiled broadly, nodding to individuals in the wide circle that had formed around them. It wasn't long before someone tapped him on the shoulder.

"Sorry, old man, but you can't keep this lovely all to yourself tonight. Mind if I have the pleasure of a dance?" The mayor of Bradford stood expectantly as Ian brought Erica to a stop.

"Certainly, Paul. Just remember she's mine," Ian said. His smile couldn't hide the overtone of jealousy. He clapped the man on the back. "Have fun, darling," he said to Victoria as the mayor swept her away. Ian looked at her for a few moments, then gave a subtle signal toward the back of the room.

When Ches Jackson came near, Monroe whispered, "I don't know what's going on—maybe nothing. But don't let Erica out of your sight." The big man nodded and moved away.

Victoria danced with a succession of admirers and fawners until she begged for a respite. Pausing for a glass of wine, she saw Benton Harper, now dressed in black tux, gliding toward her in excitement. His feet barely seemed to touch the floor.

"Erica, sugah, what did I tell you? I think the ambiance is divine, don't you? I can feel it!"

"It's a wonderful party, Benton. You've done a great job! Thanks."

"Of course, I can't take all the credit, although you know I'd like to." He paused to grin and squeeze her arm affectionately. "I think that florist—whom I cannot stand—has actually done some spectacular arrangements with creamy white calla lilies in those marvelous Lucite containers, don't you? And the musicians are helping a tad," he said, looking in their direction. "Tell me, sugah, what do you think of the cellist?" He spun her around so she could see the one he pointed out. "I think he's gorgeous, don't you? He's new and…oh gosh!…sending me a signal! See? He's looking right over here!"

Victoria thought there was something familiar about Benton's discovery. She noted the size and build of the dark-haired man, the comfortable way he wore the tux as his strong hands guided the bow across the strings of the cello. The lean face ending in a chin with a slight notch under it—*where the scar was*. It took a few seconds for recognition to dawn. Even with the glasses obscuring his dark eyes, she knew it was Blake.

Fortunately, at that moment Harper rushed away to defuse some new crisis. Victoria shook, struggling for self-control. Her throat tightened until it felt like she might choke. Her mind raced through a series of questions, trying to assimilate the fact of his presence there, in this house, in this place far away from Washington. It was as strange as finding herself there. Her heart hammered so loudly in her chest she thought someone else would hear. She *must* remain calm. If she made a careless move, both Blake and she could be in danger. She had to make contact somehow to try to explain it all to him—at least the parts she could remember. Now that she had some evidence, it might help to incriminate members of the organization. She could only hope that Blake would believe she was not in it voluntarily.

A shiver vibrated through her body when she recalled the confrontation with Ian earlier in the evening. His intimate advance had caused her to panic. Time was running out. Ian was getting too close, pressuring her. He'd soon guess her memory had come back—if he hadn't already. How would she contact Blake without endangering both of them? Ian was watching, Ches was watching, Alice and Marie were everywhere.

★   ★   ★

AT the break, the musicians walked around to stretch their legs and have a smoke. Some strolled out onto the terrace, but Blake used the time to examine the spacious room and the hallways leading from it. He'd already memorized the layout described by their undercover agent working inside. Seeing it was always better.

There was much on his mind that worried him. The report from the Washington police had finally reached him with information provided by a prostitute who was furious at being dumped some months ago by her regular customer and biggest benefactor. When Gypsy Soldana was convinced there was no chance Monroe would return, she got her revenge. Dominguez, Jackson, and Monroe had been connected with Harry Pharr, she'd said.

There was a good chance they knew something about Victoria's disappearance. The Soldana woman claimed she'd heard them planning to deal with Pharr. Had they killed him? And Victoria? Those nagging questions teamed with others concerning the Lindstrom woman to further distract him. *Was it significant that everytime he looked at her, he was struck with the thought that somehow she might be Victoria?*

He felt the keen eyes of Ches Jackson following him. After most of the guests had arrived, Jackson had moved to the end of the bar. From that spot, he had the whole room under surveillance. Blake was careful not to call attention to himself or Jackson might recognize him as Wilson. He casually pretended to study the paintings on the wall. Some were very large, Oriental works that harmonized with the furnishings. He stopped to look at a group of smaller oil paintings that he felt he'd seen before. Out of the corner of his eye, he saw that Jackson was no longer as intent upon his movements, but watching Erica instead.

Blake turned his attention back to the artwork. The first had a river flowing through it, with pink and green pebbles along its banks. The point of a white obelisk rose in the distance beyond the trees. It was signed simply, Erica. He stopped and stared at the scene, only slightly different from one he'd seen before. Cold fingers began to crawl up his spine.

Careful not to give any hint of his astonishment, he moved to the next one. A field of wildflowers—Victoria's favorite subject.

When he stopped in front of the third painting, the icy fingers reached the summit of his back and seemed to grab him around the throat as the undeniable realization took shape like some dark monster. On the canvas was a small walled garden with a solitary tree bursting with the rich green leaves of summer. Beneath the tree, a bed of golden chrysanthemums bloomed in thick profusion. A wrought iron table stood in the shade, with its one chair. A book sat on the table, beside a delicate cup and saucer. Same signature. Those cream-colored dishes decorated with tiny green shamrocks were Victoria's. The garden was hers also, the same garden he had seen only once, in the fall, when the tree was almost bare, its brightly colored leaves falling to the ground below.

He felt sick, knowing his argument with himself was over. Erica was Victoria. Blake felt his mouth go dry, while the heat of anger replaced cold fear. Criminal activity and a new identity. What the hell was going on? Had Victoria's kidnapping been staged? Had she betrayed him—and herself? It was a hateful thought, but one he couldn't ignore. A jumble of hurt and fury tore through him, shoving aside his professionalism, taking control of him. Scowling, he swung around to look for her. With a jolt he saw that she was heading straight for him, and Ian Monroe was right behind her. Although she was smiling, it was fake and the eyes that looked at him were fearful.

Damn those green eyes—eyes that were deepened by the big emerald chunks wrapped around her throat—jewels surely bought by illegal drug activities. It would seem, Blake thought painfully, this woman he loved so deeply was a smuggler and the mistress of the very man he'd spent a year trying to catch. What was her game? To head him off, no doubt. He was wary and felt the acid churn in his stomach, but he was in control of himself again as he watched her advance.

Victoria had observed him standing quietly in front of the group of paintings, saw him stop and peer very closely at each one. She had read from the change in the set of his shoulders the very moment he knew the art was hers. When he turned his angry face toward her, she almost sagged, but she knew she couldn't falter now. She and Blake were on a dangerous tightrope and one slip could mean grave trouble for both of them.

She was aware of Ian coming alongside her. Without hesitation, she kept walking.

"I want to compliment you on the music this evening," Victoria said, fighting to keep her voice steady, smiling as she extended her hand.

Startled, Blake reacted automatically, clasping her hand as the familiar, once beloved voice flooded his being. His senses were instantly alert as he felt her left hand nudge his coat pocket. He knew Jackson watched them from a distance. Ian Monroe's steely eyes bored into him over Victoria's shoulder as he added his praise of the music.

"Yes, it certainly sets the perfect mood for our party."

"I especially liked *Stars Fell on Alabama*," Victoria said. "It's so nice to dance to."

Blake played along, stifling the emotions boiling under the surface. "Well, thank you very much," he said, bowing slightly. His dark eyes were hooded, unfathomable. "It's our pleasure to entertain you."

Victoria inclined her head, still smiling as she and Monroe moved toward a circle of people just beyond them.

After a few minutes, with his stomach still turned upside down and his mind in torment, Blake headed for a bathroom. Once inside, he reached into his pocket and felt the piece of paper. The note read:

> *Blake. Help me get away. Will leave as soon as I can.*
> *Look for me in parking area. Victoria*

A day ago he would have been elated. Now, he was seething with distrust. He didn't think there could be a reasonable explanation for Victoria's association with Ian Monroe.

He had just flushed the note down the toilet when he felt the gun in his back. Turning his head, he looked into the deadly serious eyes of Ches Jackson.

CHAPTER FIFTY-FIVE

"OKAY, Wilson—or whoever the hell you are—get your hands up and in back of your head. Move against the wall. Flat! Do it now!" It took only seconds for the black man to locate the gun in Blake's shoulder holster.

Blake did not protest. The .38 in Jackson's hand sported a silencer and the agent knew the gun's firing wouldn't be noticed by party goers any more than the frequent popping of champagne corks.

"Let's go. We're going to have our own little party somewhere else." Jackson motioned with the gun for Blake to turn around. "Put your hands down and look normal. You're dead if you make a sound." He prodded Blake out the door.

As the two men emerged, a contingent of Jackson's security force—and sometime gardeners—was waiting. They formed an effective screen of black tuxedos as they herded Blake past the great room, along the south corridor and to the narrow stairway leading down.

Jackson shoved his prisoner into one of the basement rooms. Blake lurched into the small space and took advantage of a moment of opportunity. In one smooth motion, he side-stepped, spun and slammed against Jackson's arm, knocking the gun away. Swiftly, Blake landed his fist on the surprised man's jaw. It was a short victory. Two other men quickly entered and joined Jackson, forcing the outnumbered man down as they punched him. They left him on the floor, bloody and semi-conscious, with hands tied.

"You'll stay here awhile, my man," Jackson said, coolly, dabbing a handkerchief at a cut on his lip. "After the society crowd splits, you and me—we're gonna have a little talk."

Jackson motioned to one of his men armed with a 9mm semi-automatic. "Stay inside. Don't take your eyes off him." He closed the door and listened until he heard the lock click, then moved down the hall.

Another youthful, muscular guard stood at the foot of the narrow stairway. "Keep your ass on alert, Everett," Jackson cautioned him. "When you find one rat, you damn sure know he's not alone. Watch out for that other one." Then turning back to the others, Ches Jackson flashed his familiar grin. "All right, you mean muthafuckas, let's go back to the party."

★   ★   ★

VICTORIA was uneasy. It was after midnight. She hadn't seen Blake since she'd passed the note to him. The musicians had reassembled and played on without him. Some of the guests had gone and she felt a new current of danger cut through the atmosphere. Ian stood beside her, his pleasant expression fixed as always, but he said little. Across the room, Ches looked grim and watchful. He began making his way toward them.

Something was wrong, Victoria thought. It was time to get out, now, before everyone left, while there were still some distractions. She hoped Blake was out there waiting for her. What would he do, she wondered. Embrace her—or arrest her?

"The invitations are in the office, ready to be checked," Ches said quietly, as he approached. "All nine of our wholesalers were here tonight."

"Good," Ian said. "We can move the stuff quickly."

Just then, Alice approached the group. "There's a phone call for you, Mr. Monroe. Will you take it in your office, or down here?"

"Thank you, Alice. I don't think there's a quiet place anywhere down here to have a conversation. I'll go upstairs."

Monroe hurried up the stairs, unlocked the office door and went in. "Hello," he said, picking up the receiver. Kenneth Raitt was on the line.

"Ian. I got your message. I just can't believe your crew managed to ruin the fishing trip—and lost another boat in the process."

"Things happen, Kenneth. I wasn't here to supervise. Remember, you were the one who wanted me to go to Washington."

Raitt laughed harshly. "Yes. Silly of me to think you'd trained your fucking fishermen right!" He laughed again, louder this time.

There was a note of madness in the senator's voice that Monroe had never heard before. Uneasiness began to creep into his consciousness. Raitt was on something, and whatever it was, he was near hysteria. It certainly wouldn't do to have him out of control.

"Calm down, Kenneth. We're getting ready for another expedition—in a few hours. Everything's all set, and I'm going to be here to oversee it. Don't worry."

"No-o-o-o, no. I won't worry. *You'd* better the hell worry, you stuck-up son-of-a-bitch! You let something happen to Perea's load and I'll direct his Colombian bulldogs right to you." He laughed wildly. "Have you got that, Ian? Do you understand?"

Monroe held the receiver in stunned disbelief. Raitt had switched from coded conversation to talk of loads and someone named Perea. Dammit to hell, Ian thought. Perea must be Raitt's source in South America, the godfather of the cartel! And the fool just blabbed it over the phone.

"Yes, I understand."

Ian came out of the office and descended the stairs. His thoughts were in turmoil. He didn't like the situation at all. Raitt was becoming impossible to work with. Too unpredictable. Tonight's operation was as well planned as anything could be in this business.

But, now there was this undercover cop Ches had discovered right here in the house. Bad news. If the phones were tapped, Raitt's conversation could bring the operation down. They'd have to move fast now. Bring in this load and get out of there. Ches had already made some contacts, checked on some places in the West Indies and Central America where they could re-establish business. It would be a good time to cut both Raitt and Dominguez loose. And, if Victoria was beginning to remember things, he would fix that—with drugs, if necessary. He would uproot everything, change everything, but he could not give her up.

While Ches stood watchfully beside Victoria, persistent questions about the invitations kept popping into her head. She was convinced the symbols used on them were to let "clients" know what product was available. Something else was important about them, requiring that they be "checked."

Victoria saw the look on Ian's face as he returned. "Is everything all right?" she asked.

"Perfectly," he answered with a slight smile.

She didn't believe him. Her uneasiness deepened. "Please excuse me for a moment, Ian. I'm going to freshen up." She headed for the staircase and struggled to hide her nervousness even as she felt both men's eyes boring into her back. It seemed there were more stairs to climb and the distance around the balcony to her room was longer than it had ever been.

★   ★   ★

EVERETT tensed at the light footstep on the basement stairs. His finger touched the cold trigger of the weapon in his hands. It would take only the slightest pressure to fire off a significant amount of the forty-round clip. In the darkened hall at the foot of the stairs, the young man was confident as he eased himself into a position to see who waited on the top step. Only one high-heeled shoe beneath a slender ankle showed. As Everett watched in amazement, the rest of the visitor came into view. She casually descended until he stepped into the small pool of dim light spilling down from the main floor.

"Oo-ooh!" she squealed, halting instantly, as one hand flew to her mouth. "You scared me half to death!" She gaped at the gun pointing at her. "What are you doing with that?"

"Catching rats," Everett said, chuckling at her reaction. "But you don't look like a rat to me." His eyes ranged over her petite body. Black satin gleamed where her full breasts pushed outward and the skirt rounded her hips. From a distance, he'd seen this particular maid before, pretty in her daytime uniform. Close-up tonight in this party uniform, she was a babe.

Deep dimples formed in her cheeks as the young woman smiled. "I'm on my break. I just had to get away from the crowd for awhile." She ignored the gun and sat down on the step. As she did, her narrow skirt rose up high on her thighs, exposing most of her shapely legs. "Whew! It's gotten awfully warm."

Everett watched with his mouth partly open, as the maid unbuttoned the top of her uniform and spread the white satin collar apart to cool herself. Her hands rose gracefully and went to the back of her neck, lifting her dark curls up. At the same time, she stretched, arching her back. "Um-m-m," she purred, cat-like. Cleavage flanked by the shiny fabric deepened as the bulging bosom rose and fell with each breath.

The man continued to stare, transfixed, as dark lashes lifted and deep, brown eyes looked sideways at him. His right arm hung limply by his side, the forgotten gun pointing downward.

"My name's Marie. What's yours?"

"Uh...Tim..." His body had already reacted. Now, he had to battle with his mind. Hell, she was offering. There was another guard watching the cop. This wouldn't take more than a few minutes. He could say he'd gone to take a leak if Jackson came down looking for him.

Marie leaned sideways and propped herself on one elbow.

"You're one fine woman, Marie." Everett's eyes mirrored his hunger as he contemplated the firm breasts. He lightly ran a finger down the deep shadow between them. "Wanna play?"

She giggled. "I'm on a break, remember?" The voice was breathy and coy. "Not a vacation."

"Well, it's time I had a break, too. How about we take a quick break together in one of these rooms?"

Marie grinned impishly. Without saying anything more, she took Tim's hand and led him toward an empty room.

The only thing Tim Everett felt was a slight breeze from behind before something hit him very hard on the head. Marie caught the 9mm before it clattered to the floor.

"Good work, Bryant!" Marie hissed. "Right on time."

Agent Bryant's dark face smiled in the dim light. "No problem." He looked down at Everett lying on the floor. Shaking his head, he whispered, "Damn. I knew this idiot wasn't a real gardener. All the time we were planting those pretty flowers out there, he didn't want to get his hands dirty. I don't trust a man who won't get dirt on his hands."

"Let's tie him up and get him out of sight. We've got to get Harrison out in a hurry."

"Right." Bryant produced some duct tape and within moments the two had dragged their captive into the room. Bryant secured him to a pipe beneath a small lavatory.

Marie made certain Everett would be silent for the next few hours by adding a strip of tape across his mouth. Then she pulled a set of keys from her pocket and locked the door. The two agents stood in the hall, whispering as they worked out the next step of a plan.

Blake Harrison lay motionless on the floor of the small room, waiting for his head to clear. The guard had an automatic pistol trained on him. No sense in being stupid. His hands were tied in back, but at least his feet were free. He'd wait for a reasonable chance to surprise the man.

He'd heard Jackson's instructions to the guards. There should be only one stationed on the other side of the door, but Blake thought he'd heard more than one voice outside the room. His thoughts were interrupted by a knock on the door.

The guard started in alarm. "Who is it?" he asked, tensely, aiming the automatic at the door.

"It's the maid, sir. Mr. Jackson sent me down to ask if you needed anything. Would you like me to bring you something to eat?"

The curious guard opened the door just a crack, then a little bit wider. Blake lifted his head enough to confirm that it was Marie. The 9mm pointed straight at her mid-section.

"Well, I just might. What've ya got, honey?"

"Oh, my. So many good things. Roast beef, turkey, escargots."

Blake smiled at Marie's skill. He watched the guard's gun arm relax a little.

"Esker-what?"

Marie gave him one of her deepest dimpled smiles along with a giggle. "Escargots…you know…snails."

"Goddamn! Whatever you do, don't bring me no snails! That ain't food for a man." He smiled, enjoying the maid's playfulness in response to his tough talk.

Now, thought Blake. He rolled to his feet and bolted head first toward his captor, slamming him against the door frame as the gun skittered harmlessly out of reach. It didn't matter. The man was unconscious.

Instantly, Bryant pushed the door open. "You okay, Harrison?" Both Bryant and Marie stared in dismay at his bruised face.

"Never better," Blake said grimly. "Now, let's get the hell out of here!"

CHAPTER FIFTY-SIX

VICTORIA hesitated for only a moment, looking around her at the silent room. Then she grabbed the keys and hurried through Ian's bedroom into the office. She rushed to gather the invitations on his desk and retraced her steps. Locking herself in her bathroom, she rifled through the stack of cards. She didn't know what she was looking for, but there had to be something significant.

Seeing nothing on the fronts, she flipped the stack over and looked at the backs of the cards. Most were blank. The first different one she found had a pencil drawing of a trident on the back. Neptune. Was one of their contacts replying that he or she was ready to take delivery of the drugs? Looking closely, she noted a series of tiny letters and numbers, ending with a quarter moon in the upper right hand corner—in her handwriting.

Victoria looked at the front of the invitation, once again studying the design that made up the border. One sun in an upper corner, one moon in the opposite lower corner. The sun, the source of all light in the solar system. The moon, merely a reflection of that light. Understanding penetrated her consciousness. Ian Monroe's arrogant style was evident in this brilliant design. The analogy was clear: Ian is to Erica as the sun is to the moon.

The rest of the notation didn't make sense. Quickly, she examined the backs of the other cards. Eight more had different hand-drawn planetary symbols. All eight of those had similar, but not identical, numbers and letters in small print in the corner. Each series ended with the moon drawing. What a clever and invisible way to distribute the drugs each time. Send out an invitation with code markings in the border to tell what was available. Information on the back might tell the cost, date and time of meeting, location, and even who the contact was. Obviously, it was she. The wholesaler would draw his or her symbol on back and turn in the invitation at the party. That way the organization knew who was ready to accept shipment. This evidence, she thought, along with the entries in the little notebook and the ledger, should provide Blake with enough to catch the "planets" and facts to make a case against Monroe. Keeping the nine cards, she tiptoed back to Ian's office and replaced the other invitations on the desk.

Once again in the relative safety of her room, Victoria steeled herself to remain calm. Certain of what she must do, she hurriedly took off the elegant dress and changed into jeans and shirt. She carefully stuffed the little notebook and lists of names into one pocket of her shirt, then folded the invitations and pushed them into the other pocket. With those spaces taken, the ledger had to be crammed into the waistband of her jeans. It was uncomfortable but completely hidden when she pulled on a sweatshirt over it all. Scarcely breathing, she moved to the door and opened it a crack. No one was in sight.

★   ★   ★

THROUGH high-powered binoculars, Mike Chapman studied the security guards posted at each corner of Ian Monroe's big house. Jackson knew his business, Chapman thought. Situated as they were, the four men had the exterior of the house and the entire grounds covered. No one could approach or leave without their knowing it.

Blake's partner had been in the woods that flanked the house since dusk, keeping the binoculars aimed at the expanse of glass facing the bay. He and one other agent had witnessed the main events at the party, from the time Ian Monroe led Erica Lindstrom down the long staircase, to the moment the couple approached Blake.

Chapman knew him so well, he'd noticed the sharp change on Harrison's usually pleasant face. Something was out of kilter. He'd watched Blake disappear toward the back of the room, watched Ches Jackson and a group of his strong-arm men converge on that same spot. Then a few minutes later, they moved as a solid wall toward the south wing. He knew there was an outside door at the end of the hall, but they never came out. They must have gone down to the basement. Damn. No evidence of Blake again. Chapman had known then that they had Blake and were probably working him over.

That was when he'd sent Bryant to back up Marie. Agent Bryant had keys. As one of Monroe's "gardeners," he'd had no trouble getting past Jackson's goons and through that door at the end of the hall.

Now, Chapman stiffened and leaned forward, squinting intently through the field glasses. Bryant was coming out the side door. With a friendly wave, he hailed the two guards who had him in their line of vision. Then he stopped to light a cigarette. He sauntered over to the guard on the southwest corner and began talking to him. Chapman watched as the lookout on the southeast corner turned to scan the front of the house. In that moment, he saw a dark shadow, bent low to the ground, move silently away from the house. He held his breath until the dark shape was swallowed up by forest. After a few moments, Bryant ended his conversation and walked away along a brick pathway, past the garage and greenhouse, until he, too, disappeared.

In minutes, Bryant and Harrison emerged from the darkness and came noiselessly toward Chapman.

"Erica is Victoria." Blake's whispered bombshell stunned his former partner. Chapman could only stare at him as Blake continued in a tight voice. "She wants out of there, Mike." He paused. "We'll get her out. After we question her, we can decide if she's innocent or guilty."

Chapman nodded, not knowing which question to ask first, and certain there wasn't time right then, to listen to the answer. "Harding and Levin are waiting with the bass boat. They're about a hundred yards down the shore, below the bluff."

"Good. Signal them to move in closer. All we can do now is stand by," Blake said quietly. "Marie is watching for Victoria to make her move."

Chapman nodded and looked away. It was hard to see a friend suffer like that.

★   ★   ★

SILENTLY, Victoria stepped out onto the balcony and heard the buzz of voices rising up from the floor below. She'd have to walk along the wall, past the next two rooms. If no one was in the foyer, she'd go out that way. Once outside, she'd stay out of sight behind the shrubbery. In a few minutes, she'd be hidden among the cars in the parking area.

She inched forward, careful to keep away from the balustrade. Ian's curt voice drifted upward. "...Erica..." It was only a fragment of a sentence. She froze, not yet past the office. From her position, she could see Henry, still near the front door. So much for that way out. Then she heard Ian again.

"...going to find Erica."

Victoria heard footsteps moving toward the stairway. In the next seconds, she debated her chances of making it along the balcony and around the corner to the hallway leading to the narrow servants' stairs on the end of the north wing. But it was too late. Ian would be close enough to see her by then. She darted back into her room and silently shut the door, pressing her back against it, desperately wondering what to do. Her breathing was rapid and shallow, and she knew she was near panic.

Suddenly, Marie was there, standing in the doorway to the dressing room. Startled speechless, Victoria stared at her, certain the maid intended to turn her over to Ian.

Instead, without a sound, Marie beckoned.

Victoria felt like she had stepped into a dream sequence. Taking the chance, and realizing it was her only one, Victoria followed the maid into Ian's room and closed the door. Marie pulled her toward his closet. To Victoria's amazement, the closet door stood open and the clothes were shoved aside, revealing a door built into the back of it.

"Hurry," Marie whispered, opening the door to an elevator. "This will take us down to the basement." The maid shoved Victoria inside and punched the button. The door slid shut. As the elevator descended, Marie explained. "I'm Agent Menard. Harrison is waiting for you with a boat."

"Thanks," Victoria responded, exhaling the breath she'd been holding. Her mind swam with relief. Blake was waiting!

Ian reached the door of Victoria's bedroom. He knocked and called to her. When he received no answer, he repeated the knock. Impatient after waiting a few more seconds, he went in and looked around. He saw the white dress thrown over the back of a chair, but she was nowhere in sight. Puzzled and suddenly panicky, he rushed out and down the stairway. "Ches, Erica is not up there! Did she come past you down these stairs?"

"No, she didn't." Ches looked around the room at the thinning crowd. No sign of her. He'd better do some checking, he thought, although she had probably gone down to the kitchen by way of the back stairs.

"I don't understand where she could have gone so quickly." Ian spoke with a forced calm, unlike what he felt.

Ches started to speak. "Ian, she's only been gone a few…" In mid-sentence he tensed, listening to identify the unknown signal just barely entering his consciousness. A slight shudder, a faint, high-pitched whine. The elevator. He bolted toward the north hall, toward the narrow flight of stairs which led down to the basement on that side of the house, the place which had an exit directly to the beach.

The elevator had reached the lower level. As soon as the doors opened, the women rushed out and through the storage closet. "Out the back door and run toward the water!" Marie said urgently. "Good luck!"

Victoria raced to the exit and slammed herself against the release bar. The door burst open and she sprinted across the sand toward the water. An angry shout of alarm off to her right cut through the darkness and lent added urgency to her escape. Marie was no longer behind her, although Victoria knew the agent had come out the door right after her.

A rifle fired twice, followed by a shriek. Behind her she heard the door open again, then a loud thump. She didn't slow down, fighting savagely against the soft sand pulling at her feet. The few seconds since she'd left the house seemed like an eternity.

It was pitch black, but Victoria could hear the lapping of water just ahead of her. She saw the white outline of a boat bobbing up and down a few yards down the shore and changed her direction. Without warning, strong arms grabbed her and a hand clapped over her mouth, stifling the scream that rose in her throat.

CHAPTER FIFTY-SEVEN

TERROR surged through Victoria as the man held her in a vise-like grip. She struggled, twisting her body and jerking her head, but her arms were pinned to her sides and the big hand squeezing her mouth didn't move.

"Quiet! It's Blake!" he whispered into her ear. His voice was urgent.

Victoria froze. She quickly nodded her understanding. Together they raced toward the water. They heard shouts from the house, and more running feet from that direction. Two men helped them into the boat and pushed it away from shore. The sound from the electric motors was muffled as the boat moved out slowly. Soon they had gained some distance from the shore.

The sharp staccato pops of an automatic weapon firing around the house on the bluff forced the group in the boat to keep their heads down. Blake hoped it was random panic firing, but Levin had an M-16 ready in case they became sure targets. Once they were far enough from shore to be swallowed in darkness, Harding opened the throttle of the big outboard and the bass boat shot forward, heading south toward the lower edge of the bay.

Blake turned to Victoria, touching her on the shoulder. "Are you all right?" he shouted over the roar. He could feel her shivering as the wind tore at her sweatshirt.

"Yes," she answered. She scanned his face, trying to read his thoughts, but she couldn't see him very well in the darkness that surrounded them.

He rummaged under the seat. After a few minutes, he straightened up and put a windbreaker around her. "This will help," he shouted.

"Thanks," she responded numbly. There was still no indication of what he was thinking.

Lights began to appear in the distance. Safety lights on the gas drilling platforms rising out of the water, and then, buoy lights. Victoria looked toward Blake as the boat turned east into a channel cut through the land.

"Intracoastal Canal." He paused. "We're heading for Gulf Shores."

In a short while, they sped under the Highway 59 bridge. Just east of there, Harding nosed the boat into a small dock where several people milled about. The occupants of the boat were helped onto the dock and to the waiting cars. For the first time, in the glare from the headlights, Victoria saw the bruises on Blake's face.

They sped off, seeing only a few vehicles going in the opposite direction as they headed for the beach, and then turned westward. Soon the agency cars pulled into the driveway of an octagon-shaped wooden cottage perched on stilts, fifteen feet above the sand. Victoria looked at Blake with a puzzled expression.

"It's my family's beach house," he explained. "You'll be safe here." He ushered Victoria up the stairs. "Lewis," Blake called over his shoulder, as they went into the house, "find a weapon for me, will you?" The other agents remained outside in little groups, smoking and talking. There was an air of suppressed excitement. All had realized that the night wasn't over. Monroe's organization couldn't stand still, not after what had happened this evening, and the DEA couldn't let them get away.

Once inside, Victoria and Blake were silent. He felt awkward, sensing her uneasiness as well, and avoided looking directly at her.

Blake's professional training dictated his opening remarks. "Sit down there," he said, pointing to a rattan sofa as he led her across straw mats in the living room. When she sat, he leaned against the counter that divided the living room from the kitchen. "What is Monroe planning for tonight?"

Victoria stared at the floor. "They're bringing in a shipment tonight—or rather, this morning before dawn."

"Where?"

"I don't know where, exactly. Somewhere near here."

He looked at her stonily. "Weren't you in on it?"

"Well, yes, in a way. But, they didn't tell me where it would be tonight." Her hands were clenched together tightly. Almost in a trance, she noticed how the gems in the large ring winked in the light from the lamps around the room. "It seems my job was to handle the distribution for this load." After a few moments, she continued. "A plane is bringing it in from Montería in Colombia. The landing site…I…I'm not sure. I saw a map from a distance. The spot they pointed to was a narrow peninsula. The talk was about a long, straight stretch of road and a boat pickup. That's all I know."

Without further explanation, Victoria slipped the emerald and diamond ring off her finger and placed it on the coffee table in front of her. Looking away, she reached behind her neck and unclasped the sparkling necklace. She laid it beside the ring. Then she removed the earrings.

"Evidence," she said, looking straight into Blake's eyes. She pulled the rest of it from under her sweatshirt, adding it to the pile on the table. "This should tell you what you want to know about Ian Monroe's operation—except for the identity of his distributors, the nine planets. If someone can figure out the coded messages…," she paused to point to the invitations, "which I think are meeting times and places to receive the drugs, your agents can arrest them on the spot. Ian might have recorded their actual names somewhere, but I didn't find them."

As he signaled for one of the agents to come in and bag the evidence on the coffee table, Blake dialed a number. He filed his report over the phone, and when he had finished, he listened while someone at headquarters gave him an update on what had transpired at Monroe's house after the group got away in the bass boat.

"After you left, Harrison, there was a firefight in the woods," the man said. "Monroe's men covered his escape. He and Jackson left in their two boats." He hesitated, then continued. "I've got more bad news. Agent Bryant is dead, and Agent Menard is seriously wounded."

"Damn!" Blake's voice reflected outrage. Bryant had been a good agent…and Marie… They had both risked their lives to free him. "How bad is she?"

"Shot through one lung, and a leg. She's semi-conscious, but the doctors said we might be able to question her briefly before they wheel her into surgery. She keeps trying to tell them something. The medical staff thinks she wants to talk to someone from the agency. I've got a man on the way to the hospital now."

"What about Mike?"

"Chapman was hit in the arm. Only a flesh wound."

"Hell!" There was a pause. "Anything else?"

"Yes. It's big. The wiretap boys reported an interesting conversation on Monroe's phone. The caller sounded crazy, but he talked about fishing and boats and loads, and mentioned a man named Perea in Colombia. Monroe—who called the man Kenneth, by the way—assured him that the group would be fishing again tonight."

Blake let out a low whistle. The Perea cartel was one of the most powerful in Colombia. "Do they know who the caller was?" He knew what the answer would be.

"They traced the call to the Senate Office Building in

Washington, D.C.—right to the office of Senator Kenneth Raitt."

"That ties a neat bow," Blake said. Well, almost, he thought. Raitt could always claim someone else used his phone. "Thanks for the information. I'll check in later. Keep me posted if there are other developments in the meantime. I hope Marie can give us some clues about where the shipment is arriving tonight. We're trying to second guess what they'll do next, now that the organization is on the run."

"Oh, one more thing," the voice said, hesitantly, "I don't know if you want to hear this or not, Harrison, but you've got to know. The fingerprints from Erica Lindstrom's glass that Marie Menard got for us belong to Victoria Dunbar."

"Thank you," Blake said, glancing at Victoria.

As he hung up the phone, she turned to face him. His bruised face looked more severe in the strong light than it had before. She stared at him as he took off the black windbreaker with the big gold letters on the back. She saw the empty holster, emitting its own kind of presence, strapped around one muscular shoulder and lying close to his body below the other armpit. It was a very familiar sight, yet it had always unsettled her, an undeniable reminder of the dangerous life he lived.

Victoria watched him reach up to open a cabinet above the counter and remove a bottle and glass. He was still dressed in the once-white evening shirt and black pants he had worn for the party. The shirt had a tear on one sleeve and parts of it were smudged with dirt and blood. With slow movements, he poured a small amount of brandy into a snifter and handed it to her. She held it for a moment, then drank some, letting it warm her insides.

Blake sat in a chair opposite her, leaning forward with elbows on thighs, looking down at his clasped hands. Finally, he faced her, leveling his gaze directly into her eyes. "What happened, Victoria? What in the hell happened?"

She saw pain on his face, but the anger had remained as the

stronger emotion. She had the terrible feeling he wouldn't believe anything she'd say. How she wished she could put her hand on his knee, try to bring back the closeness. She opened her mouth several times, searching for a way to explain something she herself didn't understand. Finally, she whispered the only words she could. "I don't know."

"You don't know?" Blake's voice rose in the span of those three words. "That's a hell of an answer!" His eyes were fierce. "You've been working with Ian Monroe and his gang, and you can't tell me why or how it all came about? You'll have to do better than that!" His pent up rage was on the verge of erupting. He stood up and paced back and forth.

The confrontation was almost anticlimactic to Victoria. The dreaded scene was happening and it was going badly. She was limp with the release of nervous tension, almost too drained to talk. "I really don't know. Two days ago, I seemed to wake up from a long sleep. I can't remember anything that happened in between then and sometime before, when I was in a shopping mall with Susan. After that, things get hazy. I think there was something about a train. But, I can't piece it together."

Blake looked at her closely, wondering if it was a con. "Do you know a fellow named Harry Pharr?" he asked suddenly.

"No. I've never heard that name."

"How did you end up with Monroe?"

"I…can't remember."

"Cut the nonsense, Victoria!" He was shouting, standing squarely in front of her demanding answers. "Why did you change your appearance?"

"I didn't! Two days ago…I looked in the mirror and didn't recognize what I saw. Do you think that I…?" What she read in Blake's face defeated her. Tears welled up in her eyes. She brought her hands up to cover her face, unable to fight the accusations. "I'm very,

very tired."

The tears pricked his conscience. It could be the genuine despair of a woman who was mentally confused. Or, it could be the performance of the century. Right now, he couldn't decide which it was, but he owed her a fair hearing. She hadn't blown the whistle on him to Monroe. Or had she? Giving him the note could have been her way of pointing him out to Jackson. This "evidence" she produced could also be phony.

"I'll show you to a room where you can get some sleep," he said, stiffly. "You needn't worry. You'll be safe here. If I have to leave, one of the agents will stand guard outside."

Blake led her to the bedroom. He opened the door and motioned her in. "You'll find night clothes in the chest-of-drawers." He switched on the bedside lamp. "My sister-in-law always leaves some things here."

She nodded her head.

"Get some sleep." Blake's expression was unreadable. He went out, closing the door softly.

Victoria looked around at the small room furnished in wicker and linen. Feeling miserable, she drank a few more sips of the brandy and sat down on the bed. Tomorrow I'll try to talk to him, she thought, when I've had some rest. Her life had changed so radically, and so much was still unknown. She felt warm now, very drowsy— and so, so hopeless.

★　★　★

THE luminous hands on Steve Callahan's wristwatch gave off a greenish glow.

O155 hours. He'd be approaching the coast of Alabama in less than two hours. It had been a good flight. That Colombian cartel had been true to its word. The airport at Montería had been shut down tight until the plane was loaded, refueled, and he had taken off. No one gave him any trouble. And, this new Navajo was a dream airplane, real easy to handle. With the modifications done, it had greater fuel capacity, and more powerful engines to compensate for the weight of the extra fuel.

He had other worries, though. Something was brewing at the landing site. *"Be ready to unload in a hurry,"* Dominguez had warned him in his last radio transmission about thirty minutes ago. Callahan thought it had sounded like the Feds might be breathing down their necks. Damn. If things were that hot, maybe they were going to run.

As he adjusted the throttle and pitch control levers, he realized he'd better take things one at a time. For now, just staying awake was a biggie. He didn't have a co-pilot on this run. It was the hardest time, those last hours of a long haul. And, Callahan knew at the end of the trip, he'd have to do something that would present an even greater challenge. He was supposed to put this airplane down on a dark, narrow road flanked by sand and water. *Shit!*

CHAPTER FIFTY-EIGHT

"Thanks," Blake mumbled as an agent handed him a replacement weapon. He slipped it into the empty shoulder holster, barely aware of his actions as he retraced his steps to the living room. His thoughts were tortured by the fear that this woman he loved had become a criminal. It was almost a replay of his first love. Well, not quite. Restless, he picked up the phone. He wanted headquarters to patch him in to Mike Chapman.

"Hey, Mike. You okay? How's your arm?"

"Aw, man, you know me. I'm a survivor. All hell broke loose around the house after you pulled away. There were guys running through the woods with all kinds of bad-ass firearms. They couldn't figure out exactly what had happened—whether or not 'Erica' had run away or had been taken away. Monroe went berserk. Screamed at his men to find her or else. Then they spotted us and opened fire."

"Is that when you were hit?"

"Yeah. Bryant and I were pinned down on the bluff near the edge of the woods. We tried to move to a better position. Bad idea. Marie had already been hit trying to shove a stone or something to create a stumbling block out the basement door. It worked, too. Jackson tripped and fell, which probably gave you and Victoria enough time to get to the boat. But, Marie nearly bought it. She dragged herself out of sight before she lost consciousness. I radioed for help." Mike paused. "Right after that, two other boats got away—

Monroe's Bertram and a fast cigarette boat they always kept there. We assumed Monroe was in one and Jackson in the other."

"Any sign of Dominguez?"

"Nope, not tonight."

"Monroe will have to make a move immediately," Blake said. "We know he was bringing a shipment of drugs in tonight, possibly somewhere along the Fort Morgan peninsula. He might decide it's too risky after what's happened and just skip out. Have the Coast Guard keep a sharp eye out in the Gulf for those three boats in case they make a run for Cuba or the Indies. And, remind our boys—no chase plane."

"It's all covered."

"Way t'go, good buddy," Blake responded, switching into the Wilson drawl. "You're lookin' good."

"I, like, had a good instructor, man." There was a brief silence. "Uh...how are things over there? With Victoria, I mean."

"Difficult." Blake's single word, uttered tonelessly, was followed by a long pause. "It's hard to know what to believe."

"Ouch. I'm sorry to hear that. A real bummer."

"Yes, it is. Stay in touch, Mike. Send some reinforcements over here ASAP, will you? If we need them, it'll be on short notice. Meanwhile, I've got people scouting all the marinas around here, just in case he turns up. Simmons is posted at the fort. He radios every half hour. I'll sit tight until we have a clear indication from Monroe. If he makes a move, I want us to be ready to roll when that happens."

"Okay. I'm coming along, too."

"Hey, you ought to take it easy for a while."

"Hell, no, this damned arm isn't going to keep me out of the action. There's nothing going on here worth even talking about. See you soon."

Blake shook his head. With a wry smile, he replaced the receiver in the phone cradle. He left one light on and went into an empty bedroom, not realizing until then how tired he was. He lay down and felt the knotted muscles complain. As he suspected, sleep wouldn't come easily. His mind continually replayed the nagging worry that Victoria had consented to her part in the drug smuggling operation. There was no doubt she was involved, and at no time in the agency's surveillance had they picked up the slightest indication that she was being forced to do anything against her well. What had made her change so much, both physically and emotionally?

Had Harry Pharr kidnapped her? If he had, as all clues indicated, how did she get into Monroe's hands? Was it really a mental block or a convenient alibi? He remembered the cold, pale eyes staring at him in the field that day as Monroe negotiated the landing site. She had been hard as a nail and clearly one of the principals. There'd been the same business-like coldness on the night the marijuana landed. Then, as the DEA closed in, she disappeared.

★　★　★

ABRUPTLY, out of a deep sleep, Victoria sat up. Her eyes were wide open, frightened, transfixed in the lamplight. A strange foreboding flooded her senses, a dread of something about to happen.

The jagged bolt of memory came out of nowhere, splitting open her mind, replaying a part of her life she didn't want to remember, forcing her to be the main character as well as a witness to the horror. At first, the scene was blurred. A filthy man threatened her as he shoved her against the subway seat. Then her mind zoomed in for a close-up and she saw him clearly. Greasy hair, heavy gold necklace, a meanness in the eyes. No! His sour breath made her want to vomit. Was she dreaming? It must be real because something rose up in her throat. Someone was screaming.

In the next second another series of flashbacks tore through her consciousness. She lay on the pavement, feeling the cold cement on one side of her face and on her palms as she tried to push herself up. The man kicked her hard, and she felt the pain as she saw her knees draw up. *Oh, please. Somebody help me!*

Like a hurricane, this thing inside of her had hovered, dark and menacing, sending out squalls in advance to signal its approach. Now that the time had come for it to rush relentlessly forward, the images spilled forth, rolling, hurtling nonstop. Nothing could hold them back, those pictures that were cold, sharp and merciless.

Victoria's skin crawled as she watched roaches dart along the walls and floor of a rag-strewn room. The same savage man came toward her. She saw herself cringe before him, rise up, then draw back again, terrified. On he came. In horror she stared, unable to change what was going to happen, feeling the searing pain as her body recoiled from the blows of his fists against her ribs. She heard a scream again and knew it was her cry for help as she tasted something strange and warm. Blood was on her mouth and above her eye, dripping downward. Bright, bright red. Her blood. She couldn't breathe. And then, she was naked. Oh, God. The man was on top of her, tearing at her as she tried vainly to kick and fight him off.

She didn't want to see this. *No! No!* But, there it was…still there. The scene wouldn't go away. *Oh, please, somebody help me!* The weight of his body crushed down upon her, painfully pressing the air out of her lungs. She couldn't move, watching as he forced himself between her legs and surged into her roughly, painfully. She saw the searing lacerations, the agony on the blood-smeared face of the body on the floor. And she burned with rage. It could not have happened. But the speed and power of the storm tide of memories wiped out the barriers in her mind. It *had* happened. Forced to accept that reality, she began to mourn the loss of a part of her life, her untarnished spirit, her shiny expectations. Gone.

★   ★   ★

THE primeval sound woke him. It took Blake only a split second to realize he'd been asleep. Another scream tore through the night, barely human. He was up and running with gun drawn, heading for the room Victoria was in. An intruder must have gotten inside, he thought in disbelief. More cries came from the direction of her room. He could hear someone dashing up the outside steps and hoped to hell it was one of his men.

Blake burst into the bedroom with the gun pointed straight ahead. Victoria was sitting up in the bed, rocking from side to side, knees drawn up under her chin, hands covering her face. The initial screams of terror and shouts of garbled words had changed into keening, as if something had died.

Harding, with an M-16 in hand, ran in as Blake moved toward the bed. "Check the rest of the house!" Blake shouted. "Quick!" There was loud thudding of many boots on the stairs and floors of the beach house as other agents rushed in. Harding spun around and sprang out of the room, motioning the others to follow.

Blake holstered his gun and reached for her hands. "Victoria! Victoria! What happened? Did someone come in?" He tried to pry her hands away from her eyes. "Victoria?"

Blake managed to get her hands from her face, but the wailing continued. She whipped her head back and forth in frenzied motions. Her eyes were wild as she fought him, her fists beating against him in panic. "No! No! Get away from me!"

"Victoria! It's all right. I won't hurt you." He saw recognition finally register on her face. He put his arms around her, trying to comfort her, feeling her slump against him. "What was it? What frightened you?"

"The man." Her face contorted with the memory, her head still moving back and forth.

"What man? Was someone in here tonight?" Blake's voice was tense.

Harding reappeared, shaking his head. "I can't find any sign of entry anywhere," he said.

"The man...before..." Crying uncontrollably, Victoria struggled with the words, trying to communicate what had filled her mind without warning.

"Was it Ian Monroe? Did he hurt you?"

"No, another man." The sobbing stopped as she stiffened, a desperate look on her face. "The man on the Metro!" She needed to talk, the only way to rid herself of the dark memory. "He...he forced me...to go to his place. He beat me...hurt me so much." She stopped, shaking her head in despair. "He...raped me." The long-repressed grief welled up from deep inside her, forcing its way out in great wracking sobs.

Blake pulled her close to his chest, resting her head against him, letting her cry while the fury over Harry Pharr built inside him like a tower of fire.

Harding stood by, waiting. His face reflected pity as he motioned that he and the others were going back outside. Blake heard their footsteps retreating. Someone closed the exterior door quietly.

He held her for a long time, feeling her body relax slowly, until her eyes closed. After a time, thinking she'd drifted off to sleep, Blake gently laid her down and covered her. She jumped, startled by the touch of the blanket. "Please don't leave me, Blake!" Her hands clutched him in renewed panic.

"I won't leave you, baby. I'm going to stay right here." He kissed her tenderly on the forehead and lay down beside her, once again cradling the trembling body in his arms. He stroked her hair gently until she was breathing evenly. He knew she was asleep, finally, but he didn't move.

Too bad Pharr was dead, Blake thought, still feeling the anger burn deep in his throat. He wanted to resurrect the little scum and make him suffer for what he'd done. It was a long time before he was able to sleep.

CHAPTER FIFTY-NINE

"Harrison?"

The low voice, followed by a soft, but persistent knock, woke Blake. Gently he lifted Victoria's head and moved his arm. It was numb. He rose, tiptoed out, and quietly closed the door.

Harding stood in the hall. "We got the report from Marie just a few moments ago. She insisted the load is scheduled to come in tonight—not around Fort Morgan—but on the way to the fort. The plane will land on the road near the water. She said they planned to unload it right onto a boat. She didn't know the exact site."

Blake had suspected the old abandoned World War II airstrip next to the fort was the most likely place to land the drug plane. But, if the smugglers wanted to unload the stuff directly onto a boat, the road was the place. In spots, the waters of Bon Secour Bay practically touched the highway on its north side. He looked at his watch— 0315 hours. Even though, by now, Monroe had almost certainly diverted the shipment because of the DEA's interference, they still had to follow up this lead. It was the only one they had. There was the off chance the pilot, who was surely in the air at the time the melee started at Monroe's, couldn't be contacted. He might be coming in according to their original plan.

"How many Zodiacs do we have?"

"Three or four. Enough capacity to hold all of us."

"Okay. Load everybody into the boats. We'll follow the coast, then head inland due south of that small boat dock on Fort Morgan Road. It's about halfway between the fort and the intersection of Highway 59. The road is straight there for about a mile. You'd better alert the FBI, Customs, Coast Guard and local police to stand by."

"Do you want me to bring Simmons in from the fort?"

"Yes. Have him position himself in the woods just south of the dock. He can be there in five minutes. Tell him to radio in every ten minutes."

Blake opened the bedroom door once again. Victoria was sleeping quietly, lying on top of the bedspread, still dressed in her jeans. He felt a twinge of guilt. He'd said he wouldn't leave her, but he had no choice now. For Victoria's sake as well as the DEA's, he couldn't let Monroe get away. Ian Monroe was the key to it all. He was the one who could clear her name.

"Leave a man to watch the house," he whispered as he closed the door. "I don't want her to be left alone. And, Harding, call headquarters. Have them send a female agent out here ASAP. Victoria might feel better having a woman to talk to."

★   ★   ★

VICTORIA'S sleep had been interrupted the first time the bedroom door clicked shut. Even though Blake and the other man talked in hushed tones, she had heard their quick exchange. That road they were talking about…she remembered seeing it as they drove past on their way to Gulf Shores from the Intracoastal Canal. When the door opened and shut again, she kept her eyes closed.

It was impossible to stay in bed as she heard footsteps milling around and doors opening and closing, followed by the sounds of many feet tramping down the steps to the beach. Victoria felt compelled to do something herself. The DEA wanted the drug ring. She needed some answers, some proof to give them that she was innocent. Even Blake didn't believe her.

When the clatter ceased, she eased out of the bedroom. There was no sound except for the distant roar of waves breaking on the shore. A quick look around told her no one was in the house. In the living room, a dim lamp remained on. She kept away from it and stayed in the shadows. Through the windows facing the Gulf, she could see flashlights illuminating a group of men climbing into three inflated rubber dinghies.

She had heard Blake assign an agent to watch over her, likely to keep her from escaping. She squinted through the glass, scanning the dunes for her guard. No sign of him. They were probably all on the beach now, making last minute plans before the search group left in the Zodiacs. The female agent hadn't arrived yet. Victoria knew she had to make her move right then.

As she turned to leave, she noticed a map spread out on the counter. Quickly, she went to it and located Fort Morgan Road. It was barely two miles from the beach house to where it began at Highway 59. Another ten or eleven miles along the road would take her halfway to the fort, to the boat dock Blake had mentioned.

Soundlessly, Victoria went out the door and down the steps. Five cars were parked on the drive. She went directly to the one closest to the street. The keys were in the ignition. She hesitated only a moment, gauging her chances. Dunes blocked her view of the beach. Wind blew off the water creating a constant, high-pitched sound. Under that was the echoing noise of the surf. The men shouting instructions to one another on the shore weren't likely to hear anything else.

She got into the car and pulled the door gently to close it. Her right hand groped for the key. She felt cold steel and squeezed. The engine started instantly. Cautiously, she shifted into reverse and backed the car straight into the driveway across the road. Then slowly, without lights, she turned onto the beach road and headed toward Gulf Shores.

★ ★ ★

CHES Jackson stared at the haggard man looking out the cabin windows as the boat lay tethered to the dock. He hardly recognized Ian Monroe, he'd changed so much in only a few hours.

Jackson thought back to an earlier part of the night when the madness started. Erica had suddenly left the house and he'd raced after her. He frowned when he recalled how a piece of driftwood or something had tripped him a few yards outside the storage room door and he'd hit the ground hard. That was enough to give her the few extra seconds she needed to get away. When he found the two guards tied up in the basement, he knew it had all been rigged, probably by the Feds.

He also knew the organization was finished, at least in that location. As soon as the shooting started, the remaining guests had left, and by the time it was over, his security people were scattered. He'd had a hard time convincing Ian that they had to get out of there right away.

Jackson recalled the final panicky scene when he and Monroe were alone in the magnificent house on the bluff.

"We've got to find Erica!" Ian shouted. His eyes had a wild look in them.

"No! The thing we've got to do is haul ass! And fast! You know damn well some of these high-powered locals have called the police about the shooting. That's aside from whatever the Feds have up their sleeves."

"Where's the money?"

"It's packed in a couple of suitcases upstairs in your closet."

"Get it, Ches! Hurry!" Ian was shaking.

He had obeyed, racing up the stairs two at a time. In moments he brought them down and handed one to Ian.

The forlorn man stood nervously in the middle of the cavernous great room. "I called Miguel and told him to meet us right away at the spot. You and I will take the boats, and dock them on the Fort Morgan Road." Ian's words were ragged. "We'll meet the last shipment. We've got to. Too much at stake. Then I will find Erica."

"Think, man! She's probably coming out of the amnesia. She won't be the same. It wouldn't do any good to track her down. Once she starts putting it all together, we've had it. Let's get the hell out of here."

They hurried out to the pier. Occasional shots continued to echo through the trees surrounding the house as they sped away in separate boats.

That was less than an hour ago.

At the sound of an approaching craft, Monroe jerked toward the window. "Here he comes."

Minutes later, Jackson felt the boat rock slightly as Dominguez stepped on board. He unlocked the cabin door and Dominguez entered.

"What's going on?" the Cuban asked with a frown.

"Erica got away. Looks like she's gone to the Feds," Jackson answered.

"White-haired bitch!" Dominguez turned his furious glare on Monroe. "I knew she'd be nothing but trouble. Shit! We should have let her die in Pharr's apartment!"

"That's enough, Miguel," Jackson said, sharply, not wanting him to push Ian over the edge.

"Enough? I had enough of Erica Lindstrom a long time ago," Dominguez continued as his rage built, "but our fine *hidalgo* here had to have her—only he couldn't really have her because she was crazy. A real *loca*. So, he has been acting like a horny old goat locked out of the pen. Look where it has got us!"

"Shut up!" Ian shook with anger. His hands clenched into fists.

"Not until I've had my say." Dominguez' face was menacing in the dim light of the cabin. "We're going to bring in this load tonight, *amigo*, with me running the show. Me, you hear? I'm cutting out the crew. No one but us will know what we're doing. When Callahan lands that plane on the road out there, the three of us will unload—alone. We'll throw the duffel bags into the boats and be gone."

"Wait a minute," Monroe said angrily. "Half that coke is for the Colombians. If we don't deliver, they'll track us down wherever we go."

"The hell they will. I will be so far away, they will not find me. You two can do what you want with your share."

"He's right about scratching the crew, Ian," Jackson said to Monroe. "Fewer vehicles moving around on the roads, less chance of someone drawing attention to our operation. It may be the only way to save ourselves. And, as for the Colombians, we'll worry about them later."

"Damned right, I'm right," Dominguez said, fiercely, "and, remember, it is your fault the heat is on us now." He turned to face the cabin door. "We will go now, Ches. The crew is waiting at the shop. We will tell them it is off for tonight, that it is tomorrow instead. Then you and I will take the trucks and come back here."

The two men raced along the Intracoastal Canal in the cigarette boat with Jackson at the helm. The wind was chilling, yet the heat of anger still simmered inside the Cuban. Since that moment he heard Erica got away, he could barely control his resentment at Ian's refusal to see how he'd exposed the organization to risk. Damn women, he thought in disgust. They had to be dominated or they would sure as hell take over your life. He was leaving Ginger behind. No problem for him. She was nothing but excess baggage at the moment. He could see things clearly, unlike Ian. The man had lost it, lost himself.

It all came down to what he knew about people, Miguel thought. You could not trust anybody. You had to be ready at any moment to save yourself before somebody stripped you clean.

★ ★ ★

THE small force of federal agents halted about fifty yards from the road. The men crouched low to the ground. They could see the two boats tied up at the small pier on the north side of the highway where the waters of the bay lapped against the narrow beach.

Blake switched on his radio. "Simmons. Where are you?" he whispered. He touched his ear-piece and waited for Simmons to answer.

"Roughly twenty yards ahead of you. A little to your left. I'm coming over."

In moments, a shadowy figure approached. "Glad to see you fellas. I was getting kinda lonely." Simmons flashed a quick grin at the men clustered around.

"See anything?" Blake's eyes scanned the surrounding darkness.

"When I got here, two boats were docked—a cigarette boat and Monroe's big Bertram. Then Dominguez arrived in the Hatteras and boarded Monroe's boat. It wasn't long after that all three came out on deck. Dominguez and Jackson left in the cigarette boat with Jackson at the helm. Monroe disappeared below decks again. It's been quiet ever since."

"Okay, let's spread out," Blake whispered. "Simmons, take four men with you. Go across the road. Position yourselves on either side of the dock, but stay back. We don't want to spook them yet."

"Will do."

"The rest of you men will stay on this side. Scatter, but keep down and watch for my signals." Blake turned to Chapman as the force began to move out. "I want you to stay down, Mike. That arm might start giving you some trouble."

"It'll be okay," Mike responded, gruffly, but the wound had begun to throb now that the pain killers had worn off. "I don't want to miss the show."

Everyone was in position. Twenty minutes passed. Then a faint engine sound steadily intensified. A battered pickup truck drove by, slowly, as if its driver were uncertain where to stop. Finally, it came to rest several hundred yards west of where the agents hid in the shadows. They heard it turn around, then the motor shut off. Someone walked back toward them, his footfalls quiet on the roadway.

Blake stared into the darkness. He couldn't make out who it was. Medium height. Coming closer. Dominguez. He felt his muscles tighten as he watched the man walk to the pier, jump aboard the Bertram and disappear down the ladder.

In five minutes, another vehicle approached but stopped east of them, about the same distance away as the first one. Another shadowy figure walked toward the hidden agents. Heavier footsteps thudded on the pavement. The big man approached the pier and gave a low whistle. There was an answering whistle from the boat and he went aboard.

Mike leaned over and whispered to Blake. "Looks like all the players are here, my man. That was Jackson. We're in the right place."

"Seems like it."

The radio squawked in Blake's ear. It was Levin reporting from the beach house. "The lady's gone," Blake heard him say.

"I hope this is a joke." Blake's voice was flat.

"No joke, Harrison," Levin said. "When the female agent arrived, she couldn't find Victoria anywhere."

Blake exhaled sharply. "Find her, and fast! Call in as soon as you have something."

CHAPTER SIXTY

Victoria steered the car onto Fort Morgan Road, now a deserted stretch of asphalt flanked by dark pines. She punched the odometer button on the dash and drove on. Ten miles beyond that point her headlights shone on a luminous sign.

ROAD CLOSED FOR REPAIRS.

Victoria doubted it. However, it was a sure way to stop traffic. She slowed down and pulled into a narrow driveway on her right, following the double dirt tracks a few yards before stopping. They seemed to disappear into the woods. It was a good place to leave the car, she decided. She got out and tramped back to the highway.

She walked around the sign and headed west. The road lay silent. In the scant starlight, only its luminous, white center stripe was visible, an endless eerie finger pointing the way ahead.

Victoria didn't know when the steady hum of motors first became audible, but suddenly she realized the noise was getting louder. When the small plane flew overhead, the sound seemed to move in a circular pattern over and around her. Then, somewhere ahead, a faint glow appeared through the trees that hadn't been there moments before. Jogging now, she hurried toward the light.

The aircraft had almost completed its wide circle in the sky when Victoria rounded the next bend and saw a truck parked in the middle of the road, facing away to the west. There was no one in it, but its headlights were on, brightening the pavement. Much farther down the road, another glow, dimmer, shone in her direction.

Suddenly, almost on top of her, the sound of engines became a roar. Instinctively, she threw herself flat onto the pavement. She felt the vibrations roll over her and then the wash of air from the propellers. She squeezed her eyes shut as sand, kicked up in the disturbance, pelted her face.

The plane, without its lights, dipped down and settled onto the roadway just ahead of the truck. Tires squealed as it struggled to slow the forward momentum.

Shaken, Victoria picked herself up and ran forward, crouching beside the empty truck as she watched. In the distance, the tires of the aircraft squealed and finally rolled to a stop. Immediately, the pilot cut the left engine. Three men came across the road from the right, running around the tail to the left side of the craft. One of them reached up and opened the cargo door. He jumped into the plane and began tossing heavy bags onto the pavement.

There was no sign of the DEA force and Victoria didn't know what to do. She couldn't let these criminals get away. She knew she didn't have long if she intended to stop them. One engine was still running. They would unload and be gone in minutes. She needed a weapon.

Victoria raised up and looked into the cab of the pickup. In the back window, a gun rack held two shotguns. She didn't know much about guns, but one of them looked familiar. A long time ago, her father had spent many hours on army firing ranges training her in the use of one just like this. As she reached through the open window and grabbed it off the rack, she hoped she hadn't forgotten.

Her hands were steady as she checked the chamber. She could see two shells in it. The magazine could hold more—maybe five— but she didn't have time to find out how many had been loaded. A glance ahead told her the men were working feverishly. She had to hurry. The men, some with automatic weapons slung over their shoulders, relayed the duffel bags from the road to the pier only a few yards away. Still more bags were shoved out the plane's cargo door onto the road. Staying out of the twin beams of light, Victoria ran in the soft sand along the roadside. Propelled by fury, she was heedless of her own safety.

The cargo door slammed shut and the plane slowly taxied forward along the roadway. The roaring sound of the engine diminished as the aircraft moved away, while the three men hurried to move the bags off the road.

Hidden in the brush, Blake had his hand in the air to give the signal to close in when a deafening sound split the air. He whipped around to meet the new threat and froze in disbelief.

The blast of the shotgun and Victoria's sudden appearance in the lights stunned them all. "You can't get away, Ian! The DEA knows all about you!"

The relay halted, bags held in mid-air, strained faces swiveled in the direction from which the lone female voice had come. Victoria had a Remington 1100 braced against her shoulder, the barrel pointed at them. The squad of federal agents remained immobile, reluctant to move as long as she was in that vulnerable spot— directly in their line of fire. Actors on an improvisational stage, illuminated by headlights instead of footlights, poised to make the next move in reaction to the lead player.

She sensed the advantage of surprise. Now she pointed the shotgun directly at Ian. "They'll be here soon. Do you really think I'll let you get away after what you've done to me?"

"Goddamn!" Ches Jackson muttered vehemently. He swiftly scanned the surroundings. Nothing yet. But that didn't mean the sonsabitches weren't there. He couldn't see much beyond the lights. Keep one eye on the territory, he told himself, as he moved in the direction of the boats. He looked sideways at Dominguez. Mean written all over his face. If anybody did anything stupid, it would be that crazy ass.

Ian Monroe ignored the gun and stepped toward Victoria, speaking in a voice of combined relief and agony. "Erica, darling, where have you been? You don't know what you're saying. You've had a great shock." He paused, extending his arms. "Come away with me. I've got to leave for a while. Kenneth Raitt...my partner...he's ill. It isn't working anymore. But you and I, Erica, can start all over again. We can make a wonderful new life somewhere else." His facial muscles twitched, betraying his fear that she might refuse. "All I want is to protect you and care for you. You must come with me."

Jackson and Dominguez remained tense, observing the confrontation between Ian and Victoria. Both men were aware the Navajo had reached the truck parked on the far end of the road and was turning around.

"You made me your partner in crime." Victoria's voice almost choked on her anger. "A robot trained to be a criminal. You must be insane if you think I'd go with you."

★   ★   ★

STEVE Callahan pivoted the plane on the makeshift runway, readying for takeoff. He squinted at the lights on the instrument panel as he checked the gauges. Just enough fuel to take off and fly to a nearby airport. Air traffic control would note that he'd merely left one local area to land at another. People did it all the time. Without suspicion, he could refuel and then be on his way back home.

He restarted the left engine and looked up momentarily to see if the road was clear. It was then he saw trouble. A fourth person stood in the road, silhouetted in the lights, holding a long-barreled gun on the other three. A woman, he realized in astonishment—it could only be Erica. *Shit! What now?*

★　★　★

"Erica, Erica, it was much more than that." Monroe spoke, moving closer to her. She might be telling the truth about the DEA, he thought. He had to do something quickly. He'd manipulated her for so long, he was sure, in the end, she would respond once again. It would only take the right words.

"Don't call me Erica!" she screamed. "My name is Victoria Dunbar. I was kidnapped in Washington—not by you or any of these men. Who did? How did you get me?"

"It was Harry Pharr, one of Miguel's wholesalers. When Miguel and Ches found out what Pharr had done, they took you to a hospital. You were in critical condition, my darling."

"Did you have Pharr killed?"

"No! He was hit by a car while trying to run away from Miguel and Ches." Ian paused to see if he had allayed her suspicions. "I assure you I'm not a killer."

Victoria took a deep breath and pressed on. "What happened to my face? Why do I look like this?"

"The doctor said you must have reconstructive surgery. You didn't remember any of your former life. I gave you a completely new one, better…a perfect life." He paused, his voice softening. "Only later I realized I had fallen in love with you."

"You don't love me—only what you turned me into."

Ian continued talking, moving closer, arms still outstretched as if her words had not registered in his mind. "For such a long time, I wanted someone like you, my darling. How content I've felt with you by my side!" His body was almost touching the barrel of the gun she held.

He was calling her bluff, Victoria thought. And she also knew she wouldn't shoot him, even as angry as she was. The DEA had better hurry.

Ian saw the small flicker of weakened resolve on her face. Swiftly, he brought one arm down and knocked the gun sideways. It fired harmlessly as he wrestled it from her.

"Enough of the soap opera, *amigo*," Miguel shouted. He held an Uzi leveled at Victoria. He backed to the edge of the road, near the dock. "You've put this operation in danger long enough. Get out of the way. I'm not going to let you slow us down any longer."

Ian glanced around. Ches was on the dock, with an AK-47 trained on Miguel. Even if Ches fired, the Cuban could still hit Erica. Ian had the Remington in his hand. He wondered if it had any rounds left. He stepped in front of her and faced Miguel.

"Don't do this, Miguel! It's not necessary. We've been partners for a long time. Let it count for something. We can all leave here rich and begin new lives somewhere else."

"That's a laugh! This babe has already caused enough trouble. She'll end up destroying us all," Miguel snarled ominously. "I'm warning you. Move out of the way!" His finger tightened against the trigger.

The burst of gunfire from the direction of the dock hit Dominguez just as Monroe squeezed the trigger. Hit from two directions, Dominguez lurched sideways and fired. Monroe saw the flash from the barrel of the Cuban's gun and his brain swiftly informed him he would be the target before he felt the blast. It knocked him backward. Ian Monroe was dead when he hit the ground.

Callahan sat frozen in the cockpit, watching the drama unfold in the distance. To his right, he saw a dark shadow running hunched over, alongside the plane. Then another, and another. His hand dropped to the throttles and shoved them forward.

Momentarily, Victoria felt time stand still in that deadly spot on the road, even as she heard the increasing rumble of the airplane. Closer still, a boat's engines churned to life. She was dimly aware of other gunfire, and of men rushing from the tall grass on both sides of the road. She heard Blake shouting for her to get down as he raced toward her. She flattened and looked up in time to see Dominguez slumping downward, face contorted in pain, pointing his gun directly at her.

Blake fired as he ran and rolled on top of Victoria. Dominguez died on his knees, but in one final reflex, his fingers tightened. Bullets strafed the ground as he fell sideways.

Victoria felt the body covering hers twitch in violent spasms and heard the cry of pain. Frantically, she pried herself out from under Blake and groped to find the bullet holes she knew were there. Her hands discovered obscene patches of oozing stickiness on his right arm and leg. While her fingers probed for other wounds, she was aware of activity all around them.

Shouts and running feet. In the chaos, Ches Jackson had disappeared in the Hatteras. The shouting became more urgent along with a change in the background noise—the unmistakable roar of an airplane heading toward them at high speed.

Victoria looked up to see lights and whirring propellers advancing in a headlong rush along the road. "No!" On her feet in an instant, she grabbed the Remington lying beside Monroe's body. Desperately, she fired a blast at the oncoming plane. It kept coming toward them, gaining speed. It would be on top of them in seconds.

From both sides of the road, automatic weapons sprayed a hail of bullets at the plane, but it didn't slow down. Knowing there was little hope of a fifth shell in the chamber, she took careful aim and fired again. A tire exploded and the Navajo reacted as if it had been jerked sideways with a strong hand. The left wing tilted downward as the plane swerved off the road at top speed. Propellers sliced into the sand as it cart-wheeled several times and stopped at the water's edge.

Victoria sat down on the asphalt, limp and dazed, hearing the yells and exclamations only as muffled sounds. She shook with the release of tension as she turned to Blake. He was bleeding steadily. She looked up to call for help and saw Mike rushing toward them. Somewhere near her, a voice talked into a radio, calling for an emergency medical team.

"How bad is he?" Mike's face creased with worry as he saw the hole in Blake's arm. He knew the bone was damaged. But the leg seemed to have only a flesh wound.

"Thank goodness for his bullet-proof vest, or it would have been worse. There are several pieces ripped out of it, but nothing penetrated. I think these two places are the most serious," Victoria said. "We've got to stop this bleeding, and fast."

Chapman pulled off his T-shirt, wadded it up and applied pressure to the more serious wound. "Hey," he shouted over his shoulder. "We need some first aid here. Quick!"

"Good work, Victoria." Blake's voice sounded distant.

"Keep still, my man," Mike cautioned. "We'll fix you right up."

"Mike." Blake's breathing was shallow. "Pick up Raitt. Will you do that for me?"

"You bet I will! Just as soon as I can catch a flight to D.C."

Others surrounded them and trained hands feverishly tended to Blake's wounds, Victoria bent over him, putting her face against his, murmuring to him. She felt her tears flowing uncontrollably, tears of relief and tears of agony for his pain.

"I'm okay, Victoria, honey," he said, thickly. "I'm okay." He managed a twitch of a smile to reassure her.

"And, to think I believed you when you said you didn't do John Wayne," she said, trying to steady her voice.

"Aw, shucks, little lady," he said, slowly. "A man's got to do…and a woman's got to do…whatever the hell they've got to do. Ooo-oo, damn! This smarts!

CHAPTER SIXTY-ONE

The massive carved desk in front of him almost dwarfed Kenneth Raitt. He was thin and haggard. His eyes seemed to sink into the darkened circles around them. In shock, the senator stared at the television set in his office. All day Sunday, reporters had told of the seizure in Alabama of a plane and a load of cocaine, and of the death of a Washington society leader who was at the scene as the DEA closed in on the drug smuggling ring. Now, Monday morning, the reports continued with more details.

Raitt's thoughts were erratic as he scratched furiously at the itch on his arms and chest. The high-and-mighty Monroe. Couldn't pull it off. Never did trust him. Goddamn, where *do* these bugs come from? They're all over me, he thought in panic.

He loosened his tie and rolled up his shirtsleeves in order to reach the places on his skin where the itch was worse. No relief. He could see them now. Little purple insects crawling all over him! The panic increased as he slapped at them. They didn't go away, just kept crawling.

The intercom on his desk buzzed. Raitt hit the button. "What?" he shouted.

"Senator, we have a request for you to speak at the dedication of the Disadvantaged Children's Center on June 11th. Your calendar is clear." The voice of his secretary paused. "It would certainly help your campaign, sir. What shall I tell them?"

"Tell them to go to hell!" Raitt screamed and punched the machine off.

"Why doesn't she leave me alone?" he asked himself, muttering. " I know why. Trying to trick me…ruin my campaign." His face twisted in suspicion as he stared at the closed door. I'll take care of that, he thought. He stood up and hurried to the door and turned the lock.

Raitt looked around the room, staring at the tall windows with their open draperies. "People looking in. What are they looking at?" Rushing from one window to the next, he jerked the heavy curtains closed. Only dim light remained in the room.

The senator sat down once again at his desk. With shaking hands, he pulled open a bottom drawer and reached down, his fingers feeling for a small packet hidden under copies of the Congressional Record. "Ah!" he said as his fingers felt the smooth plastic. He slit open the packet and, with a small pocketknife, arranged the tiny powdery crystals in two lines on the glass top of his stately desk. He bent his head, and closing off one nostril at a time, sniffed hard. Then, he sat back, letting the euphoria kick in.

He could think a lot better now. Should he contact Perea about the payment to try to stall him? With that shipment lost, there wasn't going to be enough money right away to cover it—not only what his organization owed, but for all the value of Perea's part as well. Maybe he had been too hasty, he conceded, in buying TV time for campaign ads that began running last week. He'd used his back-up money for that. At the time, he hadn't worried, even though those tapes had cost him a fortune. Another flood of drug profits had always come in on time.

Now, he was wiped out, thanks to Monroe. Perea would not be sympathetic.

He could beg the money from his wife. No, he decided, emphatically. He'd find another way to get by this, just like he'd always gotten by after a screw-up. Congress provided the smokescreen of public trust to shield its members. Some of the smart ones had learned how to use it.

Nervously, Raitt got up again and walked to one of the windows. He parted the drapery panels just a little. Staring hard at the manicured shrubbery landscaping the Senate Office Building, he inhaled sharply. "Latinos! Perea's men!"

He closed the panels with a jerk and raced to the next window. Easing those draperies open just a crack, he looked out and saw the same thing. "Shit! They're all around! That bastard Perea wants his money now. I've got to think what to do—and these damn bugs are back again!" He scratched his neck until red lines marked his skin.

The senator hurried back to his desk. Rummaging in the drawer once again, he found another packet, opened it, and dumped the contents on his desk. He leaned forward without ceremony and inhaled deeply. Brushing his face off, he rose and wiped a hand swiftly across the desktop to clear away the grains.

Feeling a good hit this time, Raitt smiled in satisfaction and leaned against his desk. In moments the smile changed to a grimace. His body began to twitch violently and he fell to the floor. The involuntary movements continued relentlessly. Froth bubbled up in the corners of the senator's mouth. Terror registered in his bulging eyes as the agony coursed through him. And, then he was still.

CHAPTER SIXTY-TWO

FASTEN SEAT BELTS flashed high on the forward wall of the jet as it began its descent to National Airport. Victoria gently nudged Blake from his nap.

He sat up, wincing slightly, and stretched out his long legs. As well as he could with one arm in a cast, he straightened the papers in the briefcase on his lap. "Are we there already?"

"Yes, we are," Victoria said. "It will be good to get back, won't it?" She looked at him with tenderness, at the traces of gray in his hair, the lines beginning to appear in his face, and the lean, firm body of a much younger man. He had overcome the gunshot wounds fairly well. The doctors had patched bone, stitched the torn muscles and treated an infection. Now, three weeks later, he had only a slight limp and occasional discomfort from his arm. Her mind switched back to the brief period of recuperation Blake had in a hospital in Mobile— and then, a more extended rest in Gulf Shores after he was released. That had been good for both of them.

She'd had intensive therapy with rape counselors, and had felt some of her inner turmoil ease. It would take a long time to completely heal emotionally, but she was confident she'd make it. Blake's family had been wonderful to her, especially his mother. Elise Harrison had made it clear that she thought the two of them were right for each other.

Blake clicked his seatbelt into the locked position. "I'll be glad to see what's going on at headquarters. I never thought I'd say that.

Damned if that field work doesn't get to be a strain at times," he said solemnly, as crinkles appeared at the corners of his eyes. "By the way, at last report, Ches Jackson still hadn't been captured. Apparently, he made it to some place where he can hide for a while. The word on the street is that a hooker helped him disappear." Blake shook his head, thinking back to that night after Jackson had gotten away in Dominguez' Hatteras. The DEA report told that the black man had simply vanished. The Coast Guard searched for days in the swampy regions north of the canal, in Mobile Bay, and in the Gulf. "He'll survive awhile longer until his luck runs out," he added. "We'll find him. It just might take some time. He's had a lot of experience in staying out of sight."

Victoria knew Jackson's confession would have been helpful, but Ginger Kopenski had furnished a lot of information. The remaining pieces of her puzzle—information about the clinic where she'd been taken and the doctor who had treated her—had been discovered in Ian Monroe's safe in the house in Virginia, along with her ID cards. Even though the people who had heard Ian's confession that night would give convincing testimony in court, Victoria was relieved to have the tangible evidence as proof of her innocence. She thought about the other parts of the big puzzle, the "planets", those people with whom she had supposedly worked to distribute the ring's cocaine and marijuana. They were all high-powered names in the southeast—executives, politicians or society leaders. Of them, she had no memory at all. But the safe in the bay house had supplied that information and all had since been arrested.

She looked out the window as the plane swooped down on its glide path. There was Georgetown University and the Kennedy Center. One after another, rising along the banks of the Potomac in stately display, the federal buildings slid past, so close she felt she could reach out and touch them. The Lincoln Memorial, the domed Jefferson Memorial presiding over the Tidal Basin, the spire of the

Washington Monument, and farther away, the Capitol. The sight was familiar, but never had it taken her breath away as it did now.

She felt Blake's hand squeeze hers and heard him whisper, "You see, darling, they're welcoming you home."

Victoria's answering smile was confident. Blake felt a lump of emotion rising in his throat as he looked at her. He realized he could no longer recall what she'd looked like before, so accustomed was he now to the new contours of her face. She had refused more surgery to reverse the changes. "Life changes us all," she'd said, and that was the end of that. Her hair was back to its normal color and style once again, and her clothes were her own choices. He'd had the tiny turquoise-studded locket returned to her. It lay in the hollow of her neck once again, on a new gold chain.

In the past weeks, he had worried about the effects of the bitter experience on her mind, and whether or not she would be able to put it behind her. Slowly, he had been encouraged by her comments. She wanted to volunteer her time talking to young people about the dangers of getting into the drug trade. Best of all for her, thought Blake, she was eager to resume her career. Victoria had lived up to her name. She would be all right. A courageous fighter, a steady friend, and the woman whose love had restored his faith in the human race.

The jet's tires chirped as they touched the ground. The plane lurched in resistance as the pilot hit the thrust reversers. Minutes later, the aircraft had taxied to the terminal and stopped.

Blake leaned over and kissed her. "Ready?"

"I am." She said it without hesitation, flashing a smile at him as she unfastened the seatbelt.

"I want to take you to the opera soon," he said, as they made their way with the other passengers along the narrow aisle.

"Okay. But, not *Don*…"

"No, my love. *The Marriage of Figaro*…sometime after the marriage of Dunbar and Harrison."

ACKNOWLEDGMENTS

I am indebted to:

Jane Carson, director of the Rape Crisis Center in Mobile, who, in March of 1993, took time to explain the destructive impact on women of the crime of rape

Margaret Ellis and Spencer Frost, both pilots and published writers who shared their knowledge of various aircraft, and insights into flying them, while critiquing the manuscript

Maureen Conway Frost, for her guidance and critiques, and great food during the many writing group sessions

Dennis C. Smith, Jr., MD for his comments on the effects of certain kinds of injuries and their treatments

Members of the Church Street Writers' Group, steady providers of a strong base of support.

Others who read the manuscript and offered suggestions:

Linda Bennett, Martenas Godfrey, Chris Haas, Stephanie Hebert, Lanier Keller, Deborah Knowles, Barbara Mangum, Jenny Slay, Adrian Smith, Yvonne Smith, Jacob B. Waltermire, Jr., Karen Waltermire, Tammy Wittner

My gratitude goes to the following authors and their books on drug smuggling in the 1980s:

Eddy, Paul; Sabogal, Hugo; Walden, Sara. *The Cocaine Wars*, W.W. Norton Co., 1988.

Greenhaw, Wayne. *Flying High; Inside Bigtime Drug Smuggling*. Dodd Mead, 1984.

Mermelstein Max; Moore, Robin; Smitten, Richard. *The Man Who Made It Snow*. Simon & Schuster, 1990.

Rice, Berkeley. *Trafficking: The Boom and Bust of the Air America Cocaine Ring*. Charles Scribner's & Sons, 1989.

Rosenberg, Philip. *Spivey Assignment: A Double Agent's Infiltration of the Drug Smuggling Conspiracy*. Holt, Rinehart & Winston, 1979.

Wolff, Kay; Taylor, Sybil. *The Last Run*. Viking Penguin, 1989.

Other information was found in numerous issues of:
The Mobile Press Register and *The Washington Post*

ABOUT THE AUTHOR

Photo by Sheila Hagler

JEAN DUHON is a former educator and present-day globetrotter. Her travels continue to take her to a number of exotic spots in the world, where she loves learning about other cultures.

Although she was born and reared in southern Louisiana, she has lived in many places since, especially enjoying the excitement of life in and around Washington, D.C. Ms. Duhon has returned to the Gulf Coast, and currently lives in the historic city of Mobile.

Her adopted city is the setting of her first book, *Silent Invasion,* a World War II fictional tale of intrigue in America. At present, this writer is working on a third novel.

Ms. Duhon welcomes your comments. She can be reached at

jeanduhon@windstream.net